ST.

MINOTAUR
MYSTERIES

GET A CLUE!

Be the first to hear the latest mystery book news…

With the St. Martin's Minotaur monthly newsletter,
you'll learn about the hottest new Minotaur books,
receive advance excerpts from newly published works,
read exclusive original material from featured mystery
writers, and be able to enter to win free books!

Sign up on the Minotaur Web site at:
www.minotaurbooks.com

ALSO BY SHERYL J. ANDERSON

Killer Cocktail
Killer Heels

Killer Deal

SHERYL J. ANDERSON

St. Martin's Paperbacks

This is a work of fiction. All of the characters, organizations, and events portrayed in this novel are either products of the author's imagination or are used fictitiously.

KILLER DEAL

Copyright © 2006 by Sheryl J. Anderson and Mark Edward Parrott.
Excerpt from *Killer Riff* copyright © 2007 by Sheryl J. Anderson.

All rights reserved. No part of this book may be used or reproduced in any manner whatsoever without written permission except in the case of brief quotations embodied in critical articles or reviews. For information address St. Martin's Press, 175 Fifth Avenue, New York, NY 10010.

Library of Congress Catalog Card Number: 2006040884

ISBN: 0-312-94936-7
EAN: 9780312-94936-5

Printed in the United States of America

St. Martin's Press hardcover edition / July 2006
St. Martin's Paperbacks edition / August 2007

St. Martin's Paperbacks are published by St. Martin's Press, 175 Fifth Avenue, New York, NY 10010.

10 9 8 7 6 5 4 3 2 1

*To Sara and Sean,
for their love and patience
and all their great ideas*

Acknowledgments

First, I want to thank the usual suspects—our fantastic families—for their love and encouragement. I'd also like to thank our marvelous friends at Westchester Lutheran Church and School for their enthusiasm and support, especially our pastor and his wife, Fred and Sandra Masted; my beautiful Rebekah Circle sisters; my PSO buddies; and the "well-read" faculty (who gets this one first?). Thanks, too, to Judith Meyer and Molly's other fans back home at Prince of Peace Lutheran. My gratitude and affection to Doug Clegg, for believing since kindergarten that we'd get here and for all his advice along the way. Big thanks and hugs to Joel and Mary Barkow for their friendship, their legal and artistic advice, and all the great pizza. A special tip of the cocktail shaker to Ann and John Abraham, Heidi Amundson and Rick Pearson, Sherry and Bill Fortier, Diane and Chris Maeder, Allison and Bart Montgomery, and Cyndi and Tony Widmer.

I also want to thank our favorite booksellers, the grand group at The Mystery Bookstore in Westwood, California, and the fine folks at Pulp Fiction in Brisbane, Australia. And as always, our thanks to our marvelous editor, Kelley Ragland, her assistant, Ryan Quinn, and all the other great people at St. Martin's Press, and to our wonderful agent, Andy Zack.

One

"YOU NEED A DEAD BODY. A really cool dead body," Cassady suggested.

"Is that something I order on-line or do they have a department upstairs?" I asked. Believe me, if there were a way to order up a stylish cadaver in Manhattan, Cassady Lynch would know. Networking is second nature to her and with her long legs, amazing figure, and cascading auburn curls, her life is overflowing with people eager to do her all sorts of favors.

"I'm fairly sure you have to special order those," Tricia said. "Especially one that's already been refrigerated."

My two best friends and I were spending our lunch hour shopping—that's why granola bars fit in desk drawers—at the marvel that is the flagship ABC Home Store on Broadway. High heaven for shopping addicts, it is eight levels of treasures ranging from dainty little soaps to massive French country antiques. When I was growing up, one of my favorite books was about two kids who deliberately get locked in the Metropolitan Museum of Art overnight; I used to dream about doing the same. Now I dream about being locked in ABC Home. With a platinum card. That someone else pays off.

We were on the first floor, helping Cassady search for a new pair of earrings. A fellow intellectual properties lawyer at the public interest group where she works had persuaded her to attend some sort of scientific seminar that night. She was having second thoughts, but didn't want to leave her colleague hanging, so she'd decided new baubles would amp up her excitement about going.

Cassady frowned, gently enough to show displeasure but not deeply enough to start a crease. "At the risk of disparaging the mayor or the commissioner, there have been plenty of homicides in Manhattan this summer. I'm sure several of them are unsolved and worthy of your talents."

Love and murder are my favorite topics as a journalist and as a person. What with the extreme behavior, the denial of risk, the blinding focus, and the will to succeed, being in love and being homicidal aren't as far apart as one might think. Or hope. And the place where those two mind-sets intersect fascinates me most of all. But it's a dangerous intersection, and this time around, it would prove to be an incredibly costly one.

"Believe me, I've tried," I said. "Not to sound like a ghoul, but whenever I hear about an interesting case, I pitch it to my darling editor, but she keeps shooting me down."

"Maybe Eileen—and/or Fate—are suggesting you try a social crusade or a government scandal," Tricia suggested, examining a lovely pair of freshwater pearl dangles. "A less macabre route to greater journalistic glory."

As opposed to the murder route I had been pursuing. While I'm best known as the advice columnist for *Zeitgeist* magazine, I've recently—through sets of unique circumstances—had the opportunity to solve two murders. I wrote articles about both investigations that were well received, but didn't quite launch the career transformation I'd hoped for. My editor continues to scoff at my desire to formally move beyond "You Can Tell Me" and build up an investigative resume. And while I love my column and the front-row seat it gives me at the demolition derby of love, a girl needs a challenge.

"Molly's got a gift, Tricia," Cassady said firmly. "We should encourage it."

"I want to see her byline in the *New York Times* as much

as you do," Tricia agreed. "I was just hoping there was a less dangerous way to get her there."

"I don't want to work for the *Times*," I told them.

"Of course you do. Everyone wants to be on the *Times*. I don't write and I want to be on the *Times*. You're pretending otherwise because Crew Boy is there." Cassady shook her head in disbelief. "Wimp."

"Not wanting to work with Peter doesn't make me a wimp, it makes me smart."

"Oh, bumper harvest of sour grapes. It's a mammoth paper with plenty of room to avoid him. Or better yet, get him fired in as messy and public a way as possible."

Peter Mulcahey is a present rival and a former boyfriend. I was dating him—actually, in the process of breaking up with him—when I got involved with the first murder. And the detective investigating it. That dear detective is the one who christened Peter "Crew Boy." Behind his back, of course. But it does suit him. At that point, Peter and I were both working at magazines we saw as jumping-off points for our writing careers. I'm still at mine; he's jumped off to the *Times*, more through tenacious brownnosing than proven journalistic merit.

Okay, Cassady's right; sour grapes abound but still: "I don't wish Peter ill," I said, trying to make amends.

"Really?" Cassady asked. "I wish him huge ill and I never even dated the man."

"He didn't treat you well, Molly. It's our right to wish for anvils to fall on his head," Tricia said.

"I just want to figure out the next step in my career," I said, not so much to be noble as to stop talking about Peter.

"Wonderful. We'll switch to anvils falling on Eileen," Cassady suggested.

Eileen Fitzsimmons is my editor at *Zeitgeist*. We're one of those glossy Manhattan lifestyle magazines that will instruct you to "Be Proud of Who You Are," teach you "Ten Bulletproof Ways to Seduce Him," and share the need to "Get Off Your Butt to Get Your Butt Off," all in the same issue and with no sense of irony. Eileen was brought in to "put some teeth into the thing," according to The Publisher. At this point, the only place she's sunk her sharp incisors is into the tender hearts of the staff. Those who don't loathe her fear her. Best I can tell, she enjoys both reactions equally.

Eileen has been good to me. Once. Which makes me nervous, since it brings to mind Don Corleone: "Someday . . . I'll call upon you to do a service for me . . ." Eileen's goodness was publishing my second investigative article, the one about Tricia's brother's fiancée being murdered at their engagement party. Perhaps you heard about it, maybe even read it.

As part of Eileen's periodic efforts to toughen up the magazine, she asked me to write about the murder and the part I played in unraveling it. I wrote a strong piece (if I may say so), we got lots of great letters and e-mails about it, and I've been asking Eileen to let me tackle another investigative feature ever since. But she just scrunches up her nose like I'm a particularly mangy kitten, pats me on the shoulder, and sends me back to my column.

"Which brings us back to needing a body. One that will seem attractive to Eileen," I explained to Tricia and Cassady.

"Hmmm. Eileen as necrophiliac. Hadn't considered that before," Cassady said.

"Please. Like I don't have enough trouble looking the woman in the eye as it is."

"Play your connections. Get the inside scoop from your scrumptious Sherlock," Cassady suggested.

Tricia answered before I could. "Cassady, no. You know how Kyle feels about our investigations."

Hearing Tricia refer to them as "our" investigations was delightful, because I certainly couldn't have solved either murder without their assistance, insight, and support. And she was absolutely right about Kyle; he'd be appalled at the notion of my actively scouting for another murder investigation. He's very protective—of me and of his turf. He'd prefer that the two not meet. And I can understand that, even if I don't always agree with it.

Kyle Edwards and I met at a crime scene. Kyle was there

because he's a homicide detective, literally one of Manhattan's finest. I was there because I'd discovered the body. We got to know each other very well very quickly, in part because he suspected me of being the killer. I felt it might clarify the situation if I solved the murder to prove him wrong. Not exactly Cinderella, Prince Charming, and the glass slipper, but we've made it work—most of the time—and are navigating the misunderstandings, drive-by shootings, and the other events that can complicate a romance between two people in our positions.

"A man doesn't always know what's good for him. Just ask Samson," Cassady replied.

"Kyle wouldn't stand in my way if I got a great story," I assured us all. "He's just not going to encourage me in that direction."

"He's happy with you as an unfulfilled advice columnist?"

"Happy with people not shooting at me."

"So when's he moving in?"

I looked at my watch so I wouldn't have to look at either of them. "That soon?" Tricia asked.

"I need to get back." I leaned in to hug them both goodbye and was practically stiff-armed by Tricia, who glared at me mightily.

Cassady arched one eyebrow, something she does effortlessly and eloquently. "Remind me to give you lessons in how to blow people off."

"Gotta go back to the office," I insisted.

"Like you'd ever let Eileen put you on that short a leash," Cassady snarked.

"Molly Forrester, you're holding out on us," Tricia declared.

"Not at all. I'm just trying not to be premature in making any announcements."

"Announcements?" The wedding bells were ringing so loudly in Tricia's head I could almost hear them in mine. Tricia is an events planner and derives immense satisfaction, as well as a nice living, from bringing order to other people's lives. The fact that she has known me for so many years and has yet to impose any order on mine both inspires and frustrates her. Because she's a petite, porcelain-skinned brunette, people make the mistake of assuming that Tricia is delicate and, therefore, meek. She's delicate all right—the same way a spider's web is. It's also beautiful and surprisingly tenacious.

"Slow down, cowgirl. He's moving some stuff in this weekend, that's all. No significant exchange of jewelry, no contracts of any sort, just . . . stuff."

"What kind of stuff?" Cassady pressed. "You're well past the toothbrush and one change of clothes point, right?"

"Not up to me."

Cassady and Tricia turned to each other, delighted by this tidbit. "You know what that means," Cassady said to Tricia for my benefit.

"It was his idea," Tricia nodded.

"Why don't I go back to work and let you two carry on at your own pace?"

Tricia beamed. "We need to have a party."

"Great," I said. "Your place? Kyle and I will try to stop by."

"I meant your place," Tricia said.

"Oh, no, no party. This isn't an official declaration of any kind. Just a little step in the right direction."

"So, is he going to be there every night?" Cassady asked, pulling me back to where I'd been standing at the counter. I made a half-hearted attempt at resisting, in part because I really did need to get back to the office and in part because I was concerned they were going to ask me questions I didn't have answers for.

Interestingly enough, my friends weren't looking to me for answers. They were supplying them themselves. "I doubt it. He works a lot of nights," Tricia said to Cassady.

"Because we can't exactly crash there whenever we want to if he's going to be living there," Cassady continued.

"Good point."

"Not necessarily a point at all," I interjected. "He's not living there. He's moving some things in, in preparation for possibly living there at some point, but is not currently taking up primary residence."

"I thought I was the lawyer."

"You've taught me well, Obi-Wan."

"Not well enough. If I were in your Blahniks, that boy would have been installed full-time months ago and possibly wearing an electronic ankle bracelet."

"You've never been that possessive in your life."

"Never had a man that worthy of possessing."

I let the compliment hang in the air while Cassady purchased a stunning pair of Sarah Macfadden earrings, delicate interlocking hoops of hammered silver. I didn't mean to downplay the importance or the excitement of Kyle and me inching toward a more permanent relationship, but the fact of the matter was, I was nervous. I'd never lived with a man before; most of my relationships had imploded well before keys were even swapped. And I'd never been so crazy about a guy that he could make me come unglued just by walking in the door the way Kyle did. It was terrifying.

Giving my arm a squeeze, Tricia murmured, "I'm so happy for you."

"How long do you suppose it'll take me to mess it up?"

"Stop it," she said briskly, miming tossing salt over her left shoulder to ward off the Devil.

Cassady tucked her new purchase into her bag and steered us toward the door. "Much as I'd like to stay and teach Miss Molly to have a little faith in herself, now I am the one who has to get back. If I'm actually attending this Concerned Geeks Saving the World thing, I've got motions to file before I go, and motions to file before I go."

"Somehow, Frost made it sound more attractive," Tricia said wistfully as we all made our way back onto the street.

Robert Frost could have made anything sound more attractive. Save, perhaps, Eileen. She's one of those women who can stop you in your tracks when you first see her—but once you get to know her, you'll never slow down in her vicinity again. Early in her tenure, I wondered if it was possible to structure my work hours so I'd only be at the magazine when Eileen wasn't—say, in the middle of the night. But then the rumors about her never going home, just sleeping in her coffin in her office, started, and I figured I had to get used to placing myself in her path on a regular basis. Especially because I'd already seen her dismantle several careers with nicely crafted lies whispered in The Publisher's ear and I didn't want to make it any easier on her to get me fired than I had to.

Which is why my heart skipped a beat when Eileen's office door flew open just as I was walking to my desk. She stepped out with one hand extended portentously, like the Ghost of Christmas Future. A diminutive specter, barely five feet tall minus her Chloe wedges and clothed in an Elie Tahari chiffon skirt and paneled blouse, but scary nonetheless. "Just the person I was looking for," she said, curling the hand slowly to summon me.

I resisted the temptation to look back over my shoulder, knowing that anyone who had been standing there was quivering under a desk by now. "Lucky me," I said, wishing it were so.

"We were just talking about you." Eileen flicked at her spiky black bangs as though the conversation had been exhausting, then gestured vaguely at her office. From where I stood, I couldn't tell whether it contained other writers, editors, or a death squad. I wasn't in any hurry to step up and find out.

The great thing about the bull pen in our office is that lives are played out in the open; the lousy thing about the bull pen in our office is that sometimes the life played out is yours. The wall-less floor plan, with row on row of desks, makes it physically impossible to keep a secret or tell a lie. Of course, when colleagues start sleeping together, they somehow forget those facts, making coming to work much more entertaining for the rest of us.

"What can I do for you, Eileen?"

"We need to talk about the Garth Henderson article."

I ran through a couple of appropriate responses in my

head and chose the most polite one, since half the bull pen had stopped what they were doing to witness this exchange: "Excuse me?" Until recently, Garth Henderson had been a self-proclaimed "advertising rock star" known for his bold flair in both his campaigns and his social life. Then, three weeks ago, Garth Henderson became a corpse, having been murdered in one of the fancier rooms of the Carlyle Hotel. Specifically, he'd been shot once in the crotch and once in the head. In that order, apparently. No arrests had been made, but the police had spent quite a lot of time talking to his ex-wife Gwen Lincoln and to Ronnie Willis, whose advertising agency, Willis Worldwide, was poised to merge with Garth's at the time of the murder. There was tremendous pressure on the police—primarily from Garth's many influential friends—to make something happen soon and I was glad for Kyle's sake that he hadn't caught the case.

Garth Henderson had specialized in blurring the line between provocative and incendiary. His clients often got extra bang for their advertising buck because Garth's campaigns, with their hefty dose of sexuality, received vociferous attention from the media. So you not only saw his ads in the places he'd paid to run them, but on news programs and in magazines that critiqued them, often finding them salacious and inappropriate. Clients generally found them hugely effective.

The only publicly unhappy client in recent memory had been Jack Douglass, the CEO of Douglass Frozen Foods. To launch Douglass' new soy ice cream line, Garth and his agency had designed a campaign that featured a buxom young movie actress, best known for appearing on late-night talk shows in a drunken tizzy, apparently about to perform oral sex on a soy fudgsicle. The television commercial had shown her stripping the wrapper off the fudgsicle with mounting excitement, then slowly raising it to her mouth while she licked her lips. The tagline of the campaign was: *C'mon, you'll like it. You know you will.*

Sales had soared, particularly among college-aged men, but the critics and pundits had howled mightily. And Mr.

Douglass, a neo-con who was reportedly being wooed by heavy hitters to segue into a political career, found himself being excoriated by those very same wooers as the media tempest crescendoed. Even when it died down, Mr. Douglass' political future was now said to be dim at best. But Garth Henderson signed several new clients.

"The Garth Henderson article," Eileen repeated with that vinegary touch of impatience that makes us all love her so. "I have a new take on it."

Apparently, the new take included actually doing it. When the news of Henderson's death broke, all the murmurs of Gwen Lincoln's name intrigued me. That only sharpened when the police investigation seemed to stall. I'd pitched the idea of an article on the couple—and the murder—to Eileen but she'd shot it down, dismissing Garth's death as "when good divorces go bad." So why this change of heart?

As I pondered that question and whether I dared ask it, a tall, angular man with marvelous cheekbones and a wild and thick head of sandy blond hair stepped out of her office. I placed the hair before I placed the face; it was Emile Trebask, the ascendant design demigod. You can find his reflection on some surface in all his print ads, smiling approvingly as dazed teenagers who have partially pulled on the clothes he designs grope each other for the camera. It's become a game to find Emile when each new ad comes out—sort of like finding the "Nina"s in Hirschfeld's drawings. Or perhaps more accurately, the fashionista's version of *Where's Waldo?*

I was surprised to see him walking out of Eileen's office. We go to people like him, they don't come to us. Eileen smirked at my reaction, thinking I was impressed. "Molly, you know Emile, don't you?"

Of course I didn't. I'd slapped down plenty of cash over the past few years to buy his clothes, but I'd never met him. I'd have to do some serious social climbing to even approach his strata. Eileen knew that and, I suspect, was enjoying the fact. "Haven't had the pleasure, Mr. Trebask," I said, offering my hand.

He shook it gently, as though one of us might break. I'm pretty sure it wasn't me he was worried about. "Ms. Forrester, I'm so glad you're going to be talking to Gwen," he said with his famous clipped accent; it was much debated in the fashion press whether it was Swiss or Affected.

Proudly, I did not gasp. Not only was there suddenly an article on the Garth Henderson murder, but I was doing an interview with the prime suspect? What did Emile Trebask have to do with it? More to the point, what did Eileen get out of it? I smiled and said, "Thank you, Mr. Trebask," while I tried to find the connection between all these interesting questions.

"I thought the world of Garth, a terrific talent, but to try to lay it at Gwen's feet. It's absurd. Gwen could not step on an ant, much less blow off someone's balls."

At first, the last word sounded somewhere between "bowels" and "bells," so I thought he was trying to be discreet. When I realized he was being anything but, I bit the inside of my lip to maintain a professional demeanor and nodded. Mr. Trebask took that as encouragement to grow even more animated. "It's very important people understand exactly what's going on here." Since I myself was a little confused on that point, I nodded again. "Gwen's being made the scapegoat and that is not right. If we let people know the truth, then the police will have to look a little harder, won't they, and allow people to get on with their business. And their lives."

I refrained from nodding yet again while my memory frantically Googled itself for some connection between Gwen Lincoln and Emile Trebask. Then Trebask pressed a small glass vial into my hand and I remembered.

"Success," he murmured.

Lifting the vial to my nose, I sniffed gently and smelled cedar and honeysuckle, undercut with something smoky and musky. The sweet smell of success indeed.

"It's lovely," I said. Success was going to be the first perfume in the new Trebask fragrance line and Gwen Lincoln was Trebask's partner in the venture. She'd been an executive at several cosmetics firms, but equally important, her first husband had died young and left her incredibly wealthy. There'd been a fair amount of talk after Garth was killed that he'd found some weak spots in their prenup and was going to wring her out in divorce court. She'd dodged a bullet and he hadn't. Twice, actually. Or so that rumor had gone.

So had Emile come to Eileen looking for an article to prop up his business partner during a crucial time? It was a noble gesture on his part, but I couldn't figure out what Eileen was getting out of it, which was always the pivotal part of any equation involving her.

Trebask lightly touched my hand again and, for a moment, I thought he was going to take his perfume sample back. "Your piece on the murder of Lisbet McCandless was very powerful. I'm sure you'll do just as well here."

"Thank you," I said, still improvising.

"And you." Trebask turned back to Eileen. Her reptilian smile grew, consuming even more of her tiny face than I'd thought possible. "You will be an amazing addition to my celebrity model lineup at the gala."

"Emile, I'm so honored."

The pieces slid into place with slimy ease. Horse-trading was alive and well at *Zeitgeist*. Trebask was looking for help in swaying public, if not police, opinion and Eileen had bartered an article in the magazine for an ego turn in one of Trebask's fashion shows. Since he'd said "gala," it was probably the show he was putting on to launch the perfume while raising funds for the Fashion Industry Mentor Project, which encouraged at-risk youth to consider careers in fashion through internships and mentorships. I'd donated money to them before and suddenly felt very protective of the organization, imagining teeny meanie Eileen prancing down the catwalk and pretending to be a model at their expense.

But I couldn't dwell on that now, because I was grappling with the most thrilling part of this strange symbiotic seduction: I came out of it with a feature article assignment.

"Please let me know if there's anything I can do, any door

I can open," Emile said, squeezing my shoulder as gently as he'd squeezed my hand.

"Thank you, I will," I said, already brainstorming on how to give Eileen and Emile what they wanted while doing what I wanted. I would find a way.

"You understand what I need here," Eileen said flatly when she returned from escorting Emile to the elevator. I was waiting in her office, despite her new assistant's efforts to bodily remove me from the sofa—if you can call it that. Sculpted slab would be more accurate. Eileen's office is decorated like Andy Warhol and Yoko Ono attempted to set up housekeeping together. Everything's bright and shiny and bold and there isn't a single comfortable spot to sit in the whole place.

"An interview with Gwen Lincoln that mentions both the new perfume and the Garth Henderson murder, in that order," I answered. She gestured for me to elaborate. "And that points to the distinct possibility of her innocence in the latter," I continued gingerly.

"Good girl."

Not to bite the hand that was suddenly feeding me, but I had to ask. "What if she's not innocent?"

"Then you can have the cover."

I wasn't expecting that. "Didn't you tell your new buddy we'd do an article to help his friend and partner?"

Eileen leaned against her desk and swatted at her bangs again. "Molly," she said, her impatience moving from vinegar to venom, "haven't you ever said something to a man just to make him go away?"

"Millions of times. I turn them away in droves."

"Oops. Didn't schedule time for you to try and be funny this afternoon. You'd better go." She slithered behind her desk and perched in front of her computer. Not to do any work, just to remove me from her line of sight.

But I wasn't going anywhere without more information. I had to know my boundaries, especially if I was going to push them. "But you did tell him we'd write an article to help Gwen Lincoln."

"I did not. I told him we'd write an article *about* Gwen

Lincoln. Now, if he made poor assumptions about the contents and point of view, just because he thinks she's innocent, he's really the one in the wrong, wouldn't you say?"

"So I have latitude here to consider her potentially guilty and investigate accordingly."

Her icy green eyes slid in my direction for a moment, then zipped back to the screen. "Theoretically, but I doubt it will even be an issue. Why don't we just wait and see if you get that far?"

The wave of adrenaline I'd been surfing dumped me on my head. Distracted by the potential of this article, I'd stopped considering Eileen's point of view. "You're assuming I won't come up with anything."

"I'm demanding that you come up with an interview. Beyond that, Molly, I won't be holding my breath."

I knew that was less a statement about Gwen Lincoln than one about me, but I tried not to rise to the bait. "If I'm going to touch on the murder at all, I'm going to have to look into it. I want to go into this interview armed with facts and no preconceived notion of anyone's guilt or innocence."

"If that's your process, so be it. Honestly, Molly, this little hobby of yours is cute, though rather twisted, but let's pause a moment and be realistic, shall we? Garth Henderson isn't some corpse you're related to. This is a high-profile murder that has stymied the police. It's out of your league."

So Eileen's real issue raised its catty little head. She thought I was incapable of solving this mystery because I didn't have any personal connection to the crime, as I had in my previous articles. She was, in her own twisted way, telling me I couldn't do it. Which is a sentiment I take as a challenge.

"I'll do it anyway."

Eileen studied me for a long moment, then let her face slide into a sickly, curling smile like the Grinch looking down on Whoville. "I had no doubt."

She was claiming to know me so well that she could count on my hunger for a great story to override any other concerns. Maybe she was right, but I didn't want to give her the satisfaction of admitting that this early in the process. "I need to know you'll support my efforts to do this the right way," I pressed.

"Fine."

"And keep your predictions about my failure to yourself."

"Your implication wounds me."

"Yours doesn't exactly warm my heart."

"I'm trying to be frank. You want to turn that into something malevolent, that's your business."

No, that's your strength, I thought, but for a change, I had the sense not to say it out loud. "Wonderful. I'll get to work." I pushed myself off the slab and headed for the door.

Eileen sat back from the monitor and folded her thin arms across her chest. "Just keep in mind you still have to do your column and that piece on dating divorced men, too."

"I will."

"All in two weeks."

"Right."

"And be careful."

Interesting. I never would have suspected Eileen of giving a second thought about my personal safety. "Thank you, Eileen," I said, trying to sound more grateful than surprised.

"God knows I don't want you infuriating some homicidal idiot who's going to come after you here in the office and hurt someone else, namely me. Investigations aren't good for your coworkers or the carpet."

Okay, so she wasn't thinking about me at all, except in relation to her own comfort. The upside was, my suspicion that Hell remained a frost-free environment was confirmed. "I'll do my best."

"You're smiling too much and I can't bear it. Go now," Eileen said with a dismissive wave.

Back at my desk, I couldn't even sit still. This was the opportunity I'd been looking for and I was going to make the most of it. Third time's a charm and I was going to make sure this article got me where I wanted to go.

I began by making lists and notes. I'd been following the news about the Henderson investigation out of personal interest, but I wanted to assemble everything I could and make sure I was fully up to date. I needed background research on Gwen Lincoln, too, to make sure I got the most out of my interview. Gwen would be expecting puff-piece softballs, but I didn't want to miss a chance to dig deep.

I was also going to have to find out how much information the police would be willing to give me. Since it was an ongoing investigation, it probably wouldn't be much. I tried to remember who Kyle had said had caught the case.

Kyle. I needed to tell Kyle. Telling Tricia and Cassady, especially in view of our lunch-hour conversation, would be great fun, but I couldn't be sure Kyle would be as enthusiastic. He worried about me, which I appreciated hugely, so he'd probably be pretty low-key about it. But he'd be happy, too.

I called Cassady and Tricia, who were both thrilled to hear the good news. Tricia made me swear we would reconvene for celebratory cocktails at some point later in the evening; I mentioned that to Cassady, who said she was sure she'd be ready to ditch her fund-raiser quite early, so count her in.

Then I took a stroll and called Kyle from the steps of his precinct. I'm very respectful of professional space and the last way in the world I want to be perceived is as the flighty girlfriend who's forever dropping by to intrude at the worst possible time. Especially now that I might be interacting with some of his colleagues on a completely new level.

"Hey, where are you?" he asked, sounding calm and pleased to hear from me.

"Out front. I didn't want to interrupt, but I happened to be in the neighborhood."

"Why?"

"Because I have great news."

"I'll come down and you can tell me in person."

There's something so delicious about watching the man you're crazy about come walking toward you. You get that great anticipation of how he's going to feel, smell, and taste as he moves closer. But it's also having those moments when you're too far away to say anything, when you can just appreciate the marvelous way he moves with that effortless, muscular gait, the way the sunlight catches little hints of auburn in his hair that fluorescent light ignores, how the blue in his eyes shines from a hundred yards away, and the way his head tilts to one side because he's thinking about other things right up until the moment he opens his mouth and says:

"Hey."

He kissed me gently and quickly. He keeps things muted in public, especially in front of his workplace. Even as he straightened back up, I could see his eyes moving over the passersby to check who might have been watching us.

"Nice appetizer," I said.

"You want the main course, make a late reservation. I'm not finishing up any time soon."

"That's too bad. We have some celebrating to do."

"What's up?"

"I need to talk to one of your fellow detectives."

"One thing at a time. Go back to the celebrating."

"That's it. Eileen finally gave me a real assignment. I'm doing an article on Gwen Lincoln."

"What kind of article?"

"An investigative piece."

"Define 'investigative.' "

"It's supposed to be a profile on her new business, but I'm going to have to address Garth Henderson's murder."

"Why?"

"People still suspect her. Don't they?"

He pinched his bottom lip thoughtfully. "Haven't been keeping track."

"Well, I'll find out."

"What else are you going to find out?"

"Whatever I can."

Kyle smiled gently and a little sadly. I figured he was thinking of how consuming his current case was, then adding on how much I was going to have to be working to get this article done right, and figuring out what little time together that would leave us. "What makes you think Gwen Lincoln will talk to you?"

"Her business partner brokered the deal."

"Yeah, I bet."

"Eileen assigned it to me. This is a huge step forward in her perception of what I can do for the magazine."

"That's great."

He let go of his lip and I waited for his mouth to curl up into a congratulatory smile. But that didn't happen. Instead, the man of my dreams chose that moment to say those three little words that can make your heart skip a beat, make you feel dizzy, and change a relationship forever. Three little words:

"Don't do it."

Two

DEAR MOLLY, I'M CRAZY ABOUT *this guy and he's crazy about me, but he's not crazy about what I do. And I'm talking my job here, not some weird little habit or sexual idiosyncrasy. He has a really dangerous job and I support him in his work. Shouldn't he do the same for me? My job isn't nearly as dangerous as his—people shoot at him all the time and they only shoot at me occasionally—so am I out of line to want him to return the favor? Signed, Baby Got No Backup*

One of the great benefits of being an advice columnist is that everyone else's problems are much easier to solve than your own. To a large extent, that's because you're only dealing with one fragment of their lives. Also, in writing to you, they tend to tip their hand about the heart of the problem, even if they haven't recognized it as such yet. For instance, the letter that's supposedly a complaint about having to shell out too much money for a ghastly bridesmaid's dress that also refers to the bride-to-be as "that selfish, man-stealing slut" indicates there are other issues at play in that warm and loving friendship.

That's why, when I'm stressed, I write letters to myself in my head. It gives me a little perspective, so I can take a deep breath and figure out how on earth I got myself into this particular situation.

After Kyle had told me not to do the article, I was at a loss. Not that I necessarily would've known the right thing to say had I seen his request coming, but since I was completely unprepared, it took me a moment to muster up an eloquent: "Why not?"

Kyle considered his answer so long I wasn't sure I was going to get one. Finally, he said, "This one's messy."

"Why?"

"First of all, it's still open. Plus, it just has that feel."

"So you don't think Gwen Lincoln did it?"

"Doesn't matter what I think. Not my case." His jaw set and I realized this was a major part of the problem. Not only was I going to be on police territory, I was going to be on another's detective's turf.

"I'm not going to get you involved," I promised. "I'd just like to understand what's going on before I interview her."

"It's not your case either."

I was surprised at how much that stung, even though I knew he didn't mean it to. All he was doing was explaining his concerns. But while I respected that, it didn't diminish the dig. "I'd never presume to be able to solve this murder before your colleagues do."

"Of course you would," he said flatly.

I didn't want this to turn into a fight, especially because, if pressed, I had to admit that he wasn't completely wrong. But surely there was a way to make this work for all parties. "Okay. There's some small chance that in the course of writing the article, I might come up with interesting information that's eluded the police so far. But I don't intend to race your fellow detectives to a conclusion. I'm writing about a suspect in the case, that's all." He stared at me until I felt compelled to add, "Promise."

Something else was bothering him. I could see it in the tilt of his head. He finally said, "This isn't like the other times."

"The other murders, you mean." He nodded and I refrained from asking him when he'd had the chance to compare notes with Eileen. "I know. That's why it's exciting. I'm not emotionally involved. I'm doing this as a journalist and it's a chance to show Eileen I'm capable of doing more at the magazine."

"Yeah. The 'doing more' . . ."

"I only want background from the detective in charge so I can understand what Gwen Lincoln might be going through right now. That'll be it. I won't bother anyone past that."

Kyle fixed me for what seemed like at least two minutes with a piercing but unreadable gaze. Finally, he said, "You're not going to get much, it's an ongoing investigation."

"I know. And I don't mean to put you in the middle. I'll go through the proper channels and set up my own meeting. I just wanted to tell you before I did any of that."

I wasn't sure if he was squinting or wincing as he shook his head. "Let me talk to him first. He can be . . ." Kyle searched for the proper description, then thought better of it. "Let me talk to him first," he repeated. "And I'll catch up with you later tonight." He wasn't exactly sending me away, but he wasn't inviting me to follow him inside either. But to prove that point that I was going to respect the process, I didn't argue the point or try to go with him. He kissed me softly—perfunctorily, if I wanted to be neurotic about it—and went back inside.

I walked back to my office, trying to clear my head before I returned to Eileen's turf. It wasn't that hot, by August standards. You could almost feel autumn lurking around the corner. A lot of my friends disdain walking, especially in an expensive pair of shoes, but I enjoy strolling in the city. It's a great way to get out of your own head and reorient yourself to the rest of the world, most of which seems to be parading by you as you work your way down Lexington or Broadway, displaying the dazzling varieties of race, age, shape, fashion, gender, economic level, and sexual orientation that exist. My grandmother always said if you sat in one place long enough, the whole world would go by. I'm pretty sure that one place is a corner in midtown Manhattan.

Back at my desk, I felt somewhat calmer, convinced there had to be a way to make this work without fouling up our re-

lationship. Not that balance and perspective are my strong
suits, but with a little work, I was sure I could scrape some
together.

I searched out all the information I could about Gwen
Lincoln and Garth Henderson. Quite a few of the articles I
found were about their behemoth wedding six years ago,
with its bank-busting decorations, platoons of attendants,
and full week of related social events. Then there was their
equally sensational separation five months ago, with its
high-spirited accusations of infidelity and emotional cruelty
on both sides.

There were also a fair number of articles dealing with
their business acumen and market savvy, but they weren't
nearly as revealing—or entertaining. And, of course, there
were those from the past few weeks about Garth's murder,
highlighting the key facts: he'd been shot (the locations of
the wounds had come out in the gossip columns rather than
the regular reportage), security records indicated he was the
only one who had unlocked the door that night so he had
opened the door to admit the killer, room service had delivered dinner for two at 9:15 and found Garth alone and alive,
and Gwen Lincoln had come to the hotel at 10:30 and demanded to be let into his room because Garth was expecting
her and she was concerned that he didn't answer the door.
She and the assistant manager discovered the body.

These were followed by articles about the police questioning Gwen extensively, talking to Garth's partner-to-be
Ronnie briefly, and the pressure being brought to bear by
friends of all involved to solve the case quickly. Emile Trebask wasn't prominent in any of the articles, but he was
quoted in one as "supporting my dear partner in this difficult
time." I wondered how deep their partnership ran.

A flash of inspiration hit me. I grabbed my phone and
called upstairs to our sister publication, *BizBuzz,* and asked
for Owen Crandall. Owen had been on staff at *Zeitgeist,*
writing for our fashion editor Caitlin, but in a shift that ben-
efited his resume, wallet, and mental health, had recently

moved upstairs to report on the business end of the fashion industry for The Publisher's newest venture.

"Would a caramel macchiato buy me fifteen minutes of your time, Owen?" I asked him.

"Molly, the pleasure of your company is reward in itself. But throw in an espresso shot and I'm yours."

A quick trip down to street level and around the corner for two coffees to go and I was back up at Owen's desk in short order. The bull pen for *BizBuzz* was almost identical to ours, but they'd been cursed with florid red and orange carpeting that Owen described as "the lava flow," while we trod on a blue and gray weave that tried to pass itself off as faux marble. No corner could be cut too sharply when The Publisher budgeted overhead items.

"I'd love to think you came to say you miss me, but you have that glint in your eye. You're on the hunt." Owen smiled and he had a great smile. Pretty great everything, actually. He was twenty-five, chiseled, with heavy-lidded eyes and a cleft in his chin to make Kirk Douglas weep with envy. More than one photographer had come in for a meeting and wound up courting him, but Owen wasn't interested. In fact, no one was sure what interested Owen. When he was downstairs with us, he'd been the object of much sighing from both genders but stayed maddeningly aloof about his personal life, tricky to do in our forced communal existence. Rumor proclaimed Caitlin had propositioned him more than once, which had spurred his desire to move up and out.

"I don't mean to be transparent," I said.

"Think of it as honesty between friends."

"Like the sound of that. So, speaking of between friends, what can you tell me about Gwen Lincoln and Emile Trebask?"

Owen shrugged. "Gwen's the major backer for his fragrance line. He leveraged everything he had to get the clothing line going, so his pockets are more shallow than you might expect."

"Is it all business between them?"

"I knew you were digging. Sorry to disappoint you, but Emile likes them young, blond, and male, which zeroes out Gwen. A meeting of the minds and the checkbooks, nothing more. What're you up to, Molly?" Owen leaned across his desk with a conspiratorial grin. "This about Garth Henderson?"

"Not yet." I didn't want to set the gossip train racing through The Publisher's kingdom before I'd even started working.

"Too bad."

"Why, what do you know?"

"Gwen was the one who got Garth to poach Emile from Ronnie Willis. Said if she was going to partner with him, they should keep the business 'all in the family,' you know? Ronnie was furious."

"And now they're all reunited. Minus Garth."

Owen nodded and sat back in his chair, licking at the whipped cream on his coffee in a way that would have brought half the bull pen downstairs to its knees. "Isn't that interesting?"

It certainly put the merger in a new light. I'd been surprised that it was even going forward but, in spite of an acrimonious, tabloid-fodder separation and pending divorce, Garth had not changed his will. I suppose when you're divorcing someone, you're so busy wishing him or her dead that you don't think about dying yourself. Upon Garth's death, his controlling interest in GHInc. had gone to Gwen and she was proceeding with the merger.

But that meant that Ronnie Willis, who'd thought he was merging with an advertising genius, now found himself partnered with a former cosmetics executive. One who'd conspired to steal a major client from him. I was surprised Ronnie wasn't invoking some key man clause to back out when the reputation of GHInc. had always been that it all hinged on Garth's individual brilliance. There had to be some other inducement for Ronnie to go forward. More than recapturing Emile Trebask.

"Where'd you hear this?"

"Someone who works for Ronnie. And even more interesting, I hear he's quite happy that the merger's going forward."

So Emile and Gwen wasn't the pairing to dwell on, it was Gwen and Ronnie. "Any other client fallout?"

Owen shook his head. "Sitting tight so far. I also hear the staff at Garth's place is solid, but Ronnie's people are nervous."

"You'd think Garth's people would be nervous, since their boss is the one who just got perforated."

"Yeah, but that's love and this is business."

"You think it's love? You think it's Gwen?"

"Why else shoot him where she shot him?" He gestured to his lap with a quick flinch.

"To plant that thought in everyone's mind."

Owen wagged his head a moment, rolling that thought around. "Hadn't considered that. So you don't think it's Gwen."

"I think I'm keeping an open mind. Besides, that's not what my article's about," I hurried to add, seeing the grin spreading across his face.

"Of course not. But if you find you need to share some suspicions, you know where to find me. And how much I cost." He toasted me with his coffee cup as I headed for the elevator.

Back at my desk, I read until my eyes crossed, then loaded up all the paperwork, trying to suppress college flashbacks, and decamped for drinks with Tricia and Cassady. Of course, meeting them for drinks could induce college flashbacks, too, but of a happier sort. They were the ones who dragged me out of our dorm suite the night I was suffering writer's block on a paper about Coleridge. Claiming to be my own visitors from Purlock, they took me to the neighborhood café where we ate hot pastrami sandwiches and drank kamikazes until I felt sufficiently inspired to go home and finish the paper. Thank goodness there hadn't been any opium dealers on campus. That we knew.

As Tricia and I settled in, the conversation turned to another crucial wrinkle in my investigation. "Kyle will get over it," Tricia assured me. "He's being protective and just needs some time to get used to the notion." We were at 5757, in the Four Seasons, waiting for Cassady to slip away from her science seminar and join us. I have a fondness for hotel bars; they tend to be quieter and people mind their own business because they're concentrating on business negotiations, vacation plans, or illicit affairs. This grand place, with its cozy tables in an airy space, was perfect for the kind of furrowed-brow discussion we were having.

"Kyle's just assuming I'm going to dig too deep and get into a mess."

Tricia framed the base of her cocktail glass between her delicate hands. "Now, he does have a certain amount of past experience on which to base that. So you really can't blame him."

And I couldn't disagree with her either, which painted me into a corner. "I'm learning from my mistakes as I go."

"Which we all applaud."

"And how better to see what I've learned than to test myself?"

"Are you rehearsing on me?"

"Depends. How convincing am I?"

"I'm always won over by simple earnestness. You're going to have to put something extra in the mix to sway Kyle."

"I should concentrate on persuading him I won't get into trouble this time."

"Excellent plan. And when you're done, you can persuade my mother I'll be married by Thanksgiving."

One of Tricia's great advantages in life is that she can completely snark you out and it takes a moment for you to realize that's what she's done. Even when it sinks in, you look at that porcelain goddess face and those huge Bambi eyes and think: *Did I hear her right?*

I thumped my hand over my heart. "*Et tu*, Tricia?"

"Molly," she continued smoothly, "if you're going to turn this interview with Gwen Lincoln into your investigative breakthrough, which I've been assuming all day is your intention, you need to commit to it. No matter what anyone else thinks, does, or says. And I speak these words with great sweetness in case any of them need to be eaten at a later date." She toasted me with her tequila mockingbird, then sipped it in punctuation.

I mustered an appreciative smile. "You're absolutely right."

"Thank you."

"He's just being protective."

"Probably."

"He'll come around once I get to work."

"Possibly."

"You're supposed to be fanning the flames, not dampening them."

"No, that I'll leave to her." She tipped her glass ever so slightly in the direction of the door, where Cassady was gliding in. An odd expression danced around Cassady's face, as though she were trying not to smile and not quite sure why she'd want to, all at the same time.

"You didn't wait for me," she sighed as she sat down.

"Comment or complaint?" I asked.

"Observation. An empirical one, at that."

I nudged Tricia. "She's been with scientists, learning new words."

"She's picked up worse things in the course of an evening," Tricia said.

"How many rounds behind am I? I'm surprised. It's usually a man who'll get started without you." Cassady looked past us, searching for the cocktail waitress and pretending not to see Tricia's grin.

"How hideous was it?" I asked.

"Actually, not so much. Interesting, even. I got into a pretty intense discussion with one of them afterward."

The waitress swept by and paused expectantly. Cassady has that kind of timing. It had taken us twenty minutes to order our drinks, but now, Cassady'd barely had time to decide where to set down her bag and she was ordering a metropolitan. The waitress left and Cassady leaned forward on the table, chin in her hands. The odd look was still on her face and I couldn't quite decipher it.

"Were you discussing science or how a pocket protector ruins the lines of a good jacket?" Tricia joked.

"Physics."

Tricia and I exchanged a look. "Physics," I repeated. Cassady's always had wide-ranging interests and her work often places her in fairly esoteric company, but I couldn't recall her talking about physics before. If pressed, I'd say the most scientific thing I've ever seen her do was walk into a party and instantly analyze the number of potential hookups in the room. But that's not science, it's math. Calculus, even.

"Where's Kyle?" she asked with a sly smile.

"Hang on. You can hurt people changing subjects that fast. Tell us more about discussing physics."

"Especially since Kyle isn't coming because he doesn't approve of Molly's new assignment," Tricia said.

"Not so much disapproval as a lack of wholehearted enthusiasm," I amended.

"Is he being protective or obstructive?" Cassady asked, more of Tricia than of me, supposing that I'd be a bit biased.

"The latter in service of the former," Tricia replied.

"So what're you going to do?"

"Write the article and trust that he'll understand."

"And you'll do just the article. No extraneous digging around or up or in or whatever the proper preposition would be in this case. Which, as a journalist and a sleuth, I would expect you to know," Cassady teased.

" 'Sleuth.' What an interesting word," Tricia said.

"Much sexier than 'reporter,' " I said.

Cassady nodded. "I believe it's Latin for 'pathologically curious.' But you didn't answer my question."

"I'm pretty sure you didn't ask one."

"Will you just do the article?"

"Now you're asking one."

"And you're still not answering."

"I'll do whatever it takes to write the article," I said crisply. "Now tell us about the science lesson."

Cassady thought a moment, then offered, "Everything in the world is connected in unexpected ways."

There was also something unexpected in the brilliance of her smile. "Ah. Are we talking about the science lesson or the scientist?" I asked.

"I'll let you know tomorrow. After lunch."

"I don't think I can stand the suspense. Don't we at least get vital statistics?" Tricia asked.

The waitress returned with Cassady's cocktail and she let us sit in anticipatory silence until the waitress withdrew. We were hugely intrigued, she knew it, and she enjoyed it. "As I said, let's wait until tomorrow and see if it's worthwhile information. Tonight is about the next step in Molly's career. To forward strides," she toasted.

"And to unexpected ways," I returned.

A surprising combination of the two capped off the evening. After relaxing conversation and even more relaxing cocktails, I made my way home and surrendered to jeans and a Tom Petty T-shirt, my favorite reading clothes. Dabbing a drop or two from Emile's vial behind my ears for inspiration, I threw a bag of popcorn in the microwave and dove back into my stacks of research.

Gwen Lincoln was taking shape in my mind as a strong, determined woman who had met her doppelganger in Garth Henderson and the combined intensity had been too much. Was it possible that there was a limit to how much of any one emotion a relationship could hold? Almost sounded like a physics problem for Cassady's new friend.

At a time when mega-agencies dominated advertising, Garth Henderson had prided himself on staying small and focused—a niche agency. Originally, GHInc.'s clients had been up-and-coming fashion folks. He'd had a good eye and most of his clients had done hugely well and stayed with him, which paid off handsomely in all sorts of ways.

Ronnie Willis and his agency were cut from similar cloth,

with slightly less sparkle. Ronnie's clients and his campaigns for them had been more hit-and-miss than Garth's, but there were occasionally brilliant campaigns and clients—like Emile Trebask—so a merger between likeminded artists had made sense.

But now, with Garth gone, what was Ronnie gaining, other than a precariously poised client list, by going ahead? Was his own agency in that much trouble, that merging with a dead man's company was better than staying solo? Or did he have faith in Gwen's managerial abilities being able to translate from one field to another? Emile Trebask and Ronnie Willis were both placing a lot of faith—and a lot of money—in Gwen Lincoln's hands. It made me want to meet her all the more.

I was so deeply immersed in my reading that the sound of a key in the front door caught me unawares and literally made me jump. I scrambled to the door, surprised to glimpse Kyle through the gap as the chain went taut. I fumbled it open and he paused uncertainly in the doorway.

"I didn't think you were home."

"I wasn't expecting you." That sounded awful, so I added, "So soon." I glanced at my watch, surprised to see it was a little after ten. "Oh, it's later . . ." I gestured feebly to the stacks of reading. "I lost track of the time."

He closed the door gently behind him. "This okay?"

Kyle had had his own key for about a month now. Danny and the other doormen adored him, so he came and went like any other resident of the building, even though we hadn't reached formal consolidation. He had clothes, toiletries, and CDs here, but I wasn't sure what the official tipping point was. Sports memorabilia on my bookshelves? Changing the answering machine to something cute about "*we're* not here"? Return-address labels with both our names? The ultimate was certainly his giving up his apartment—I had the better deal for price and location—but I knew we weren't there yet. How would I know when we'd arrived?

"I'm really glad to see you," I told him, trying not to sound too anxious.

"Sorry about this afternoon," he said, not taking his jacket off. He had about ninety seconds to take it off or I was going to get nervous, no matter how unattractive it might be.

"Me, too." He reached into his jacket, but left it on, and took out a folded sheaf of papers. Hefting them in his hand for a moment, he debated with himself one more time before holding them out to me.

I leaned in and kissed him rather than taking the papers, because I wanted to and because it was important to show him I cared more about seeing him than about whatever papers he'd brought. His response was warmer than it had been at the precinct, but there was still a fair amount of reserve. And the jacket wasn't budging, so I slid my hands inside it to ease it off.

"New perfume?" he asked, his mouth against my ear.

"Like it?"

"Interesting."

"It's Gwen Lincoln's new scent."

He took a deep breath, but I wasn't sure if he was checking out the perfume again or sighing. "I should go back," he murmured and I stopped with my hands in back of his shoulders. "I wanted to bring these by, see how you were doing." I slid my hands back out of his jacket and he laid the papers directly into my hand, watching for my reaction.

While the papers were clearly important, I was still more concerned about him. In the year we'd known each other, we'd been through more than our share of ups and downs; the more we fell for each other, the more the downs hurt. I didn't want this to become one. "Can you come back here when you're done?"

He gave me that look that somehow travels down the optic nerve to the muscles at the back of the knee and makes them go soft. "May I?"

"Please."

He nodded vaguely. His attention seemed even more focused on the papers than mine was, to the point that he tapped them with his finger so I'd open them. Unfolding the sheaf, I discovered copies of incredibly official papers. The affidavits of probable cause that had been filed for the search warrant for Gwen Lincoln's apartment the day after Garth Henderson's murder.

I felt like he'd brought me flowers and chocolates. Even better, because it went against the grain for him to do this, but he'd done it anyway. Maybe I could convince him to be excited about the article after all. If I didn't make a fool out of myself and overreact right now. "Thank you very much," I said with sincerity and, I hoped, not a trace of joyous squealing.

"These are public documents, I'm not leaking anything to you," he stressed. I nodded my understanding. "And if you wind up needing to talk to Detective Donovan, there's still some work to be done there. Work you're going to have to do."

Detective Donovan. "I'll take it one step at a time," I promised. And meant it.

He laughed a little, which delighted me. "Hey, a new approach."

I deserved that, so I returned the laugh. But I really was determined to be different this time. It was important to both of us for a lot of reasons that I handle this article carefully. "I appreciate this very much."

"Even when I don't approve, I still believe in you," he smiled.

"Appreciate that very much, too."

He took my face in his hands and kissed me with heat and gentleness wrapped into a delicious, dizzying combination. I tossed the papers behind me, hoping they were heavy enough to sail all the way to the coffee table, and slid my hands back inside his jacket.

I got the jacket off and then the shirt. "Do you really need to get back?"

"Yes," he said, lifting me off my feet and walking toward the bedroom.

"How soon?"

"Try and watch the clock."

I didn't even try. I did attempt to get up with him at about midnight, but he advised me to stay right there until he returned. He had some paperwork to finish so it could be on his lieutenant's desk first thing, but he'd be back. Kyle's a night owl bordering on insomniac and swears he does his best thinking in the middle of the night.

I didn't argue with him. I even thought I might fall asleep, but after the door closed behind him, the apartment got oppressively quiet and my mind started revving back up. After all, if he'd gone to the trouble of bringing those papers over, wasn't it rude to let them languish on the coffee table—or even worse, the floor?

They actually had made it to the table. I scooped them up and curled into my favorite seat, a well-worn leather club chair I'd inherited from a friend who'd moved in with a vegan, and started reading.

The affidavits were fascinating. I'd never seen these documents before, with their crisp, detached delineation of the facts that led the police to believe they would find the murder weapon and/or other incriminating evidence in Gwen Lincoln's apartment. There was, first and foremost, the fact that she'd found the body. Even though she had discovered it in the company of a hotel assistant manager, whom she had threatened with all manner of legal and physical damage if he did not open the door and let her in to see her soon-to-be-ex. Garth was living in the hotel while the divorce proceedings were being hammered out and Gwen had, allegedly, come by to visit him with legal documents. There were the proper phone records showing she had called him earlier in the evening to confirm when she was coming by, but the police believed all this could be ascribed to the careful crafting of an alibi, that she had in fact made the calls, then come to the hotel and shot him, then returned home until the appropriate time to leave again and publicly discover the body. The only people willing to vouch that she'd been home at the time of the murder were a maid with a long history of employment with Gwen and of drinking (cause and effect?) and a doorman who had been interviewed at home, where he was recovering from cataract surgery.

Moving down the damning list, there were several statements from colleagues of Garth's, describing screaming matches between the two of them that included Gwen spewing death threats. Once, according to the statements, she even specifically suggested "shooting him where he lived and she didn't mean his heart." There were other statements from friends, neighbors, and associates with further examples of the utterly heartless and completely ugly things people who used to love each other are capable of saying when the love is gone.

Additionally, there were statements referring to how Gwen stood to profit from Garth's death (though no mention of how she didn't really need the money), how she'd believed she deserved a piece of the company because of all her "inspiration and support," and how unhappy she'd been at the pending merger with Ronnie Willis' agency, though the reasons why weren't clear.

It was also fascinating to see how high-strung statements took on a life of their own when they were part of an official government document. I wondered how damning some of my grander statements to ex-lovers, ex-friends, and current colleagues might seem in that context. My mother used to warn me not to do anything I'd mind seeing on the front page of the paper the next morning, which made me reconsider reckless behavior more than once, but I'd never imagined something I'd done turning up in official police documents prepared for a judge. Intimidating to consider.

It had to be intimidating for Gwen, too. She hadn't been arrested yet mainly because the murder weapon hadn't been recovered and she had no guns registered in her name, and her fingerprints weren't found in the hotel room. There was nothing concrete to tie her to the murder scene—yet—but nothing concrete to tie her somewhere else either. And then there was the fact that she had seemingly gone out of her way to threaten her ex on a number of emotional and hyperbolic occasions and had gotten particularly virulent just before his death. Forensically, she looked okay. Emotionally, she looked awful. In my limited experience, it was the emotion that counted in the long run.

Somewhere around the quotes from the neighbor who commented on Gwen's temper and the employee who said Garth was actually afraid of Gwen in the days before his death, I drifted off to a light, fitful sleep filled with dreams about a frenzied Gwen Lincoln throwing dishes at Eileen in the kitchen of the house my aunt and uncle rent in the Outer Banks every August. When I woke up at 7 A.M., I had a stiff neck and a smiling homicide detective on my couch.

"Should've made a bet with you before I left," he said, scooping the last bit of oatmeal out of his bowl. Kyle was showered, freshly dressed, and ready to leave again. I felt hugely cramped and rumpled by comparison. "I knew you wouldn't be able to resist."

"So this was an exercise in temptation?" I stretched my way out of the chair and rubbed at the knot in my neck.

He smiled apologetically. "I thought about moving you back into the bed, but didn't want to wake you. We both needed our sleep."

"Thanks, I guess."

"And the papers weren't about temptation. It was an attempt to meet you halfway," he said, rinsing his bowl in the sink. He's much neater than I'd expected a guy who's always lived by himself or with other guys to be. He says his mother and sisters deserve the credit.

"What can I do to reciprocate?"

"Just remember you promised to stay out of trouble." He grabbed his jacket, scooped me up for a kiss, and was out the door before my head cleared. The boy certainly knows how to make an exit. Unfortunately.

Three

GOING AFTER A STORY IS sort of like going after a guy. When you're used to doing all the pursuing and all of a sudden you're the one being pursued, it can be a little disorienting. It can also make you question what you were after in the first place and how badly you want it.

I thought about staying home a few hours to finish going through all my research, but decided it was smarter to be in the office, close to Eileen and whatever mischief she might be brewing, and another coffee run for Owen if I needed more background. I'd barely dropped the hundred-pound stack of papers on my desk when the intercom line on my phone rang.

"It's Suzanne. Could I see you please?"

I took a moment before answering because I was debating whether to speak into the phone or turn around, look the ten yards to Suzanne's desk outside Eileen's door, and just yell, "What?" Trying to start my morning off as politely as possible, I said, "Be right there" into the phone, then strode to Suzanne's desk in under three seconds.

Being Eileen's assistant is a tough gig and Suzanne Bryant made sure we all knew it, wearing the squinted eyes and pinched smile of a martyr who can endure her pain as long as others notice her struggle. She'd only been on the desk a couple of weeks, so we were cutting her some slack due to the freshness of her suffering, but I was starting to sense a little enjoyment of the role on her part. This one bore watching.

"It's awfully early in the morning for me to have already done something wrong," I said to test the waters.

"Who said you'd done anything wrong?"

"Am I not being called to the principal's office?"

"That's not really fair, to Eileen or to me," she huffed.

"I never intended to be unfair to you," I promised her. She cast a significant look at Eileen's door, but I let my statement stand as is. "Did you need something?"

Suzanne handed me a message slip. "You better hurry. She's waiting for you."

"Eileen?"

"Gwen Lincoln."

The message slip had a Central Park West address on it. Only catch was, I'd been planning on calling and setting up the interview with Gwen Lincoln once I'd finished all my research. It hadn't occurred to me I'd be summoned at her convenience.

"Why are you still here?" Eileen shrilled before her office door was even fully open.

"I just arrived."

"Emile called minutes ago and said they were ready to see you. Go quickly, before they change their minds."

"Emile *and* Gwen?"

"That's not a problem, is it?"

Actually, it was sort of a problem to have other people dictating that the first interview of my first real investigative assignment had to happen before I was fully prepared, but I knew there was no room for argument. Making sure Suzanne had my cell number in case of another imperial summons, I threw a tape recorder and notepad into my bag and flew back downstairs and into a cab. Jotting my questions down in as organized and clear a manner as the lurching of the vehicle would allow, I managed to catch my breath by the time I arrived at Gwen Lincoln's apartment.

She promptly took it away again. I'd seen pictures of her,

but was still unprepared as she stepped into the doorway of her apartment's drawing room. It was a high-ceilinged room done in creams and golds and she was a luminous redhead, clear-skinned and statuesque, dressed in an amazing yellow Versace suit and a wicked pair of orange patent leather Brian Atwood pumps that showed off her yoga-sculpted legs to great advantage.

I was perched on the edge of the brocade settee to which the maid had directed me, still trying to decide what nonchalantly professional pose to strike, when Gwen appeared. She looked me over boldly and smiled. I tried to figure out what amused her more—my outfit or my look of surprise.

She strode over to me and I stood instinctively. Instead of offering her hand, she picked up the recorder from where it sat on the cushion next to me and flipped it on. "Molly Forrester," she said into it with a tone that implied if that hadn't been my name before, it was now. Tossing the recorder back to me, she indicated with the flick of an acrylic nail that I should lower myself back to the settee.

"Ms. Lincoln, thank you for seeing me."

"Did I have a choice, kiddo? That was never clear to me." She was in her mid-forties, but the "kiddo" seemed more a reference to our relative social standings than our ages. Taking the armchair across from me, she called, "Emile!" in the general direction of the doorway and I swore I heard it echo through the immense apartment. She turned back to me with a practiced smile. "It's his party, he should be here."

Her anger crackled across the gap between us like static electricity. It's wrenching to be suspected of murder—been there, felt that—and I can only imagine how much more difficult it is when you have a deep emotional connection to the victim. But the statistics do bear out looking at the spouse or significant other first; they usually finish quite high in the motive-means-opportunity trifecta. But Gwen Lincoln was casting herself neither as a wounded innocent nor as a potential liar covering her tracks. She was flat-out furious.

Not the smooth, polished beginning to the interview I'd been imagining for the last eighteen hours. I could feel the weight of my expectations, Eileen's doubt, and Kyle's worry sitting right on my chest, making it difficult to take a deep breath, so I sat up as straight as I could and forced myself to inhale slowly and evenly. "My understanding from Mr. Trebask was you were interested in talking to me," I said diplomatically, not wanting the interview to evaporate before it even began.

"Emile thinks he can take care of me. That can be highly entertaining in a man, but it can be tiresome as well," she said. She opened a heavy silver box on the end table next to her. "Cigarette?"

"No, thank you."

"Mind if I do?"

"It's your home."

"That doesn't stop people from lecturing me," she said, taking out a cigarette and lighting it with a dramatic flourish. "Everyone thinks they know what's best," she said, with a chill that made me fret for anyone who tried to tell her anything at all.

Emile Trebask chose that moment to enter, wearing crisp trousers and a perfectly pressed shirt from his new collection, with a cashmere sweater over his shoulders, frat-boy style. I wondered if he ever wore anyone else's clothes, which then raised the question of underwear, since he didn't design any. Not wanting to dwell on that, especially as I shook his hand, I switched to wondering if I should have put on some of his perfume. No, too calculating. And Emile was the one to leave the calculating to, as best I could tell. "Molly, thank you so very much for coming."

"Stop pretending any of this is voluntary, Emile," Gwen said, blowing smoke in his direction.

"I am so glad we have our party manners on," he responded, arranging himself on the arm and back of her chair like the spineless cat in *Peanuts*. "Thank God this isn't the story Molly came to tell."

"Why don't you tell it, then, so she gets the right one?"

There was a flash of anger in his eyes, but it vanished quickly as he leaned over and kissed her on top of the head—ever so lightly, not mussing her hair at all. "You can relax, Gwen, you're among friends."

"That's the real horror of a situation like this, you know," she said to me with a new urgency in her voice. "I can think of better ways to learn who your real friends are. Some of mine should have been given speeding tickets for how fast they distanced themselves when Garth got himself shot."

An interesting way of looking at being murdered—something he'd brought upon himself through provocation or perhaps carelessness. Definitely lacked even the lawyer-recommended dose of sorrow at the passing of a spouse, estranged or not. "You feel your friends have abandoned you?"

"They've given her space in which to grieve," Emile amended.

"Or they've gone out of their way to insist on my innocence to all who'll listen."

"That must be comforting," I attempted, watching Emile out of the corner of my eye. At the rate his body was stiffening, he was going to be back on his feet in moments.

"I should be flattered that a friend is so eager to prove me innocent of murder?" Gwen's eyes narrowed thoughtfully.

"What would you prefer I do?" Emile asked, standing up.

"Have a little faith that my innocence is apparent on its own."

Since I'd read the police documents and knew otherwise, I withheld comment. But when the pause that followed got to be awkwardly long, I suggested, "I'd like to know about the genesis of the perfume."

Gwen looked away from us both again, tapping the ash off her cigarette, so I looked at Emile. "How did you two wind up business partners?"

"Let me tell you the most frustrating part of all of this," Gwen continued, ignoring my effort to at least raise the supposed subject of the interview. "Garth's barely in the ground and everyone's already forgetting what a first-class shit he was."

Had I known her even five minutes longer, I might have suggested it was those sorts of comments that made Emile worry about her perceived innocence or lack thereof. "I didn't realize that was Mr. Henderson's reputation."

"It wasn't. It was his personality. His reputation was the charmer, the deal maker, the lover." She snorted derisively and a wisp of smoke snaked out of her nose. "He thought because he could find people to hang on his every word that they were worth hanging on. He never understood that some people will do anything if you pay them enough and mistook their love of their paychecks for love of him." She took a pensive drag on her cigarette. "Maybe some of them made the same mistake."

Emile sighed heavily, making sure Gwen heard it as well as I did. "Molly, it has always been a dream of mine to have a fragrance line. To complement the clothes."

Gwen was the one who stood now, pacing over to the marble fireplace and its stunning oil of her in a green velvet strapless Valentino ballgown, hair cascading over her bare shoulders. The picture was somewhere between a royal portrait and a Hollywood cheesecake shot. "Emile, stop conducting," she said, grinding her cigarette out in a crystal ashtray on the mantel with such force I expected the ashtray to shatter.

"You must get past the notion that everyone who wants to talk to you wants to talk to you about Garth." I could hear the effort he was making to keep his voice even, but Gwen didn't seem to notice.

"Maybe I need to talk about Garth. Has that occurred to anyone?" I was going to be touched, but then she did this Lana Turner spin-and-lean on the mantel and I wondered if they'd rehearsed this whole scene before I arrived.

"Fine, talk about him, darling, just make sure you work your way back around to Success when you're done weeping." Emile dropped into the chair she'd vacated, folded his hands, and waited.

Had I misread this relationship? I'd honestly thought that he was looking for a soft profile to build her some goodwill, if not clear her name. Was he really more interested in the perfume than in her innocence and using her momentary infamy for his own ends? Or was this a case of her image potentially overshadowing the perfume's? Or his? Or wasn't this about money at all?

"I can't get past this on command," she snapped.

Emile nodded wearily—they'd had this conversation before. "You've forgotten that you hated him, but not that you loved him."

Sliding away from the mantel, she walked toward me. "You can use that if you'd like. It's quite good."

Answering a summons was one thing, but I wasn't going to take dictation. I needed to do some steering here and get this visit back on productive ground. "Not being able to forget him—do you think that will pose any difficulties when you and Mr. Willis are running the agency?"

Emile smoothly intercepted that one. "It's going to be a difficult transition for everyone, Garth's top creative team most of all. They were devoted to him," he said gently.

"Devoted? Good Lord." Gwen extracted another cigarette from the silver box. "It was like some sick teen fan club, I hated going over there. You expected some of those girls to walk into presentations with 'We Love Garth' written on their palms with ballpoint pen."

I did my best not to get distracted by the memories of long-lashed and deeply dimpled Brent Shaw in tenth-grade English that that image conjured up. "Who didn't love him?"

Emile looked at me sharply, but Gwen gave me a half-smile. "Was I supposed to be keeping a list?" she asked.

"But you wouldn't be on it if you did."

"Didn't I make that clear?"

"Not completely. When Mr. Trebask said you hadn't forgotten you loved him, you said it was a good line, not a true statement."

Now I got a full smile, but it was icy. "What are you implying?"

"Nothing, except that with some people, even when they're maddening, there's a part of them you still care about, connect with."

Gwen dropped the cigarette back in the box. Her whole

face changed for just a moment, softening in a way I hadn't imagined possible. "Yeah," she breathed, "the bastards." Reconsidering, she took the cigarette out again and let the lid of the box fall closed, her face hardening again, but that one naked flash had been enough. She still loved Garth Henderson, no matter how many reasons she had to hate and/or vilify him. But there was that whole "thin line" issue—just because she still loved him didn't mean she didn't kill him. "Let me tell you, Ms. Forrester," she said, her voice having hardened, too, "if I'd killed him, there wouldn't be anything left."

"Gwen!" Emile objected.

Another statement aching to file itself in an affidavit. But then again, if she was being so injudicious with me, there was an excellent chance she was also being truthful. A liar would be more careful. "Do you have a theory about who did kill him?"

"Another list?"

"That many possibilities?"

She took a deep drag and fixed me with an intense look. For the first time, I recognized the woman I was accustomed to seeing in newspaper and magazine photos. "Actually, no."

"Why not?"

"His life was filled with dependent people. Which is one of the reasons I left. I wanted to be in a marriage, not a cult."

"It was my understanding," I said gently, "there was indiscretion on both sides."

She laughed with unexpected richness. "Aren't you polite."

And it was agonizing. I wanted to cut to the chase, but I could tell Gwen Lincoln was accustomed to being in the driver's seat and challenging her was sure to be counterproductive. I could also sense Emile Trebask's blood pressure creeping up as the conversation continued to hover around the murder and not the merchandise. "I was trying to be appropriate."

"Miserable, isn't it?"

I couldn't help but smile. "I just haven't had a lot of practice."

"Don't bother. People are going to judge you unfairly no matter what you do or say, so why not do and say what pleases you? You'll never please them."

"Thank you. Did you kill your husband?"

Emile sprang to his feet. "That's enough."

Gwen laughed even louder this time. "Good girl. No, I did not. Emile, sit down."

Instead, Emile stood over me. His hands swirled futilely in my face a moment, then buried themselves in his pockets, but not before I saw they were trembling. "Ms. Forrester, I asked you to do this article to support Gwen in our new business venture, not to cause even more ridiculous speculation about Garth's death."

"Emile," Gwen said, her voice soothing, "let's rethink this. What's going to get our beautiful venture more attention—a polite little chat where we avoid the elephant in the room or an article that will have everyone talking about us?"

Was it as apparent to Emile as it was to me that he had lost control of this situation? Was this typical of their relationship or was she just being tenacious about this particular subject? She seemed to be burning to say something, but waiting for me to ask the right question. Putting a patrician hand on Emile's shoulder and easing him back into the chair, she sat on the arm as he had before.

I pursued. "If you didn't kill him, do you know who did?"

"No," she said. Emile tensed as though he were going to get up again and I wasn't sure for a moment if the "no" was to him or to me. But she was looking right at me even as she slid her arm around his shoulders, either to comfort him or hold him in place. "Isn't this nicer than wasting our time playing games? And this is what you really need to know, not how Emile and I got together or why we picked this scent or what's next on our agenda."

"All of that's important, too," I said honestly, looking at Emile. I wanted to get the best information possible for the article, but it would all be for naught if Emile got too upset and narced me out to Eileen, who would take great delight in canceling the article. A little voice in the back of my head did question whether Gwen was putting on a show for me, but I still didn't sense any insincerity on her part. Her hands were rock steady, even if Emile's weren't. What was he so nervous about? "But I would like to get back to dependence. Do you feel these people were emotionally or financially dependent?" I asked.

"Both. His little fan club at the agency couldn't live without him on either level. And if Ronnie Willis thinks he's just going to slip into Garth's place—in the agency and in their hearts—he's delusional."

"Why?" The joining of the two niche agencies had created a lot of buzz in the volatile advertising world, but it had all been positive.

Emile must have felt we were headed back to solid ground, because he answered that one. "They were spinning it as a merger, but Garth was actually bailing Ronnie out. Ronnie was about to lose some major clients until Garth dangled the merger in front of them."

"Does that include you?"

Emile shrugged grandly. "I was already gone. Ronnie's terrific, but he wasn't keeping up with me. I wanted more, and Gwen assured me Garth could provide that."

"Accepting Garth's offer made Ronnie crazy," Gwen added with a tight smile, "but at least it let him cling to his illusions of power. The only thing worse than wanting power and never getting it, is having it and losing it. It drives people to extreme behavior."

I looked at Emile, waiting for him to tense up again, but despite the fact that his business partner had just accused someone of murder, he did nothing but trace the crease in his pants leg with his finger. Was he agreeing with her or ignoring her?

There hadn't been much in the police paperwork or the press accounts to bolster the theory of Ronnie Willis as a suspect. He'd been questioned because of the merger, but it had been brief and unproductive. According to a statement released by his lawyers, anyway. Besides, even if it were painful for him to cede some of his kingdom to Garth Henderson, if

Ronnie Willis had been on the brink of financial collapse, why would he have harmed the man who was rescuing him? "Mr. Willis doesn't gain anything by Mr. Henderson's death. He still shares control of the company. With you."

"You're assuming he's capable of rational assessment," Gwen answered. "Again, you're being far too polite. I don't think poor Ronnie has ever fully accepted just how fragile his position is. It's not too, too difficult to imagine him seeing himself taking over and guiding the new agency to great heights."

And apparently not too, too difficult to imagine him with a gun in his hand. I thought of a drowning swimmer who, in his panic, fights so hard that the lifeguard is the one who drowns. Could Ronnie Willis have turned on Garth Henderson, his savior, out of frustration or envy or panic? Had he known that would leave him with Gwen Lincoln as a partner instead?

"Do you anticipate any difficulties working with Mr. Willis?"

Emile covered his face with his hand, but Gwen smiled sadly. "Ronnie and I have been traveling in the same circles for a while. We aren't close, but I think we have a foundation to build on. Of course, the idiot called me the morning after Garth was killed and remembered to offer his condolences first, then told me he wanted to make sure Emile and I were going to stay with the firm because he'd be sure to take great care of us. 'In Garth's memory.'" Eyes closing briefly, she shook her head. Even a woman who believes you should always say what you want to say had her definition of being inappropriate.

When she opened her eyes again, they were brimming with tears. She tried to blink them back, rather than call further attention to them by wiping them away. "I identified the body that same morning. Now that's part of 'Garth's memory,' too."

Emile was up out of the chair in a flash, linen handkerchief at the ready, arm around her. "You don't have to talk about this part at all."

Gwen accepted the handkerchief, but pressed on, her voice surprisingly strong. "They tried to show him from an angle that minimized the damage I could see, but it was still so . . . And his mouth, his beautiful mouth . . ."

"His mouth?" All I knew about was the two gunshots.

"Cut." She drew two nails down her top lip, indicating vertical slices on either side of the fulstrum. "I wanted to kiss him good-bye . . ." She drew in a shuddering breath and in a sudden sweep, walked out of the room.

Not sure if that was my exit cue, I rose slowly. Emile stared at the floor for a moment, then looked out the door. When he looked back at me, he was smiling apologetically. "I had hoped this wouldn't happen." I started to blurt out an apology, but he wasn't talking about me, thank goodness. "I wanted her to do this article because she needs to be think-ing about other things, but everything is still Garth, Garth, Garth. He certainly screwed us over here."

So he was blaming the dead guy, she was weeping for him, and I was trying to keep my head from spinning. I'd re-alized this wasn't going to be a simple profile, no matter how much Emile wanted that, but this was turning out to be more of a maze than I'd expected. Hoped for, even.

"If she's not back by now, I'm going to have to go get her and this could all take a while. Why don't I call you at the magazine and we'll set up a new appointment."

I gave him my cell phone number, explaining my erratic presence at my desk, and he walked me to the front door. "You see she still loves him."

"Yes."

"Too bad there's not an off switch for that. But then, life wouldn't be nearly as interesting if we could control our emotions, right?"

A fascinating spin on a survivor's grief, so I just nodded. My gut told me Gwen Lincoln wasn't responsible for Garth's death, but I was still troubled by how hard Emile was working to make sure I believed that.

Emile shook my hand and I was out in the hallway, ring-ing for the elevator in one fluid sweep. As I descended, I considered my next move and decided I needed to talk to Ronnie Willis.

I'd promised Kyle I wouldn't try to outrun the detectives on this case. I'd promised Eileen I'd concentrate on Gwen Lincoln. But if the goal was to write about Gwen Lincoln's innocence, wouldn't it help to prove who was guilty? And what, dared I think, could it hurt?

Four

I DON'T LIKE TO LIE. Particularly because I'm not as good at it as I might be. So I attempt to do it as infrequently as possible and to confine it to exchanges with people who deserve it. That's why it was so nice, at last, to be in a position where I was digging into a story and could tell the truth about who I was and why I was digging. Or most of the truth, anyway.

The pleasure of making my first official call as an investigative journalist was only marred by having to listen to a hideous instrumental version of "Brass in Pocket." Aside from forcing me to confront the gritty cultural question of who'd thought it was proper to reduce such a great song to a series of airy clarinet riffs, the call was successful. I started off with the communications director of Willis Worldwide, explaining to her that I needed to speak directly to Mr. Willis because I was a magazine reporter doing a profile of Gwen Lincoln and was interested in Mr. Willis' feelings about going into business with her. The hope that other, more illuminating information might also come to light, I kept to myself.

The communications director parked me on hold, leaving me with the song. Fortunately, the interlude was brief and she was soon back to tell me that Mr. Willis happened to have a brief opening in his calendar if I could come to his office in an hour. Sign me up.

The offices of Willis Worldwide were only a few blocks away on Madison, so I had time to go over some of the questions raised by my brief stay with Gwen. Did Ronnie see this business arrangement as a merger of equals or was he aware of the perception, in Gwen's mind at least, that Garth had been saving him? Could he go forward without Garth and with Gwen? And where did he stand on the issue of Gwen and her guilt?

Still refining my questions as I got off the elevator, I was completely unprepared for what was behind the receptionist's desk. Not the petite brunette with the headset, pierced eyebrow, and tongue stud, which had to make answering the phone and saying "Willis Worldwide" eight hundred times a day even more enjoyable. The poster on the wall behind her. A huge blow-up of the ad that had made Ronnie Willis an advertising sensation fifteen years before. A Somalian boy of no more than six looked straight at the camera with searingly sad eyes. His emaciated frame was draped in a woman's spangly gold evening wrap, but his malnutrition-distended belly poked through. The caption read: DOES THIS MAKE ME LOOK FAT?

The posters had been part of a fashion-industry-backed campaign to raise funds for African famine relief, but the explosion that issued forth from the TV pundits, talk radio ranters, and op-ed exorcists had not paid much attention to that part of the story. Instead, Ronnie Willis had made a name for himself in advertising by angering, insulting, and outraging people. He had proudly embraced it as his modus operandi ever since. He and Garth were kindred spirits, but if what Gwen Lincoln had told me was true, Ronnie's magic touch had faded while Garth's had continued to shine.

The impatient clicking of a tongue stud against teeth brought me back to attention. The receptionist frowned at me expectantly.

"Hi. Molly Forrester, here to see Ronnie Willis."

"Really."

Not that an icy attitude is uncommon in the ranks of Manhattan receptionists, but this was a stronger dose than I was expecting. I'd smiled at her as I'd approached, looked her in the eye when I spoke to her, and been warm and polite in tone. Now I tried to keep my return "Really" cheerful. What had I done to earn the coolness?

"You don't seem his type," she continued.

"Excuse me?"

"You called just a little while ago, right? And he moved stuff around to see you right away. I figured that meant you'd met him at a club last night or something but, like I said," she sniffed, "you don't seem his type."

"I'm interviewing him for a magazine article," I said, not sure why I felt I had to explain myself to her. At least it got a smile in response, though I couldn't be sure if it was because she'd been right that I wasn't his type or because a magazine writer was more interesting than a day-old club date.

"Which magazine?" Interest piqued, she leaned forward. As the V-neck of her tee gapped, I caught a glimpse of a tattoo that looked suspiciously like a tentacle rising out of her cleavage.

"*Zeitgeist,*" I answered, taking care not to look directly at the tattoo or any other part of her chest while I waited for her to say something cutting about the magazine. She was not exactly our target demographic.

"Oh, right. 'You Can Tell Me.' I knew I recognized your name." She punched a button on her console and said my name into her headset as I tried to imagine her reading my column in line at the tattoo parlor. "Ronnie's assistant'll be right out. Have a seat."

She indicated the low-slung sofas to her right, but I had to hover a moment longer. "You've read my column?" I asked, trying to sound offhanded and not surprised. Meeting people who know my column—especially unlikely candidates—is a wonderful way to get perspective on the letters and my advice. Of course, they aren't always pleasant encounters, like the sales clerk at Good Guys who read my name off my credit card and proceeded to chew me out in front of the entire store because I'd allegedly encouraged his girlfriend to move out and stick him with half the rent, a three hundred dollar phone bill, and an STD. I was quite sure I hadn't given that specific advice, but he'd been equally sure I was lying.

Fortunately, the receptionist seemed more bemused than angry. "Yeah. People can be so screwed up."

"True."

"That one last month, about the cow who was stealing all her sister's boyfriends? I so know who wrote that one."

"I keep all that confidential," I said preemptively.

"I respect that, I wasn't trying to get you to tell or anything, it was just so clear to me that it was pretty wild to see it there in print and think, 'Hey!'"

She smiled with great satisfaction and I nodded back, happy she had no issue to settle with me. "As long as you don't want me to name names, I'm always happy to discuss the column," I said.

"So are you really here for an article or did Ronnie write you a letter?"

"I'm doing an article on Gwen Lincoln, but Mr. Willis is part of the story." I almost didn't finish the sentence because of the odd look that crossed over her face when I said Gwen's name. It was more than concern she might lose her job because of the merger, but I couldn't quite identify it.

She sat back in her chair and fiddled with the neckline of her shirt, as though trying to tuck the tentacle back down out of sight. "Yeah. Have fun with that."

Before I could ask her what exactly she meant, a silky voice called my name. A catwalk castoff slouched her way down the hall toward me, her brown hair as long and straight as her body, her face blankly beautiful. "This way please," she said, pivoting to go back from whence she came without pausing, leaving me to scramble to catch up. I threw a look back over my shoulder at the receptionist, but she turned away. I was going to have to get back to her.

The hallway walls were painted an unsettling shade of deep orange and adorned with other framed ads created by

Ronnie and his agency. They were all familiar, but as I looked around, I didn't see one less than three years old. Had someone forgotten to cycle in the new hits—or hadn't there been any?

Ronnie's assistant deposited me in a conference room featuring floor-to-ceiling windows with nothing in front of them and withdrew. The space was nearly filled by a mammoth conference table of highly polished cherry and severe matching chairs. An immense plasma screen on one end of the room was balanced by whiteboards on the other. Everything else was glass—glass walls on one side, windows on the other. It made the whole room feel like it was suspended, rather than being connected to the rest of the building. It wasn't a completely pleasant sensation. I eased past the table, wanting to check out the view, but the closer I got, the more I felt I was tipping forward, on the verge of falling through the glass and plummeting twelve stories to the hum of Madison Avenue below.

"Wanna jump?"

Startled, I turned quickly as Ronnie Willis slid into the room. He was taller than I'd expected from his publicity photos. His thin face was very boyish, despite the deep creases at the corners of his eyes. A neatly trimmed beard and mustache obscured the lines around his mouth. A few bold strands of silver poked up in his thick black hair and his eyes were a warm, mossy green. He was one of those men who, feature by feature, are quite attractive but somehow the whole package doesn't hold together the way it should, draping a sense of awkwardness over him.

"Should I?"

"Seems to cross most people's minds," he shrugged. He slid his hand across mine in greeting. "Ronnie Willis."

"Molly Forrester."

"Hope you don't mind, my babysitter wants to horn in." He gestured vaguely to the doorway, now filled by a severe young woman in a black MaxMara suit and a terrific pair of Jimmy Choo kidskin slingbacks.

Meeting her halfway, I shook hands with her. "Paula

Wharton, communications director. We spoke on the phone," she said in a tight, unhappy voice.

"Nice to meet you in person."

Ronnie sighed. "I don't have anything to hide about what Garth and Gwen mean to me, or about anything else in my frigging life for that matter, but Paula's got to monitor me anyway. Thinks I don't know how to behave, especially around women." He winked at me with overblown zeal, then bugged his eyes at Paula, awaiting her reaction.

She glanced at him without smiling and sat down at the far end of the conference table. Ronnie leaned his forehead against the window, looking straight down to the street. His jacket shifted oddly on him and, for a moment, he looked like a scarecrow peering down from his perch at the worms in the field. "Does make you kinda dizzy, doesn't it."

"I was actually worried about falling, not thinking about jumping," I said, not eager to return to the window.

"Wind up on the sidewalk one way or the other," he said, forehead still on the glass. "What's the difference?"

I couldn't tell whether he was trying to provoke a reaction or was genuinely philosophizing. A glance at Paula didn't help; she was keying something into her BlackBerry. I wanted Ronnie to be relaxed and speak freely, but wasn't sure that could happen with Paula acting as watchdog. But maybe if I played his game a little, that would help. "Isn't the difference control?"

"Yeah, right," he snorted. "Like that's not the greatest illusion in life."

"Yet your profession is all about control. Controlling what we want, what we think we need. Which controls our spending, eating, socializing . . ."

He swung back from the window. "Ohmigod. You're on to us and now I have to kill you." Paula's head snapped up. As old a joke as it was, it was truly startling in this context. I couldn't manage a laugh in response and Ronnie winced. "Sorry. That was stupid, wasn't it. You're here about Garth and I'm making . . . See, that's why she's here. I am an asshole sometimes. Please, have a seat." Suddenly all knees and elbows, he pulled a chair out from the conference table for me.

I didn't sit down right away. I'd heard tales of Ronnie's goofy charm, but this seemed more like antic desperation, tap dancing before the music even started playing. Paula put away her BlackBerry. "I'm actually more interested in Gwen Lincoln," I reminded him.

Ronnie drummed his hands on the back of the chair as though he needed to bring it to my attention that the chair was available. "Yeah, but that still means you're here about Garth. He was the link between Gwen and me. I'm gonna do everything I can to preserve the relationship now that he's gone, but it'll never be the same. Just gotta hope fortune'll smile on the brave. Or at least not crap all over me."

"You're not confident of the success of the new agency?"

"Sit down and we'll talk about it," he said with a surprising edge to his voice. More than impatient, he was now troubled I hadn't taken a seat. Or that I was asking the wrong questions. Not wanting to anger or annoy him, I sat down, putting my notebook and tape recorder on the conference table. Somewhat relieved, Ronnie swooped around the table to sit facing me, giving me a smile, then glancing at Paula.

"Future of the agency," she prompted.

"Yeah. I know I'm damn good and so are my people. Garth's people are tremendous. Gwen's wonderful. But how many things in life really turn out the way we expect?" Ronnie shifted in his chair, having some difficulty getting comfortable.

"Ronnie's just being alert and cautious, as any good leader would be, about the process of mixing two companies. Especially in light of the tragedy," Paula elaborated. Ronnie looked as though he were going to disagree with her assessment, but then his mouth shut and he nodded in agreement.

"My bond with Gwen is what really matters, what I want most to save," Ronnie said, working to focus.

Not exactly the impression I'd gotten from Gwen. "Is it in danger?"

"It's hard to do business with friends, that's all. Not that I could ever replace Garth for her or Emile or any of them, but I gotta do what I can to protect them all."

"Protect?"

"Whoever did this to Garth—who knows who else they're angry at? Gwen could be in danger, too."

Glancing at Paula, I found she was already watching me for my reaction. "Danger from whom?"

"The maniac who did this. Until he's caught, Gwen needs to stay vigilant. We all do."

Everything I'd read or heard whispered or whispered myself had examined Garth's murder as a single act, driven by either passion, which made Gwen the front-runner, or money, which shone a light on Ronnie. No one had yet suggested that Garth was the first on some sort of list. I checked Paula for her reaction, but she was looking at her boss steadily. This was not a new theory to her, but I couldn't tell how much credence she gave it. Was it serious or just Ronnie trying to make himself a larger part of my story? Or Ronnie thinking he could stay out of the suspect column if he listed himself under "potential victims"?

"You think you're at risk as well?"

"Shit, yeah. I've already spoken to the police about it."

"Do they share your concern?"

Paula glanced down at the tabletop and Ronnie's nostrils flared briefly. "They're prepared to look into it."

I assumed that meant no. "Mr. Willis—"

"Ronnie."

I acknowledged the gesture with a nod, but couldn't quite bring myself to say it out loud. Something about his deliberate boyishness combined with the diminutive name smacked of trying too hard and made me uneasy. Was he covering up guilt or something else? "Do you have any suspicions about who might mean all of you harm?"

"None. That's what's so frigging terrifying. It could be anyone. You have any idea of the number of hearts we touch, minds we change each and every day with our work? And if just one of them is sick, twisted, desperate, and takes issue with us, what can we do? Apparently, we can die all alone in a hotel room, well before our time. Or we can be alert and ready."

I half-expected him to draw a pistol out of his waistband and wave it at me, but thankfully, he just smacked the table for emphasis. Not to be unsympathetic—losing someone close to you to murder is cataclysmic, especially if you believe it puts you in harm's way as well—but Ronnie's manic behavior seemed out of proportion. Unless there was someone impacted by the merger who could loathe Garth and Ronnie equally and see Ronnie as a viable next target. "Given your concerns, is it safe to proceed with the merger?"

Ronnie looked queasy for a moment, then nodded. "I sure hope so. It's what's best for both firms. And I know it's what Garth would've wanted."

"We're straying from the point of the interview, aren't we?" Paula asked pointedly.

The point of the official interview, sure, and I couldn't think of a way to stay on the topic of Garth's death that wouldn't arouse Paula's suspicion and further inflame Ronnie's paranoia.

"Right," Ronnie said. "Let's dish about Gwen." Paula cut him a warning look, but he reached over and patted her hand sloppily. She slid her hands into her lap, out of his reach.

"I'd like to get your impressions of Gwen as a businesswoman, moving forward with both the agency and her venture with Emile Trebask in the shadow of her husband's death," I said.

"Ex-husband," Paula corrected.

"The papers were never signed."

"Unsigned papers'll change your life," Ronnie said lightly, making a visible effort to relax now that the conversation was moving away from the shooting. Though he professed affection for Gwen, he apparently didn't fully embrace the thought of being her business partner.

Running Garth's company—without Garth—potentially put Ronnie in an enviable position in a hugely competitive field. But could he maintain that position? The aging posters on the hallway walls made me wonder. "Even with Ms. Lincoln's involvement, are you comfortable taking Mr. Henderson's place?"

Ronnie shook his head emphatically. "I'm not gonna try. He was one of a kind. But I can keep the firm moving ahead on the path he laid. As long as I still have those girls."

"Those girls?"

Leaning back in his chair, Ronnie flashed me a grin. "You haven't met the Harem?"

"Ronnie, don't—" Paula attempted, but Ronnie shrugged her off.

There was a joke here I wasn't in on, a fact Ronnie seemed to enjoy a great deal. "I'm afraid I haven't had the pleasure."

"Garth had an eye for beauty and an eye for talent. And a knack for finding both in one place. His creative directors are some of the most exquisite young women in advertising. The rest of us jealous bastards call them the Harem."

Visions of Bond girls danced in my head. Why, yes, she's a nuclear scientist, but she's a swimsuit model, too! Still, given GHInc.'s track record, whoever these lovelies were, they had to know their stuff.

"You don't approve," Ronnie noted, making me aware I was not controlling my facial expressions.

"I'm sure I just don't appreciate the joke fully," I said diplomatically.

"That statement's not for attribution," Paula said firmly.

"Relax, Paula, Molly isn't here to get us into trouble. Besides, it's not like it's a secret."

"It's less than professional," Paula said, without indicating whether she was referring to the nickname or his delight in it.

"Thing is, they're the soul of that agency. I'm just hoping I can inspire them to anything like the heights Garth led them to. God knows I miss Garth, but I still have a company to run, a reputation to sustain, and I am gonna use each and every asset at my disposal to make sure that happens. Anyone brave enough to come along for the ride is absolutely welcome." Paula caught his eye and he took a deep breath. "Everything I have is in this now and I'm gonna make it work."

Did he want pity or respect? Or both? I did feel for him, the sum total of his professional life hanging in the balance because of Garth's death. But a man with that much hanging in the balance was a man that much more likely to take desperate steps. Had he created the situation he was now proclaiming he could overcome? Brimming with questions I couldn't ask, I went back to the subject at hand. "What does Gwen think of the . . . creative directors?"

Ronnie's thin lips twisted. "She recognizes them as a tremendous business asset," he said with an utter lack of conviction, sounding like he was quoting from an annual report.

Again, I tried to home in on the source of his discomfort. "Were any of them anything more to Garth?"

Before Paula could object, Ronnie answered smoothly. "I never name names. That way, no one's ever tempted to do it to me."

"Are you married?"

"Why, are you?"

"No."

"That's nice to know."

"But completely irrelevant."

"Not at all. I like to know everything possible about the people I'm talking to, don't you?"

"That is part of being a reporter."

"Tell me something else about yourself."

"I'm very anxious to ask you more questions about Gwen Lincoln."

"She's not easily distracted, is she, Paula?"

"What're you trying to distract me from?"

Ronnie laughed, but it came from too high in his chest to be real. I'd caught him and he didn't want to admit it. What didn't he want to talk about?

"Tell me more about the Harem," I asked, trying to sound playful.

Ronnie shook his head. "I'm not gonna waste your time

rambling. You wanna know about Gwen. What else can I tell you about her?"

I wanted to talk about Gwen and the Harem, even more so now that he didn't. I needed to come at him sideways. Remembering the odd look on the receptionist's face, I asked, "How long have you known each other?"

I could've sworn what flickered through his eyes was admiration. I'd hit on the very thing he didn't want to talk about. "We were acquainted in the days before she married Garth."

"Acquainted" struck me as an evasion Bill Clinton would've been proud of. I had to press. "Ever anything more?"

His smile went a little rigid. "Yes. Now we're very good friends. And about to be successful business partners."

"You've forgiven her for stealing Emile Trebask from your agency?"

"Makes me admire her business savvy that much more."

"And now that you're all back together again, it doesn't really matter."

He leaned forward, his gaze cool and direct, and I knew whatever he said next, it was going to be a lie. "True."

"When does the merger become official?"

He leaned back again, waving his hand dismissively. "Any day now. We put everything on hold when Garth died, of course, but the lawyers are smoothing out the last few details. And some redecorating's being done over there before we move in."

"Are you involved in the campaign for Success?"

"Of course. We're all very excited about it. The campaign and the perfume. The print campaign will be previewed at Emile's gala. Awesome work."

"So you're looking forward to the future."

"You bet."

"No regrets about having to give up your autonomy and individual creative vision to merge with a company that's now less than what you were expecting?"

Ronnie stared at me for a cold moment, lacing his long

fingers together in front of his face. "You're way too young to understand the true meaning of a question like that."

"I understand whoever killed Garth Henderson took more away from you than a partner. Do you think that was the goal?"

Fear dashed across Ronnie's face and his hands fell away. "No. This isn't about me."

"And yet you're concerned you could be next."

"As a loose end, not a primary target. I didn't do anything wrong."

"And Mr. Henderson did?"

Paula tapped her pen on the table. "I don't see how idle speculation could possibly add to a profile of Ms. Lincoln. Perhaps you'd like to e-mail me the rest of your questions and we'll reply in kind." Interestingly, Paula seemed more upset with Ronnie than with me, but whichever, she was pulling the plug. She stood and waited for Ronnie to do the same.

He hesitated, then rose slowly, his face settling back in that same "here comes a lie" expression. "Let me say one last thing. I'm gonna miss the hell outta Garth, but I take comfort in the fantastic possibilities of my new partnership with Gwen Lincoln, a woman of tremendous business instincts and creative drive."

I flipped off my recorder and slowly gathered up my things. Now I was certain he was hiding something, but I also knew if I pushed it, Paula would make sure I never talked to him again. "I appreciate your candor and your time, Mr. Willis. I'll be in touch, Ms. Wharton."

I shook both their hands. Hers was the same rote jiggle she'd given me when she'd entered. But Ronnie, who had barely bothered on the way in, now held my hand in a death grip. "I don't need to tell a smart one like you how delicate all this is," Ronnie said, that hint of fear creeping back into his voice.

"I don't want to cause trouble for anyone," I assured him, thankful that no one who knew my track record was around to dispute that.

The slouching assistant materialized to escort me to the

elevator. I said I could find my way, but she insisted. I wasn't sure if they were worried I'd get lost or if I'd steal something on the way out. I had hoped to chat with the receptionist again, but she wasn't at the desk, replaced by a young man who sat up so straight with his hands folded on the desk that I suspected electrodes in the chair or drugs in the coffee.

Back down on the street, I paused to turn on my phone and consider the potential guilt of Ronnie Willis. He was hiding something, but was it related to Garth's death or some other aspect of the merger? Were professional or personal demons haunting him?

Before I could formulate an answer I was happy with, my phone rang. It was Tricia, wondering if I'd heard from Cassady. My head was so full of Ronnie and Gwen that it took me a moment to remember Cassady's lunch with the physicist.

"Maybe they aren't done yet," I suggested, heading back toward my office.

"It's almost three o'clock," Tricia said.

"Maybe it's a good lunch. Or the service is slow."

"I'm just so intrigued. It's not like her to withhold so much information. Speaking of which, how did your interview go?"

"Interviews, plural."

"Tell me, tell me."

I was beginning to when my call-waiting beeped. "Hang on, let me see if this is Cassady."

"I'll hang up and you can three-way me back in."

Tricia did just that and I picked up the second line just before it escaped to voice mail. "Hey, you," I said, not bothering to look because I was so sure it was Cassady.

"Hey, yourself."

It wasn't Cassady and I could hear him chuckling as I groped for a clever response and failed to find one.

"Of the many things I love about you, the fact that you haven't changed your cell number is pretty high on the list right now," he continued. "I need to see you."

"Why?"

"Many reasons, but primarily because we seem to be working on the same story."

Which is, I swear, the only reason I agreed to have drinks with Peter Mulcahey.

Five

"WE CAN'T ALLOW THIS TO happen."

"It's just drinks."

"I've lost count of the number of disasters that have begun with that phrase."

Tricia and Cassady had arrived at my office hoping to swoop me off for cocktails and I had stunned them with the news that I was otherwise occupied. With Peter. Stunning the two of them is no mean feat and normally I would've taken a certain amount of pride in the accomplishment, but there was that little gnawing feeling in my stomach that knew their misgivings had some merit.

"Why on earth?" Cassady asked.

"He says we're working on the same story."

"How would he know?" Tricia asked.

"I haven't figured that out yet."

"All the more reason not to see him," Cassady said. She leaned against the desk of Carlos, the editorial assistant who camps out next to me, and I could see the muscles in his neck clench as he resisted the urge to lean back into her.

Tricia took my chair, but Cassady's side. "You know Peter, he's trying to steal information and sources from you. He always wants someone else to do the hard work."

"So maybe I'll beat him to the punch and steal something from him."

"Do you have a suspect yet?" Cassady asked.

I glanced around the bull pen to determine how many eavesdroppers were on alert. Carlos was mesmerized by Cassady's cologne, but plenty of other ears looked a little too perked up. "Of course not. I'm just doing an interview and the whole point of the interview is that she isn't a suspect," I clarified for all within hearing range.

"Maybe you do need to see him," Tricia said suddenly.

"Traitor," was Cassady's response.

"He has information about what she's doing that she didn't think was public. She needs to at least figure out what his source is. If there's a leak, we need to know."

Cassady thought about that one briefly. "I really hate that there's a good reason for her to spend even two minutes with him."

Tricia shook her head. "It's like Eva Marie Saint having to shoot Cary Grant in *North by Northwest*. Just part of the intrigue."

"But they wound up together at the end of the movie."

"Don't worry about that," I assured Cassady. "Peter is ancient history and will stay that way. But I do want to find out how he knows what I'm doing. And if he has any insights into this story that he's willing to part with."

"Just be careful what kind of bargain you strike with him."

"You think that poorly of my self-control?"

"The mother of us all fell prey to a snake. I hate to see any other woman make the same mistake."

"Perhaps we should chaperone," Tricia suggested as we made our way to the elevator.

"It's really all right," I assured them both now. "I'm over Peter—"

"But he's not over you," Cassady interjected.

"Of course he is. This is professional taunting, nothing more. I'll check for leaks, see what else I can learn, and be out of there in record time."

"But not too fast," Tricia suggested.

"Snakes don't deserve good manners," Cassady said.

"But if we are going to be working the same turf," I said,

assuming I was getting Tricia's point, "it makes sense not to antagonize him."

Tricia nodded and Cassady sighed in capitulation. "All right. But mark my words. You're going for cocktails with a man you used to sleep with, a man you then dumped, who now has something you want. What good can come of it?"

"Thank you for the warning and a special thank you for issuing it in a crowded elevator. Good evening, everyone," I said with a smile to the rest of the passengers as I let Cassady and Tricia exit ahead of me. I tried to think of the variety of smirks I saw as moments of unexpected joy my friends and I had been able to bring to our fellow Manhattanites. That's better than dwelling on the concept of people laughing at you on their way home.

Cassady stepped to the curb, raised a hand, and a cab stopped. She's gifted that way. "If you don't call us by eight, I'm sending the SWAT team in," she vowed, opening the door for Tricia.

"Speaking of calls, how'd lunch with the physicist go?"

"Gee, I'd love to tell you, but you have other plans. Guess it'll have to wait."

Tricia leaned back out of the cab. "Be careful."

"As always."

She and Cassady rolled their eyes at each other as Cassady got into the cab. "Eight o'clock," Cassady reminded me.

"Sooner," I assured her as they drove off. I hailed another cab for myself—not with Cassady's ease, but eventually—and headed down to the Flatiron Lounge.

The only thing I handle with less confidence than current boyfriends is former boyfriends. In my relationship with Kyle, I was exerting supreme effort to relax and enjoy the natural progress of things. Until that little voice started whispering that there is no natural progress, that a relationship requires guidance and training and cultivation. Or is that roses? I wonder sometimes if it's the downside of being an advice columnist—you become so acutely aware of the myriad ways people screw up relationships that it seems impossible to take a step without detonating a landmine. The shoemaker's shoeless children and all that.

But the care and feeding of an ex is a whole different obstacle course. Normally, I move on and pretend neither to care nor consider how he ever thinks of me, mentions me, spits when he sees me coming, etc. But it's a pretense because I do care, I do consider, especially when I did the dumping. It's as Dorothy Parker said, in reference to her heart being broken, "Once there was a heart I broke; And that, I think, is worse."

Not that there was a chance I'd broken Peter's heart. I was pretty sure it was unbreakable. But I had dumped him pretty abruptly because Kyle had taken my breath away and I regretted not being more civil about it. The burning question was if I was about to pay for that.

He was waiting for me at the bar, half-leaning, half-perched on a stool like he owned the place. I saw him first, which gave me a chance to absorb the fact that he looked really good, in that effortless, Nautica-ad way of his. He was wearing his golden hair shorter, which suited him, and had gotten a lot of sun—probably sailing with his cousins at Martha's Vineyard—which made his pale blue eyes stand out even more. Or maybe it was the cobalt blue lamps above the bar that electrified them.

I was surprised by a butterflyish sensation in my stomach. What was there to be nervous about? Other than letting him play me into making a fool of myself. Or doing it all on my own. He was up to something, had to be, and I needed to be on guard.

One thing at a time. Taking a deep breath and walking up to him, I debated how to greet him. A handshake might be too cool, but a hug and a cheek kiss might be too insincere. What would Barbara Stanwyck do? No, that didn't help, because she would have shot him rather than break up with him and wouldn't be in this position in the first place.

Lucky for me, he spotted me as I approached and dropped me a mocking bow, which left me no alternative but to offer my hand. He took it, kissed it lightly, then put his other hand over it as he straightened up. "Good to see you, Molly," he said.

"Good to see you, too, Peter. You look great."

"Just trying to keep up with you." He kissed my hand again and swept me onto a bar stool. "What'll it be?"

"Scotch mist, please."

I watched him carefully as he ordered, trying to remember what had first attracted me to him. Probably that I'd never dated anyone like him—he was very Ivy League and I am anything but—and he was a charmer par excellence. We'd had a lot of fun, but it had all stayed pretty close to the surface, whereas with Kyle, things had gotten so deep so fast, it still made my head spin sometimes.

He turned back, blatantly looking me over. "Thanks for meeting me."

"You made it pretty hard to resist. How'd you know what I was working on?"

He pulled a mock frown. "Do we have to talk business right away?"

"I'm sorry, is there something we should discuss first?"

"Sure. Weather. Politics. The cop."

"Do I get to pick?"

"You still with him?"

"Which candidate are we talking about?"

"The cop."

"Yes."

"How unfortunate."

"Not at all."

"For me."

He gave me a lazy smile to show he didn't mean it, but I decided to take the opportunity anyway. "Peter, I am sorry."

"Wanna come back?" he asked, his smile growing.

"Sorry about how I handled things, I meant."

"If I forgive you, wanna come back?"

I couldn't help but smile in return. "You don't want me back."

"What makes you think so?"

"Because you're willing to say so."

"How can you write that column and be so wrong about something so basic?"

Before I could say anything, his hand was behind my neck and he was kissing me with startling vigor. I was literally gasping when he let me go.

I didn't appreciate Peter playing around like this, but experience told me that coolness made more of an impact on him than anything else, so I was careful not to overreact. I went for a Scarlett O'Hara response, fanning myself with a coaster from the bar. "Oh, now that changes everything. Want to take me home right now?"

He frowned. "You don't kiss the same way anymore."

I snuck a quick lick of my bottom lip, trying to tell if I had any lipstick left at all. What was he up to? This was taking the game a bit far, even for him. "It has been awhile, Peter."

"Have you thought about me at all?"

"Of course." I smiled. "You and the weather and politics and the cop."

He laughed as sincerely as Peter ever laughs at anything. He's more of a grinner, more apt to say "That's funny" than to actually chuckle.

"Please don't try to cloud my judgment when you brought me here to answer questions," I said, trying again to move the conversation into professional waters. "How'd you know what I was working on?"

"I have a friend in Ronnie Willis' office and she mentioned you interviewed him."

She. The assistant or Paula? "What else did your friend tell you?"

"Nothing."

The assistant. "So what makes you think there's anything I can tell you?"

"Because I know how your mind works. I want to know who you think killed Garth Henderson."

God bless the bartender, who appeared at that moment with my Scotch mist. I slid it quickly toward me so I could look at something other than Peter for a moment. "That's not what my article's about," I said.

"Bullshit."

"I'm doing a profile of Gwen Lincoln." I took a sip and looked him in the eye while I could.

"Because she's a murder suspect."

"Because she's a role model for our target demographic."

"And the murder?"

"An unfortunate loss she's coping with as best she can while she moves forward with her new business ventures."

"C'mon, Moll, you can't even say it with a straight face."

"I am hoping to make it sound a little less movie-of-the-week when I actually write the thing." I put the glass down in case my hands got unsteady when I asked him the next question. "So you're doing an article on the murder?"

"Yeah."

"Why the switch? I didn't see your byline on any of the articles I read."

"No, the switch is bigger than that. I left the *Times*."

I tried to play down my surprise. "Really?"

His eyebrows drew together. "You don't keep as close an eye on me as I do on you."

One surprise after another. "So where are you?"

"It may turn out to be a hugely stupid move, but I signed on with Quinn Harriman's start-up."

"*Need to Know*? Congratulations." Quinn Harriman was an investment banker turned publisher. His first effort, a magazine for gourmands, was growing nicely and his newest venture was being touted as a magazine for "the good guys." While it was being surmised that this was some sort of anti-lad mag comment, what precisely made one a good guy hadn't been spelled out too clearly in the promotional material. But if Peter was one of them, it was bound to be interesting. And open to debate.

He shrugged. "It's a risk, but I didn't like the paper as much as I'd thought I would, so I'm eager to dive into the next thing."

I'd never seen it before, so I didn't recognize it right away. Peter was being humble. What could have happened at the *Times* to cause this? When I was dating him, his definition of humility had been acknowledging that there might be one or two men in the city more fascinating than he was, but only one or two. Peter's irresistible force must have finally encountered an immovable object. There was another story to investigate. But this one first. "So you're doing an article on the murder itself."

"Premiere issue, setting the tone, no pressure. Quinn thinks it has all the ingredients for a great cover story—money, power, sex—"

"Sex?" I asked innocently, prodding for his theory.

"The killer vaporized his nuts, Molly. Sex figures into this somewhere."

"I agree. What's your deadline?"

"Two weeks."

I raised my glass in a sympathetic toast. "See you on the newsstands." I tried to picture his cover story next to my cover story and wondered what Eileen would say—or shriek—when she found out. I'd sprint across that burning bridge when I came to it.

After we'd both had a sip or two, I decided to count on his newfound humility not having reduced his ego by too much and ask, "So, in your story, who killed Garth?"

He'd been waiting for me to ask. Ego intact. "Your girl."

"Excuse me?"

"Doesn't everyone suspect Gwen Lincoln?"

"Do they?" But looking straight into his twinkling eyes, I wasn't completely sure if he was presenting his real theory to get my reaction or if he was giving me a cover theory so I wouldn't know what path he was actually following.

"You don't agree."

Maybe it was worth offering up a piece of my truth to elicit something from him. "Why would she bother?"

"Crime of passion."

"Old news, they were already getting a divorce. Besides, she was equally unfaithful."

"So?"

"Killing over a trespass you're committing yourself strikes me as a very male thing to do."

"Harsh."

It was my turn to shrug. "And a stake in the agency isn't worth killing for. Let the divorce lawyers work that one out."

"Then who did kill him?"

I immediately thought of Ronnie Willis' desperate song and dance, but I wasn't about to say so—in part because I wasn't completely sure, but mainly because I was too competitive. "Guess I'll have to read your article to find out."

"Because that's not what your article's about."

"Right."

"You don't even have a casual theory?"

"I just got this assignment, Peter, I'm still meeting the players. In fact, I should go."

"Have dinner with me."

"Thank you, but no." The fun of seeing him again was dissipating under the weight of his agenda, plus I now had extra homework to do. I slipped off my stool, but he stood even more quickly and stepped into my path.

"Because of the cop?"

"Because I think it's the smart choice. Thanks for the drink."

Peter stepped back, for the moment at least. "I did think since we might be crossing paths on this, it'd be a good idea to see each other, make sure everything was okay . . ."

Make sure I wasn't ahead of him on the story, that sort of thing. "Wonderful idea. Great to see you." I debated for a split second, then kissed him lightly on the cheek and turned to leave.

"One more question before you go."

I stopped, waiting for the punchline. "One."

"What do you make of Ronnie's whole 'working with the woman I love' deal? I mean, even if you're just doing a profile of Gwen, this must enter into it, right?"

I did not want to have to tell Peter Mulcahey that I didn't know what he was talking about. But then again, I didn't have to, because his smile told me that he knew. "Ronnie didn't phrase it that way to me," I said neutrally, half-expecting a trap.

"That's okay, he didn't say it to me either. But my source says he keeps saying it when he's on the phone to her—"

"To Gwen?"

"Who else?"

"How good is your source?"

"Inside there pretty good, why?"

"There are other women at both agencies," I said, remembering Ronnie's enthusiasm for the Harem.

"Yeah, but they're all gonna report to him. That's not 'working with the woman you love,' that's having a great fringe benefits package." Peter grinned, enjoying his view of corporate relationships, but I was too distracted by the cascading dominos of thought he'd set in motion to be offended.

Could Ronnie have wanted Garth out of the way both as a business partner and as Gwen's partner? But Gwen and Garth were getting divorced, so that was already taken care of. And the company was stronger with Garth at the helm. But those were both rational considerations and how often is murder a rational act? Still, thinking of Gwen's expression when she talked about Ronnie and vice versa, these were not people in love. If Ronnie was proclaiming the glories of loving the one he worked with, he was either snowing somebody big time or in love with someone else. Could that relationship have enough meaning to provoke a homicidal confrontation? Was there a triangle at the heart of this merger? Had Garth been Ronnie's rival in love as well as business?

It was time to visit the Harem.

Without tipping my hand to Peter.

"You're ahead of me, Peter. I didn't pick up on anything between Ronnie and Gwen. Maybe they both felt it wasn't appropriate for the piece I'm doing. Or that it would be impolite to publicize their romance so soon after Garth's death."

"Impolitic is more like it. Neither one of them can afford to attract any more attention from the cops. But speaking of cops and attention, I should let you go, right?" He stepped out of my way, content to let me leave now that he had established that he was indeed ahead of me on the investigative path. The fact that he might be headed in the wrong direction hadn't occurred to him, but then again, it rarely did. And if I tried to warn him, he was going to think I was jealous, so I could refrain from saying anything with a relatively clear conscience.

"I should be leaving," I agreed. "But I'm sure we'll be seeing each other again."

"I'm counting on it," he said, scooping up my hand and kissing it again. He smiled, more genuinely than he had yet, and watched me as I walked out of the bar. I know, because I glanced back over my shoulder as I exited. Just out of curiosity. Honest.

Six

"YOU HAVE GOT TO STOP telling these people the truth."

It actually pleased me that Tricia's mood had improved enough for her to lecture me. When I'd called her after leaving the Flatiron Lounge, she hadn't been very happy.

I'd stepped outside and told myself the need to take a deep breath was only about the change in temperature from inside and had nothing to do with Peter Mulcahey. The city was trying to release the heat it had gathered during the day and I needed to do the same. Absorbing so much information and suppressed emotion in one day had left me a little light-headed and the Scotch mist with no dinner had nudged that along nicely. I wanted to track down Tricia and Cassady, see if they'd eaten yet, and sort out the day's events and facts. I thought about calling Kyle, but he was never done with work this early and, besides, I needed to talk to someone about Peter. Kyle was not the ideal candidate.

But as I took my phone out of my bag, I felt like a coward for coming up with a reason not to call Kyle. I had nothing to hide: I'd met Peter for professional reasons and anything else that had happened had been Peter's doing, not mine. If I told the story right, Kyle might even be amused. Or not.

The call went straight to voice mail and I tried not to feel relieved. I left a cheery message to say that I was meeting Cassady and Tricia and hoped he'd call me when he was done. After hanging up, I went through the automatic review process my brain initiates every time I leave a message: How dorky did I sound? Did I say everything I needed to? Did I say more than I needed to? Did I remember to say good-bye?

To shut my brain up, I called Cassady. Her phone went straight to voice mail, too. My batting average was terrific tonight. I left her a message about it not being even close to eight o'clock and how could she have given up on me so soon, and then, before the review process could even start, tried Tricia. Her phone rang at least and I decided that, if I got voice mail from her, too, that it would be a divine sign to go home, get into my pajamas, eat Frosted Flakes for dinner, and either reevaluate my life or watch *Sullivan's Travels* on DVD.

Tricia answered on the third ring. "How'd it go?"

"Peter was just feeling me out."

"Did you say 'out' or 'up'?"

"Give me some credit."

"Just asking."

"Where are you guys? Please tell me you haven't eaten yet."

"Well, I can only speak for myself, but I am at Lotus and I am starving."

"Where's Cassady?"

"She left me."

"To go to the bathroom?"

"To meet the physicist."

"You're joking."

"I wish I were. I haven't been abandoned so blithely since Doug Crandall, sophomore year of college."

"I hear he's bald and bitter now."

"Thank you, but the fact remains, I've been tossed aside. Let's meet somewhere for dinner and make a voodoo doll of the physicist with our breadsticks while we're waiting."

This was highly irregular for Cassady. There was a line between canceling out on girlfriends because you got a competing offer from a man and leaving a girlfriend midevening to go to a man. A true girlfriend didn't cross it without a very good reason. Cassady hadn't offered a reason at all, simply left. And then there was the fact that, "She just had lunch with him."

"Compounds the crime, doesn't it."

Hidden agendas abounded—Cassady, Peter, Ronnie Willis. I needed to sit down and ingest something fortifying before I attempted to make sense of them all. "I'll be right there."

"No, I want a change of scene. And dinner."

"Where should we meet?"

"On the blasted heath around a cauldron."

"Not with just two of us."

"Then, we should at least go to the Village. Employees Only in twenty minutes."

"Make it thirty."

"You're closer than I am."

"You're not making allowances for my lousy cab karma." Cassady can stop a cab with less effort than it takes to blink. She barely gets her arm above her waist and they're queuing up. Tricia has a more forceful but not much less successful approach. She flings her hand out like she's starting a *Matrix* shockwave and a cab stops. Me—I raise, I fling, I lunge, I walk a lot. Cassady says I need to develop a more Zen approach. I was afraid that meant imagining myself as large, yellow, and peeling at the edges, but she said I didn't have to picture myself as the cab, I had to project an aura of being worthy of a cab.

But here's one of my big problems in life—worthy worry. I worry I'm not worthy—of cabs, cool boyfriends, great jobs. Which makes me try harder at all of the above, but also to fret pretty consistently about what's poised to go wrong. At least it gives me a heightened awareness of where and why things can explode in relationships, which figures heavily in the column and in my investigations.

Now if I can just find some non-Freudian explanation for my dislike of the subway.

"That one's not pathological, it's practical," Tricia assured me as I finally took my seat next to her—thirty-three minutes later. Naturally, she'd had no transportation trouble and had arrived well before me. "Now tell me about Peter and the interviews."

"First things first. What's up with Cassady?"

"Hormones," Tricia sniffed. "It borders on the unseemly."

"My father once told me never to play pool with a physics major, but he never said anything about having sex with one."

"Which would be unseemly times two."

"The sex?"

"Your father talking to you about such things. And I'm not implying that Cassady has already leapt into bed with the Unknown Scientist, I'm coming right out and saying she's being adolescent."

"Really? What did she say?"

"Nothing." Tricia paused, eyes widening as she watched me absorb this information. "Not a word."

This was huge. When Cassady met a new man, we got a complete dossier that would put the CIA to shame at the first debriefing. A physical, psychological, and romantic assessment from a woman with a ruthless sense of what she likes and does not like in all areas, especially men. But for her to offer no information, no opinion was completely out of character. "Maybe she just doesn't have a sense of him yet," I attempted.

Tricia's nose twitched with derision. "And that's why she abandoned me. She needed to go get a sense of him. Perhaps we need to get a sense of him and figure out why he's making our dear girl do things that are so unlike her."

I paused with my glass halfway to my mouth. *Things that are so unlike her.* I knew Tricia was talking about Cassady and, while I shared her concern, I found myself suddenly picturing Gwen Lincoln in all her lemony composure. When I'd interviewed her, I'd been painting a picture already framed by all the research I'd done: capable businesswoman, perfect hostess, always in control. But what if she'd gotten into a relationship that had changed all that—especially if she'd gotten into it on the rebound from a relationship that had gone hugely sour, so she was looking to feel something completely different, be something completely different. What if Gwen Lincoln and Ronnie Willis *were* an item? What if they'd killed Garth to form a more perfect union, if our founding fathers would pardon the turn of phrase—a merger on every possible level?

I set my glass back down and Tricia gasped, a not fully unhappy sound. "What is it? What did you just figure out?"

I filled her in on my interviews with Gwen and Ronnie, and then on Peter's parting shot. She wanted to go back and talk more about Peter, but I insisted that could wait. The day's final tally had been that I wasn't impressed by the possibility of Gwen killing Garth by herself or Ronnie doing it by himself. But the two of them together was an equation I hadn't run yet. I still needed to get into GHInc. and talk to the Harem to get a sense not just of their worth to Ronnie, but what they thought of him—or more specifically, him with Gwen.

That's when Tricia rebuked me for my honesty. "If you tell people you might be publishing what they say, they're not going to speak very freely."

"I'm not expecting a confession in the middle of an interview, Tricia. I need a sense of the dynamics between these people to see where the breaks in the chain might have been."

"Still," she insisted, "you should be more devious. And I only suggest it because I know you have it in you."

"I'm saying 'thank you,' but I'm thinking a much more devious phrase that only differs by a few letters."

Tricia sighed. "How can you be offended when I am so clearly complimenting you? Your ability to weasel information out of people is enviable—"

"Does that make me a devious weasel?"

"—and I'd hate to see you lose sight of that because you feel like you have to approach everything as a formal journalist now."

"I do have an article to write."

"Which will be much more delicious if you do it your own way," she said with heartfelt enthusiasm. "I'm not suggesting you go all Jayson Blair or anything, just sneak up on these people. Get them to talk about things they shouldn't be talking about."

She had a point. I was so smitten with my officialness that I was forgetting the impact it had on the people I was interviewing. Naturally they were going to go out of their way to present me with a beautiful façade that was suitable for publishing, especially in a magazine like ours that specializes in beautiful façades.

I promised Tricia I'd rethink my strategy before my next interview, we ordered dinner, and she moved on to her next agenda item. "So how's Peter?"

"Fresh coat of paint, but no real renovation." I told her about his leaving the *Times,* the new magazine, and his pretending to miss me so I'd share information with him.

"How sure are you that he's pretending?"

I laughed to show us both how sure I was. "Tricia, please. He's stooping to conquer, that's all."

She shook her head, not buying it but declining to argue the point. "Did you find your leak?"

"Not mine. He knows someone in Ronnie Willis' office—his assistant, best I can tell. She told him I was there. So no worries."

"Good. Then there's no reason to see him again."

I shook my head emphatically. "Wasn't planning to."

"Yes, but what's Peter planning?"

My inability to answer was rendered moot by a passing patron, who stumbled as she passed our table and fell into Tricia as Tricia had her champagne cocktail to her mouth. The woman was profusely apologetic and Tricia, who had managed to splash only the table, not herself, laughed it off. I was the one who was stunned, staring at the parallel pink lines that now ran down across Tricia's lips. Just like the cuts on Garth's mouth Gwen had described. Had someone hit him as he'd had a glass to his mouth? Someone he'd be relaxed enough to have a drink with—like Gwen or Ronnie?

As Tricia tidied up and the waitress brought her a fresh drink, I tucked that thought process away, declared a moratorium on Mulcahey, and shifted the conversation back to Cassady for a while. We agreed that we were very happy she might have found someone so compelling; we just wanted to meet him and hold his confirmation hearings soon.

Once I returned home, delightfully full of seafood salad and Tricia's colorful thoughts on physicists, the subject of Peter had slithered down my consciousness list to a slot somewhere below Eileen and above the national debt. The thought that kept nudging its way up the charts—with a bullet, as it were—was the notion of Gwen and Ronnie being in cahoots.

I went to pull out my notes and discovered a Post-it on top of the stack. *Check the freezer before you start working. I'll be late.* I wondered when Kyle had made an appearance and a snide little voice in the back of my head suggested perhaps while I was sitting in a bar with another man. I reminded the little voice I had nothing to feel guilty about, but when I opened the freezer and saw the pink-and-white cup, the guilt was there nonetheless.

At some point in his travels that day, my marvelous detective had stopped at a Baskin-Robbins and gotten two scoops of jamoca almond fudge, then brought them home and put them in the freezer for me. Jamoca almond fudge is what I will dine on in Heaven and Kyle, a mint chocolate chip guy to the core, found my choice baffling. But he didn't try to dissuade me, which I deeply appreciated. We had enough of those points of contention.

I got out a spoon, determined to slowly go through both the ice cream and my research, savoring the first and looking for anything that hinted at a relationship between Gwen and Ronnie in the second. The dessert was terrific, but the research came up short. Aside from a couple of postmortem comments about the adjustments that were going to have to be made at GHInc. because of this unexpected partnership, their names rarely came up in the same article. If there was something going on, they were hiding it well.

I did find a picture of the Harem in a magazine article about Garth. I'd looked at it before I met with Ronnie and noticed that the group appeared to be the agency's portrayal of a collection of young women in advertising rather than an actual staff, they were so demographically balanced and highly polished. But looking at them again with "the Harem" bouncing around in my mind, there was suddenly something about them that suggested a *Playboy* pictorial: "The Girls of GHInc." I could see why Ronnie was so taken with them.

I dug Emile Trebask's card out of my purse and dialed his number. If I left a voice mail tonight, he could call me back as early as possible in the morning and I could take advantage of his offer to help to arrange a meeting with Garth's staff as soon as possible.

"Hello?" his smooth voice said in my ear.

It took me a moment to realize I had the live guy, not his voice mail. "Mr. Trebask, it's Molly Forrester from *Zeitgeist*." I looked at my watch. Still in the office at ten o'clock. Impressive. Or obsessive.

"Good evening, dear Molly," he said pleasantly.

"I didn't realize you'd be working so late, I thought I'd get your voice mail. Am I interrupting?"

"I'm not at work and you're not interrupting. I gave you my cell number for just such an occasion." Cool. I had Emile Trebask's cell number. I tried to imagine where he might be, but since he didn't offer, I thought it better not to ask. "I'm so glad you've called," he continued, "it shows me you understand how important it is that we continue to communicate during your process."

Some little part of my journalistic ego chafed at that, but since I was calling the man to ask for a favor, I was in no position to complain. "Thank you."

"You don't have any concerns about today, I hope. Gwen and I, it's a passionate relationship."

"It's evident you really believe in each other," I said, even though his grand insistence in her innocence was one of the things that made her so suspect. The best friend doth protest too much. But keeping Tricia's advice about deception in mind, I moved on to asking my favor. "I'd like to talk to the creative directors at GHInc., get a sense of how they feel about Gwen coming in—"

"They're thrilled."

Or at least they would be by the time I met them, I surmised. "It would be terrific for our readers to see Gwen as a role model in the—"

"The mother hen teaching her chicks. Wonderful." He laughed, but it was cut short as someone grabbed the phone from him.

"Molly Forrester," Gwen Lincoln said in that same assertive tone. "I shouldn't need to point out that I do not wish to be portrayed as a mother hen, a den mother, a mother superior, or any other damn maternal figure to this collector's set of brains with boobs."

An interesting contrast to Ronnie's assessment of the Harem. But before I even opened my mouth to attempt a response, the phone changed hands again. "We're at dinner, it's been a long day," Emile said hurriedly. "Tomorrow morning, ten o'clock, GHInc. The whole team will be there for you. And when you've spoken to the girls, then perhaps you can speak to Gwen again." Once she's a little more sober, no doubt.

"Thank you, Mr. Trebask. That sounds ideal."

"I told you, Molly, it is my pleasure to help you. Anything I can do to ensure people are seeing the real Gwen. I want to protect her future, even if someone has savaged her past."

"Nothing wrong with my past," I heard Gwen complain hoarsely. "Mistake erased."

"Good night, Molly. We'll see you tomorrow morning." Emile hung up and, I hoped, hustled Gwen out of whatever public space they were in before she said anything else provocative, incriminating, and/or embarrassing.

Guilt is a fascinating thing, even more intriguing in the

people who should have it and don't than in the people who do or even the people who don't need to have it and do anyway. A notion driven home by Kyle suddenly returning home. I jumped; not just because I was thinking for a brief moment about Peter, but because it had taken me weeks to learn to leave the chain off so Kyle could come in without knocking, but it still startled me when he did.

I put the phone down to greet him with a warm smile and a warmer kiss. He returned both, then nodded in the direction of the phone. "Didn't mean to derail you."

"No, I just finished. Work."

"Pretty late."

"Setting up something for tomorrow."

"How's it going?" he asked with a commendable lack of judgment.

"It's been an interesting day."

"That can cut both ways. Want to tell me about it?" Quite often, Kyle doesn't want to talk about a case he's working on, sometimes because there's confidential information involved, but mainly because he tries to carve out some space in his life where all that doesn't intrude. And then he winds up with me, who has no walls—normally—but he's still a gentleman about giving me the out.

Tonight, I wondered if maybe I should take it for a change. Not just because the subject was a sore one, but because the day had included Peter. But then again, if I didn't say anything about Peter and it came out later—and that's one thing that investigations will teach you, sooner or later the things you work the hardest to hide come out anyway—it was just going to be that much more uncomfortable. And it really was not a big deal that I'd seen him, so why didn't I just come out and say so?

I had my moment. I felt it, the opening, the rising energy, just like when you're bodysurfing and you know that if you dive in right now, you're going to fly and if you hesitate, the surf is going to pick you up and smack you down and you're going to come up with sand in your teeth and a significant loss of dignity. But I hesitated anyway, overthinking how casual I should be about "Oh, not much, just had drinks with an old boyfriend," and an odd expression scrunched up his face, blowing my concentration completely. "Why, how was yours?" I asked.

He shrugged, his odd expression resolving into a smile. "Not bad. Closed the Seidman homicide."

"Kyle, that's great!" This case had bedeviled Kyle and his partner for months now. Even as they were required to move on to other cases, they kept spending every spare moment going back to this one, certain they had the killer and just needing that extra piece of the puzzle to prove it. "We should celebrate."

"Ben and I grabbed a drink before we came home." Ben Lipscomb was Kyle's partner, a big rumbling bear of a guy with great insight and greater patience. "Thought I'd finish up the celebration with you."

"Wanna go out? Your victory, your call."

He pinched his lower lip, then released it to smile lazily. "Let's stay in."

I dove into creating an impromptu celebration, beginning with drawing a nice warm bath and insisting that he sit and let me scrub his back and pamper him while he told me about discovering the final piece of evidence that tied the suspect to the crime scene, then working the confession out of him. He so rarely talked at length about his work that I was captivated by both the story and his eagerness to share it with me. His eagerness to share the bathtub with me was endearing, too, as was his chagrin after he pulled me in and I told him that my sweater was dry-clean only. Its survival wasn't really that important in the grand scheme of things, but he got points for folding it gently, soggy as it was.

After we toweled off, I made black Russians, wishing desperately that I had a fireplace we could curl up in front of—not because it was chilly but because it seemed the classic thing to do. We made do with lots of candles on the coffee table and curling up on the floor. And on the couch. And in the bed.

It wasn't until the next morning, when I was on my way

to the GHInc. offices, that I remembered I hadn't told Kyle about seeing Peter. I filed it away, still suffused with the glorious feeling of our night-long celebration and the adrenaline of my approaching interview.

GHInc. was on Seventh, Garth having built his business with fashion clients and wanting to play that for all it was worth. Stepping off the elevator was like walking onto the set of *Julius Caesar* as directed by Ridley Scott—everything was heavily textured stone and dramatic lighting, sound bounced around in an eerie but intriguing way, and the young lady behind the altar-like arrangement of stone slabs that I assumed was the reception desk had the sweet, beatific smile of a vestal virgin. Or someone doing some pretty serious self-medicating. The icon above her was the agency logo. No reproductions of ads here; perhaps that was the agency version of, "If you have to ask, you can't afford us."

"Welcome," the vestal virgin intoned. "How may I help you?"

After I explained who I was, another temple attendant was summoned to escort me to the conference room. I followed her across the slate floor to mammoth double doors she threw her whole weight into opening. The inner sanctum, no doubt.

The Harem awaited within. Even more stunning in person, the six of them were arranged around the conference table as though waiting for another photograph to be taken. They all looked to be in their late twenties, give or take a few years for good genes, makeup, or lighting. Behind them, someone had cannily placed mock-ups of print ads for Success. Over various images of beautiful young women in various stages of dressing—or was it undressing—in front of beautiful young men ran the bold statement: *Get it.*

An African-American woman with caramel skin, green eyes, and perfect posture was the first one to rise and offer me her hand. She was taller than I was, even without the Miu Miu pumps, and wore a gorgeous mauve Bottega Veneta pantsuit. "Ms. Forrester?"

"Molly."

"I'm Tessa Hawthorne. Welcome to GHInc."

"Thank you." I stepped closer to her to shake her hand and caught a scent it took me a moment to identify. I sniffed again.

Tessa smiled. "Success."

"I thought so."

"We're all wearing it. A welcoming gesture to Gwen. In addition to the fact that it's a terrific fragrance."

"We're not all wearing it," a smoky voice corrected from the far side of the table. She was an athletic-looking brunette with heavy-lidded brown eyes and thin lips, dressed in a white Ellen Tracy blouse and a black Dana Buchman skirt, the pleats of which she was pressing between her fingers.

"Wendy Morgan. Wendy's allergic," Tessa explained.

"Lindsay, too," Wendy, the brunette, said defensively.

She pointed across the table to an angular blonde with deep blue eyes and sharp cheekbones, dressed in herring-bone slacks and a silk blouse with a cutwork collar. The blouse was sapphire blue, heightening the impact of her eyes. She glanced up at me, nodded, then immediately returned her attention to the legal pad in front of her, from which she was methodically tearing long, thin strips of paper. "Hi. Lindsay Franklin. I can't wear any perfume, never have been able to," she said.

"She still tried, when we first got the samples, and broke out in awful hives," Tessa said, wrinkling her nose. "Made me itch just to look at them. For days."

"Tessa," Lindsay said, uncomfortable with the memory or the attention.

"Why'd you try it if you knew you were allergic?" I asked.

Lindsay smiled ruefully. "I keep thinking I'll find one I can wear and wouldn't it be nice if it were a client's? Sort of the reverse of Wendy's problem. She can wear every perfume except this one."

" 'Wendy's allergic to Success.' Want to know how many times we've made that joke since we started working on the campaign?" Wendy spoke sharply, but the rest of them just smiled, which led me to believe it was Wendy's normal tone.

"One-third of a group having an adverse reaction to a product is problematic, but we've had the manufacturer do broader testing and it's an anomaly," Lindsay explained. "Most women will wear Success with no trouble at all."

Tessa shrugged. "Lindsay's husband used to be a lawyer, so she's always covering our bases, protecting us from the downside of everything."

"It's not because she's married to a lawyer, it's because she's married," Wendy said. "The rest of us have maintained our independence."

Lindsay gave Wendy a practiced, tolerant smile. "I can't imagine that has any impact on what Molly's here to talk to us about, so why not just let her have a seat and ask her questions?"

To distract me from the tension crackling between those two, Tessa introduced me to the other three: Francesca Liberto, a petite, raven-haired beauty with flawless olive skin; Megan Carpenter, a gently freckled redhead dressed in a skintight lime green Juicy Couture sweater and matching leather skirt; and Helen Woo, an Asian-American beauty with close-cropped black hair and piercing eyes. They all greeted me cordially, unruffled by the interplay between Wendy and Lindsay.

As I shook hands with each of them, I noticed several of them wore the same Tiffany charm bracelet—a silver heart dangling from a thick silver chain. "Your bracelets are lovely. They all match?"

Everyone but Tessa shook a matching bracelet down from her sleeve for me to see. "A gift from Garth when the merger was announced," Helen explained, holding her charm up so I could read the inscription. GARTH'S GIRLS ROCK. Apparently, "the Harem" wasn't suitable for engraving. Or maybe they didn't know that's what the outside world called them. "And in recognition of an exceptionally profitable year." She beamed at her cohorts and I half-expected them to launch into a cheer or at least a sorority song.

"Yours isn't back yet, Tessa?" Wendy asked.

Tessa shook her head, embarrassed. "I broke mine," she

explained to me. "Caught the clasp on something and pulled it right off. I kept forgetting to take it in, now I have to remember to go pick it up."

"Garth's Girls. Is that a name he gave you or did you choose it yourselves?"

"Who can ever remember where an idea starts," Tessa said quickly. "We work as a group, think as a group, take credit as a group."

"We are the Borg," Wendy suggested. She seemed eager to stand out from the crowd and even more eager to get this gathering over with. I couldn't tell whether she felt she had other things to do or if she wasn't eager to discuss the topic at hand.

"I appreciate all of you taking the time to talk to me."

"Command performances are our specialty," Wendy said, earning a dark look from Tessa.

"Emile called this morning and let us know you wanted to talk to us about Gwen taking the helm here at GHInc. Of course, we're delighted to have the opportunity to discuss it with you," Tessa said smoothly, like she was drafting a press release as she went along.

Helen was more tart. "We love Gwen and we're thrilled she's going to be our new leader. She even has a bracelet, if she wants to start wearing it again."

"Garth gave her one of these bracelets?"

"He said he owed it to her for getting Emile to move over here," Tessa explained. "And because she'd been his 'main girl' for so long." Not exactly a winning term of endearment, especially because the infidelity stories had gotten so much play during their separation. Was he complimenting her or insulting her by lumping her in with the women in his office?

"I don't think she wears it anymore," Francesca said. The quick exchange of glances around the table said they didn't blame her for that choice.

"Their split, then the merger, then losing Garth—it's been a crazy year," Lindsay offered.

"But still very profitable, so far," Francesca said.

"Have you been spending a lot of time with Gwen in her new position?" I asked.

"We'll have her up to speed in no time," Tessa said.

"She and Ronnie Willis have been working very hard to set up a smooth transition, so we've just been pushing on ahead," Lindsay explained.

"Which we're quite capable of doing," Wendy said, her voice growing more brittle with each pronouncement. There was barely contained fury in her, but it was hard to determine whether it was directed at someone in particular or there for all to share.

"This must be incredibly awkward."

"Replacing the dead guy, you mean?" Wendy leaned back in her chair as though she were peering under the table to see if her legs were long enough to kick me. "Of course it's awkward. It's hideous. And I'm betting it's not exactly her idea of a good time either."

The rest of them continued to look at me with polished smiles, waiting for the next question. It was the Thanksgiving dinner dynamic: Everyone knows Uncle Fred gets a little crazy when he has his sherry, so no one reacts to it anymore. Still, I had to wonder if this was how Wendy always comported herself or if part of her fury stemmed from Garth's death. Perhaps she was one of the palm-inscribers Gwen had spoken of so disdainfully.

"I would've done anything for Garth," Lindsay said with quiet firmness and most of the rest of them nodded in pained agreement. Only Wendy got up and turned away, studying the view of Seventh Avenue through the window behind her. "We're all looking forward to working with Gwen but, as you can imagine, it will take some time for us to feel the same way about her." She yanked on her newest strip of paper with a little extra firmness.

" 'Cause if she can have us that easily, then we're just sluts, right?" Wendy said. She was still looking out the window but I could hear the tears in her voice.

Megan did cry, dropping her head into her hands. Helen slid a comforting arm around her. "Knock it off, Wendy," Helen requested.

"It's been very difficult. He was the heart of our process,

we're still trying to learn how to exist without him," Lindsay said. The others nodded, even Wendy.

I've had good bosses, I've had hideous ones. I've even had bosses die on me. But I've never had a boss who came close to inspiring this level of emotion in me. Had I been unfortunate or were these gals nuts? Gwen had used the word "cult." "Coven" seemed to fit even a little better. Part of me wanted to laugh in anticipation of the punchline I hoped was coming, but between Wendy's agitation, Megan's tears, and Lindsay's paper tearing, and the general air of anguish in the room, I couldn't deny that this emotion was uncomfortably real.

I also couldn't be sure how reticent they'd be about talking about the actual murder. "It must be hard to get past what happened to him, to stop thinking about it," I said, trying to ease into it.

Megan's sobs deepened, but no one else rushed to respond. After a moment, Tessa said, "We miss him every day, so we can't help but think about it."

Wendy finally turned back from the window. "And now we're working with her, which is also a pretty pointed reminder."

"Wendy, don't," Lindsay said quietly.

I immediately looked back to Wendy to see if I could figure out what she was doing that she wasn't supposed to be doing. Thankfully, Wendy cleared that right up. "Sorry. I'm not supposed to accuse the new boss of murder."

Tessa rocketed to her feet. "Wendy, she doesn't know you well enough to recognize your poor attempts at humor."

Wendy stiffened. "Don't sweat up your pretty little blouse worrying she's going to write something about my accusing Gwen. Come off it, Tessa, she's not even going to mention the word 'murder' in her article. Gwen will be referred to as 'the former wife of the late Garth Henderson' or some elliptical crap like that, right? I mean, no offense to you," she swung her napalm gaze in my direction, "but we're all in the image business, right? We might as well be honest with each other, even if we aren't going to be honest with the public.

This is one of Emile's parlor tricks to make Gwen look good and I defer to his clout. But I want it known that this is bull-shit and I'm here under duress."

A series of looks ricocheted around the room like that insane drinking game where you wink at each other and whoever misses the sequence has to do shots. They were checking on each other's reactions, trying to silently decide who was going to react and how strongly. A fascinating sociological exercise, but it was moving too fast for me to keep up. I got a sense that Lindsay and Tessa were the locus of the network, but they weren't looking at each other at all.

As long as accusations were being flung and Wendy was so totally wrong about why I was really there, I thought I'd add my own spice to the stew. "So, Wendy, when you accuse a new boss of murder, it's Gwen and not Ronnie you're accusing?"

Wendy's head snapped back as though I'd thrown my tape recorder at her. "Ronnie Willis?" She laughed gratingly. Francesca tried to pull her back down into her seat and failed. "That'll be the day. That's Ronnie's whole problem, he's not a killer in any sense of the word."

"Do you like anyone here, Wendy?" I asked.

"Including you?"

I had to smile. Partly because I admired the clarity of her rage, even if it was broadly directed. But mainly because I was sure Tessa would clear the room if it appeared I was taking Wendy too seriously and I wanted to know what else Wendy had to say. Especially about Ronnie.

"What do you really want to know, Ms. Forrester?" Lindsay asked, taking one of the strips of paper and curling it around her finger. There was a certain even pressure to her tone that was calming to the rest of them. Wendy actually sat back down. They were a tightly knit group with convoluted dynamics but the broad strokes were apparent: Tessa was the leader, Wendy the troublemaker, and Lindsay the peacemaker.

What I really wanted to know was what, if anything,

made them worth killing for. But I asked, "As I said, how do you feel about Gwen Lincoln as your new boss?"

This time, everyone waited for Lindsay to answer, even Wendy. But it didn't feel like deference as much as tiger cubs waiting for the mama to have the first bite before they pounced. "I don't envy anyone coming in here to fill Garth's shoes. But if you're going to attempt to replace the irreplaceable, Gwen Lincoln and Ronnie Willis are an excellent place to start."

Frustration was nipping at my heels. They were too contained, too polished. Even Wendy. They had circled the wagons and, with the glibness of minds accustomed to creating slick images and phrases, were keeping me at bay. I was about to retreat when the vestal virgin burst in, face flushed and placid demeanor blown to smithereens.

"Help!" she squeaked.

"What's wrong?" Tessa asked. She and Lindsay got up immediately, hurrying over to the receptionist. The others rose more slowly.

"Mr. Douglass . . ."

"Jack Douglass is here?" Tessa asked. The receptionist nodded frantically. Tessa looked at Lindsay. "Do we have a meeting?"

"No," Lindsay answered, but it didn't really matter because at that moment, Jack Douglass, CEO of Douglass Frozen Foods, stepped into the room and while he may not have had a meeting, he did have a gun.

Seven

"AM I INTERRUPTING?" CASSADY ASKED breezily, then continued before I could tell her that she actually was. "And feel free to hang up on me, since I deserve all the righteous snarks you toss my way because I was selfish and impetuous last night and I'm actually sorry."

"Much as I enjoy the rare treat of you apologizing, this isn't an ideal time to chat," I explained.

"Then meet me for lunch and I'll still be full of remorse, I promise."

"I'm not sure I'll be free for lunch. In fact, I think the detective I'm with would like me to get off the phone right now."

Cassady sighed lightly. "Tell Kyle to be patient and learn to share."

"It's not Kyle."

Cassady sighed deeply. "Molly Forrester, what have you done?"

Yeah, well, what I had done was get just the slightest bit carried away by the sight of Jack Douglass with a gun in his hand. Most of the Harem had frozen in horror. Megan had started weeping again, Francesca had screamed, and Wendy had uttered a very colorful, convoluted exclamation that began with "Holy" and ended with "Mother of God," but went some decidedly profane places in between.

"Mr. Douglass," Tessa had attempted, but at that, the paunchy but still dapper man in the doorway had raised his small but vicious-looking gun higher, as though he were drawing her attention to it because she certainly wouldn't have spoken had she seen it when he first stepped into the room. Absurdly, I was checking the reflection of the wall sconces on his balding head, noting that he didn't seem to be sweating in the least. I figured that was good because it meant he was somewhat calm and wasn't sweating bullets, as it were. It had to be to our benefit that he was calm. Didn't it?

Lindsay tried next. "Mr. Douglass, there's no need—"

"I'll decide what I need!" His voice was much tighter than I would have hoped for; "calm" was definitely on its way out. With his free hand, he dragged a handkerchief out of his pants pocket and wiped it across his bald spot. He wasn't calm, he was just buffed dry. "You people pretend to know, but you don't! And now look!" He stuffed the handkerchief back into his pocket as he strode into the room. We receded from him like a wave pulling back from the beach.

There was a telephone designed for conference calls sitting on the middle of the table. It looked like something off the *Star Trek* bridge—some synthetic spider perched in the middle of the table, awaiting orders. I stepped in close to Lindsay, so we were shoulder-to-shoulder and blocking Douglass' view of the phone. Sneaking one hand behind my back, I flailed my fingers at it, hoping Wendy or someone else on the far side of the table would see the gesture. After a moment, I heard the faint squeak of the phone being moved on the table.

Unfortunately, so did Douglass. He turned in our direction and I stepped forward to distract him. I'd like to say I was being brave and cunning, but it was blindly instinctual and when both he and the gun turned in response, my stomach went liquid with regret. But once I was committed, there was nothing to do but improvise and hope someone behind me was dialing 911.

"Mr. Douglass, let's discuss this."

"Who the hell are you?"

"A neutral party."

"Then get out of here. Now. I have business to attend to." Lindsay stepped up beside me, shoulder-to-shoulder again. I was impressed and grateful. "Mr. Douglass, whatever your concern—"

"My concern? How about my work, my life? My board of directors wants to get rid of me. Because I was foolish enough to listen to you." He swung the gun slightly past us at this point and I turned my head just enough to see Wendy was the one in the line of fire. She responded by going alarmingly pale.

"The campaign's tracking very well," Lindsay said gently.

"But they're embarrassed. They doubt my moral rectitude. You told me it would work!"

"It did work. It increased your sales." Gwen Lincoln had stepped into the doorway behind him, improbably cool and collected and agonizingly alone. I wasn't expecting a SWAT team, but a little uniformed presence, even the security guys from downstairs, would have been very welcome right now.

Douglass spun on her. "Doesn't matter if it's not my company anymore!"

In one of those amazing moments of synchronicity, Lindsay and I looked at each other and dove at Douglass in unison, like we'd practiced the maneuver a thousand times. I aimed for his arms and upper body, she went a little lower, and we all the hit the stone floor with such force that I thought my lower jaw was going to shatter into dust. We slid across the cool smoothness of the floor until Douglass' head hit the corner of the conference room door, just past Gwen's feet. I heard the gun skittering away, the other women in the room screaming, and my pulse pounding in my ears. But the sound that surprised me most was the soft giggle coming from Lindsay, a desperate, giddy sound that would have been infectious if I'd had any breath left in me at the moment.

Which is how I came to be sitting across from an unsmiling police detective when Cassady called. At least things were less chaotic than when the police first arrived, with

Douglass streaming blood from a gash in his scalp, Gwen trying to calm the troops, the Harem wailing in various keys, and Wendy hyperventilating over having been the one to pick the gun up off the floor. My hands had even stopped shaking.

Now statements were being collected, so we were all divvied up into various nooks and crannies of the office. I was still in the conference room with Detective Hernandez, a very serious woman with unreadable dark eyes and marvelous dark curls corralled into a ponytail at the nape of her neck. She'd been polite enough to let me answer my phone when it rang, but I didn't want to abuse the privilege.

"So," she said as I put my phone back down on the table, "you were saying you've never met Mr. Douglass before?"

"I was here to interview the creative directors for an article I'm doing. I've never met any of them either."

"What were you thinking when you decided you should or could take Douglass down?"

I'd had this sort of question posed to me innumerable times in my adolescence, so I knew the answer. "I wasn't thinking."

Detective Hernandez didn't seem familiar with my father's favorite line of reasoning. "Excuse me?"

"It just kind of happened," I explained. "I was worried things were going to escalate before you had an opportunity to respond and he turned his back on us and Lindsay and I just had one of those unspoken agreements and . . ." The displeasure on her face would have been perfectly easy to understand even if I hadn't already seen the expression on Kyle's face more than once. "In retrospect, I see that it was foolish, but at the time, it seemed like an appropriate response."

"You're lucky you didn't get yourself or somebody else shot."

"Yes, I know. I'm sorry."

She shrugged. "Don't have to apologize to me."

Yet I felt like I needed to apologize to someone. Maybe I was really just hoping someone would say, "It's okay," but

Detective Hernandez had passed on that opportunity. "I couldn't stand there and not do anything," I offered.

To my surprise, Detective Hernandez nodded. "Understood. Just don't make a habit of it, okay?"

There was no point in trying to explain that her advice was a little on the belated side. I just smiled and said, "Thank you."

Detective Hernandez's partner, Detective Guthrie, stuck his head in the conference room door. He torqued an eyebrow, she nodded, and he entered. "Visitor from the one-nine," he told her. He had the bearing and haircut of a man who had served in the military before becoming a police officer, but he gave me an unexpectedly sweet smile.

"What's he want?" Detective Hernandez asked with a not so sweet frown. Detective Guthrie jerked his thumb at me and both Detective Hernandez and I looked at him in surprise. I took me a moment to realize that Kyle had somehow found out I was there and had come either to make sure I was all right or to drag me out before I could cause any more trouble. Detective Hernandez gave her partner a puzzled shrug and he stepped back into the doorway to signal down the hall.

"I'm sorry," I said, aware I was apologizing again but not getting any resistance this time. "It's my boyfriend."

"What is?" Detective Hernandez turned to me sharply, like I'd suddenly switched languages on her.

"The one-nine. He's a homicide detective over there and someone must have called him about my being here and he wanted to check on me because," I said, gesturing to the man walking in the door, "that's not him at all."

Detectives Hernandez and Guthrie exchanged one of those partner looks that smacks of "we're the only sane people in the room" as I frowned at the tall blond walking toward me with a knowing smile. He diverted his glance to Detective Hernandez long enough to shake her hand and introduce himself as Wally Donovan, then offered his hand to me. I shook it automatically, still adjusting to his not being Kyle.

"Hope you don't mind, but I'm working the Garth Henderson murder and when I heard things had gotten a little dramatic over here this morning, I thought I'd come over and check out any overlap."

Detective Hernandez quickly brought him up to speed on the events of the morning, based on the interviews she'd done, while I studied him as surreptitiously as possible. So this was the difficult detective Kyle had wanted to keep me away from. I'd assumed that he was an older detective, someone who'd object to me as an interloper or see me as a distraction in Kyle's life. Maybe some of that stemmed from guilt. I'd also pictured him as small, dark, and antisocial and that probably stemmed from many Humphrey Bogart and John Garfield movies. He was, in fact, tall, blazingly blond, and almost gregarious. The suit was rather high end for a detective and as he pulled out his notebook, light bounced off his nails. A detective who got manicures. New one on me.

"So, Ms. Forrester, how do you think the events here this morning relate to your probe into Mr. Henderson's death?" Detective Donovan asked. I didn't need to see the expressions on the other two detectives, I could fill those in for myself.

"That's not why I'm here."

"Peter Mulcahey led me to believe otherwise."

I held back the laugh and the sigh. "What's a nice detective like you doing with a guy like that?"

"He and I go way back."

"He and I go not so way back and my question stands."

"If we're going to start judging each other by the company we keep, let's talk about Kyle Edwards."

"Let's just talk about all the reasons that talking about that's a bad idea. It's much simpler."

"I got a question," Detective Hernandez interjected. "Why don't you two go buy each other a drink and let me work my case?"

"You're not matchmaking, are you, Detective Hernandez?" He grinned at her, but she didn't so much as think of smiling back. Behind him, Detective Guthrie rolled his eyes.

I didn't stop to consider any other possibilities why Kyle

didn't want me around this guy, I leapt at an opportunity to get more information on the murder. Not unlike the way I'd leapt at Jack Douglass—without thinking where I'd land. "Nevertheless, a good idea. What say we visit the scene of the crime. Bemelman's Bar in the Carlyle at six o'clock, Detective Donovan? We can continue our conversation then." I scrawled my cell number on a business card and held it out to him.

He pocketed it. "Do they serve dinner there?"

"We don't have that much to talk about." I stood, turning to Detective Hernandez. "May I go now?"

"Please do."

She stood, too, so Detective Donovan was the only one in the room sitting. In fact, he leaned back in his chair. "Detective Hernandez, I'd like to talk to Mr. Douglass. His actions this morning put his relationship with my victim in a whole new light."

"Why, when they're actions he took after your vic was already dead?"

"From what I've gathered, he's not too happy with the agency. Maybe he's been feeling that way for a while."

Detective Guthrie gave Detective Hernandez another one of those partner looks and she nodded. "You can talk to him when we're done with him. He's getting his skull glued back together. You can ride along to the hospital with us if you want."

"Who cracked his skull?"

I made a beeline for the door, not eager to have that conversation again or to give either Detective Donovan or me a chance to change our minds about meeting up later. "Thank you, nice to meet all of you."

Out in the reception area, I hesitated, not quite clear on the layout of the offices. I needed to hunt down Gwen and get a reaction from her, but stopped at the sight of Lindsay sobbing in the arms of a handsome young man on one of the stone benches. Unsure whether something else had happened after the police separated us to take our statements, I approached cautiously. "Lindsay?"

They both looked up. He had a lean face dominated by big brown eyes and unruly eyebrows that were drawn together tightly at the moment. Tapping him on the chest, she sniffed and said, "My husband Daniel. This is Molly Forrester."

"So you're the other heroine," he said, making the last word sound as much like "idiot" as he possibly could.

His anger was understandable. "I owe you both an apology. It was a stupid thing to do and I shouldn't have dragged you along with me, Lindsay."

"I was going to do it with or without you," she said quietly.

"Lindsay," he said, sounding more like an impatient tutor than a distressed husband.

She dabbed at her eyes with the last dry spot on the tissue in her hand and I noticed her cuff drooping oddly; she'd ripped her blouse in the melee. "Your blouse, what a shame," I said.

Daniel inspected the tear and shook his head. "One down, four to go."

Lindsay managed a small smile. "I have this blouse in five different colors. I couldn't resist."

"It looks great on you, I can see why." Maybe it was some foxhole-bonding thing, but I was liking Lindsay. Then she grabbed my hand and pulled me down on the bench next to her. "Do you think Jack Douglass had something to do with Garth's death?" Now I was liking her even more.

"Lindsay," Daniel repeated.

"Why, do you think he did?" I asked, causing Daniel's brow to furrow even more deeply.

"After the ad launch, he was furious about his political friends backing off, even angrier than he was today. Garth told him all that mattered were his sales figures and how the ad was tracking."

"Typical," Daniel interjected.

"Jack went off about how wrong that was, how Garth had ruined his life, his reputation," Lindsay continued. "Garth said he'd calm down eventually."

"When was this?"

"Right before Garth died. A week, maybe."

"Did you tell the police about it?"

"Sort of. They asked us about disgruntled employees, business rivals—"

"Like Ronnie Willis?"

Lindsay's eyes widened. I'd mentioned him as a rival, but Lindsay was zooming off in a whole different direction. "Oh. Ronnie said Garth's death was only the beginning. I didn't believe him, but . . ."

So Ronnie was flinging the paranoia around more freely than I'd realized. On some level, he'd probably be pleased rather than threatened by Douglass' meltdown, seeing it as vindication of his theory. But I didn't buy it. How careless was it for Douglass to blast in and do this if, in fact, he had killed Garth? Hiding in plain sight was one thing, renting a billboard was another.

Ronnie's theory rang especially hollow as I watched Gwen enter the reception area, flanked by another detective and Wendy. She was masterfully poised for a business-woman who had just encountered a gun-wielding client. Not that I expected her to be a quivering mass of nerves, but she could at least look a little rumpled. Actually, what she looked like was a woman who had exactly what she wanted. The question was, how had she gotten it?

"How did we not see this?" she asked expansively, not being clear who the "we" encompassed. "All the finger-pointing that's been going on and it never occurred to me."

"To point the finger at Jack Douglass?" I asked, not to be difficult but to be sure I understood her train of thought.

"To suspect him in the least. He's such a gentleman and this is not the way you'd expect a gentleman to settle his grievances."

I nodded, thinking of Aaron Burr and Alexander Hamilton, but not wanting to send her down that path.

"You weren't here for his fudgsicle meltdown or you might think differently," Wendy said.

"You think Jack shot Garth?" Lindsay asked.

Wendy pursed her lips, then quickly pressed them together again, automatically fixing her lipstick. "I don't know about that, but he was practically foaming at the mouth." She tossed a glance at me. "He's the one who called us sluts."

"I still think it's quite fertile ground for the police to explore while the rest of us get back to work," Gwen declared, sweeping us all with an imperious look that ended on Daniel. "Do you work here?"

"I'm Lindsay's husband, Daniel," he said, offering his hand. "Lindsay called me and I ran over to make sure she was okay."

Gwen blinked slowly. "Weren't we just talking about gentlemen? And here's one in our midst." She patted his hand before releasing it, then gave Lindsay a smile. "You're a lucky girl, Lindsay. And how fortunate you're in a position to drop everything and race over here, Daniel," she said, packing an impressive dose of condescension into a short statement.

"Daniel's director of development for Rising Angels," Lindsay explained with a touch of defensiveness. Rising Angels is a terrific nonprofit that works with children whose parents are in prison, getting them mentors and tutors and taking them to educational and cultural events. Really noble work. "He's only a couple of blocks from here."

"This is an expensive neighborhood for a nonprofit," Gwen observed.

"Our offices are over at St. Aidan's, they donate the space, it's the only way we can swing it," Daniel explained. He gave Lindsay a quick peck on the cheek. "I do have to get back. Take it easy." He nodded to the rest of us and hurried out.

"He doesn't like to talk about work that much, he feels like people think every conversation is a request for donations," Lindsay said with an odd mixture of apology and pride.

"Why is it the guys who are working hardest to make the world a better place are the ones who don't like to talk about work?" I asked.

"You married to a do-gooder, too?" Wendy asked.

"I date a police detective."

They all reacted to that, Gwen more sharply than the others. I was hoping she'd say something that would hint at how uncomfortable and/or guilty that made her feel, but instead she leaned in with a startling intimacy. "Then work your magic to find out where they are with Jack Douglass and why they hadn't questioned him before."

I knew the answer to the second part: because you look so much more guilty than he does. But my answer was, "He's not on this case."

"Still. Cops talk to each other, don't they?" I didn't answer, not about to tell her that if I ever was going to summon up the nerve to lean on Kyle for information, it would be for my article about her, not to provide her with the inside scoop on where she was ranked on the suspect list. My silence didn't sit well with her. "Have I gone too far? God knows, the last thing I need right now is an aggrieved journalist evening the score in a major publication. If an apology is what you seek, consider one offered." She took a deep, shuddering breath. "I must have a cigarette. Who will descend with me?"

"I will," Wendy offered promptly.

"Wait here," Gwen commanded and strode back toward her office, either to get her cigarettes or to smack a few more people around before taking her break.

Lindsay tugged at Wendy's sleeve. "What do you think happened with Jack?" I realized they hadn't had a chance to talk since the to-do, so I hung back quietly, eager to hear their take.

Wendy glanced at me, hesitated more for show than for conscience, then answered with a grim smile. "Gwen happened. She called him this morning and told him she wasn't going to honor the discount Garth had offered him when he got so upset about the fudgsicle campaign. She said the agency had delivered on its promise and any collateral damage was his problem, not hers."

Lindsay gasped, while I envisioned Gwen in a chef's coat and hat, stirring a great big stewpot with a roaring fire underneath it. Lindsay voiced my question. "Are you saying she provoked him?"

"I'm saying she's trouble and we have to be careful. I'm beginning to think we have no idea what she's capable of. And if you print a word of that," Wendy said, looking daggers at me, "I will deny it and drag you through courts until you cry for mercy."

"Wendy," I said gently, "you're going to do really well in business once you learn to speak your mind."

"I think the fact that people are showing up in my workplace with weapons gives me the right to speak frankly, don't you?"

"I'm not sure I see a direct correlation, but I'm not a constitutional scholar."

"Wendy, what should we do?" Lindsay asked, but Wendy didn't have a chance to answer because Gwen was striding back to us, a cigarette already in her hand.

"Here's a question for you all. How do I break this to Ronnie?" Gwen stopped beside us, tapping her cigarette against a beautiful sterling case. "He needs to know what happened, but I'm worried his fantasy coming true might be a bit much for him."

"It's not his fantasy, it's his fear. And it looks like it might be well-grounded," Wendy protested.

"But Ronnie was nowhere in sight and I didn't hear Jack Douglass ask for him once. Do you think that will hurt Ronnie's feelings?"

It was Wendy who looked like she was hurt. Why would Gwen's riffing on Ronnie bother her? Then again, she wasn't taking it all with the same grain of salt I was, that most of this cavalier attitude about Ronnie was to cover up how close Gwen and Ronnie really were. It didn't bother me to hear her mock Ronnie's conspiracy theory because I didn't think Ronnie really believed it himself. Had Wendy bought in? Then again, Wendy wasn't exceptionally fond of Gwen, so perhaps she was throwing in with Ronnie to stake out territory as the new regime took form. There are women who prefer to work for men. With the past few female bosses I've had, I'm ready to give it another try.

"Molly, my dear," Gwen said, "what must you think of us now?"

"It's been an interesting morning," I agreed. "And I wasn't quite finished with the interview when Mr. Douglass arrived."

"I am so sorry." Gwen glanced at her watch. "Do you need everyone and when do you need them?"

"I could sit with you, see what I can fill in if that might be easier," Lindsay offered.

"Lovely. You two kindred spirits work it out and let me know how it goes." Gwen caught Wendy by the arm and swept her off to the elevator.

"I don't mean to butt in," Lindsay said quickly in their wake, "but I would be happy to help."

"I appreciate that."

"Maybe we could do drinks after work or something."

Why is it that you can go for great stretches of time and no one wants to see you, then suddenly everyone wants to see you at the same time? "I might have something then already, but let me call you later in the day and we'll figure it out. Thanks for this morning. It was memorable."

Lindsay grinned and gave me a quick hug, startling but sincere. "Pretty amazing, that's for sure."

I clacked across the stone floor and rang for the elevator. Lindsay gave me a quick wave and headed back to her office. There was such a fascinating array of personalities in the Harem, I could understand Ronnie's fascination with them, looks and talents aside. But killing to control them seemed extreme for Ronnie. If he was involved in this, there had to be some other motive.

I was trying to imagine the conversation as Gwen told Ronnie about Douglass when my phone rang. "Hey, you," I said, seeing that it was Kyle.

"Can you talk?"

"Sure. How are you?"

"Fine. How's your day going?"

"Pretty wild, actually."

"Can't wait to hear about it. Wanna have drinks after work? Say, six o'clock at Bemelman's?"

No matter what I said, it was going to be the wrong thing. Gwen was right: Cops talk to each other. And men pick all the wrong times to share.

Eight

AS I MAY HAVE MENTIONED, watching the man you love walk up to you is a thrilling, wonderful thing. Unless he's angry. Then it's a thing that makes you contemplate a convent, assumed identities, maybe even celibacy.

On the phone with Kyle, I'd asked if I could call him back from the office. When he hung up without answering, I'd taken that as a yes. His fuming presence on the sidewalk outside my office building contradicted that.

"I can explain," I said as he approached, immediately kicking myself for not having a stronger starting position.

"Don't doubt it. I've never known you to be without an explanation." His eyes, normally breathtakingly warm, were hard and cold. I've seen Kyle mad before, but it's generally been in defense of me. Being on the receiving end was tough.

"He sought me out," I persisted.

"He holding someone you love hostage and forcing you to meet him?"

That took me by surprise. Hyperbole doesn't come naturally to Kyle, so it was an indication of his anger that he was going for the grand. "He's not forcing me to do anything."

"Jack Douglass needed five stitches and might have a cracked vertebra in his neck," Kyle countered, switching tracks on me.

"That all happened before Donovan even showed up. He had nothing to do with it."

"Except if he'd closed his case, Jack Douglass wouldn't be running around with a damn gun."

"You don't know that Jack Douglass killed Garth Henderson."

"And you don't know that he didn't!"

Now I was starting to get angry. I loved my job and I wanted the man I loved to respect that—and me. I wasn't saving the world like he did, but I was trying to make a difference. "Okay, I didn't turn down the opportunity to talk to Donovan. But he made the offer and I'm trying to do my job."

"Makes one of you."

"What?"

"He's a lousy cop, Molly. He plays politics instead of working a case and this could be the one that blows up in his face. I don't want to see you get dragged into some stupid, humiliating mess because he's a jerkwad."

"How does his being a bad cop threaten me, other than his giving me lame information?"

"You can't stay out of harm's way when you're working with a good cop, what's gonna happen with a shitty one?"

My father says certain efforts are like banging your head against a brick wall: it's so nice when you stop. I hadn't realized I was carrying a little knot of resentment in the pit of my stomach until it unfurled in a rush of warmth. I'd misjudged Kyle's motives completely. He wasn't trying to keep me off his turf, he was trying to keep me safe. "I'm not going to team up with him," I said quietly, "I'm just going to talk to him. Get his perspective."

Kyle shifted unhappily. "I'm not asking you not to, because that wouldn't be right and because you wouldn't stop anyway," he said flatly, "but I am gonna tell you, it's a pretty lousy idea. There's no way the department's not going to look bad here and I hate to think of you being part of it."

"Part of the mess or part of pointing it out?"

"Both. I got two words for you: O.J."

I could almost see the gremlins scurrying at our feet, dragging the bricks and mortar in to start building a wall between us. "Do you want me to cancel with Donovan?"

"Damn it, I want you to be a nurse."

Stunned, I stared at him while I tried to figure out a more intelligent response. I knew this was about safety, about conflicts of interest, but it was still hard to hear him saying he wanted me to be something other than what I was and certainly something other than what I really wanted to be. He took in my expression and shook his head, struggling with his own thoughts. I couldn't bear to think where this conversation might go, so I wrenched it in a new direction. "Is this about the uniform?" I asked after a moment.

"Yeah," he said, trying to muster a smile, "it's all about the uniform."

"The shoes, too?"

"Nah, I hate the shoes."

We both stared at our own for a few moments. Battle lines had been drawn, but we were crawling toward the DMZ. Leave it to me to thump on a landmine to see if it'll go off. "I so hugely admire what you do and I'm sorry Donovan doesn't do it as well. But I want to understand as much about the case as I can."

Kyle's eyes came up slowly, some of their warmth restored. "Don't let him play you."

I nodded. "I won't."

Kyle's hand shot up behind my head, his fingers twisting in my hair as he pulled me to him with a sudden and almost painful firmness. Startled, I tilted my face wrong and our teeth collided. I committed to the kiss anyway, but he laughed and released me, throwing his arms out in surrender. "When our timing's off, it's really off."

I laughed back, tapping my front teeth, hoping we were on solid footing again, at least for the moment. "Good way to lose a tooth."

"Ask your new friend Donovan about that," he said, stepping away from me.

"About what? Are you telling me you've kissed Wally Donovan?"

Kyle sighed and said, "Call me as soon as you're done," before heading down the sidewalk, vanishing around the corner before I could say anything else. I felt like I'd successfully swerved to avoid a pothole, though I wasn't quite sure my wheels had regained traction yet or how close to the shoulder I was. But I was pretty sure we'd kicked up some serious gravel.

I was still working on getting back to cruise control when I got upstairs to the office, only to be greeted by someone sitting at my desk. Since I come and go all day, people often snag my desk for a moment or two to grab a phone call, talk to the people who sit near me, or eat particularly fragrant lunches in a place where they won't have to contend with the fumes for the rest of the day. So someone being in my chair wasn't that startling, it's just that the person in the chair usually works at the magazine. Today's squatter worked at Willis Worldwide. At the reception desk.

Having enraptured my neighbor Carlos, she was deep in conversation with him, the two of them leaning into each other so they were almost forehead-to-forehead. While she was being earnest, he was trying to figure out where her tattoo started. Nevertheless, it gave me a moment to rack my brain in a futile search for her name. Had she ever told me? I didn't think so. Had I ever asked? My bad. Why was she here? I couldn't imagine. Her System of a Down T-shirt and Diesel jeans were both tight enough that I could tell she wasn't carrying a weapon, unless it was nestled down among the tentacles, and that gave me hope I could handle whatever had brought her to my desk.

"Hope I'm not interrupting," I said by way of greeting, setting my bag on my desk. She jumped up so suddenly Carlos almost snagged his nose on her décolletage, but he snapped his head back just in time.

"Remember me? I'm Kimberly, from Ronnie Willis' office? I'm sorry I came by without calling, it was kind of an impulse and I hope it's okay because you sort of said I could," she said as Carlos frowned at me for intruding on what he had thought was a promising discussion and rolled back to his own desk.

"Of course, Kimberly, it's nice to see you again," I said, resisting the impulse to say her name three or four more times so she might think I'd known it all along. I couldn't remember saying anything that might encourage her to drop by unannounced, but given the events of the morning, I wasn't eager to disgruntle anyone. And if Kimberly was bringing me pearls of wisdom from Willis Worldwide, I was eager to check them out.

"It's just, there's this situation I wanted to ask you about, these friends of mine, and I was coming over this way anyway, so . . ." She shrugged at the machinations of Fate and her acceptance of them. Intrigued and puzzled, I suggested we move to the conference room, disappointing Carlos but guaranteeing me as much privacy as one ever gets at *Zeitgeist*.

Our conference room is a nook of blond wood and linen accents, a little homier than the Willis conference room. Kimberly ran her hand appreciatively along the highly polished table before curling up into a chair as though we were settling in for quite the chat. I thought about sitting across the table from her, make things official, but decided to sit next to her and make things more friendly. Much easier to pick people's brains when they think you're a friend.

"So what can I do for you, Kimberly?"

"I've been thinking I should talk to you, ever since you came in to see Uncle Ronnie."

I blinked slowly, not sure if I should betray surprise. While her incongruous presence at the front desk now made slightly more sense, I was sure she hadn't mentioned they were related and neither had Ronnie. What other secrets might she have to share? "What did you want to talk to me about?" I asked, trying not to sound too hopeful.

"This situation." She clacked her tongue stud on her teeth a moment, weighing a decision. "With some . . . friends of mine."

"So you mentioned out front. Could you be more specific?"

Clack, clack, another decision. "Remember that letter that we were talking about, the one you can't tell me about who wrote it, but I still know?"

I nodded enthusiastically to cover my disappointment that her business call was about column stuff, not about my interview with her boss. I'd be attentive enough to be polite, but move her gently but firmly along so I could get back to work. "Right."

"This is actually about someone else."

"Okay." I glanced at the wall clock because glancing at my watch would have been rude. She had three minutes to get to the point.

Clack, clack. "Suppose you were working with someone you knew pretty well."

"Okay."

"Maybe even someone you were, like, related to."

I didn't know how to make it clearer to her that she had my full attention now, short of announcing it on the office intercom. I leaned in like she was about to tell me a delicious secret. Oh please, oh please. "Okay."

"So you know things about this person that no one else knows."

"Such as?"

"That his wife broke her mother's best china platter over his head at Easter dinner because she found out he was having an affair and now the whole family is going to have to find a different place to have Easter because Granny's not going to let them back under her roof all at one time, ever again, because she's still pissed at them. Or something like that."

Plausible deniability is just as important in a family as it is in government. You promise to keep a secret, but then you realize it serves the greater good to let that secret slip, yet you want to still be able to sit at the table, should Granny ever invite everyone over again, and not feel like a traitor. Kimberly wasn't playing around, she was making a deal with her conscience—and I was the beneficiary of that deal.

"I bet it would be hard not to think about that every time you saw that person. Especially if it had only happened last Easter," I added, looking to establish a time frame.

She nodded, her mouth pulling into a thoughtful frown. "And then what if you found out that this guy you were so close to was about to start working with the person he'd had the affair with?"

Granny could've broken the platter over my head at that point and I wouldn't have even blinked. "I think I'd be concerned," I answered carefully, "especially if the man and the woman were supposed to work together really closely. Like partners or something."

"Exactly."

I wanted to shout "Goal!" or at least throw my arms up in the touchdown signal, but I kept my hands folded in my lap and considered how it changed my view of the world to know that Ronnie Willis and Gwen Lincoln had had an affair as recently as last Easter. It meant passions were high and fresh when Garth and Gwen began their divorce and Garth and Ronnie began their merger. Did Garth know any of this? And was that why he was dead? "It's a tricky situation," I said after a deep breath.

For the first time since we'd sat down, Kimberly looked me in the eye and I could see she was trying not to cry. This was hard for her, but I knew if I told her she'd done the right thing or said anything to verify directly that she was ratting out her uncle, she'd bolt and not only would I never get to talk to her again, she might tell her uncle he needed to stop talking to me, too. "I don't know what to do."

"It's not your responsibility to do anything," I assured her sincerely, placing my hand on hers. She'd given me a fascinating new piece of information, the least I could do was try to help her find some peace of mind.

"I don't want to see anyone else get hurt."

I held my breath as I asked the next question, like a child approaching a butterfly poised on a flower. "Anyone else?"

"It took his wife months to stop crying and it would be

awful to have her go through that again if things started back up, don't you think?"

"Absolutely." I dared take one step closer to the butterfly. "Did anyone else get hurt?"

"Granny's still pissed about the platter."

"What about the partner? The woman? Did anyone in her life find out? Or get hurt?"

She started to shrug, then stopped with her shoulders drawn up so she looked, for a moment, as though she were drawing herself up to lunge at me. I held my ground and her gaze as solidly as I could.

Her eyes got huge and wounded and wet. "That's not what I'm saying at all. Not that I'm saying anything to begin with. I came to ask you your advice, how to handle this, not to have you think terrible things about him. I love Uncle Ronnie."

"Of course you do or you wouldn't be here trying to find a way to help him," I answered quickly. "You want to protect him, right?"

"He didn't do anything bad." Tears coursed down her cheeks, dragging rivulets of mascara behind them. "I came here to find out how to keep him out of trouble, not get him into it."

I tried to ease her back into her fake perspective again and give her a chance to catch her breath. "But suppose there's someone he knows, someone he used to be close to, who did do something. And now he's getting close to her again. I can see why you might get worried."

The tears continued to flow as Kimberly tried to process the thought that Gwen Lincoln could have committed murder for dear old Uncle Ronnie. I squeezed her hand. "It's nothing you put in my head," I assured her, "I'd wondered it before." She'd just helped me solidify the motive, but I couldn't tell her that. Poor kid was upset enough already. "If you wrote me a letter, I'd tell you to keep the communication lines open with this man and make sure he knows that you want to help him. Don't press him, just let him know you're on his side. And stay away from her."

"When did you start giving relationship advice in the flesh, Molly, and what's your going rate? Shouldn't your clients pay the magazine directly?" Eileen had appeared in the conference room doorway, not unlike the monster swinging suddenly into view in *Alien*: You knew she was around here somewhere, but you tried to forget about her until she blocked your way out.

"Excuse me, I'm just taking a moment to speak with a friend," I told her, squeezing Kimberly's hand again in reassurance.

"Spend all the time you want with her. You've got more free time than you know what to do with because I'm killing the article." She turned her icy grimace of a smile to Kimberly for a moment. "Waterproof mascara, dear. It's not a new invention." And she slithered out of sight again.

Much as I would have liked to leave Kimberly there in the conference room and tackle Eileen in the hallway, I forced myself to be a grown-up and a professional and see Kimberly to the elevator, by way of my desk so she could grab some tissues and Carlos could give her his card. I made her promise she'd call me if she needed to talk about this again and I made her promise she wouldn't talk to anyone else about it. "There are people who would use this against Ronnie," I whispered.

"You won't?"

"I won't," I promised, readjusting my theory to feature Gwen in a big fat solo.

The moment the elevator doors closed, I flew back to Eileen's office as fast as my kate spades could carry me. Suzanne made a noble effort to get up and bar my way— more for the martyrdom points than out of any genuine affection for Eileen—but I didn't slow at all and Suzanne, smaller and less committed than I, ducked back out of the way and let me barge into Eileen's office. She even closed the door behind me as I proclaimed, "Eileen, I just got started!"

"And look at what you've already done!" Eileen grabbed

her bony hips with her bony hands and stood her ground. I pulled up before I ran her down.

"I've been interviewing people. And they're the ones that keep bringing up the murder, not me," I said, wanting her to appreciate the effort it was taking on my part to play by her rules. "As a matter of fact, someone just gave me a very tasty tidbit and I'd like to get to work at pursuing it because it'll have a major impact on the article."

"There's no rush, since it's canceled."

"Eileen, please don't do this."

Eileen shook her head in frustration, sending her chandelier earrings swinging madly. "I told you I didn't want you turning this into something involving people charging into the office with guns."

I took a fraction of a moment to plug in those new coordinates. But now that I understood what her real issue was, we could fight more fairly. "The Jack Douglass incident was unfortunate. But I'm fine, thank you very much for asking. More importantly, I had nothing to do with his appearance this morning and he didn't come here."

"No, but this could be his next stop."

"I don't think he could care less about the two of us or even pick us out of a lineup. The really crucial thing here— I don't think he's involved in Garth's death."

"That's not what Ronnie Willis says."

Of course not. If Ronnie was covering for his lover Gwen, Jack made a very handy scapegoat. "When did you talk to him?"

"He called me. Hysterical. Gwen told him about the whole drama and he thinks he's next on some sort of corporate hit list."

Of course she did and of course he did. "Which, other than telling me a lot about Gwen and Ronnie's relationship for the article, doesn't have anything to do with our happy little group here at *Zeitgeist.*"

"On the contrary. Ronnie wants Emile to cancel the gala and we cannot let that happen."

If I had to reset my coordinates one more time, I was going to fall off the map. Right over the edge where it says: *Here there be dragons.* And they draw a little picture of Eileen. Belching smoke.

"Why not? It could be an intriguing development to include in the article on Gwen—the impact of scrapping the gala on the perfume's launch, her new business profile, her relationship with Emile. It's pretty interesting. And beyond maybe having to delay an ad for Success for one issue, we don't have any investment in the gala anyway."

"Speak for yourself, you selfish girl."

Oh, yes. How foolish of me not to have Eileen's debut as a runway model in the forefront of my mind where she believed it belonged. I once heard a story about an actor who played the doctor who escorts Blanche to the sanitarium at the end of *A Streetcar Named Desire*; legend has it he told friends the play was about a dedicated doctor who rescues a troubled young woman after she has a breakdown. The heart of the story all depends on where you're standing on the stage. And where would Eileen ever be but front and center?

But what was getting lost in Eileen's solipsistic tantrum was what Ronnie thought canceling the gala would accomplish—for him, Gwen, and/or Emile. Ronnie apparently thought he'd be presenting himself as a glittering target to Jack Douglass or anyone else in on the grand conspiracy if he went out in public. But canceling was such a mistake for Gwen and Ronnie's ascendancy to running the agency and hurtful for Emile, as one of their prized clients. "How could killing the article help that?"

"He wants to let sleeping dogs lie."

"Let sleeping-around bitches get away with murder, more like it." Didn't Gwen and Ronnie realize that canceling the gala would draw more attention, not less, to them? It would look like guilty consciences rather than prudent management. "Besides, I'm not the only one talking to these people. Peter Mulcahey's doing a piece that's supposed to be the cover article for the premiere issue of Quinn Harriman's new magazine."

I now have a pretty good idea of the look on Catherine the Great's face right as the horse fell. "Quinn Harriman?!" Eileen shrieked. "That rat bastard thinks he's going to muscle in on *my* story?!"

There were so many follow-up questions to ask—whose story was it, why shouldn't he, and why specifically was he a rat bastard—but I didn't want to risk killing the momentum that was oh so tenuously shifting back in my direction. "Listen, this is your call. If you want to pull me off the story and just cede the territory to Peter and Quinn—"

"Do you think I got where I am by rolling over for self-important men?"

Rolling over, sitting up, and begging all came to mind, but, in an impressive feat of self-restraint, not to mouth. "All I'm saying is, personal safety carries a lot of weight with me and I understand if you're too concerned about Jack Douglass to pursue this story. I'm sure Peter and Quinn will do a great job with it. Let them take the hit."

"I'm not going to let them take anything that should be mine."

"Are we talking about the hit or the story?"

"The story, of course. Aren't you paying attention? Do you still suspect Gwen Lincoln?"

"As the bumper stickers used to say, 'Now more than ever.'"

"You are a child of the suburbs, aren't you."

"I'd like the opportunity to pursue the theory that Gwen Lincoln killed Garth Henderson knowing that she would get half the agency, which she would then run with her lover, Ronnie Willis."

"That's not possible."

"Why not?"

"Because I've never heard a word about the two of them being together and no one in Manhattan is that discreet. It's impossible. There's always a doorman or a stylist or a maitre d' who gets the ball rolling."

"All the better to scoop them with, my dear."

"Can you prove this?"

"Not if you kill the story and chain me to my desk."

"Then go forth and verify." She flicked her fingers in the direction of the door and I happily scooted that way. Only to have her command my departing back, "And while you're at it, fill a table for the gala."

"Excuse me?" I faltered in the doorway.

"Don't worry, I'm not expecting you to buy the tickets, just make sure there are smart, beautiful, interesting bodies in each chair."

A cheering section for her turn on the catwalk, no doubt. "The assistants never get to go to that sort of thing—"

"For good reason. Who wants to spend an entire evening with them? This table is your responsibility. You must have a few presentable friends. I think I've met one. So bring them along. Eight seats."

This wasn't the time to protest that I hadn't planned to attend, that Kyle hated this sort of thing, or any of the other objections that bubbled to the surface. This was the time to grab my barely saved story and run.

Looking back, this was probably also the time to quit the magazine and save myself, but you know what they say: Never look back, something may be gaining on you. And besides, those slacks don't look as good from behind as you think.

Nine

Now that most of the American blood supply is 50 percent caffeine anyway, Starbucks needs to team up with the Red Cross and put some of those blood donation chairs in their corner cafés, so you can recline slightly and have the java of your choice pumped straight into your veins through an IV, while you chat or make inappropriate phone calls or write angry poetry on your laptop.

In the absence of such technological advances, I was left to gulp down a vanilla cappuccino as fast as its scalding temperature permitted and hope I'd reach the saturation point quickly. Tricia watched me with great concern, sipping slowly at her chai tea latte to let me know her sense of harmony was a little less precarious than mine. She'd been in the neighborhood, dropping off fabric swatches with a client, and had, with her marvelously instinctive sense of timing, called me to see if I could sneak out for a coffee break. While she'd been very sympathetic about the day's craziness thus far, she had told the barista to ignore my request for an extra espresso shot in my cappuccino.

"Why are the things we want most the things that turn out to make us the most crazy?" I asked.

"I believe it's tied to original sin," she answered. "The whole Tree of Knowledge thing. 'Careful what you wish for' and all that."

"I'm pretty sure that's not what the serpent says."

"Much suffers in translation."

"I want to get this right, Tricia."

"I know you do. And I know you will. You just need to be patient. You've got an awful lot of people with their own agendas cluttering up the path, but you'll clear them away."

"Which would you kill for, love or money?"

"Does it have to be an either/or?" asked the woman I couldn't imagine killing anyone.

"Just seems to me that if Gwen killed Garth for the company, Ronnie knows about it. If she killed him for love, Ronnie probably wasn't in on it. It was more spur of the moment."

"How 'spur of the moment' is it to visit your soon-to-be-ex in a hotel with a pistol in your handbag?"

"Maybe she carries it with her all the time. And totes an RPG instead of an umbrella."

"That, you'd think the hotel staff would've picked up on."

Either a new idea or the first dose of caffeine hit me. Sitting up a little straighter, I asked, "What do you suppose they did pick up on? The initial reports said the police didn't find anything helpful on the lobby video."

"You haven't been to the hotel yet?"

"I talked to the VP of operations and confirmed that their video hadn't turned up anything and that the cardkey readout said no one had opened the door but Garth. Doesn't hurt or help Gwen."

"You need to go over there and nose around."

"And how do I explain that in terms of a profile of Gwen?"

"What did I tell you about telling the truth? Stop it!" Tricia exclaimed.

"I thought the nicest thing about being official would be that I didn't have to lie anymore," I said as we settled into the back of a cab and headed for the Carlyle Hotel.

"It's not so much lying as selectively representing the truth," Tricia said firmly.

"Still, I want to be proud of what I am, what I'm doing, and not slink around and pretend I'm something else."

"But you slink so well," Tricia said, with a mocking purr to her voice, "which is one of the things I love most about you."

"Yeah, yeah, I love you, too."

A loud sniff from the front of the cab startled us. Our cabbie, an immense, ruddy Irishman with unruly red hair struggling to break free of a Notre Dame baseball cap, gazed at us by way of the rearview mirror and wiped away a tear. "You should be proud of what you are," he told us, "and don't lie to yourself or to the world. You love each other and that's all that really matters. 'Cause without that, what is the world but a vast and lonely place?"

Tricia started to explain his error, but I squeezed her arm and told him, "You're so right. People in love get so silly, don't they?"

He nodded. "You can go ahead and kiss her. I don't mind." He grinned. "I don't mind at all."

"We're a very private couple," Tricia said, "and we'd prefer you keep your eyes on the road."

I winked at him in the mirror and took Tricia's hand. She tried to pull her hand away, but I wouldn't let go. She looked out the window so she didn't have to look at me and, probably, crack up, and we rode that way all the way to the hotel, where our cabbie tearfully wished us a long and happy life together. I threatened to hold Tricia's hand on the way into the hotel, but she was ready to move on to a new game. The question was, which game would give us the bigger prize?

After a few scouting patrols around the magnificent lobby, its floors so shiny I felt like I was walking through a stream, we acquired our target. A lanky young bellman, either the soul of industry or the poster boy for ADHD, was zipping around, straightening cushions and flower arrangements when he wasn't taking guests and their bags upstairs. I felt very Holmesian when I pointed him out to Tricia and remarked that such an eager young man might be open to earning a little something extra for helping us in our quest.

After a brief, quiet consultation on method, we made our approach. As he fussed with a flower arrangement that was nearly as tall as he was, Tricia said, "Excuse me. You look very busy, but I hoped you had a moment."

He nearly snapped to attention, but the effect was more a high school drum major than the military bearing he was trying to convey. "Yes, ma'am, I'm Jimmy. How can I be of service?"

"This is a little awkward," she said quietly enough that he had to lean in to hear her. I dipped my head in, too, and we stood clustered like three kittens around a bowl of milk.

"Would you like me to get the concierge?" Jimmy asked, equally quietly.

"No, we'd like to be less official," Tricia told him and his pimply forehead creased thoughtfully.

"We're trying to get into a secret society," I whispered, "and all we can tell you about the initiation is that part of it requires visiting famous Manhattan crime scenes."

"Oh, sure," our young friend said, seeming completely familiar with a group I could've sworn I'd made up. "You want the suite where the councilman got arrested with all the blow and the chicks, or the one where that rock singer almost drowned his girlfriend in the tub?"

I paused a moment in appreciation of the complex lives people lead. "Actually, the one where Garth Henderson was killed." Jimmy frowned more deeply than before, so I elucidated. "The ad guy who got shot in the head and the lap."

"Oh, sure," he said again, as though remembering a beloved teacher from grade school. "That one's new, haven't gotten so many requests yet. So you two wanna get in and, ya know, spend some quality time together in there?" He winked at us and I tried to figure out just what it was about the way Tricia and I were carrying ourselves that had everyone assuming we were a couple. But if it was helping, fine, let him think it.

"Can you really get us in there?" Tricia asked.

"If it's not occupied, no problem. If it is, takes a little work."

"How much work?" I asked, knowing I hadn't been to the ATM in a while and trying to remember what, if anything, I had in my wallet.

Tricia was faster than I and was already slipping him a twenty. "See if it's occupied and then we'll talk."

Jimmy bowed to her slightly and strode off in search of information. "How did you get so good at that?" I asked.

"Making men do what I want?"

"I'm always impressed by the power you have to cloud men's minds but actually, I was referring to the elegant slippage of cash."

"My mother raised us with a twenty in one hand and a martini glass in the other. She still insists that what you cannot sway with one, you can sway with the other."

"And yet, you turned out remarkably well."

"Good nannies."

"I owe you twenty bucks."

"The meter's running and the adventure's young, dear heart." She looked at me with sudden sharpness. "Have you talked to Cassady today?"

"She called in the midst of the Douglass madness so I had to ask if I could call her back, but every time I've tried, I only get voice mail. And I'm not even sure why she called."

"Not like her."

"No, it's not."

"I haven't had any luck either. Maybe she's in court and forgot to tell us. Also not like her, but understandable."

"When do we start worrying?"

"I never cease to worry about either of you," Tricia said, pleased with herself. "When do we go track her down and confront her face to face about her delinquent return of our phone calls so we're reassured that she's not lying dead in some wretched alley, you mean?"

"I was hoping to keep the hysteria level a little south of that but, yes."

Tricia glanced at her watch, then pointed to Jimmy, who was rapidly returning. "Let's see how long it takes us to finish up here."

Jimmy hustled back, sweeping us up and moving us to the elevators in his enthusiasm. "We have a small window of opportunity during which a friend of mine is on that very floor with a housekeeping cart and a passkey." He punched the elevator button, smiling expectantly.

I was already digging my wallet out of my handbag. It lacked the subtlety of Tricia's palming bills, but we seemed safely past the point where subtlety was required. "Were you working the night it happened?" I asked, impressed I actually had cash. Usually, my wallet's filled with credit card receipts, business cards, and Post-it notes. I started with two more twenties, not wanting to inflate the market needlessly. He took them graciously and allowed us to enter the elevator ahead of him.

As the doors closed and he pushed "7," he said, "Yeah, I was there that night. First big shitfest since I started here. Place was crawling with cops like you wouldn't believe and the guests are getting all hysterical, the ones that aren't grabbing their cell phones and cameras, ya know, and we all had to talk to the cops which is always hard 'cause people got secrets and all, so things were buzzing around here for quite a few days after."

"People have secrets?" Tricia asked.

"Some of my fellow staff members have business deals with certain people who come and visit the hotel that they'd rather not have to discuss with the cops, ya know?"

"So other than call girls and dealers, were there any other interesting people sighted that night?" I asked.

The elevator doors opened with a "shush" and the bellboy's voice dropped in response as he ushered us out onto the seventh floor. "That's the weird thing. Nobody remembered seeing anybody out of the ordinary. Or anybody at all. Mr. Henderson had lots of people come see him and those babes who work for him, they were in and outta here all the time. But that night, nothing. Not until the wife shows up and raises a ruckus and the assistant manager opens the door and—boom, there it is."

I wasn't sure if he was referring to Garth's body or to the door to room 734, before which we now stood. He rapped on the door with a knuckle arpeggio and before I could ask another question, the door opened.

"This is Rhonda," Jimmy explained.

His playmate was not the giggly young lady I'd imagined, but a large, damp, and unsmiling woman who plucked the proffered twenties from my hand without meeting my eye. "Don't sit on the beds, don't touch the flowers, and for God's sake, don't use the toilet." She coughed tubercularly. "And no smoking."

She lumbered away and Jimmy grinned at her. "She's a riot. But she's right, ya gotta be quick."

We walked into the beautifully appointed room and I tried not to gape. Before I came to New York, the Holiday Inn was the top tier of my hotel experience, so I still tend to be awed by the sheer lushness of a luxury room. This one was no exception, though I felt some disappointment in how perfect the room was again, how every trace of the crime that had occurred here had been erased. Not that I'd expected anything to be left, with the hotel anxious for people to forget about their association to the incident, but it still seemed sad that such an awful thing could happen to someone and then simply be scrubbed away.

Jimmy pointed to the writing table and armchair in front of the window. "He was in that chair when they found him. Well, not that exact chair 'cause the original one was trashed on account of all the blood and all. The housekeeping girls were pretty worked up about making sure they got the blood outta everything else—there was big talk about having to pull up the carpet, things like that. But they did a nice job, you can't hardly see nothing. Hope that doesn't kill the experience for you."

"No, not at all," I assured him, "it's really more about just being in the space." Tricia and I moved around the room as though inspecting it, but the room didn't matter at all, it had been scrubbed raw since the murder and had nothing left to tell us. It was the color commentary from the bellboy we'd come for. "So you and the other bellmen were on babe watch with Mr. Henderson and his employees?"

"Hell, yeah. You could tell what day of the week it was by which of the babes came by with work for him. Francesca on Monday, Helen on Tuesday—"

Garth was killed on a Friday. "Who had Friday?"

"Free night. Guess he liked to keep that one open for social things, ya know? But then he'd dive right back in on Saturdays with Lindsay and Sundays with Wendy. Poor bastard worked way too much, but I guess it takes some of the edge off to be doing it with knockouts like them."

That was the question that suddenly parked itself in the forefront of my mind. Was Garth Henderson "doing it" with one of his knockouts? Had Gwen Lincoln come to see him and managed to surprise him with one of his "girls"? Gwen's views on infidelity seemed flexible enough that even if she were having an affair with Ronnie Willis, she could be enraged by finding her husband *en flagrante* with a protégée.

"When they found him, were the beds made up?"

"Chocolates still on the pillow."

Not the kind of detail likely to occur to you as you throw the bedclothes up and pretend to the rampaging ex-wife that nothing's going on. Besides, what I'd learned about Garth, he struck me as the sort who'd flaunt his conquests, not cover them up. "Any sign of anyone else?"

"Nope. Room service brought up dinner for two, but it hadn't been touched. There was a drink on the table, that was it. Hell of a way to go, all alone like that."

"All alone except for the person who shot him. Twice," Tricia pointed out.

"Yeah, there is that."

"What's the talk on the hotel staff? Who do you all think did it?"

"Chuck in room service, he's running a betting pool. Even money's on the wife."

"Who are the long shots?"

"A hooker. That new business partner. The mayor."

"The mayor?" Tricia asked, offended on several levels, including the fact that her father did a lot of work for him.

Jimmy shrugged. "Darnell, one of our bartenders at Bemelman's, he always bets on the mayor, no matter what you're betting about. Says it's a political statement."

I tried to imagine Gwen Lincoln standing here, facing Garth and some horrible realization that made any other resolution inadequate, and pulling the trigger. Twice. And then having the impressive presence of mind to come back to the hotel a short time later and help "discover" the body.

"So everybody's betting on her, but no one remembers seeing her that night—until the body was found," I said, partly thinking out loud, partly for clarification from Jimmy.

"Yeah, bugs me, too. Maybe we're just so used to seeing her around that it didn't register. Or that she comes over so often, she knows how to get by everybody."

Unfortunately, that made sense. It was easy enough to do the math. Anger multiplied by love divided by divorce plus gun equals dead guy.

Unless I was wrong.

It hit me with that cold, clammy certainty that pours over you at the instant the locked car door closes and you see your keys still in the ignition.

Unless I'd been looking at the wrong relationship in Garth's life. Unless the variable of love represented not his wife, but one of the reasons he left his wife. Unless the person who loved Garth enough to kill him was someone else who came to the hotel regularly, knew its routines and his. Unless the person who killed Garth Henderson was a member of his Harem.

Ten

"DEAR MOLLY, WHY DO I *have such a hard time admitting that I'm wrong? And why is it only about certain things? I actually don't have that much of a problem admitting that I'm wrong about facts, but when it comes to feelings—don't hold your breath. Does this mean I'm passionate or I'm stubborn? Does this mean I'm wrong more often than I want to admit or I'm right so often that I'm out of practice? How do I learn to let go of the feeling without taking down a bunch of other feelings, maybe even a whole relationship, with it? Would it be easier never to say I'm wrong? Signed, Objectively Subjective*

When I realized I might very well have been pursuing the wrong theory about Garth's death, I had a sudden and intense desire for fresh air. Almost as though I was dishonoring Garth by bringing my bad theory into the room where he died. My suspicions about Gwen and Ronnie had been primarily intellectual, but this one I felt deep in the pit of my stomach, that raw and spiky nausea that comes with migraine headaches and guilt attacks.

"No one saw any of the 'babes' that night?" I asked Jimmy again, just to be sure.

"Nope." He shook his head and checked his watch, but Tricia straightened up from her inspection of the carpet near the death chair and looked at me sharply. Picking up on something in my voice or manner, she knew I'd switched tracks.

"What?" she asked impatiently.

"Just clarifying."

"No, you're not. You're formulating a new theory and I don't see it. Share."

I didn't want to be rude to Jimmy, who'd been marvelously forthcoming from his particular point of view, but I also didn't want to discuss a newly germinated possibility in front of him. "Nothing to share."

Her top lip curled in the beginnings of protest, but then she looked at Jimmy and clamped her lips together, realizing. "Fine."

Jimmy's housekeeping friend banged open the door, startling us all. "Housekeeping," she barked reflexively. Giving us all a sullen glare, she declared, "You gotta go now."

"Checkout time so soon?" Tricia said with a pleasant smile.

"You two got what you needed?" Jimmy asked solicitously, as though we were going to be coming back regularly and he wanted to be sure we parted friends, despite the housekeeper's grim demeanor.

"I think so," I told him, not explaining that it was what he had told us rather than shown us that was really helpful.

"What about your souvenir?" Rhonda growled.

"Excuse me?" Tricia said with the offense of a woman who doesn't even take the free shampoo, much less consider packing the towels and bathrobe.

"Don'tcha gotta prove to your club you were in here?" She grabbed a tented card from the bureau and held it out to me. It was a service survey, asking for feedback on our stay at the Carlyle. A rough but bold hand had filled in the room number and signed, as housekeeping supervisor, Rhonda. I thanked her and took the card. "Oughta be collecting stamps or taking dancing lessons," she said, leading the way back out into the hallway.

Jimmy escorted us back down to the lobby. Still eager to be of assistance, he wondered if there was anything else we needed. What I did need was for him to remember seeing one of the Harem the night of the murder but that wasn't going to happen, so it was time to move on. We thanked him graciously for his help, he wished us great success in our secret society, and we made a quick yet graceful exit.

Outside, we paused. More correctly, Tricia grabbed me and wouldn't let me so much as make eye contact with a cab until I answered her questions. "What is it? What did you figure out?"

I explained the new coalescence of my theories. "It just kept bugging me that everything Gwen got out of the murder she could have gotten out of the divorce. She's just a little too pragmatic for the 'if I can't have you' histrionics."

Tricia considered that thoughtfully and eased the pressure on my left arm. "So what's the protégée's reason for blowing him away?"

"I'm still working on that part. Mind if I work on it in the cab?"

"Not if you don't mind if the cab takes us to Cassady's first." Tricia nodded to the doorman, who signaled for the next cab in the queue to advance.

"My not minding has been taken for granted," I said, following Tricia to the cab. "You really think we should go to her apartment?"

"She's not answering at the office or on her cell and before I jump to any assumptions about her lack of well-being, I'd like to make sure she isn't in bed with the flu or otherwise detained. It's just not like her to go this long without calling either of us."

Tricia was right. Cassady was the kind of friend who would literally call to say hello—and only hello—on days she was too busy to chat. Even if she were in court, she would've texted one or both of us with some wry comment about the proceedings, just to touch base. And the fact that I had explained I couldn't talk that morning because of an incident involving police other than Kyle and she hadn't called me back at least three times since, pressing for details, was a definite sign that something was up.

As we rode up to the West 70s, Tricia and I returned our attention to my new theory of the murder. Everyone agreed that the Harem was hardworking and dedicated, so it wasn't hard to imagine one of them having a superbly deep emotional commitment to the agency. The kind that overwhelms your life, casting such a deep shadow that not much manages to grow in its shade. If that utter devotion were capped by an affair with the CEO, and the CEO then hurt her in some way . . . But what way? He was getting a divorce, so he was about to be "free." Had she been looking for something more?

"Were they worried about their jobs at all, with the merger going through?" Tricia asked.

"Not that I've uncovered. Ronnie Willis makes it sound like they're the whole reason he wanted the merger. And I still think we're dealing with an element of passion, given the way he was shot."

"So, when you sleep with your boss, what's the breaking point?" Tricia tilted her chin up at me expectantly.

"I don't know."

"Roger Leary."

"I did not sleep with Roger Leary!" Roger Leary was a self-proclaimed Casanova and semitalented jerk who had somehow worked his way up to editor at *Scoop,* a brassy, biting weekly mix of gossip and fashion. All I can say in his defense is he gave me my first decent magazine job. Given the kind of guy he is, it's not enough to get him into Heaven, but it's all I've got.

"Of course you did."

"No, I did not."

"Then why did you stay in that grotesque job so long?"

"Because I was hoping to sleep with Matt Grovesnor, the assistant editor, but that never happened either. Besides, if I had slept with Leary, don't you think I would've mentioned it?"

"Not necessarily. There are some secrets so shameful that

they don't come out until years and years later, even among the best of friends."

"Like you and Sam Burnett." Sam was a slick and slippery GOP centurion who'd worked on a campaign with Tricia's dad back when we first got out of school and Tricia still thought she was going to do that kind of work, too.

"Exactly."

"Seriously?! I was just guessing. How long?"

"Only three times."

"What was the breaking point?"

"They sent him to New Hampshire to put out some fires before the primary and I found I didn't miss him in the least."

"Not exactly a passionate commitment."

"To the job or him. Bet your girl has both."

I agreed. I just had to figure out which one of the Harem was such a go-getter that she'd kill her boss for derailing any of her plans.

But there was another go-getter on the agenda first. The cab dropped us in front of Cassady's charming old building and the doorman greeted us warmly, confirming that Cassady was home. He called to let her know we were on our way up and she was standing in her apartment doorway as we got off the elevator. Wearing jeans and a sweatshirt.

I've seen Cassady naked more often than I've seen her in jeans and a sweatshirt. This is a woman whose idea of bumming around is Banana Republic chinos and a James Perse tee, with a spritz of cologne instead of perfume. Even more perplexing was the MIT emblazoned across the sweatshirt; I couldn't think of anyone we knew who had gone there.

"We should've brought you soup," Tricia exclaimed.

"I'm not sick," Cassady said, leaning on the doorjamb and watching with a sly smile as we advanced. "I wanted to work from home today."

"Were you going to tell us?"

"I might have mentioned it to Molly if she hadn't been too busy wreaking new havoc with New York's finest."

"I called you back and you didn't answer," I said in self-defense.

Cassady stretched luxuriantly, like a cat preparing to move to a sunnier spot. "I've been bad."

Tricia and I stopped, reacting to the same low trill in her voice. "Are you alone?" I asked, amazed I hadn't considered this until now. Several pressing matters were vying in my mind, true, but I still felt inattentive.

Cassady pointed inside her apartment like a car-show model. "It's safe to come in. Trust me."

Inside her apartment and away from neighbor's ears, we dropped our handbags and our pretenses. "I've been worried about you," Tricia proclaimed.

"Yes, it was wrong of me not to let you know I was fine and just otherwise occupied. I apologize," Cassady said, giving Tricia a brisk kiss on the cheek and heading for the kitchen. "Sadly, it's not cocktail hour yet. What form of caffeine can I offer you until it's five o'clock?"

"Did the physicist go to MIT?" I asked, anxious to unravel and put aside this mystery since there was more than one on the table.

"He did. For about three decades, judging from the stack of degrees he carried out of there."

"So he's an older man?" Tricia asked, floating delicately to a semi-flopped position on Cassady's sofa.

"Yes, he's Molly's age," Cassady called in from the kitchen. I'm three weeks older than Cassady and those three weeks may be her favorite part of the year. "But he's educated to a ridiculous extent, so he seems even older."

"So what was it about this graying gravity that swept you off your feet to such an extreme that you stayed home from work and turned off your phone?" I asked.

"He's got a great sense of humor."

Tricia and I groaned in perfect harmony, honed by years of Cassady's checkered romantic track record. All of her greatest debacles began with that sinister phrase: "He has a great sense of humor." Not that Tricia and I didn't value that trait in a man. It's just that it's so tough to make Cassady laugh that she's willing to overlook a host of other, major imperfections—bad manners, massive debt, a wife—to stay with a funny man much, much longer than is prudent. Invariably, the breakup ratchets her criteria up even higher and the next guy has to try that much harder.

"When do we get to meet him?" I asked.

"I'm not sure."

"Excuse me?" Tricia sniffed. "Have we been found wanting?"

"No, not at all, it's just that he's actually kind of shy and I don't want to spring the two of you on him. It might be overwhelming."

"Was that a compliment?" Tricia asked me as Cassady returned from the kitchen with a carafe of iced coffee, cream and sugar, three different flavors of Italian syrup, and glass mugs. She set the tray down and we began to assemble our own concoctions, giggling like kids with a junior chemistry set.

"Aaron is a gentle soul and I want to take care in introducing him to the two of you."

"Is he a physicist or an orchid?" Tricia asked.

"You two remember Heisenberg's Uncertainty Principle?" Cassady asked, as though it were a logical response.

"Isn't that the one that proves whatever outfit I select, I'm not sure what shoes to wear with it?" I attempted.

"No, no, it's the one that says the more a man claims he wants to commit, the less certain you can be about what he's really after," Tricia said.

"The principle states," Cassady, who slept through more science classes in college than both Tricia and me combined, explained, "that the act of observing a subatomic particle affects the behavior that's being observed, making it impossible to determine both direction and velocity."

Tricia didn't seem any more certain of how we were supposed to respond than I felt. "That strikes me as sad, actually."

"No," Cassady said with a sly smile, "it just means that since I'm still trying to determine direction and velocity—"

"You don't want us to observe him until you're sure where you're going and how fast you're going to get there," I hypothesized.

"Precisely."

Tricia pouted. "That could take ages."

"Let's stick with the scientific mode and examine past data. When has it ever taken Cassady ages to make her mind up about a man?" I asked.

Tricia drew herself up in mock defensiveness. "That doesn't pertain to this experiment because we've never had the variable of skipping work and wearing grubbies for a man before."

Cassady laughed. "Just a little longer, please. Just a little."

"How about all the way until Friday? Say, Emile Trebask's gala?"

Cassady sniffed the air. "Do I detect an ulterior motive?"

"Not at all. I've been given the task of filling a table for the gala and of course I'd love the two of you to come with the gentlemen of your choosing and it strikes me as a grand time for us to meet Aaron. Besides, as a physicist, he can explain the black hole of fashion that will be created by Eileen's debut as a model."

I laid out the twisted road to the runway and Cassady laughed heartily. Tricia sat back, jingling the ice cubes in her glass. "So you and Kyle, Cassady and Aaron, and me and . . . Hmmm."

Cassady arched an eloquent eyebrow. "The list of possibilities must be long and varied, as usual."

Tricia shook her head. "The list is boring. You're both going to be there with someone you've deemed special and I'm going to wind up there with someone I've deemed tolerable."

Cassady jumped to her feet. "If ever there were a call to the hunt, that's it. What do you say, gals? Cocktails at a few of our favorite haunts, see what's in season to spice up Tricia's list?"

Tricia shook her head. "You still have work to do and Molly has an appointment. I'll think of someone, not to worry."

"You could always go back and throw money at boys in fine hotels," I suggested.

We brought Cassady up to speed and I explained the delicate nature of that evening's meeting with Detective Donovan, which I was now looking forward to even more, since I had a new theory in mind.

"Are you going to share this new theory with Detective Donovan?" Cassady asked.

"It wouldn't be very responsible of me until I have more to back it up with."

"But you are going to get together with Detective Donovan."

"Let's choose our verbs carefully. I'm going to meet Detective Donovan and we are going to exchange information. It's all business."

Tricia brightened. "Maybe she needs backup to make sure it stays that way."

Cassady smiled eagerly. "Are we volunteering?"

"I could make myself available. But I will not be seen anywhere outside this building with you until you're properly dressed," Tricia said.

"All can be arranged."

"And just so we're clear," I interjected, "it's him you don't trust, not me, right?"

"Do we dignify that with a response?" Cassady asked.

"A direct ego stroke would suffice."

"We just think it's so wonderful that you have this assignment that you've wanted for so long, we don't want anything or anyone to mess it up," Tricia offered. "And, pardon me for saying so, but if Kyle doesn't like him, you need to be on your guard."

"Or accompanied by one or two," I admitted. Not only did I appreciate the notion of Tricia and Cassady coming along, I could see the benefits of demonstrating to Detective Donovan from the beginning that this was a brief interview and nothing else.

Cassady left us to shower and change. Tricia and I lingered over our coffee, knowing it would be at least half an hour before we could get access to a non-steamed-up mirror. We both called in to make sure our offices were surviving without us, then returned to the mysteries at hand.

"Why all the secrecy, do you suppose?" I asked.

"He's either married, ugly, or so delicious she thinks we're going to devour him on the spot. Which could be fascinating, because she isn't usually all that possessive."

I nodded slowly, thinking back over Cassady's former flames. Tricia was right; Cassady wasn't generally possessive because most men were so smitten by her that their attention was incapable of straying enough for them to be distracted by anyone else.

But a possessive woman might go to great lengths to keep a man to herself. Or keep him from being available for someone else. Gwen had seemed anxious to discard Garth; had one of the Harem seen that as her opportunity and then, when rebuffed, lashed out with a gun? I reviewed the group in my mind: Most of them were fairly intense, with the exception of Lindsay and Francesca, but all of them spoke of Garth with reverence, even if Wendy's statements were laced with anger. Was that the grief talking or was it something else?

Cassady emerged a surprisingly short time later, dressed beautifully in a silk wrap blouse and pencil skirt. Detective Donovan was in for quite a surprise.

He reacted with grace and a big grin when he approached our table at Bemelman's a few minutes after six. The place was already filling with the anxious hum of the worker bees, as glamorous, professional, and transient as they might be, released from their hives and swooping down in search of the evening's nectar. The ritual is fascinating to watch when you have no vested interest in anyone's success or failure and we were having a delightful time handicapping the action at the bar when Detective Donovan walked up.

"This is a surprise," he said, standing over us and giving Tricia and Cassady such blatant lookings-over that I wanted to put my arms around them or at least drape my jacket over them.

"Detectives probably don't like surprises," Tricia replied in a silky tone that led me to believe she would have stiff-armed the jacket had I offered it.

"Actually, we love them. Especially the nice ones," he said, sliding down into the chair next to her.

"But isn't the real thrill in uncovering?" Cassady asked.

"Uncovering a surprise is better yet," he answered, smiling so fully that his ears moved with the effort.

"I don't mean to intrude, but Cassady Lynch and Tricia Vincent, this is Wally Donovan," I said, perhaps the most surprised of the four of us. Not that both of them can't be masterful flirts, but it was unusual for Tricia to dive in so quickly. It's generally something she works up to slowly, but this was flirting a la Porsche—zero to sixty in the bat of an eyelash.

They all shook hands and I swore Detective Donovan started to kiss Tricia's hand, then thought better of it. And I don't think my little cough of disbelief was what derailed him, just his inner sense of rhythm, which was telling him to slow the hell down. I was hoping Tricia's might speak up, too, but her mouth was set in that small pucker of determination she gets when she sets her sights on something or someone. One of my bodyguards was apparently all too willing to throw herself on the grenade, should the grenade be similarly inclined.

"Thanks for meeting me," Detective Donovan said to me, remembering the original purpose of our gathering.

"I hope you don't mind that I brought my friends along," I said, making it clear I knew he didn't mind at all.

"Not at all, as long as you don't mind if we talk business for a moment. It's pressing, but this morning wasn't the best."

"How is Mr. Douglass?" I asked.

"Still in the hospital."

"Goodness, Molly, what did you do to the poor man?" Cassady asked. She settled back into her chair, deferring to Tricia in the battle for Detective Donovan's attention.

"I didn't think he was hurt that badly," I said with a

twinge of remorse. I had only wanted to disarm the man, not wound him for life.

"They suspect a concussion. He's also on psych review while Hernandez and her crowd sort out charges." Detective Donovan leaned in, dropping his voice. "If you own stock in his company, better hope your broker's still at the office, 'cause you want to sell fast."

"Have you talked to him?"

"Preliminary. Little too doped up."

"Do you think he killed Garth Henderson?" Tricia asked. Coming from her, it sounded like the slightly awed question of a woman flirting with a detective. Coming from me, it would have sounded like a challenge. Perhaps she was just playing with him to help me out.

Whichever, it worked. He shifted slightly in her direction. "I haven't discounted him yet."

I thought about scribbling a note on my napkin and sliding it over to Tricia, but she didn't need it. "Have you discounted anyone?" was the perfect follow-up question she anticipated and asked for me.

"The four of us," he answered. "And Ronnie Willis."

"Really?" I asked before I could stop myself. "Why Ronnie? And why not Gwen?"

"I interviewed Willis and he's just not a killer. He's too freaked out about his future. That's not a guy who could pull a trigger. And I know it's a woman, so I gotta keep Gwen Lincoln on my list."

"How do you know it's a woman?" Cassady asked, leaning back in out of genuine interest in the discussion.

"I was at the crime scene. There was evidence."

"Such as?"

Detective Donovan smoothed his tie several times, letting us know what was coming next was difficult for him to say. "That's pretty valuable information."

"What are you suggesting?" I asked, more sharply than I'd intended, but he seemed to be leading up to something unsavory.

"There's a business arrangement to be made here."

"You should know," Cassady said, on the same train of thought I was, "I'm a lawyer and as an officer of the court—"

"Ladies, ladies," Detective Donovan protested, his smile getting decidedly crooked, "you can't think that I'd come here and propose something illicit."

"So much for my plans for the night," Tricia said, trying to lighten things a bit—but it didn't help. Kyle had warned me that Detective Donovan wasn't a good cop, but I hadn't understood he might be a dirty cop.

"I'm talking about a book deal."

All three of us gaped at him. His crooked smile nearly did a cartwheel as it twisted yet again while he waited for one of us to say something.

I was the most articulate first. "What?"

"I think there's a great book in this case and I'm looking for a journalist who'd like to write it with me."

"Shouldn't you solve the case before you start franchising it?" Cassady asked.

"We're getting closer all the time," Detective Donovan said earnestly. "But I thought it would be invaluable for my co-writer to be as close to the process for as long as possible."

Pieces of information swirled around inside my head, like that arcade game where the air blows the bumblebees in little gusts and you have to grab them up and put them back in the hive. "That's why you've been talking to Peter Mulcahey?" I asked, grabbing as fast as I could.

"I've been talking to him because we're old friends. Back in the day and all that."

"Have you talked to him about the book?"

"I ran it past him, but he wasn't interested."

"That tells you a lot, when Peter takes a pass," Cassady muttered.

"I think you and Molly working together could be a very interesting idea," Tricia said, placing her hand lightly on the detective's arm. I started to protest, but the very pointed toe of her Stuart Weitzman pumps found the sweet spot in my right shin and I stopped to silently contemplate if I'd ever walk again.

"What do you think, Molly?" Detective Donovan asked.

I swung my legs toward Cassady and away from Tricia. "It has possibilities. But only if you really think you're on to something. I can't devote a lot of time to a case that's going to stay open until it's cold."

Detective Donovan's gaze moved from one of us to the next to the next, sizing up the table before placing his bet. "The crime scene stank with perfume. Expensive stuff, not call girl stuff. That's why I'm not eliminating any of the women in his life."

I deliberately waited a beat before asking, "Was it Success? The perfume?"

For a detective, he didn't have much of a poker face. "What makes you ask that?"

"It was a prominent product in Garth's life."

"Yes, it was Success. Gwen Lincoln ID'ed it for us that night. She was wearing it, too."

"Of course she was wearing it, she helped create it," Cassady said. "But she's not the only one who wears it."

"It's not in stores yet."

"No, but Garth's agency has samples," I said. "The people who work for Emile Trebask have access. Emile's been handing out samples all over town. I have some. You can't suspect Gwen just because of her perfume."

"It's not just the perfume, it's the divorce and the merger plus the perfume, right?" Tricia asked him. He nodded.

"What about the tooth?" I asked.

A frown rippled across his brow. "I don't think I want to divulge that until our relationship is clarified."

"Gwen told me his mouth was cut. Someone else told me there was a problem with his teeth. They were chipped, right, or broken? Because someone hit him in the mouth hard enough to cut his mouth and chip his tooth?"

"Have you seen the size of the rings Gwen Lincoln wears?" he asked, balling his hand into a fist—for demonstration purposes only, I hoped.

"There are a lot of women in this town with heavily encrusted hands," I replied.

His eyes narrowed. "You can't be this sure it's not Gwen unless you've got a suspect of your own."

I shook my head. "I can discount one suspect without naming another."

"Imagine that, Donovan," growled the voice behind me, "my girlfriend's a better detective than you are."

Eleven

ONCE, I THOUGHT IT MIGHT be a very impressive thing to have two men fight over me—duelists maybe, or gunfighters, or even just two guys willing to punch each other out over the question of my honor, my beauty, or even my ability to bake a cherry pie (much of this has its roots in my fascination with American folk music growing up). Interestingly enough, two homicide detectives going toe to toe over my forensic instincts had never appeared on that list.

It wasn't so much that they were asking each other to step outside as that they got so animated in their discussion that Tricia, Cassady, and I decided in the interests of decorum, discretion, and potential property damage to usher them outside so they could cool off. A public scene wasn't going to help anybody.

"Subcontracting your cases out now, Donovan?" Kyle spat as Cassady took him by the arm and walked him several feet away.

"Not hiding behind a bunch of skirts, that's for sure," Detective Donovan snapped as Tricia did her best to walk him several feet in the opposite direction. Which left me standing in the middle, trying to catch my breath and assimilate the facts I'd learned before chaos erupted again.

My theory that it was one of the Harem girls was looking

better all the time. All the Harem girls had the perfume. They knew the hotel routine. Garth wouldn't hesitate to let them into his room. It all still worked. I just had to figure out which of those bracelet-wearing advertising Amazons had snapped.

Or at least snapped off her bracelet.

Could the bracelet be the key? Pushing my theory forward, I hoped I was taking a stride, not a leap, to focus on their sterling badge of honor. It was clearly significant to all of them, yet Tessa wasn't wearing hers when I met with the group. What if she hadn't broken it? What if she just couldn't bring herself to wear it after she'd destroyed the man who'd given it to her, especially with what the bracelet meant to the rest of that tightly wrapped and tightly knit group? But what could have driven Tessa to the breaking point?

I had to figure out a way to talk to Tessa alone, but first, I had a mess to clean up. But where to start? Did I thank Kyle for being so supportive but ask him to rein it in a bit? Or did I tell Detective Donovan that while I appreciated his desire to make himself a star, I wasn't sure I was the one to help him?

I decided to approach Kyle and Cassady first, mainly because I could hear her laughing from where I stood and I was anxious to discover what part of this she found amusing. Probably my part, but it was worth confirming. As I walked up to them, she bit her lip guiltily. Kyle was still pretty grim.

"Is it one I've heard before?" I asked.

"It's not even a joke," Kyle said.

"I'd always thought that pissing contests were about distance, but Kyle was explaining that they're about duration. It makes so much sense, I don't know why I didn't see that a long time ago," Cassady said, still chuckling.

"You all right?" Kyle asked tersely.

"I'm fine. And I appreciate your coming, even though it wasn't—"

"Yes, it was necessary. Can we go now?"

Cassady looked at me even more expectantly than Kyle did, reacting to the toughness in his tone. "I can grab Tricia and we'll talk to you guys later," she volunteered.

"Sounds good."

Kyle almost did a double-take, he was so unprepared for my agreement. He knew I still wanted to talk to Detective Donovan, but I knew Detective Donovan wasn't going to be at all forthcoming in front of Kyle. Besides, Detective Donovan didn't seem to be following my path of reasoning at all, so I felt under no obligation to offer him my theory. Yet.

"Thanks for joining us, sorry it was so brief," I said to Cassady as we hugged each other good-bye. "Tell Tricia—"

"Tell her yourself," Tricia said, walking up behind me.

I turned and looked past her for Detective Donovan, but he had disappeared. "We're going," I said.

"Detective Donovan asked me to apologize to all of you and said if he could be of any further assistance, feel free to call him," Tricia reported, handing me one of the two business cards in her hand. I looked quizzically at the second and she smiled. "This one's for me," she said, tucking it into her bag.

"Do you have dinner plans, Tricia?" Cassady asked with a touch too much enthusiasm.

"No, Cassady, I'm free," Tricia responded in kind.

"These two kids are headed home for the evening, I would hope, so wanna grab a bite with me?"

"That'd be great." Cassady and Tricia went off, arm-in-arm, to find a cab.

"And then there were two," I said quietly, mainly because I couldn't think of anything of substance to say that wasn't potentially inflammatory.

"Did they leave because of me?" he asked, watching them walk away.

"Of course not, why would they?" I answered sincerely.

"I came in and busted up your party."

"Didn't Cassady explain that they came with me precisely because you said you didn't trust Donovan, so they wouldn't let me see him alone?"

"But you still had to see him." I started to answer, but he held his hand up to stop me. "I want you to write a great article. I tried to stay away. But I thought about you getting mixed up with that cretin and I . . ." He sighed and looked up and down the street. "Wanna eat around here or closer to home?"

I slipped my arm through his. "We could order in."

"No, it's okay. I can be social."

Good thing, too, because a voice called out my name and we were suddenly shaking hands with Lindsay and her husband as I introduced them to Kyle. They'd just stopped by Ronnie's office so Lindsay could drop off some artwork and were on their way to eat at Girasole, a little farther north. They invited us to join them. Much as I wanted the opportunity to talk to Lindsay, I was going to politely decline. But Kyle accepted their invitation, much to my surprise and their delight.

The low-ceilinged, warmly glowing restaurant was a great place to talk and I was pleased Lindsay wanted to. "I'm so glad we ran into you," Lindsay said, reaching across the table to pat my hand once we were settled in. The charm on her bracelet clinked against the tabletop and I seized the opportunity.

"Such a beautiful bracelet."

She caught the charm in her right hand, as though apologizing for the sound. "I love it. It means so much, especially now that he's gone."

"I'm surprised Tessa hasn't made a point of getting hers back from the jeweler. Wouldn't you miss yours?"

Lindsay snuck a look at her husband, who was explaining his work at Rising Angels to Kyle. "I really would," she said, dropping her voice.

"Is that a secret?"

"Daniel doesn't like the bracelet. He calls it my sterling shackle, says it's a symbol of servitude. Daniel's a little anti-authority."

"But he's a lawyer."

"Was a lawyer. Because he wanted to save the world. He's much happier in a nonprofit environment where he's calling the shots and seeing tangible evidence of his work. Which helps balance the fact that it's the same hours for half the pay." She made a face that she probably intended as wry, but it looked pretty weary.

I glanced at Daniel myself. "You work pretty hellacious hours, too, I bet."

"Usually. I'll probably go back to the office after we eat. But I love it. It's just hard because I'm trying to compete—I mean, keep up with the rest of the group and they don't have the obligations I have. And once we start a family . . ." She trailed off, glancing over at Daniel. I expected it to be one of those longing looks of love that make single women gnash their teeth, but it was a look of pained sadness.

I've seen that look before, so I stepped carefully into delicate territory. "Are you hoping to start soon?"

Lindsay looked back at me quickly, smiling with effort. "Hoping. Trying. Praying. The whole range."

I nodded sympathetically, having watched friends struggle with doctor's appointments and ovulation predictors and cruel calendars. "Does it qualify as irony," Cassady asked once, "that all our single friends are praying not to get pregnant while all our married friends are praying to conceive?"

Lindsay took a deep breath. "So where are the two of you on the whole range?"

I laughed in surprise. "I'm not sure we can even see the range from here."

"Really? You truly have that 'great couple' vibe."

"Thank you," I said, trying to figure out how to get the conversation back to her and the Harem and as far away from my romantic future as possible. "You guys do, too," I said, desperate for a segue, then pressed on before she could respond. "So at work, you're the only one who's married, but aren't any of the rest of them in relationships?"

She shrugged. "Some of them are, but the job always comes first. My father used to tell me, 'Never work for a man who doesn't want to go home at night.' Women who aren't anxious to get home are even worse." She smiled, but there was a startling edge to her pronouncement and I could imagine more than a few testy exchanges between her and some of her cohorts. She seemed to catch the edge herself because her smile and voice both lightened as she said, "I think the real reason Tessa hasn't gotten her bracelet back is because she had such a rough time drinking for her charm."

"Drinking for it?"

"It was this bizarre game Garth had us play at the party. When we unwrapped our bracelets, the charms were separate. He dropped each charm in a champagne glass and we had to drain it and come up with the charm in our teeth without spilling anything. If you didn't get it all in one move, you had to do it again and again."

"And, like any good drinking game, it gets harder the more you try because you're getting blitzed."

"Tessa wasn't just blitzed, she got sick. In front of everybody. Garth picked on her about it for days afterward and she didn't take it well. Things were kind of prickly between them for a while."

"I can imagine." And I did imagine. I pictured Tessa making a mess out of herself, trying to excel at yet another task from the boss, and failing at this one to the point of embarrassment. And then I remembered Tricia getting hit with the champagne glass to her mouth and wondered what might have happened to her front teeth had she had a sterling silver charm between them at the time. Then I imagined Tessa again, this time exacting revenge on a man who had humiliated her by hitting him in the face while he tried to drink for his charm. Which would be exceptionally hard to do with someone pointing a gun at his head or his crotch.

The urge to leave the table was overwhelming, but I didn't know where to go. Could I come up with a reason to track Tessa down? Could I enlist Lindsay's help to do that? Should I compare notes with Detective Donovan? Should I tell Kyle I had a headache and ask him to take me home? Or should I sit there and pretend that this was no more interesting or shocking than anything else Lindsay had said, lest she get suspicious and somehow alert Tessa?

I decided to stay put, let the idea percolate, and see what else I could get Lindsay to divulge.

"Had Tessa and Garth made up when he died?" I asked, trying to sound not much more than politely interested.

"I think so, but still—I'd bet that when she looks at the bracelet now, it brings back the negative as much as the positive. That would be hard." She rubbed her own charm between her fingers, an automatic gesture I'm not sure she was aware of. She frowned suddenly. "You won't put any of this in your article about Gwen, will you?"

"No," I said, figuring it was the truth because if I was right, the article wasn't going to be about Gwen anymore. "Do you think you'll all stay together once Gwen and Ronnie have things running smoothly?"

She thought about that for a moment and my ears drifted over to check on the guys, who were discussing music. "I really don't know. I think some of them are hoping things will be different, that we'll be less equal, you know?" Lindsay said after a moment.

"More personal recognition?" I asked, thinking of Wendy's Borg comment.

"I think the team's more important, but that's not a very popular point of view. Especially with Gwen and Ronnie coming in, everyone's jockeying for position." She cut herself off, tucking her bracelet into her sleeve, then folding her hands on the table.

"Tessa seemed to be setting the tone this morning," I said, trying to ease the conversation back to her again.

Lindsay paused again, fingers slipping up her sleeve to adjust the bracelet again, and smiled. "Can't hold her champagne, but otherwise, Tessa's strong. She got us all focused again after Garth died, helped Gwen make the transition. She's still a step ahead of everyone. We'll just have to catch up."

Kyle threw his arm over the back of my chair, startling me. "Can you believe this?" For a split second, I had the absurd notion that Kyle and Daniel had been talking about the murder, too, and Kyle had reached the same conclusion I had. But I knew better. Still, what could the problem be?

"What's wrong?" Lindsay asked, taking Daniel's hand.

Kyle sighed for effect. "Daniel says Dave Matthews is better than Tom Petty. Molly, you gonna let him get away with that?"

I looked Kyle in the eye and got the nonverbal message loud and clear: He wasn't enjoying his conversation with Daniel anywhere nearly as much as I was enjoying mine with Lindsay and he very much wanted me to abandon mine to bail him out of his. Of course, I was piecing together a mystery and he was trying to be polite to a guy he'd just met, who struck me as a bit of a cold fish. So since Lindsay'd already given me a great deal to chew on and I owed Kyle big time, I frowned at Daniel in mock horror and said, "Sacrilege!"

Daniel laughed. "Prove me wrong."

I smiled back and committed to finishing the meal without betraying what I was really thinking about. I gave an impassioned defense of my favorite rock star and Daniel countered for his. The four of us laughed and joked, and the rest of the meal passed in that pleasant, gentle group banter Tricia calls Cocktail Party 101—discussions of favorite movies, bands, TV shows, and books but never politics or religion.

The most interesting aspect of the evening was the feeling that we were gliding across the surface of everything. It was more than my being distracted by the new information on Tessa. It was the dynamics of the four of us. Some people you connect with immediately. I'd felt that Lindsay and I had done that in the office but now here, with the guys with us, I felt as if we were backing up. Maybe I was just tired—it had been quite a day.

Kyle declined coffee and dessert with no nudge from me, telling them that I got very cranky if I didn't get my fourteen hours, and we parted company in front of the restaurant with us heading for a cab and them saying they wanted to stroll a while before they headed home. I told Lindsay I was sure I'd be talking to her again, maybe even drop by the office in the morning with follow-up questions for the article. And for Tessa, but Lindsay didn't need to know that.

I tried to keep my excitement under wraps, but once we were in the cab, it sort of leaked out. "That was amazing."

Kyle groaned, dropping his head back against the seat. "It was excruciating. That guy has the personality of a dial tone."

"I'm sorry."

"If you'd resisted the Tom Petty challenge, I would've gotten up, thrown you over my shoulder, and carried you outta there."

"As exciting as that sounds, I'm very glad you resisted."

Kyle rolled his head to look at me. "What'd you figure out?"

"I think Detective Donovan is on the wrong track."

"I told you that already."

"And I think I'm on the right one."

Kyle watched me patiently, waiting for me to continue, but I wasn't sure I should. "And . . . ?" he prompted.

"Do you really want to know? Isn't this the conflict of interest we've been trying to avoid?"

"The conflict of interest is me helping you work on another cop's case. I'm not helping you. I'm listening to your theory. Maybe."

"And that won't cause a problem?"

"Knowing you, yes, it will, but a kind I probably haven't even thought of yet."

I wanted to take offense, but that's hard to do when it's the truth that's being flung in your face. So I took a deep breath and laid out my theory about Tessa killing Garth, including the charm bracelets, the champagne glass, the perfume, and the party humiliation. Kyle's head rocked up and down on the edge of the seat as he listened, staying with me right up until the party. "I don't buy it."

"Why not?"

"It's not a motive for murder. Now, if it's the tip of the iceberg, you may be on to something. But I don't think you've got it yet."

"So what do I do?"

Kyle sighed. "Keep . . . working on your article."

"Do I have to tell Detective Donovan any of this?"

I could see the amusement in Kyle's eyes, even though he was gazing at the ceiling of the cab. "I like the spirit of co-operation in that question."

"I'm not trying to be difficult."

"Yeah, it's effortless for you and it's one of the sexiest things about you." He swung his body across mine suddenly, hungry kisses roaming over my face and neck as he pulled me against him. It was a delicious, dizzying moment until he started chuckling in my ear. I thought about biting him, but he moved away too quickly.

"Are you picking on me?"

"Sweetheart," he soothed, rolling back into his original position, "I was just trying to get you to stop thinking for a minute. But I know how hard that is when I'm limited by our surroundings and our audience."

"Don't mind me," our cabbie urged.

"You're not trying to get me to stop thinking," I protested, "you're trying to get out of answering the question."

"She's got you there," our cabbie said.

"Does she tip you extra for the help or do I tip you extra to stop?" Kyle asked him.

"Should both try it and see what happens," the cabbie answered.

Kyle pinched his bottom lip. "Molly, I don't ever want you to withhold evidence. But you don't really have evidence. You have conjecture."

"Which I tried to share with him and he wouldn't listen."

"Because you're really wasting his time until you have more to go on."

"And should I?"

"Should you what?"

"Go on."

"Like there's another option."

Now I was the one who sprawled across him. The cabbie hummed happily until we arrived at my building and we both tipped him generously.

In the morning, my theory held up to the toughest test: I was still as excited about it as I had been the night before. Even with Kyle challenging me on every conceivable point as he bolted down breakfast and headed out the door. His parting request was a simple one: that I call and warn him if I was going to come see Detective Donovan. I agreed, knowing I needed to plan my "casual follow-up" with Garth's Girls.

But first, a different follow-up with other girls. I had to call Tricia and Cassady and fill them in on the interesting developments of last night—and discover I'd missed the most interesting one of the bunch.

"He's very sweet," Tricia said in a way that made "sweet" a thing to be cherished, not demeaning or condescending at all.

"You met Aaron and I missed it?"

"You had more pressing matters to attend to."

"Still. I feel like I'm the only one who couldn't stay awake long enough to see Santa Claus."

"Trust me, Molly, he does exist and he's very charming. I really don't see why she was so skittish."

"Because they've only known each other for a few days. This is whirlwind, even for her."

"All the better to meet him early then."

"Before the gala?"

"You'll have to discuss that with her."

Which I arranged to do by having Cassady meet me for coffee on her way to a client meeting. Cassady's idea of a big breakfast is having real milk in her coffee, but I was able to tempt her with a piece of my cream-cheese-and-carrot muffin. "It's vegetables," I told her. "And calcium."

"I'd be more persuaded if I hadn't heard you give similar speeches in defense of chocolate cake."

"Eggs, flour, milk. And chocolate promotes serotonin production and we all need more of that. Would you like me to get you a chocolate muffin?"

"No, thank you. Just tell me what Tricia said about Aaron."

" 'Sweet.' " She wrinkled her nose, but I hurried to assure her, "In a really good way. So I want to meet him now."

"You and Kyle free for dinner?"

I did owe Kyle a pleasant dinner after he'd gotten stuck with Daniel for such a long time the night before. I told Cassady I'd check with Kyle, then filled her in on my new thoughts about Garth's death. She nodded excitedly, actually eating another piece of muffin as she listened. "What a great idea."

"Tessa?"

"No, making him choke on his own pride, as it were. I have a few former bosses I'd like to see swallow more than that, believe me. My question is, was she sleeping with him, too, or is this strictly some sort of thwarted ambition thing?"

"I'm thinking both, which explains the two shots."

"Very creative. No wonder it's such a good agency."

"I don't think they'll be adding it to their list of credits."

Cassady's business meeting was only a few buildings past mine, so we brushed off the muffin crumbs and headed toward work. The air was muggy, so we both walked with that anti-sweat posture where the elbows are turned out slightly to keep the underarms as well-ventilated as possible while still keeping the shoulders square enough not to lose the handbag. As long as I didn't have to answer my phone, I could stay cool.

Or unless I saw someone I wasn't prepared to see. Peter Mulcahey was pacing the plaza in front of my building and while he didn't seem to have worked up a sweat, I felt droplets on the back of my neck at the sight of him. I thought I'd dealt with him and dismissed him and couldn't imagine what had brought him back to me. Of course, I work in a very large building and there was always the hope that he hadn't come to see me at all, that this was all an unhappy coincidence. But that hope wilted in the heat as Peter strode up to me, barely taking time to acknowledge Cassady as he did so.

"What's going on?"

"Hello, Peter," Cassady said before I could.

"Cassady, excuse me, I'm not trying to be rude—"

"Just happens, right?"

"And sometimes even without provocation."

They were never fond of each other and this was not the ideal situation for them to catch up. "There something I can do for you, Peter?" I asked.

"Tell me why Detective Donovan won't take my phone calls."

"Maybe he ran out of free minutes."

"I'm serious, Molly."

I tried to remember anything I'd done or said that Peter could point to as proof of my complicity in Detective Donovan shunning him. "I talked to him last night, but I didn't say anything that would make him cut you off."

"Other than the fact that he was wrong," Cassady pointed out.

"You were there?" Peter asked.

"But we didn't talk about you. Much," Cassady said charitably. "Molly just offered a different point of view."

"He wants you to write the book, doesn't he? Let's write the book together," Peter said suddenly.

I wasn't feeling as charitable as Cassady. "That's a bad idea for so many reasons, Peter."

"We'd be a great team."

"I think we've already proven the fallacy in that. Besides, he told me you weren't interested."

"Lying bastard."

A wonderful thing to hear about a detective who's provided you with crucial information. But I wasn't going to let Peter shake me up, I knew I was on the right track. "I don't care about the book, Peter."

It would have been a more persuasive statement had Cassady not looked at me like I was losing my mind even before Peter did. Peter's smile hardened. "I don't know what you and Donovan are up to—"

"Nothing!"

"—but I'm going to figure this out before either one of you. And then I'll write the damn book myself." He took a moment to remember his manners. "Nice to see you, Cassady."

"Always a pleasure to see your true colors, Peter," Cassady said, waving in farewell.

Peter stalked off and I tried to remember if I'd ever seen him genuinely angry. One of my problems with Peter had always been that his emotions were contained to the point of not being sincere. Maybe we'd just never dealt with anything that was sufficiently important to him.

"Why is it never the pleasant ones who come back to haunt you?" Cassady asked.

"Then it wouldn't be haunting."

"What's Kyle think of him popping back up?"

I didn't say anything. I didn't have to. Cassady's known me too long and has that telepathic polygraph old friends develop; she can feel my pulse change from across the room. "Oh, Molly," was all she said, but with that deep disappointment your mother uses when you've spilled hot chocolate down the front of your satin Christmas dress five minutes before leaving for church.

"Not intentionally. I'll tell him."

"When?"

"When the time's right."

And I should've known then, but I had to learn it again the hard way: Like an unfamiliar highway exit ramp, the right time is something you usually only recognize after you've missed it.

Twelve

DEAR MOLLY, WHY IS IT *so difficult to keep a promise? Is it some sort of performance anxiety thing, where the pressure gets to be too much? Is it because we make them in the heat of the moment and when that cools off, the promise loses its appeal, too? Or is it because we make promises about things we know we can't achieve, but we'd still like to get points for good intentions? Signed, Cross My Heart and Fingers*

"We had a deal," my editor growled.

At least I thought it was my editor. It was about the right size and the proper level of antagonism, but the shape behind the desk was swathed in an absurdly large amount of white terry cloth and where the face should have been, there was a bright blue oval.

"Maybe I should come back when you're done. I don't want to undo all of Suzanne's hard work by making you yell at me," I said, throwing a sympathetic look at Suzanne. Her martyrdom was genuinely earned this morning, since she was in charge of giving the tiny bundle of shroud and fury a facial, right there in her office.

"It's all right," Suzanne whispered, picking the already hardening blue goo off her fingers.

"Any particular reason you didn't go to a spa or a salon?" I dared ask.

"And be seen in public like this? Are you insane? And don't try to change the subject. I'm upset with you."

"I'm sorry," I said, in the interest of saving time.

"I would hope so. You promised me a sensational cover story about Gwen Lincoln. Now you're saying she might be innocent?!"

"Wasn't that the original hope, the reason Emile asked you and The Publisher to make room for the article?"

"But Quinn Harriman's going to have the real killer on his cover! Of his first issue!"

"Assuming Peter Mulcahey figures it out in time, which is not a given." This whole exchange was my mistake. I should have known better, when summoned into the inner sanctum for an update, than to be truthful and specific. I should have just assured her that I was working hard, that I had no ideas about Gwen's guilt or innocence, then complimented her on something and eased my way out. But no, in my excitement, I'd overshared.

"And we're going to be stuck with the Widow Lincoln on ours!"

As intrigued as I was by the image of Gwen dressed as Mary Todd Lincoln, I couldn't stop to consider it. This was no time for pride or subtlety. My article was slouching toward the scrap pile and I had to lure it back to safety. "Of course, she'll be wearing a headline that says 'Eileen Fitzsimmons Set Me Free'."

It was like releasing a helium-filled balloon—you let the gas escape, then wait a moment until it stops flinging itself around the room. Eileen's eyes opened as wide as the hardening facial masque would permit, so I continued. "If the magazine proves Gwen is innocent, doesn't she have you to thank? You're the one who assigned the article," I said, trying not to grit my teeth. Better to have written and have credit stolen than never to have written at all.

Eileen's head wobbled slightly as she let the idea bounce around and become her own. "Maybe Gwen and I could be on the cover together," she suggested.

"How Oprah of you. Want me to call a photographer in right now, take a few practice shots?"

"I have very delicate skin," Eileen protested.

"Which is why you're protecting it from the entire visible light spectrum, I get that."

"Fine, be one of those disgusting girls who swipes with a little soap and water and glows for days. Some of us must be pampered."

Momentarily distracted that Eileen had, in her own way, complimented me, I faltered for a moment, then refocused. "So I'm going back to work now, on helping you save Gwen. I'll keep you posted." I gave her a wave and a smile as I backed out of sight. She might have tried to smile back, but it was hard to tell through the mask.

I alighted briefly at my desk, uncertain as to my next move. Which made me think of Cassady's new beau and his buddy Heisenberg. If observing the particle changes the behavior of the particle, I was going to have to sneak up on the atom if I had any chance at all of splitting it.

Since I needed to talk to Tessa, I asked for Lindsay when I arrived at GHInc. Now that we'd had dinner together, it appeared natural for me to want to see her, talk to her again. I was banking on her maternal reputation being well earned, and that part of the mothering instinct would be she was the one who kept tabs on everyone, listened to their problems, and refereed their arguments. If I could get her to share those sorts of stories with me and tell me everything I needed to know about Tessa—preferably without even realizing that's what she was doing—I'd be that much closer to the atom without the atom knowing.

Fortunately, Lindsay was delighted to see me, greeting me in the reception area with a warm hug. She ushered me to her office, which was immaculate and streamlined, as I would've expected, its main adornment a large, ornately framed picture of her and Daniel on their wedding day.

"Such a nice picture," I said, surprised by the wistfulness I heard in my own voice.

"Thanks. We really enjoyed seeing you guys last night. Daniel had so much fun talking to Kyle."

I smiled politely. "Kyle enjoyed it, too."

"We'll have to do it again. Have a seat," she said, moving several large bags off her sofa to make room for me. "Sorry, Francesca cleaned out her closet and brought me all the goodies for Daniel's thrift shop."

"Daniel has a thrift shop?"

"Rising Angels does. In the basement at St. Aidan's. It's a really fun place. I'll take you over there one day if you like that kind of shopping."

"Haven't met a kind I don't like. That's so sweet," I said, sitting on the now vacant buttery leather, "Francesca supporting Daniel's work that way."

Lindsay started to make a face, then caught herself. "You're right, it is."

"You don't think so?"

"No, I do, I do. The whole group is very supportive, we're all there for each other. It's just with the thrift shop, I sometimes think they bring it here to me so they don't have to deal with it themselves, make a trip out of the way or anything." She pressed her lips together, then smiled. "I'm sorry, I don't really mean that, I shouldn't have said that."

I wanted to tell her that people who said things to me they weren't supposed to say were my favorite people in the world, but I refrained. "I understand," I said instead. "It's tricky when you feel friends are taking advantage of you."

"So, what brings you by this morning?" she asked brightly, thinking she was changing the subject when really, she was just reinforcing it.

"I heard a rumor and I wanted to run it by you," I said, dropping my voice to a confidential level. "I won't name names in the article, but who is it that's thinking about leaving?"

I immediately regretted my approach because Lindsay looked as though I had gut-punched her. "One of us? Leaving?"

"Maybe there's nothing to it," I said quickly, hoping I hadn't torpedoed the conversation before it even began.

"Maybe that's why Francesca's cleaning out her closet," Lindsay said, giving one of the bags a little kick. "After all, when do you clean your closet this thoroughly—when you lose a lot of weight, which she hasn't, when a man moves in, which hasn't happened, or when you're getting ready to move, which she would only do for a new job because she's got this great rent-controlled place in the Village." Lindsay kicked the bags again, her sadness swiftly giving way to anger. "I've worked so hard to keep this group together and—" She gave the bags a third, decisive kick and the toe of her pumps popped a hole in one. Pulling up short, she planted herself in her desk chair like a kid being put in the corner.

"Why's it up to you to hold everyone together?" I asked quietly while I tried to figure out whether I'd missed something about Francesca. But Tessa was the one with the absent bracelet, the one I wanted to know about. "I thought Tessa was your ringleader."

Lindsay's eyes flashed and I thought she was going to kick me this time. "Did Tessa tell you that?"

"No, but the dynamic when I came—"

"Tessa likes attention, so she thinks she deserves it and she'll do just about anything to get it. It was really sort of sad with Garth, the whole Electra complex. He played into it, enjoyed it, but that was a little sad, too."

Here was the first run in the perfectly smooth pair of pantyhose. Now, if I could just tug in the right direction, the runs would multiply. "Think it's going to be hard for Tessa, with Gwen and Ronnie?"

"I'm sure she already has a plan for Ronnie," Lindsay said, her jaw setting. "She's going to have a tough time with Gwen, though. They rub each other the wrong way."

"Why? Think there's some sort of jealousy there?"

Lindsay shrugged. "Like Tessa wants to be in charge and resents Gwen? I hadn't thought about that, but I can see it."

"I was thinking on a more personal level. If Tessa's feelings for Garth were a little less Electra and a little more, say, Cleopatra."

I expected either assent or denial from Lindsay and I was silently cheering for the former. What I got instead was such a naked look of pain that I almost blurted out an apology without knowing what I'd done. But while I was still groping for a response, Lindsay said in a low, tight voice, "I'm really not in a position to comment on the personal lives of any of my coworkers."

If it was exactly what I was looking for, why did it hurt so much to hear it? I guess I'd been hoping for a catty narc-out, but this had a self-flagellating quality to it, like she was blaming herself for not having caught on to whatever was going on after hours—maybe even during hours—and where it might end up. "Garth and Tessa were having an affair?" I asked gently, just to be sure I was interpreting properly.

Lindsay's expression didn't change at all, but her voice got more jagged. "You're not going to put this in the article, are you? I don't see how it helps anyone to know."

"I just want to understand the emotional landscape Gwen's entering," I said with the conviction available at a moment's notice.

Lindsay shook her head. "You really don't want to get into this. Tessa's so good at what she does, the rest shouldn't matter."

Before I could press further, Lindsay's office door flew open and Wendy stepped in, eyes wild and wet. "Moron said no!" she exclaimed, not registering my presence on the sofa. Lindsay looked at me instinctively and Wendy turned, her shoulders sagging at the sight of me. "Sorry. Didn't know you had company."

"Want me to give you a moment?" I asked, standing. I could even wander down the hall and try to bump into Tessa while they sorted this out, whatever it was.

"I need so much more than a moment, it's not even funny," Wendy replied. She pivoted back to the door. "Later, Lindsay."

"Wendy, let me make some phone calls," Lindsay said with a bright trill to her voice I wouldn't have thought possible a moment before.

"Whatever," Wendy said, vanishing back out into the hall.

"She's trying to get a loan, and Daniel and I know a lot of financial people because of all his fund-raising, so I've been trying to hook her up," Lindsay explained, easing the door closed behind Wendy.

"She seems pretty discouraged."

"Her last boyfriend stole her credit cards and trashed her rating, so she's still recovering," Lindsay said. She forced a smile. "That's why we're all so good at our work. We're running away from issues in our personal lives."

"What are you running away from?" I asked, looking at the wedding photo again. "You seem to be doing great."

Lindsay shook her head, her lips folding together again. "We want something we can't afford and it's . . . It gets hard."

That quality was back in her voice; this wasn't a trip to Europe we were talking about. "I'm sorry," I said simply, wanting to pry but refraining.

"In vitro," she said so quietly I could barely hear her. "Not the sort of thing people give you a loan for."

That's why she'd looked so pained at dinner and why she'd been happy to change the subject. Even though I was just getting to know her, I felt for her. Here I was thinking she was all set, with a job she loved and an adorable husband, but she was looking at things I hadn't even begun to consider and discovering she might not be able to have them. She made good money, but he didn't if he worked at a nonprofit; from what I'd heard, millionaires could go broke trying IVF. "Daniel gets so upset. He spends his days fixing other people's lives, taking care of other people's children and we can't . . ." She paused, sniffing, and I groped for the right response, but she spoke again before I did, her voice trying to gain strength. "It's one of those weird cases where Daniel and I are both perfectly fine, but there's something about his sperm and my eggs that they just won't take and it's what we want most, but it's just so hard and so expensive and—" She stopped, literally shaking herself free from that train of thought. "I'm sorry."

"No, I didn't mean for this to be painful, I . . . I'm sorry." I squeezed her hand and she smiled slightly in appreciation.

The door flew open again and Helen stuck her head in. Lindsay laughed shortly. "A closed door has a lot of meaning around here."

Preoccupied, Helen nodded to me in greeting. "Sorry, but Wendy's having a meltdown and we could really use your magic touch, Lindsay."

Lindsay nodded, not pointing out to Helen that she was having her own moment of despair, just smiling bravely. I assured Lindsay I'd be fine, maybe even visit the ladies' room while she and Helen tended to Wendy.

I trailed after them down the hall, getting close enough to the conference room door to see that Francesca was already in there with Wendy, handing her a mug of something steamy and talking to her in a low, soothing tone. I felt somewhat envious, thinking of how lovely it would be to work with other women who were so supportive, so willing to put their own work aside to help a colleague through a rough personal moment. That qualified as blood in the water in my office and the boss loved a good feeding frenzy. Kept her teeth sharp.

Almost as sharp as the teeth Tessa bared in an insincere smile as she walked up beside me. "I didn't know you were here. Is there a problem?" Tessa followed my line of sight to the conference room door and sighed unhappily, but made no move to join the gathering.

"Lindsay said I could drop by if I had any more questions, so I did."

Tessa folded her arms across her chest and I could see both wrists were still bracelet-free. "We should keep things slightly more formal than that. Does anyone else know you're here?"

"Are we talking about notifying lawyers or just security?"

Tessa's grip on her own arms tightened, the silk of her

blouse crimping under the pressure. "I'm just looking to ensure a smooth and consistent flow of information. We're all very anxious to have this article present Gwen to best advantage. That may sound selfish, but it's just practical. We're in the midst of a crucial transition."

Tessa was almost trembling with the effort to keep her emotions contained and I found that curiously emboldening. "Do you think Gwen minds that you slept with Garth?"

Tessa's angry claw shot from her arm to mine before I could step out of range. "Let's talk in my office."

She propelled me down the hallway and into an office that was the same size and layout as Lindsay's. Tessa's accents were different—a dramatic dried flower arrangement and framed vacation snapshots on the credenza—but otherwise the offices were impressively democratic. Not until the door had latched behind us did she let go of my arm. "We believe in discretion around here," she said crisply.

So my sin was not the question but where I'd asked it? "Excuse me."

"Who told you?"

Wrapping myself in my journalistic mantle, I decided to bluff her. "I'd rather not reveal my sources at this point," especially because they were named Intuition and Hunch.

"I'd appreciate the opportunity to know the agenda of the person who singled me out so you know the kind of biased information you're getting from that source."

What fascinated me most at this point was that she wasn't even trying to deny it. What also fascinated me was the phrase, "Singled out?"

"Or have you already talked to the rest of them and I haven't heard about it yet? Is that what Wendy's crying about?"

Why my accusing Tessa of having slept with Garth would make Wendy cry was beyond me. I needed to start again. "Perhaps you didn't understand my question."

"I understood it quite well and my off-the-record answer is: I don't think she could be bothered to give a flying damn. But now that I've been gracious enough to answer your question, perhaps you could answer mine. Who singled me out?"

Dawn comes more slowly some mornings than others. "Are you saying someone else was also sleeping with Garth?"

Tessa glared at me with frustration, like a teacher losing patience with a truculent child. "I'm saying we all were."

Thirteen

MY UNCLE MIKE SAYS HE misses the Cold War because at least in those days, you knew which direction the bombs were coming from. It's the ones that catch you watching the other horizon, sneak up behind you, that do the real damage. And you don't have to be a retired CIA agent to appreciate that.

Even as the mushroom cloud began to dissipate, I was still having trouble grasping what Tessa was telling me. After a fumbling moment, I repeated back slowly, "You all did?"

"Not at the same time, obviously," she said petulantly.

That took care of one batch of images I was trying to keep out of my mind. "Still," I said, "I'm just trying to be clear. All of the creative directors were having affairs with Garth?"

"Everyone but Lindsay. Garth would never have slept with a married woman," she said with a tone that implied such a distinction made him a man of irreproachable moral character and she would proudly defend his memory on that point.

"But the rest of you?" I said with a tone that made it clear I didn't find much defensible here.

"You can't understand."

"Probably not, but I'd really like to give it a shot."

Tessa's hands moved to her hips, as though she were holding herself back. Or together. "We didn't know at first and then when we did find out, no one wanted to stop because we were all afraid someone else wouldn't quit and that wasn't fair."

On one level, I was impressed by her ability to look me in the eye and say these things with the same crisp professionalism she no doubt employed to address a client's concerns in a meeting. But at the same time, I couldn't believe she was as dispassionate about the situation as she was trying to sound. And I couldn't believe what this did to my suspect pool. Just when I thought I was swimming the final lap, about to touch the side and score a medal, I was in the deep, deep end with only Tessa's missing bracelet as either a life preserver or an anchor.

"Do you mind if I sit down?" I asked.

"Actually, yes. Yes, I do," Tessa replied, getting more flustered as I got more confused. "I don't want to talk to you anymore." She marched over and opened her office door, waiting impatiently for me to exit.

I sat down anyway, which flustered her even more. She flapped the door a time or two in case I wasn't leaving just because I hadn't noticed it was open. "Tessa, I don't think you want to end this conversation when I still have so many what I hope are misunderstandings about the situation."

"I don't care what you think. Get out."

"Don't you care what my readers think?"

"My lawyer will be at your office by the time you get back there."

"I'm not saying I'll put it in the article—I am trying to be positive about Gwen, after all, and it doesn't paint a very pretty picture of her to discuss her ex-husband's bizarre take on 'employee contributions.' "

Tessa slammed the door, but it had one of those catches on the hinge that slowed its arc at the last moment and prevented it from making a very satisfactory sound. While I wasn't comfortable with the fury in her eyes, at least I was still in her office. And there were no weapons in sight. "I.

Didn't. Know." Her tapered fingers clutched her sleeves again and I was sure this time, the silk was going to rip.

In return for her not bouncing me, I tried to ease up. "You thought you were the only one?" I asked gingerly.

"I was in love with him," she said with a strength and simplicity that impressed me. "When I found out about . . . the whole situation, I knew most of them were doing it for political reasons. To get in good with him, get ahead, whatever. But that was never part of it for me. I loved him."

"Did you think he was leaving Gwen for you?"

After the firmness of her declaration, the bitterness of her laugh caught me off guard. "I'm so much smarter than this, but I wished, I hoped. Even while I knew better." She surprised me again by sitting on the couch and looking me in the eye. "And I'm sure that disappoints you because it's not nearly as good for your story—spurned lover now forced to work for widow, or whatever spin you were going to put on it."

Actually, it was the homicide spin I was going for, but admitting that would get me tossed out of her office for sure. I had to ease her into that corner without her suspecting. I held her gaze and asked, "How did you find out about everyone else?"

"The damn bracelets."

"He gave them to everyone."

"Exactly."

She was still a step ahead of me and seemed quite content to wait there until I caught up. "And though everyone getting the same gift isn't that unusual in a corporate setting, you found it strange?"

"I didn't get anything else," she said, as though I'd just stubbed my toe on the Rosetta stone and still not seen it.

"Because he didn't single you out for special treatment, you decided everyone was getting the same treatment?"

"You have to admit, it was pretty suspicious."

I'd been hoping for something more concrete. If this was some crazy theory of hers, all based on Garth being a bad gift giver, I was wasting my time. "But the theory breaks down because Lindsay got a bracelet, too."

"Which is why Wendy wigged out."

Absurdly, all I could picture was one of those old horror movies where they're trying to do a telepathy experiment so the heroine who's hearing voices can prove she's not losing her mind, but the lab assistant keeps holding up a test card and the heroine keeps misidentifying it. I was trying so hard to get Tessa to talk about Garth's murder—and eventually admit to it—but each time, she turned in a new and unexpected direction. I was staring at a picture of a ball and she kept saying "key." I tried again. "How does Wendy fit into this?"

"She was the one who made us all realize what was going on. When Garth didn't give me anything extra, I was sad but that was it. I kept it to myself. When she didn't get anything extra, she was furious."

"That seems to be her default mode."

"You don't get Wendy. She's brilliant. A pain in the ass, but brilliant. And yes, she has a temper, but that's part of her brilliance—her passions are so large and persuasive."

Tessa was slipping into pitch mode, like Wendy was a product she was promoting. "Statement withdrawn," I said, to get her back on track. "So what happened?"

"After we got our gifts, Wendy was throwing her magnificent tantrum in her office and Francesca and I went in there to find out what was wrong. Wendy said she was sleeping with Garth and the least he could do was give her some little thing on the side to acknowledge that."

I refrained from pointing out that she had already been receiving something on the side, whatever the size, and instead said, "And that's when you realized you weren't the only one."

She nodded. "And when Francesca started sobbing, I realized it was worse than I'd thought."

"What happened?"

"Wendy went from office to office and got everyone to confess. Not a fun day. Not even for Lindsay, who I think was very embarrassed about the whole thing."

"Weren't the rest of you?"

"There were a variety of reactions. More anger than embarrassment, I think."

"What did you decide to do?"

"Well, first we were so upset some of us wanted—" The words went through her brain just a moment before they went out her mouth, so she had time to gasp them back in. "I don't mean that. No one meant it. No one did it. We didn't do it."

"As a group. But one of you did it individually."

"No. Never. No one wanted to even leave him, much less hurt him. I thought about telling him it was over, but Wendy started telling us all that we had to break up with him, then Helen figured out that Wendy wasn't going to and said she wasn't going to give Wendy that kind of advantage and so we made an agreement."

"To kill him."

"Stop it! No! To pretend that nothing had happened."

I tried to picture them vying for his affection—if there was any real affection involved—each now aware of the others and trying to knock them out of competition. But then, somebody hit the breaking point.

"Did anyone's situation improve?" I asked, trying not to sound judgmental.

Tessa shook her head, but she knew the connection I was making. Someone had hoped she could change his mind, become his favorite if not his exclusive. And when that failed, she snapped. So whose breaking point had been reached? "That's when I put my bracelet away. I told the others it was broken, but I just couldn't do it anymore. But I never told Garth because—"

"He was murdered."

"Stop it. You're trying to provoke me, but I have nothing to confess, other than being really naïve and stupid and loving someone I shouldn't have."

She was perceptive, I gave her credit for that. And she had an answer for everything. But did that make her innocent or just well-prepared?

While I contemplated that, Tessa shifted her attention to a

different aspect of our exchange. "You can't put this in your article. It'll look so horrible out of context."

"It is context. It's the reason one of you killed him."

The panic in her eyes was already dying down, replaced by cold calculation. "But think of how Gwen would look if you included this in your article."

"Because she's your victim or because she's his victim?"

"You'd portray her as a woman oblivious to huge problems in the two areas your readers care about most—work and love. There'll be a lack of identification for your readership which can only negatively impact your article, your magazine, this agency, and our joint interest in the launch of Success perfume."

I considered applauding, then worried it might encourage her. "Tessa, you're not pitching me an advertising campaign."

"Every mention in the media is advertising," she replied, that cold gleam in her eye working its way to the demonic end of the spectrum. "I have a brand to protect and I'll do anything to protect it."

"Even kill?"

"I mean suing you or destroying your magazine. You don't care who killed him, you're just using his death as emotional leverage to get us to talk about Gwen in some sensational way so you can make that miserable bitch interesting."

"May I quote you on that?" I said, rising and showing myself to the door to save her the trouble. "Or would you prefer that I say, 'Unnamed sources at the agency say she's a miserable bitch,' something along those lines?"

"I'm going to tell our clients to stop advertising in your magazine."

"I'm going to tell my readers to stop patronizing your clients."

She glared at me, I glared back, and I could swear I heard Ennio Morricone playing on the Muzak in the hallway. Instead of reaching for a pistol, I put my hand on the doorknob. No tumbleweeds blew by and Tessa didn't backpedal, so I opened the door and left.

I needed to walk. Fresh air and time and the reassuring

clamor of Manhattan traffic to clear my head. This was the first time I'd investigated a crime where my respect for the victim was destroyed and I wasn't sure how to absorb that. I felt ill. I wasn't sure what bothered me more: what Garth had done or that I'd actually found myself thinking, *I see why he's dead.*

Not that the women didn't bear responsibility, too. They'd been knowing, consenting participants, even more so after the bracelet revelation, and whatever their reasons—love, advancement, exercise—they'd kept it going. Until one of them shut down the party. The question had to be why. If finding out you're sleeping with a serial dog isn't enough to stop you, it's not enough—by itself—to make you pull out a gun. What else had been going on?

I didn't make a conscious decision where to walk. I did think about calling Tricia or Cassady at one point, but I was still trying to sort it all out and thought it would be better to talk to them later. We were supposed to be going shopping for the gala after work and I hoped I'd have a newly constructed theory by then. But with all of that going through my head, I was going on autopilot and rather than winding up back at my office, I found myself standing in front of Kyle's precinct.

By the time he was coming down the front steps, I still wasn't sure why I was there. But as he walked up to me and I grabbed him by the lapels and kissed him, hard, not caring who might see us, I knew I was there just for that. To reassure myself about decent men and good relationships and absent agendas.

Kyle extricated himself from my grasp and searched my face. "What's wrong?"

"I just needed to see you."

"What happened?"

"Something had to happen?"

"Yes."

There was no point in trying to pretend he wasn't on to me. "I've been operating under some false assumptions."

"That sucks," he said sympathetically.

"I thought I knew what kind of guy Garth Henderson was."

"Found out something you don't like?"

"Yes."

"Too bad."

He said it flatly, but it still jabbed me. "Excuse me?"

"You play this game, Molly, you're going to find out stuff that turns you off. People don't kill each other when things are going well. Uglier it is, more important it is. Chances are, it's why the person's dead."

He was right. I wanted to imagine that this was a devilish puzzle, where everything would fit neatly together sooner or later, but it wasn't going to be neat or pretty or simple. "It's just, if I was so wrong about him, what else am I wrong about?"

"Maybe nothing." He pinched his lip and was quiet for a long enough time that I started to get goose bumps on the backs of my arms, worrying what he was going to say next. "Come in and talk to Donovan."

"You told me to stay away from him unless I had something concrete."

"I told you to stay away from him because I was ticked with both of you."

You know those spots in the funhouse floor that suddenly drop an inch, just when you think you're almost to the exit? My instinct was to reach out and grab him to keep my balance, but my hands balled up instead. "Thanks for letting me know."

"He thinks this case is some sort of audition for a life in the media and you're encouraging that, whether you know it or not. Doesn't serve either of you."

"I'm trying to do my job. Don't blame me because you think he's not doing his," I said, trying not to sound as shrill as I felt.

"Fair enough. But what is your job, Molly? Writing about Gwen Lincoln or solving Garth Henderson's murder?"

"Are you making a point or putting me in my place?" I said, caring less about the shrill thing now.

"If you've got significant information," he continued, not

even acknowledging my question, much less answering it, "it has to be handled properly."

I resisted, not to be petulant, but because I wasn't quite sure the information that Garth Henderson and the women had been involved in a situation that icked me out met Kyle's criteria. It rocked my world, but I was well aware he'd seen much, much worse on an easy day. Suddenly feeling very awkward standing there with him, I grew anxious to leave. "I should dig a little more, make sure it's significant before I bother him. Or you. Sorry. I'll talk to you later."

I walked two whole steps away before Kyle grabbed my arm with surprising firmness. Not sure whether he was stopping me from going, or just stopping me from going before he'd had his full say, I still had no choice but to stop. "Does the information clear his prime suspect?"

I considered that as objectively as possible, distracted somewhat by the pressure of his hand on my arm. "No, damn it," was my analysis. It didn't clear Gwen. If anything, it put her back on the Suspect Top Ten, returning higher than she'd left due to a much more densely populated motive than I'd assigned to her before.

"Why is that a problem?"

"Because I was sure Donovan was wrong, and now I'm not."

"Lousy feeling."

"Yes, it is."

"Sentiment'll foul you up faster than just about anything." For a horrible moment, I thought he was talking about us. Maybe he was, in part, because he looked at me long and hard before he continued, "Can't fall in love with a theory."

Back to Heisenberg's theory. Does the act of falling in love with something change your ability to relate to it? Is it impossible to love something without changing it? While I could appreciate the scientific fascination of the question, the emotional application seemed too treacherous to even consider at the moment.

"Don't get hung up on hating a suspect," Kyle went on.

"Liking someone doesn't make them innocent. And disliking someone doesn't make them guilty."

I nodded slowly and he released my arm, only then seeming to register he'd even grabbed me in the first place. "Sorry to have bothered you," I said, half-hoping he'd assure me I was never a bother.

"Don't worry about it," he said instead. "I want to know what you're up to."

"So you can tell Donovan?"

"So I can keep track of you," he said, his jaw setting, "and encourage you to tell Donovan when it's appropriate."

"I'll get back to you on that," I promised. Leaning in to kiss him good-bye, I felt a wave of sadness wash over me, but it ebbed before I could determine where it had come from.

He stood on the steps and watched me walk down to the corner. I knew him well enough to know he wasn't going to tell Detective Donovan I'd come by until I said I was ready, but I also knew it nagged at him that I had information I wasn't sharing. Especially because my tendency is to share everything, whether he likes it or not, and this deviation from my norm made him really uncomfortable.

And it's not that I was trying to keep something from him, it was that everything was such a jumble now I couldn't begin to explain it all to him or to Detective Donovan. I needed to find a spine to hang this new knowledge on, so I could step back and see what sort of creature it was after all.

Was I letting my judgment of the people involved interfere? Was I not looking at Gwen as closely as I should have because she was bold and successful? Disregarding Ronnie because of his glib boyishness? Excusing Tessa because of her earnestness? Missing someone else entirely because I was confusing instinct with impression?

Much as I wanted to return to GHInc. and work my way from office to office like some crazed trick-or-treater, banging on doors and asking for motives, I knew I had to be better armed before I went back there, too. So I went to my building, overshot my floor, and prayed that Owen was in his office.

He wasn't, but I found him two doors down, playing trashball with Kevin Bartholemew, his editor. Kevin was a doughy fellow with a wardrobe that hadn't evolved much since high school—chinos in need of ironing and oxford shirts with fraying collars. He had a chronic sinus condition that caused him to snort continually in a teeth-gritting register, but he had a zesty sense of humor and he played trashball with his writers, which made him an enviable boss in my universe.

"Molly Forrester!" Kevin cheered as I stuck my head in his office, a gathering place for tottering towers of paper and books. "Say you've come for me and not the pretty boy."

"I'd never presume to come for you, Kevin," I smiled, "though I dream of it constantly."

Kevin laughed so heartily that Owen missed his shot. "She wants something, but how can we resist?"

Owen picked up his ball and tipped his head at me. "Don't look happy, Moll. Girls at GHInc. giving you a hard time?"

"What are you doing hanging out with Dracula's widows?" Kevin exclaimed.

I was relieved that Owen looked as surprised by the moniker as I was. "I'm writing a profile of Gwen Lincoln."

Kevin banked a large wad of newspaper off the wall near me and into the trash can. "Poor thing."

"Me or Gwen?"

"Both of you, actually. That's one weird group of babes over there. And Ronnie Willis thinks he's gonna slide in there and 'shake things up.' Gonna have an estrogen-charged mutiny on his hands, is what's gonna happen."

"Why? He told me they were the agency's greatest asset, he was crazy about them, yadda yadda."

"Gotta be crazy to think he's going to keep them all. Garth controlled them by keeping them all equal. Rumor has it, Ronnie's talking about putting one of them in charge."

"No one mentioned that to me," I said, perplexed.

"Announcing D-day in advance defeats the purpose."

I've seen people kill for love and for money. Was I now

seeing the intersection of the two? I held my breath while Owen took his next shot, then asked, "During the merger, was there any talk about who's getting equity stakes in the new entity?"

Owen frowned as his ball hit the rim and bounced out. "Ronnie and Gwen. That's it. Garth was going to hold most of it, of course, and that's been a major delay—Ronnie and Gwen dancing around who gets how much of that piece of the pie."

I scooped up the ball, tossing it from hand to hand. "So they're both getting more than they were expecting when the deal started."

"You'd think they'd be happy, but there is no happiness in Manhattan. There is only the momentary sating of hunger," Kevin said with a grin.

"And we all know how cranky hungry people get," I said, taking my own shot. "And if someone promises you a piece of the pie and then takes it away, don't you wind up even more hungry than you were to begin with?" The ball teetered on the pile already in the trash can, but when it slid down, it stayed inside.

"The gods of trashball say you're on the right track," Kevin said, stomping down the mound to make more room before his next shot.

"You think Garth's death is tied to equity in the agency?" Owen asked. I was gratified to see that glint in his eye that reporters get when they smell a story brewing.

"I don't know yet and I'd appreciate your not scooping me," I said, backing out of the office.

"Hey, we're all one big journalistic family, aren't we?" Owen looked to Kevin for confirmation.

"I don't mind the two of you helping each other out, I just don't want to have to kiss Eileen at the next company function," Kevin said.

"I'll protect you, I promise," I told Kevin as Owen raced up, caught his arm through mine, and rushed me down to his desk.

We were on the same wavelength. If someone wanted a

piece of the action badly enough to kill for it, there was probably a pressing financial incentive. Maybe even big enough to have some public aspect to it, like legal filings. If we could find it, it would not only strengthen my theory, it would give me a persuasive entrée to that suspect. I promised Owen to share access to people and information and marveled how easy it was to offer that to someone I liked and respected.

Hopping from search engine to search engine, we found nothing on Tessa, to my chagrin. Lindsay wasn't a candidate, but we checked her out anyway and only found a mention or two of events for Daniel's group she'd attended. We discovered Francesca shared her name with a sixty-four-year-old microbiologist with a rather freaky Web site about an endangered breed of turtle. Helen had been a track star at UConn and was very active in alumni activities. Megan hosted a fan site for *That 70s Show* that was a little on the obsessive side, but nicely done. And just when I was about to think this theory was going to produce nothing but another brick in the wall, we learned one more thing. Two weeks after Garth Henderson was murdered, Wendy filed for bankruptcy.

Fourteen

"I'M NOT SURE I CAN do this."

Tricia and Cassady looked at each other in alarm. Tricia
even put down what she was holding to offer her hands to
me. Cassady asked, "You want me to get you some water?
Or maybe water back on a Glenfiddich neat?"

I shook my head. "I don't know. I'm not sure what's
wrong with me. But something must be. I don't feel like
shopping."

Tricia's expression grew even more grave and she returned the exquisite Lanvin one-shoulder dress she'd been
looking at to the rack. "We can always shop later."

"We can also wear something we already own," Cassady
said.

"If we must," Tricia said with a peppy sigh of sacrifice.
"But let's take care of one crisis at a time."

We were supposed to be looking for dresses for Emile's
gala and had begun our pilgrimage at Saks. I don't go to
very many of these sorts of affairs, so my closet held limited
possibilities; I don't even visit the evening-wear department
without several friends and good reason. Tricia and Cassady
traveled in formal-dress circles more frequently, but were always willing to reexamine their wardrobe options. Besides,
there is something delicious about rustling among the fancy

dresses, feeling the sleek fabrics, and imagining that the dress which will make you irresistible, cover all your figure flaws, and therefore make itself worth its obscenely high price tag is on the next rack. Sort of the grown-up, or at least adolescent, version of playing dress up. Which is why it's most successfully done in the company of other women. Playmates.

Yet though I was the one who had suggested the shopping excursion, I now found I didn't quite feel like playing. Mainly because I couldn't get Wendy off my mind. I'd tried to see her at the office and been told she was out, visiting a client. I'd left her messages with the receptionist and on her voice mail but hadn't heard back from her. My efforts to loiter and "run into her" had been rebuffed by Tessa, who'd materialized in the lobby and asked me to make specific appointments for any further interviews—and to make them through her. Whether protective, controlling, or paranoid—or all of the above—Tessa was guarding the temple door now.

Gwen had not been in the office and, after a moment's deliberation, I'd decided it was better not to drag her into a territorial skirmish at this point, to hold her in reserve until I was sure I was closing in on the truth. But to do that, I needed to get to Wendy.

On a playing field leveled by all of them being involved with Garth, Wendy stood out because of her financial situation. Love and money. Had she been getting enough—any?—of either from him? The timing suggested she had gone to him for help and/or a piece of the agency's equity, he'd refused, she'd flipped out and killed him, and then, without options, was forced to file for bankruptcy. But suggestion wasn't enough.

Especially because my cell phone rang. I grabbed it, hoping it would be Wendy, eager to talk to me. Instead, it was someone I wasn't eager to talk to. "Hello, Peter."

Cassady scowled and hissed, "Hang up on him. Right now. Or I'll have to track him down and show him storage ideas for his phone he's only dreamed of."

I held up a placating hand, certain I could dismiss Peter quickly. "What can I do for you? Or not do for you, as the case may be?"

Cassady reached to take my phone from me, but Tricia restrained her, leading her off a few steps so the two of them could watch me, hawk-eyed, but also whisper back and forth without interrupting my conversation.

"I didn't mean to ambush you this morning," he said, sounding pretty close to contrite. Very close, for Peter.

"Yes, you did."

"No, really, I meant to persuade you. Maybe even seduce you. Never ambush you. And I wanted to apologize for that."

"Thank you." This sudden outpouring of gentility was beyond fishy, but I had to admit—I was intrigued to see where it was leading. "That why you're calling?"

"In part. I also wanted to apologize for the fact that I'm about to scoop you so bad, you won't know what hit you."

"Excuse me?"

"And I want you to know, while you're sitting up late at night, trying to cover this story without mentioning my name every other paragraph, I'll be wishing it could've been different."

"Oh, Peter, you were so close to convincing me you'd gotten a black market sincerity transplant and then you had to go and spoil it."

"I am sincere. In wanting you to know I am soooo close."

"But are you closer than I am?"

We listened to each other breathe for a moment, trying to parse the silence. For an insane moment, I remembered why he'd been so fun to date—he'd always been a challenge. And now he was offering another one. No way could I let him win.

"See you on the newsstands," he said after a moment.

"Not for long. We'll be sold out."

I hung up, probably just as he did, and looked at my friends. I knew they wouldn't approve, but I expected them to be somewhat amused. Tricia, however, had her hands on her hips and Cassady was checking her watch.

"You told him you were close," Tricia scolded.

"I am."

"Not close enough," Cassady said. "We need to get you and Wendy in a room together and get this thing worked out."

"It's not a divorce settlement, Cassady," I said as she scooped her hand behind my back and guided me without subtlety toward the exit.

"Actually, in a way it is—you're talking about a woman who is trying to get everything she believes she's owed out of a man before her relationship with him is over," Tricia said, falling in beside us. We were marching to the exit when a white Armani gown caught her eye. She stopped to sigh and we followed suit.

It really was gorgeous, though the price tag and the slit to the thigh took it off my list of possibilities. "If you're going to show that much leg, why wear a long dress?"

Cassady flapped the dress so the mannequin's leg flashed into view and then disappeared again. "It's all about hinting at what they want and teasing how available it might be."

Tricia laughed, but I was thunderstruck. That's what I was doing wrong. Rather than just asking Wendy if we could talk, I needed to flash a little leg. Tempt her. And what better way to tempt a woman to talk than to offer her the chance to talk about another woman?

"Tessa means well but she's in for a rude awakening," Wendy told me an hour later as we sat at the bar in Bar Americain. Just as I'd hoped, after ignoring multiple messages requesting that we get together for a chat, she'd responded to a message asking for background, aka dirt, on Tessa.

I'd selected a fairly open and boisterous place so she wouldn't feel I was expecting a furtive exchange of information in a clandestine setting. If I treated her like an innocent party, she might trip up and reveal herself to be anything but.

Tricia and Cassady had offered to escort me, but I worried Wendy would somehow feel she was being set up. Which she was, but I wanted to delay that realization as long as possible. I'd promised them I'd call them as soon as I was done meeting with Wendy and we'd regroup then.

"Why?" I asked, trying not to stare as Wendy repeatedly stabbed the orange slice in her old-fashioned with her cocktail straw. Cassady's suggestion of Glenfiddich neat had stayed with me and I took a sip of exactly that while Wendy formed her answer.

"She thinks she's in charge. Thinks she's going to run the whole show. But Gwen and Ronnie are just hanging back until all the contracts are worked out and then, pow. They'll be running things to the nth degree." Wendy took a long sip of her drink, then set it back down and resumed her attack on the orange.

"I can't blame her for trying to step forward, after all this time you've been kept in an artificial equality," I said with an extra helping of sympathy, meant to provoke a reaction.

Wendy looked up at me so sharply that I thought someone behind her had dropped an ice cube down her back. "What are you talking about?"

Tessa hadn't told any of them that she'd told me. Interesting. "I know about the arrangement," I said quietly, reaching out to tap the charm on Wendy's bracelet.

She stood up, ready to bolt. "You made a huge mistake," she said huskily, "talking to that she-devil when you could've talked to any one of us and we would've told you . . ." "The truth" were the words she couldn't bring herself to say. I could see some of the conviction draining out of her as she considered what exactly she could have told me. I had a sudden, deep sense that Wendy's anger was a protective covering over a fragile core and I needed to proceed cautiously.

"At least stay and finish your drink," I said gently. "Tell me your side of things."

Wendy took a shuddering breath as I willed her back onto her bar stool. After a moment, she sat down, but the fragility went back under wraps and the straw went back into the orange.

"My side of things? Yeah, that would be interesting for your article on Her Majesty's new reign, wouldn't it? Because there are some of us who work hard, do anything," she glanced up to make sure I was clear on what "anything" included, "to advance ourselves, build our careers, and we're stupid enough to believe promises that are made and then when those promises are broken and we complain, somehow we come out looking like the bad guy."

Taking a chance, I said, "Seems to me the only bad guy is the one who killed Garth."

I waited for her to explode in angry defensiveness, but her eyes filled with tears and she drained most of her drink in one gulp. As she set the glass back down, she pulled together a wry smile. "The one who ruined my life." She licked her lips lightly. "You gonna figure out who it is?"

"Maybe. You have any thoughts?"

"Only about what should happen to them when they're caught. I think it's time for boiling in oil to make a comeback, don't you?"

"I don't mean to diminish your loss, but has Garth's death really ruined your life?"

"Your roots are showing."

I don't color my hair, so I couldn't figure out what she was talking about. "Excuse me?"

"Somebody told me you started as an advice columnist. This the place where I get the pep talk about picking up the pieces and carrying on?"

I had to smile at that. "No, this is where I ask how much of a future you thought you would build with a man who was sleeping with everyone you work with."

"We had a deal," she said, with enough ragged force that the people sitting around us stopped talking for a moment and looked over instinctively, then returned to their conversations.

"What was it?"

She shook her glass, listening to something much further away than the jangling of the ice. "Does that even matter now?"

"It seems to. Very much."

The wry smile came back, more genuine this time. "My mistake." She put the glass back down. "I'm over it. Rebuilding my life. But if Tessa thinks she's going to be queen bee when this drops, she's more of a head case than I ever gave her credit for."

"Giving her a run for her money?"

"That's just the thing—not her money, is it?" Wendy stood, picking up her bag and looking down at me with narrowed eyes. "I'd love to stay and chat, but I've said all I'm going to say about Tessa."

"We can talk about other things," I assured her.

"No. I don't think we can. Thanks for the drink."

I watched Wendy walk away, not so much studying her icy, angry demeanor as pacing myself so I could get up and follow her without attracting attention.

"You're kidding, right?" the cabbie said when I slid in the back and asked him to follow Wendy's cab. His voice said Boston or just south of there. His license said Bruce Hennessey. He was a tall, spindly guy who had to hunch over the wheel to keep his head from scraping the roof of the cab.

"Actually, I'm not," I said, almost tipping over as he screeched away from the curb, apparently accepting the challenge. "Don't people ask you to do that all the time?"

Bruce leaned forward, intent on his course, and it looked like his nose could almost touch the windshield, his neck was so long. "Idiots ask me constantly, then bust up laughing like they're the only ones who ever thought of making that joke. But you don't strike me as an idiot, so I thought I'd check."

"I appreciate that."

"So who is it? Your lover?"

"No, someone else's."

"This a triangle?"

"That's an excellent question, but if it is, I'm not part of it."

"Good thing. Triangles get messy. My cousin Wyatt was messing around with his neighbor's wife and it got so nasty." He shook his head and yanked the cab into the next lane without batting an eye.

I gripped at the upholstery and tried to look cool. "The neighbor found out?"

"Yeah. It was awful."

"People get hurt?"

"Worse. The neighbor dumped his wife and now Wyatt's stuck with her."

He entertained me with other stories from Peyton Place until we stopped in front of a gorgeous building on Riverside Drive. He rolled forward into a shadow and we watched Wendy walk up to the door and be greeted with familiarity by the doorman. She even stopped to chat with him.

"Nice place," Bruce said. "This where she lives?"

Could explain the bankruptcy. "I'm not sure."

I reached forward with the money and Bruce grabbed my hand. "I'm not gonna hear about you on the news when I get home tonight, am I? 'Cause if you're gonna go in there and do something stupid, I'm gonna drive away right now and drop you somewhere you can't do no harm."

My initial alarm dissipated into appreciation. "I just need to talk to her. I promise, I'll be kind and careful."

Bruce nodded slowly. "Okay. 'Cause I can pick you out of a lineup."

"I'll take that as a compliment," I said, sliding out of the cab.

Improvising on the way, I ran up to the door, just as the doorman was closing it behind Wendy. "Wendy! Wendy!" I called. "Wait!"

The doorman opened the door again and called in for Wendy. She stepped back out, then looked daggers at both of us when she recognized me. "Go away, Molly."

"Just one more question."

"No, Molly."

The doorman stepped forward protectively. "Want me to call Mr. Willis for you?" he asked Wendy.

I actually felt dizzy as all the thoughts swirled together. Wendy couldn't afford a place here. It was Ronnie's place. This was how she was rebuilding her future. She'd moved from Garth to Ronnie, securing her position in the new regime before the merger was even finalized. Did that mean Ronnie and Gwen had broken up or was Ronnie emulating Garth and balancing them both, as it were? Or did

Wendy not care, since she'd been through this before with Garth?

I don't know that it's possible to admire amorality, but you can certainly give props to naked ambition—and apparently, naked was how Wendy's ambition expressed itself best. "I think it would be very helpful to have Mr. Willis be part of this conversation," I told the doorman.

"If we call anyone, it's the police," Wendy snapped.

"What a lovely idea! Let's make it a scene. I love making scenes, don't you?" I fished my cell out of my bag and flipped it open. "What should I tell them is happening? Were you planning on hitting me or—"

Wendy grabbed me by the arm and dragged me inside with her, calling back over her shoulder for the bewildered doorman to ignore her drunken friend. Inside, it was like the lobby of a resort hotel with glistening marble, brass accents, lots of ferns. Elegant and echoingly empty.

Wendy snatched my phone away from me. "What's it going to take to get you to shut up and ignore all this?" she hissed, watching the elevators lest one suddenly spit out someone she knew.

"A conversation with you and Ronnie."

"No way."

"Okay then. Good night, Wendy." I took back my phone and headed to the front door, hoping she couldn't tell I was walking as slowly as possible so she'd have plenty of time to stop me.

"Wait. I thought you had one more question."

"I'm pretty sure I have my answer," I said, gesturing to her surroundings. "I'll just fill in the rest for myself."

She was still frowning as we walked into Ronnie's picture-perfect apartment on the second floor. She had her own key, which said a great deal about the relationship, and she let us in without calling out to him, which said even more. I thought the apartment was empty until Ronnie swung out of a doorway and pointed a pistol at us.

Wendy shrieked, which made me feel better about wanting to do the same thing. Ronnie quickly pulled up the gun with one hand and reached out to her with the other. "I'm sorry, baby, I'm sorry. I didn't expect you so early." He pulled her to him, rubbing her back and stroking her hair while she caught her breath. I stroked my own hair and tried not to hyperventilate. Men pointing guns had become too much a part of my daily routine, but I still wasn't used to it. I was going to write a big check to the Brady Campaign once I got paid for this article.

Ronnie quickly seated us in his exquisite living room with its river view and highly polished woods, and whipped up a pitcher of martinis. All with the gun either in his hand or lying within reach, which I found highly disconcerting. "Mr. Willis," I finally dared, "could we put the gun away?"

"Not at all. I'm in danger. You've chosen to follow my sweet girl home, so you're in danger. I need to protect myself and those around me, don't I?"

"You can't think Jack Douglass is still after you," I said, wincing because it sounded ruder than I'd intended.

"Jack is a cog in the wheel and it's turning, running, getting ready to grind us down," Ronnie said, handing me a martini with his gun-less hand.

So the enemy was closing in but we still had time for a cocktail? Ronnie's perception of reality might be skewed to a greater degree than I had considered before. "Why do you still think someone wants to kill you?" I asked, setting my glass down untouched. I wanted to stay sharp for this conversation. Even if Wendy had killed Garth, now that she was sleeping with Ronnie, didn't that make Ronnie safe? Of course, she'd been sleeping with Garth before she killed him. Maybe Wendy had a hard time breaking up with men.

Wendy chugged down her martini. Her hands were trembling and I wasn't sure if that was from my closing in on her or because she believed Ronnie was in danger. Or maybe Ronnie was in danger because of Wendy and I'd thwarted her plans by showing up when I did. But if she'd killed Garth because he'd gone back on his deal with her, she wouldn't kill Ronnie now, when he hadn't had the opportunity to deliver on the deal, would she? And she wouldn't do it in front of me, would she? Because then she might have to consider me a disposable witness and we didn't want to go there. Maybe I needed a sip of martini after all.

"So how much do you know, Molly Forrester?" Ronnie asked, finally perching on the edge of the couch, his martini and his gun each balanced on a knee.

"What do you want to tell me?"

"I was looking forward to a bright, new future working with Garth. Now I'm being dragged down by his death. Obviously, I had nothing to do with it."

"Do you know anyone who did?" I asked, knowing he wouldn't out Wendy, but wondering if he harbored any suspicions.

To my surprise, he looked directly at her. She shook her head forcefully, eyes screwed shut, begging him not to speak. This was a conversation they'd had before. "Gwen Lincoln is the only one who benefits directly," Ronnie said in a silky whisper, still watching Wendy.

"Oh, Ronnie," she moaned.

"Wendy thinks we're going to lose the agency completely if Gwen is arrested," Ronnie said, picking up the gun and petting the barrel in a way that made me nervous and nauseous. "Final negotiations will get held up, papers won't get signed, all that sort of thing. She's very protective of the agency."

Wendy erupted. "I poured my soul into that place and I am not going to let it fade away because some people can't keep their pants or their lips zipped." I wasn't sure whether she was accusing Ronnie or Garth or both, but Ronnie was unruffled by the statement. "It's going to be my agency—"

"Our agency," Ronnie corrected, a little less silky this time. This is what he meant by "working with the woman he loved"? He and Wendy staging a coup and somehow easing his old lover, the widow of her old lover, out?

"Of course," she said, hurrying over to snake her arms around his neck and kiss him heartily. Even then he kept the gun clutched in his hand, which was making me increasingly nervous. I even shifted in my seat, trying to ease myself out of the line of fire should Ronnie suddenly shoot.

But then there was a shrieking, hair-raising scraping sound out on the balcony and the gun swung immediately in that direction. Ronnie nearly dumped Wendy off his lap as he stood, hurrying not to the french windows but to the light switch near the hallway door. Wendy and I were still reacting and she was whispering, "What was that?" when Ronnie plunged the room into darkness.

Ronnie hurried back to where we sat, pulling us wordlessly to the floor so the sofa shielded us from anything or anyone who might come in through the french doors. He crouched beside us, but not as low. I could smell the adrenaline sparking off him. He was eager for a confrontation.

"Could be anything—" I attempted.

Ronnie hushed me vigorously. Wendy went into a fetal crunch, her knees and forehead against the front of the sofa, hands on the back of her neck, like the old educational films about protecting yourself from a nuclear attack. She was trembling again, but from fear or tension or guilt, it was impossible to tell.

I took a deep breath and mentally listed all the benign causes of the sound I could think of and imagined how much we'd all enjoy Ronnie's reaction when the truth was revealed and he realized it was nothing but a cat or a neighbor moving flowerpots or a car down on the street. But then another sound inserted itself into the cacophony in my head, clear and riveting and unexpected, like Joni Mitchell joining in with Neil Young's "Helpless" from offstage in *The Last Waltz*. But this wasn't someone breaking into song. This was someone jiggling the knob and trying to break open the french doors.

Chaos happens so quickly it's hard to sort out, even much later. Ronnie stood with his gun out and shouted an impassioned but unintelligible warning. I jumped to my feet, clinging to the idea that everything was still okay and screaming for Ronnie not to shoot. Wendy stayed on the floor and screamed from there.

Though everything else seemed to be happening too fast, I could swear I could see the bullet as it left the gun, flew across the room, plowed through the glass, and plunged into Peter Mulcahey.

Fifteen

FRIENDSHIP HAS MANY LEVELS. CASUAL friends, who you'll speak to pleasantly when you run into them but you wouldn't hunt them down or cancel other plans for the pleasure of their company. Good friends, who can be trusted to keep a secret, an appointment, and your purse while you're on the dance floor. And then there are great friends, who appear at any hour at any location just because you ask them to and ask no questions. Not until they arrive, anyway.

"Are you the one who shot him?"

I was so glad to see Cassady walking across the surgery waiting room toward me that I hugged her before I even attempted an answer. She was dressed simply in a cotton sweater and chinos, which made me feel better about having interrupted any grand event when I'd called and asked her, with a minimum of hyperventilation and even less explanation, to come to St. Luke's Hospital because Peter'd been shot. I did mention that the police would be coming and going. Graciously, she'd said she'd be right there and withheld all further comment until now.

"My moments of wanting to shoot Peter are behind me," I said, releasing her reluctantly. I was still more rattled than I wanted to admit to anyone, including myself, and it was reassuring to anchor myself to her for a moment.

"I wouldn't have blamed you, I was just clarifying."

"Ronnie Willis was the one who shot him and he doesn't seem the least repentant about it, which is a whole different story."

"Ronnie Willis? Why were you and Ronnie Willis and Peter Mulcahey all in the same place—with or without a gun?"

I took a deep breath in preparation for diving into the explanation, but Cassady wagged her finger at me to hold it. "Before you start, this is Aaron."

The breath escaped me in a little puff of surprise. In my disarray, I hadn't registered the man standing slightly behind Cassady, hands in his pockets and head cocked to one side. My hand shot out of its own accord. "Thanks very much for coming, Aaron. Nice to meet you."

He gave me a slightly uncomfortable but still pleasant smile and shook my hand. He wasn't at all what I'd expected—not that I'd been sure what to expect. I'd resisted the leather-patched-tweed-jacket stereotype because Cassady would have glided right past that, but I'd had no theory beyond that. Aaron was a little shorter than Cassady—who wasn't?—and leanly built, with prominent cheekbones and long, tapered fingers. He wore black jeans and a heather gray merino polo, but the casual elegance was undercut by the red Chuck Taylors. His brown hair was tightly curled and his eyes were deeply, warmly brown. I immediately understood Cassady's new interest in physics. "Sorry for your difficulty," he said in a rich, rolling voice.

"Thank you."

"Is Tricia coming?" Cassady said, tapping on my hand so I'd let go of Aaron.

"Voice mail."

"Me, too. Well, you'll just have to repeat yourself when she gets here because I'm not waiting. What the hell happened?"

I gave them a synopsis of the evening, concentrating on the events at Ronnie's, and occasionally glancing over at Aaron to see how this was all striking him. He listened with interest and without judgment. Cassady took care of the judgment, shaking her head and even rolling her eyes a time or two. She sighed heavily when I explained about Peter having just come out of surgery and the various groups of detectives with whom I'd been chatting while I was waiting.

"Why on earth was Peter on the balcony?" Cassady asked.

"Pursuing his theory that Ronnie killed Garth. Looking for evidence, even though Ronnie wouldn't talk to him and the doorman wouldn't let him in the building."

"I won't speak for you journalists, but in legal circles, we call that 'breaking and entering,' " Cassady explained.

"I think 'trespassing' is being discussed at the moment, since he never got the opportunity to break or to enter." The detectives involved so far had plenty to listen to, talk about, and consider. The original duo had responded to the apartment and been told by various people at various levels of hysteria that this incident was related to other cases: Peter insisted they consult with Detective Donovan because of the connection to Garth's death and Ronnie wanted them to talk to Detective Hernandez because of his Jack Douglass conspiracy theory. I'd tried to advance the theory that it was all a misunderstanding, a function of overzealous reporting, but they were so underwhelmed by that line of reasoning that they let me follow Peter to the hospital.

Ronnie and Wendy followed quickly behind because Ronnie had started having chest pains while the paramedics were treating Peter. I'd checked in on him while Peter was in surgery and he was feeling better, though tethered to an impressive amount of equipment. Wendy started screaming at me the moment she saw me, which got me booted out of the E.R.

Just before Cassady and Aaron had arrived, Detectives Hernandez and Guthrie had checked in on me; they were back downstairs now, conferring with the latest additions to their specialized fraternity. Detective Donovan had yet to show, and I wasn't looking forward to his arrival. Perhaps the current detectives would have dismissed the need to talk to me further by the time he got there. Not that my timing is ever that good, but I always hope.

"So what are we waiting for?" Cassady asked now. "Not that I don't love hanging out in hospitals with you, Moll, but the kind of shots they dispense around here is not the kind you need."

"I wanted to talk to Wendy again before I left."

"Good idea, because she's going to be so open to sharing right now," Cassady said grimly.

"How could she make any of this my fault?"

"You suspect her of killing Garth, don't you?"

"Yes, but I didn't tell her that yet. And I certainly didn't tell Peter. Peter came of his own accord and Ronnie shot Peter of his own accord and I'm an innocent bystander in all this."

"The addition of a quark to any defined space impacts results whether there is a visible interaction between the particles or not," Aaron offered.

"I'm some sort of particle?" I wasn't sure whether it was a compliment or an insult, but given the way my evening was going so far, I was willing to formulate a hypothesis or two.

"A reactive agent is my guess, but it's early," Aaron said with far too much enjoyment for a guy who had only just met me.

"Your name's come up once or twice," Cassady explained.

"Let me take care of this nasty little situation and I'll tell you a few stories in return," I promised Aaron, who kept smiling.

"We came to rescue you and take you away from all this. Let's go," Cassady said.

"I really need to talk to Wendy. Should probably talk to Peter, too," I said, knowing how well that would go over. Sure enough, Cassady responded with a withering glance. "I tried to see him in post-op before, but they tossed me out. Of course," I said, suddenly inspired, "now that his brother is here, we really should try again, don't you think?"

Before Cassady could protest, I slipped my arm through Aaron's. Smiling bemusedly, Aaron willingly walked with me to the senior nurse who guarded the entrance to the recovery area like a Beefeater in white polyester. The nurse was intimidating in girth and manner, exuding that vibe that insanely busy people get which says, "Is it really worth bothering me?" We bravely paused before her and Aaron mellifluously said, "You're treating my brother, Peter Mulcahey."

"Waiting for a room," she said, doing her best not to acknowledge me.

"Could I see him?"

Now the nurse frowned at Cassady and me. "Can you control your backup singers?"

"His girlfriend and my wife. I'll do my best," Aaron answered. I wanted to turn around and catch the expression on Cassady's face, but I didn't dare throw off anyone's concentration.

The nurse sniffed skeptically but led us down the hall, the people in the curtained areas popping in and out of view like vignettes of suffering and rejoicing, to the back corner where Peter was propped, naked from the waist up, a huge expanse of thick gauze taped to his side and tubes peeking out from multiple locations. His grin as he saw us was positively lopsided and when the nurse announced that his brother had come, Peter, who has only sisters, nodded sleepily yet enthusiastically. "Hey, bro!" he greeted Aaron.

The nurse gestured for us to stand close around the bed and started to close the curtains behind us. "We gave him something for the pain. It affects people differently." She paused behind me, speaking sternly. "Only a few minutes and if you cause any trouble, I'll have those police back in here to haul your pretty little butt outta here for good." With a pointed flick of the curtains, she withdrew.

"A reputation already. Nice work," Cassady whispered.

"Thanks for coming to get me, guys, it means so much to me," Peter gushed as though he were hosting a birthday party rather than sporting a bullet wound.

"Peter, we're not taking you home."

"Please? I'll be good."

"They have to keep you for a while," I said gently.

"No, they don't. I feel much better now."

"Ask him again when the morphine wears off," Cassady suggested.

Somehow, I felt responsible for Peter's condition and wanted to do something, perform some act of penance. "There anyone you need us to call?"

Peter fumbled to take Aaron's hand. "My brother's here and that's all that matters."

"Knock it off, Peter," Cassady suggested.

Peter swung his bleary eyes in her direction. "Did you know I got shot? Are you the one who shot me?"

"Sadly, no," Cassady said. "Gotta say, this is sure to yield valuable information, Molly. It's a good use of your time."

I gestured for her to be patient just a moment longer. "Peter, what did you think you were going to find in Ronnie's apartment?"

"The Pentagon Papers," Cassady muttered.

"The gun. And I found it! The hard way!" Peter was increasingly heavy-lidded and thick-tongued. The strength it had taken for him to rouse himself from the surgery sedatives was ebbing quickly.

"No, no, different gun." Ronnie had turned the weapon over to the police immediately; it was a 9mm and Garth had been shot with a .32.

"Oh, then the original merger agreement. Kimberly said it changed and Ronnie was really, really pissed." Peter sank back into his pillows, drained.

It took me a moment to place the name. "Ronnie's niece Kimberly? The receptionist? She's your inside source?"

"And you're my best girl." Peter let go of Aaron's hand and grabbed mine, squeezing much harder than I would have thought possible in his chemical haze.

"That's very sweet," I said, trying to extricate myself, but his grip was like a Chinese finger trap—the harder I tried to get loose, the harder he held on.

"I love you, Molly." Peter yanked on me, trying to pull

himself back up out of his pillows, but he wound up knocking me off balance. I caught myself, bracing my hand on the bed. Which is why I was leaning over him as Tricia entered. With Kyle.

"Are we interrupting?" Tricia asked with classic Vincent aplomb.

"Damn, my family's gotten big," Peter drawled, his eyelids at half-mast.

Tricia stood in the gap in the curtains, looking at Peter with concern. Kyle stood behind Tricia, one hand in his pocket, the other to his bottom lip, staring at me. I had no idea why he was there. I hadn't called him. Which, I realized, was going to be a problem because I'd called Tricia and Cassady, but I hadn't called him. And I hadn't called him because I knew I was there with Peter and I didn't want him to know I was there with Peter and I also didn't want him to know I was hanging around people with guns again.

There are searing, formative moments in my life that continue to play in my mind so vividly that I literally flinch when I remember them: throwing up onstage in the third grade Christmas pageant (I still get stage fright); thinking Tom Garrett was asking me to the prom when he was seeking my advice about asking my best friend (I now ask a lot of questions before I answer one); and walking in on a college suitemate in the midst of a ménage à trois (I always knock first). This moment was etching itself into my memory as though a branding iron were pressed against what little gray matter I possessed.

"Does this look like a place to have a party?" The senior nurse flicked the curtains back imperiously and pointed to the exit.

"We're family," Cassady attempted.

The nurse gave us a sickly sweet smile to assure us she knew we were, in fact, liars. "Sweetheart, you could be Jesus Christ and the Apostles and I'd still throw you out. Too many of you in here. Go away and let him rest."

"Can Molly stay?" Peter asked mournfully.

"No," Cassady and Tricia answered for me. They pulled me out of his reach and hustled me down the hall. Aaron and Kyle brought up the rear. I heard Aaron describe himself as "Cassady's new friend" and held my breath when Kyle paused before saying he was my boyfriend. Maybe he wasn't as angry as he looked.

"Why'd you bring Kyle?" I whispered to Tricia, trying to sound calm and curious.

"He was with me when I got the message. It would've been even more awkward to shake him."

"He was with you?" Cassady repeated, not quite as quietly as I would have preferred.

"He wanted to talk. About what to get Molly for her birthday."

"Six months away," Cassady pointed out.

Tricia shrugged and started picking her cuticles, a sure sign she was lying.

Somehow, I'd plopped Tricia right in the middle of something I wasn't even sure I knew about myself and I didn't want to keep her there any longer. As we exited back into the waiting room, I turned to Kyle and asked, "Could we talk for a minute?" I pointed to a grouping of chairs away from the main traffic patterns of the room.

"Can I join in?" Detective Donovan asked.

"No," Kyle said before I even registered that Detective Donovan was standing there. Kyle took me by the arm and walked me firmly over to the chairs I'd pointed out. "Are you done?" he asked quietly as he released my arm.

"I'd like to talk to Wendy—"

"You don't understand my question."

He let the statement hang in the air between us so I could study it, fully appreciate all its dimensions, and realize why my answer was wrong. It took me a moment, but then my error shivered through me. Kyle wasn't talking about my being done for the moment. "You mean, am I done with the article?"

"I mean, are you done trying to get yourself killed?"

I almost protested that no one was shooting at me—for a change—but I was learning enough to keep that observation to myself. "I just want to cover the story," I said simply.

"And what does Mulcahey want?"

"To beat me to it."

"What else?"

"Nothing else."

"Then why didn't I know he was back until now?"

"Because I didn't think it was important." Which was true. Possibly not completely true, but somewhat true. There might be other blocks, Freudian or otherwise, involved, but in the greater scheme of things, especially in the scheme of Kyle and me, it wasn't important. "I've been trying to get rid of him," I said, hating that that wouldn't be clear to Kyle.

"I could see that." He nodded, not looking at me.

There was something in his voice I hadn't heard before. "Are you being snarky?" I asked, not doubting that he was capable but surprised that he'd go there.

"No, I'm being frustrated." Now he looked at me and his blue eyes were blazing with a passion I would've been delighted to see under more pleasant and intimate circumstances. "One thing you learn early on as a cop, it's really hard to protect someone who doesn't want to be protected."

"That's not it," I protested, "I just want to see this story through. You know what I have riding on this assignment."

"Too much."

While I groped for breath and an answer, Detective Donovan inserted himself into our tête-à-tête, which felt like it was verging on a mano a mano. "Sorry to break this up, Edwards, but I need to talk to Ms. Forrester, since she's such a great detective and all." Some people can't be snarky; they're too mean and it leaches all the humor out of anything they say, especially when they're trying to be funny. It's like trying to drive a car with no lubrication—you just get high-decibel screeching.

I was prepared to leap in and defend myself, saving Kyle from the trouble, but he spoke first. And told Detective Donovan, "She's all yours." He walked away, throwing back over his shoulder, "I gotta go back to work," and I honestly wasn't sure whether it was for my information or Detective Donovan's.

I wanted to run after him, yell, and/or cry, but none of those options seemed particularly viable while Detective Donovan was standing in front of me with his notebook open and Kyle was disappearing down the hallway without even half-glancing back. I chewed on the inside of my lip for a moment to refocus, then gave Detective Donovan my most professional smile. "What can I tell you, Detective Donovan?"

"Was Mulcahey at Willis' apartment looking for Willis or for you?"

"There's absolutely nothing going on between me and Peter Mulcahey," I told Detective Donovan with all the bite I'd held back from Kyle. "I had no idea he was going to . . . do whatever he was trying to do. There's no conspiracy here to be uncovered, Detective. It's an unfortunate collision of people on intersecting paths, that's all."

"So why were you there?"

"Working on my story."

"Wendy says you followed her."

"I felt she was hiding something. Like her involvement with Ronnie. Which she was."

"Why, do you suppose?"

"So she doesn't look like an opportunistic slut to her coworkers."

Detective Donovan's eyebrows wriggled briefly, but he refrained from further comment. "And is she?"

"I don't know yet. What do you think?"

"I think you're off-track. This still sticks to Gwen Lincoln and as soon as we find the gun, we'll be able to prove it."

"No wonder you like Wendy. She and Ronnie will not only endorse your candidate, they'll probably campaign if you ask them nicely."

"But you don't agree."

The problem was, I wasn't sure anymore. Something about seeing Wendy screaming on the floor in the fetal position had shaken her validity as a murder suspect. But it still made sense that it was one of Garth's Girls. The perfume, the injuries which could have been from someone forcing him to drink for his charm, the two gunshots . . . Gwen would have been more to the point, because she was killing out of anger. Garth had been killed more slowly, deliberately, out of vengeance.

"You're not sharing," Detective Donovan continued, incorrectly interpreting my silence.

"I don't know anymore," I finally said, honesty being the shortest distance between two problems or something like that. There was also the chance that if he thought I was stumped, he'd back off a bit.

This time, his eyebrows just knotted. "We don't have to be on opposite sides here."

"I didn't know there were sides. Just points of view," I said politely.

"Yeah, well, there are sides and I like people to be on mine," he stated with no politeness at all. "If you and Mulcahey aren't going to play nicely, I don't want you playing at all."

"Then maybe I better take my ball and go home," I said, endeavoring to end things on a pleasant note.

"Don't go any farther than that."

"Detective Donovan, are you asking me not to leave town?"

"Telling you, Ms. Forrester. Good night," he said and walked away. But his attempt at making a forceful and intimidating exit was undercut by his stopping to turn back and salute Tricia, Cassady, and Aaron with a tip of his notebook to his forehead.

Cassady swept the other two over to me immediately. "Was he nasty or seductive?"

"I'm not sure he was either. Or can be either," I said.

"He's not without his charm," Tricia said.

"His charm is at home in his attic," Cassady countered.

"I'm sorry you feel that way," Tricia said, "because I asked him to be my guest at the gala."

Sixteen

THE TRUE ALLURE OF A martini glass lies in its creation of the illusion that you could lean forward and plunge your entire face into it, bathing yourself in the cool, refreshing liquid of your choice that shimmers there, and wash away cares, tears, and maybe even a wrinkle or two. Or, in more dire moments, stick your head in and shock yourself awake, like the crazy guys in the movies with the sinks filled with ice cubes. I contemplated the Rob Roy that shimmered before me and decided, while the whisky facial was tempting, my current problems would be best addressed by pouring the whole thing down the front of my blouse because it would give me a splendid reason to go home and throw things around my apartment for a couple of hours instead of attempting to carry on a conversation with Tricia, Cassady, and Aaron.

After Detective Donovan's departure, I'd pressed my cell phone number on the post-op nurse and begged her to call if Peter needed anything, and we'd decamped to the Lenox Lounge to attempt to take stock of the evening. Even in such cool and classic art deco surroundings, with smooth jazz floating in from the Zebra Room, it was a frustrating task. I felt somewhat like a camp counselor with fifteen minutes to go before the parents drove up, trying to figure out how I was going to explain that all my campers had wound up drunk, pregnant, or communist in the short time they'd been in my care.

While it was tumultuous in my head, it was relatively quiet in the club. We'd reached that quiet part of the evening when people are either eating dinner or getting a second wind, not pushing quite so hard to charm their companions or conserving energy to look for new companions, murmuring rather than shouting, pacing themselves for the final leg of the marathon and kindling the desire to cross the finish line with someone full of excitement and potential. This particular race doesn't necessarily go to the swift, but often to the slick or clever or persistent. Still, it's hard to opt out and say you're not going to run.

Cassady and Tricia were allowing me time to gather my thoughts because they were engaged in a fierce debate of their own, centered on, as Cassady delicately put it, "What the hell were you thinking, inviting that vulture to the gala?"

"Aaron," Tricia said in response, "I'm sure you've already discovered that one of Cassady's more endearing traits is her tendency to beat around the bush."

"Tricia," Aaron replied, matching her tone uncannily, "I've found that the best way to control the results of an experiment is to limit the number of variables introduced." He gestured for her to keep it between the two of them and turned to me. "Too many variables diffuse your attention. Follow one thing at a time, right?"

Though my experience with physics was limited to some pretty shaky experiments in high school, I knew what he was getting at. You had to be sure of your hypothesis going into an experiment and seek to prove only that, or you cluttered your mind and endangered the experiment with extra interactions and reactions which were more measurable in how distracting they were than in how they impacted the results. You wound up proving nothing.

Was that my mistake with Garth's death? Had I gone in with the wrong hypothesis and now lost sight of the original question in my drive to get the facts to conform to my suppositions? Oddly, when I'd been looking at people I knew as murder suspects, it was such a shocking concept that I'd had a hard time committing to suspecting anyone. This time, trying to follow the twisted relationships, I found everyone similarly tainted and no one emerging as the leading suspect. No one had an extraordinary reason to kill Garth; they all had equally good ones.

So was I missing someone's reason or had I missed a suspect altogether? If I was going to salvage either the story or my ability to tell it, I needed to shed some biases and take a fresh look at all the players. And while I appreciated Aaron's empathy, the one guy I really wanted to discuss all this with was probably at home that very moment, changing the locks or at least short-sheeting the bed.

But I'd have to dwell on that cop later, because Tricia and Cassady were getting quite animated in their discussion of the other one and I felt some responsibility for keeping that from getting out of control.

"He's not even that cute," Cassady was protesting as I returned my attention to their conversation.

"Don't try to be quaint. That's not the only reason to ask a man out," Tricia answered.

"Of course not, but in this case, there are no other redeeming qualities in evidence," Cassady said.

Now it was my turn to lean in to Aaron. "Should you be exposed to trade secrets so early in your association?"

He smiled. "Education is never wrong. Painful sometimes, but never wrong."

Cassady arched an eyebrow at both of us. "And I suppose this all makes sense to you."

"It's too much to ask that other people's decisions make sense," Aaron answered.

"Though I hesitate to ask, I'm sure she has her reasons," I agreed.

"Why would you hesitate to ask?" Tricia frowned.

Now I hesitated to answer, hoping to minimize the number of people I loved who would be angry with me by midnight. "Your reasons are your own," I sidestepped. The idea of Detective Donovan joining us at the gala was noxious, but I clung to the notion that Tricia knew what she was doing.

"Hasn't it occurred to anyone that it is possible to date for the common good?"

I was comforted that neither Cassady nor Aaron seemed to understand that one any better than I did. "I must have been sick and missed that week in Social Studies," I said after a moment.

"Maybe I asked him to the gala simply so we could keep an eye on him while keeping an eye on a number of suspects all at the same time."

"Economy of effort. Commendable," Aaron said.

"Seriously?" I blurted. "You asked him out to help me finish my article?"

"You'd do the same for me," Tricia said confidently.

"I'm not so sure," I said, then hastened to revise my statement when she looked at me with dismay. "I mean, now that you've introduced me to the concept, yes, I would, but I'm not sure that particular form of sacrifice would've occurred to me on my own."

"Does bring a whole new meaning to 'above and beyond,'" Cassady said tartly.

"My faith in your taste in men is restored and I thank you all for your support and assistance," I said, toasting them. But before I could get my glass to my lips, my eye was caught by something both unexpected and somehow not altogether surprising—the sight of Wendy and Lindsay walking across the room toward us, glasses in hand.

While Manhattan is densely populated enough that you can go for days without bumping into people you know, there is also the neighborhood effect, in which you tend to trip over the people who live and work on the same circuit you do. I supposed that it wasn't that surprising for us to cross paths with Lindsay and Wendy here, since we'd come straight from the hospital and they probably had, too. And yet, this wasn't exactly across the street. We'd bypassed other places to come here and it seemed a little odd that they'd picked it, too, as famous as it was. It seemed even odder that, given the evening's previous events, they intended to join us. I was happy to see Lindsay, but I never would've expected Wendy to be interested in a friendly drink.

So perhaps she wanted a less than friendly one. "What are you doing here?" Wendy asked sharply as they stopped before us.

"Collecting signatures for a petition to stop rhetorical questions," Cassady responded.

"Hi, Lindsay. Wendy, how's Ronnie doing?" I asked quickly, scrambling to climb to higher ground. "I'm so sorry—" I began, remembering a moment too late the insurance company warning not to say you're sorry after an accident because it can be used later to indicate you believed you were in the wrong.

"You should be," Wendy replied, proving the insurance companies right.

"I'm so sorry the strain is taking a toll on him," I said, determined to clarify that I was in no way apologizing for my actions.

"They're keeping him overnight, monitoring him for a bit," Lindsay said smoothly. "I'm sure it's just a precaution and he'll be fine and Wendy can finish getting him up to speed in no time."

Wendy furrowed her brow at me, knowing putting her finger to her lips would be too obvious. No one knew? I wasn't sure whether that merited applause or a psych evaluation, but it was impressive. Deciding to keep my peace in order to keep the peace with Wendy, I sat back in my chair and waited for her to make the next move.

"I think he'll be all right, at least until that miserable friend of yours turns his life into utter hell," Wendy said.

Nice move. "I don't know that Peter'll be in a hurry to do that," I said. "He's got some issues of his own to straighten out."

"He's the criminal!" Wendy said emphatically, but Lindsay hushed her gently and eased her into a chair she had somehow spirited away from the table next to us. They were going to join us without even asking, not that we would've sent them away, but letting the question hang in the air would have at least given us all the opportunity to acknowledge how awkward and unproductive this encounter was going to be.

"It's a difficult situation all the way around," I said as Lindsay pulled up her own chair. I made introductions around the table as she settled herself and Wendy at the table in the maternal manner her colleagues had mentioned. I half-expected Lindsay to hold her drink for her while Wendy took a swig. We all let the uncomfortable silence settle on the table for a moment, then I took the first plunge, wondering if I could make investigative questions sound like small talk. "So, Lindsay, how'd you get caught up in all this?"

"I called Wendy about a client problem, she told me what had happened, where she was, and I wanted to come see how I could help. When Ronnie was settled in, I thought a drink might help relax her. Great minds run in the same channel," she said with a diplomatic smile to all of us. "Your friends have joined you, too."

The thing was, I knew how happy I was to see my friends and I wasn't sure how happy Wendy was to have Lindsay with her. She was accepting the ministrations, but didn't seem to be deriving a lot of pleasure from them. Not that Lindsay seemed to mind; she was serenely attentive, like a lady-in-waiting pleased with her station in life. Or the gawky girl who gets to hang with the cheerleaders because she's tutoring them all in math. Maybe part of Lindsay's mothering the other Girls was her way to fit into their little cult, since she hadn't been participating in the main event.

"The true measure of a friend is that you can call her from a hospital, a police station, or a wedding chapel," Tricia said, trying to find a comfortable groove for the conversation, "and she'll come, no questions asked." She shot me a look across the table, confirming with a nod that she was willing to do all three.

Lindsay smiled in agreement. "That's what makes our little group so special. We'll do anything for each other. Right, Wendy?"

Wendy's face crumpled suddenly as she struggled not to cry. "Right," she said quietly, then took a deep breath and composed herself as best she could.

Lindsay squeezed her hand encouragingly. I wondered how much she really knew about what her friends were willing to do for each other, to each other, with each other.

Wendy suddenly steeled herself sufficiently to announce, "Listen, Molly, I want to be perfectly clear about one thing. If you screw things up for Ronnie, I'll destroy you."

"Don't take this out on Molly," Lindsay said.

"Amen, sister," Tricia nodded to Lindsay.

"I'm being completely sincere," Wendy said to all of us, but with her glare focused on me.

Cassady rapped on the tabletop. "As a lawyer, I'd like to advise you against saying inflammatory things that people will take huge delight in testifying to at a later date."

"Are you threatening me?" Wendy asked.

"No, because I'd rather not stoop to your level," Cassady answered.

"Women are fascinating," Aaron interjected.

"Wendy, what do you think you're going to accomplish by being belligerent with me?" I asked, wishing it sounded more diplomatic than it did. The volume in this little discussion was creeping up and we were starting to get those slow, sidelong looks from people at the other tables, the ones that communicate just how big a jerk they think you're being without a single word.

"And what are you going to accomplish by decimating Ronnie?" Wendy continued.

"I'm not trying to hurt Ronnie, I just want to know what happened to Garth, and if either of you is involved, that's part of the story," I said emphatically.

"Ronnie didn't do anything!" Wendy proclaimed, now officially too loud and drawing full-on glares from surrounding tables.

"Wendy," Lindsay breathed.

"And I didn't do anything either!"

"Wendy," Lindsay repeated, a little stronger.

"Maybe Ronnie's been right all along," I said. "You don't suppose Gwen shot Garth so she could be with Ronnie and then decided to go after Ronnie when she realized he was cheating on her with you?"

"Wendy!" Lindsay exclaimed, now shocked and disapproving.

Wendy sprang to her feet, knocking into the table. Aaron and Cassady steadied as many glasses as they could as Wendy spat out, "You bitch!" For a moment, I wasn't sure whether she was addressing Lindsay or me, but then she sailed the remains of her champagne cocktail at me and wiped out any doubt, along with my Anne Klein blouse.

I leapt to my feet, as did Tricia, Aaron, and Cassady, while Lindsay pulled Wendy back into her chair. I'd hoped to provoke a reaction that got me information, not a dousing. But in trying to pull Wendy up short, I'd pushed her over the brink. Perversely, the size of her reaction confirmed my doubts about her potential involvement in Garth's death. If she had something to hide, wouldn't she be more controlled, more wary? But she was in dress rehearsal for a nervous breakdown and wasn't holding anything back.

Or was her long day's journey into hysteria all a show for my benefit? These women were trained to sell; maybe Wendy was selling me an image of herself. I had a sudden vision of her in some allegorical medieval painting, "Woman as Innocent."

Tricia and Cassady swarmed me with napkins while Aaron watched in fascination. I was pretty sure there wasn't one law of physics to cover the elemental clashes that were occurring in the orbit of our table. Wendy dissolved into tears and Lindsay went back into mothering mode, patting her hair and murmuring to her. Lindsay glanced up briefly to catch my eye. "She's had a very hard day."

My patience with the Girls was wearing thin. "I haven't exactly been on vacation."

"But you can move on from this."

I couldn't go anywhere at the moment, since my friends were toweling me dry, or at least patting me damp, but I knew what she was trying to say. "And you can't?" I asked her over their bowed heads.

"We're . . . invested."

"You should all quit and go to medical school," Cassady suggested.

Lindsay's gaze suddenly focused with laserlike intensity. "You can't possibly understand, so don't bother to condescend."

Tricia, Aaron, and Cassady looked to me for a reaction, but I wasn't sure how to react. I knew Lindsay was just trying to protect Wendy, but I also knew that by extension, she was trying to protect the rest of the group and the agency and her future. The mother tiger was lying down across the mouth of the den and no one was getting in or out.

Reviewing options quickly, I decided to go with the friendly smile route. "Might be time for everyone to get a good night's sleep," I said with a nod to Wendy, who was still quietly weeping. Lindsay nodded slowly, not convinced, but I was anxious to get us all out of there. Not just because my blouse was starting to get downright chilly but because I was starting to get that gnawing in the pit of my stomach that told me the pieces weren't fitting together the way they were supposed to. I needed to get away from Wendy's weeping and Lindsay's mothering and the cacophony of the day and take stock.

"Excellent idea. You're going to catch a cold," Tricia warned. "Or make a lot of new friends." Aaron politely averted his eyes as I tried to get a sense of how transparent my blouse had become.

"Can you get her home?" I asked Lindsay, wanting to leave things on a friendly note with her, at least.

"Won't be the first time," Lindsay said with a patient smile.

"Wendy—" I attempted, but she stood up, grandly sweeping her hair back from her teary face.

"Do you have any idea what you've done?" Wendy asked. "We were all managing until you came along," she went on without giving me the chance to clear my throat, much less defend myself. "We were building a new future and you've wrecked it."

"All I've done is try to find the truth. Want to tell it to me so we can all move on?" I shot back, angry that Wendy kept trying to make some of this, any of this my fault. And even angrier that she might be right. Still, when the house of cards comes down, who do you blame—the person who built it or the person who slammed the door?

"I have told you the truth," Wendy insisted. "You know more about my life than my best friends do. Like that? You get off on that kind of thing? 'Knowledge is power' and all that crap?"

"I only want to understand what happened."

"I didn't do it. That's what happened. Why would I? I was happy. I loved my life. And now I so completely don't. How stupid would I be to put myself in this situation?"

It was a valid question, assuming she was telling the truth, which was an assumption I still wasn't comfortable making. I let it go unanswered.

"We'll see you at the gala tomorrow night," Lindsay said with a Stepford smile as she took Wendy by the arm. "And I trust, for the sake of the hard work and reputations of all involved, that it will be a pleasant gathering." There was a chill of warning in her voice and as she turned her back on us, marching Wendy to the door like a recalcitrant toddler, I wondered if I'd underestimated her.

"Typical night out, ladies?" Aaron asked pleasantly as Lindsay and Wendy vanished out the front door.

"Oh, this is nothing," Cassady assured him. "There's usually at least some significant property damage."

"The blouse doesn't count?" I asked.

Tricia patted my arm. "My dry cleaner works miracles. I can take it to him."

"Let me see what I can do."

Tricia smoothed my hair back from my face. "Honey, I

say this with all due love and respect, but you look awful. Let us take you home, make you some soup, rub your feet . . ."

"She has work problems, not the flu, Tricia," Cassady pointed out.

"A good foot rub is never wrong," Tricia responded.

"Excellent point," Aaron agreed.

As tempting as it was to invite them all back to my apartment to eat, regroup, vent, whatever was required, I had an overriding concern. Who was going to be there—or not be there—when I got home? No matter his mood, Kyle wouldn't appreciate an audience or a wait when there were issues to be discussed. I needed to go home by myself and clear a few things up. My head, most of all.

I took advantage of Tricia's saying I looked like hell—it's not what she said, but it's what she meant—to ask them for a raincheck and head home on my own. I thanked all three of them for coming to my aid, packed them off in a cab, and hurried off. To an empty apartment.

He'd said he was going to go back to work, but his shift should have been over by now. I called his cell first, but it went to voice mail and I didn't leave a message. I called his office and his partner, Ben Lipscomb, answered.

"Rough night," Ben said, his deep, rumbling voice tinged with concern. He's a pretty intimidating guy physically, but one of the most serene souls I know.

"Yeah, kinda crazy. And he's upset with me which makes it worse."

"I heard."

Which made it even worse. Kyle didn't discuss our relationship much and if he'd been telling Ben, things were really rocky. "Can I talk to him?"

"Not right now."

I sighed. I'd wanted to explain about the day, talk to him about Lindsay, but now I realized all I really wanted to do was tell him I was sorry I hadn't been honest with him. "Won't come to the phone or can't?" There was enough of a pause for me to figure out the answer for myself. "I don't want to put you in an awkward position, Ben, even though I'm getting really good at that. Could you just tell him I called?"

"I will. You get a good night's sleep. As the psalmist says, 'Joy comes in the morning.'"

Since there was no way to reach through the phone and hug Ben, I thanked him and hung up. If he was telling me to get a good night's sleep, he was telling me Kyle wasn't coming home tonight. Whether it was because of a case or because of how I'd handled things remained to be seen. And fretted over. Joy was only going to come in the morning if the boyfriend did, too.

Which meant that I had two mysteries on my plate now: how to identify Garth's killer and how to untangle my relationship. And maybe a third: Which of the first two was going to be easier to solve?

Seventeen

DEAR MOLLY, IS IT TRUE *that we always hurt the ones we love? Is it because the ones we love stay around long enough for us to make mistakes that hurt them or because the ones we love notice when we do something hurtful and everyone else ignores it? Or is it that we test the ones we love to see how much they love us and that never ends well? And why is it twice as painful when they hurt us back? Signed, Vulnerable Valentine*

I was not built to operate on two hours and fifteen minutes of sleep. I believe my optimum is eight, though I never reach that unless I'm ill, vacationing, or sedated. I attempt to average six, supplemented by periodic infusions of caffeine during my waking hours. On those occasions when I don't get at least four, I've been known to be impatient, humorless, and intolerant of the foibles of my fellow man. Those are the days I should stay home, or at least hide behind my sunglasses and coffee cup all day while my brain cells strain to shake off their stupor, but those are the days I go out into the world anyway and wind up in trouble.

I awoke to an empty apartment, silent answering machine and cell phone, and a feeling of dread. It was seven thirty and there was no way around it: I had to figure out how badly I'd trashed my relationship, get a handle on my story, see what the fallout was with Wendy and company, and reassure Eileen while she prepared for the gala.

I so should have stayed home.

Pacing until I'd crashed the night before, I'd attempted to figure out how to handle Kyle and how Wendy had talked her way off the suspect list. Somewhere around 3 A.M., on my second bag of microwave popcorn and my third playing of Bonnie Raitt's *Home Plate,* I'd decided I needed to stick to my work and give the problem with Kyle some time, because if I neglected my work to fix that, as soon as it was fixed, I'd just have to turn around and go back to the article, which could potentially undo all the work with Kyle. And I might know how to proceed on the article, but I definitely didn't know what to do about him.

When the alarm clock went off, I woke without any answers and with a crick in my neck. I subjected myself to the hottest shower I could stand, which loosened my neck a little but didn't help with the holes in my theory. I forced a frappuccino and a nectarine into my stomach and then forced my body into a khaki skirt and a lawn blouse, hoping that some chemical interaction between all those natural fibers would somehow infuse me with the energy and goodwill I needed to go forth. Before I headed out, I called the hospital and was told that both Mr. Willis and Mr. Mulcahey were resting comfortably; I assumed that "comfortably" was more the hospital's term than theirs.

I debated about calling Kyle and leaving another message, but I knew I could trust Ben to have delivered the one last night, which left the ball in Kyle's lap. I was just going to have to wait. Not a hobby of mine.

But other people like to wait. Or wait for me, anyway.

In reviewing the night before, I'd decided I needed to have another conversation with Kimberly, Ronnie's niece, and figure out why she was feeding some information to Peter and some to me. I wasn't buying the worried niece persona anymore. She wanted something. Everyone in the solar system that rotated around Garth Henderson seemed to be constantly angling, looking for the move ahead, the step up, the inside information.

Maybe on some level all human interaction is a series of negotiations: What will it take to make us work together, sleep together, stay together? But it seemed to me that, for good or ill, a significant aspect of the social charter requires wrapping the bartering in a certain amount of sincerity, honest emotion, and a desire for meaningful interaction. With this group, it was the bare rapaciousness that was unnerving. And the thought that only micrometers separated them from anyone else I knew. Myself included.

I tried not to dwell on that last thought as I made my way to Willis Worldwide, opting out of my usual sport of people watching to ponder Kimberly's angle on all this. Was she acting on behalf of her aunt, in defense of her uncle, or did she have some interest all her own?

I was so intent on those thoughts, I was walking with my head down to focus. Not the way to walk down the street in Manhattan. It's like a wide receiver running his route with his head down—you miss too many options, too many threats, and you can't plan an alternative route in time if you're blocked. I should've kept my head up. Then I would have seen Lindsay coming.

Instead, I ran into her before I even realized she was there and started apologizing before I knew it was her. Not that I stopped apologizing, but the shock of recognition made me stammer a moment.

"Molly. Small world!" she said cheerily, as though we'd last seen each other at a spring tea to celebrate someone's engagement.

"Tiny," I agreed. Now, I'm a big fan of synchronicity—things happening for a reason—and had Lindsay been a man on whom I had a crush, I would have taken this third chance encounter in a row as a sign from Heaven that I should pursue him vigorously, or at least ask him to lunch. But because she was, instead, a woman affiliated with a murder I was investigating, I took it as a sign that there was no chance to this at all. "Where are you headed?"

"I'm picking up some material from Ronnie's team for a new account," she said, leaving me to consider asking why neither office had assistants or messengers available for such tasks. She pointed down the street. "I'm also picking up my shoes for tonight."

Tonight. The gala. I couldn't even summon up a smile. Did I really have to go? I didn't have shoes or a dress, I hadn't spoken to my date in over twelve hours, and the prospect of watching my boss strut her stuff, no matter how noble the cause, was less than enticing.

Lindsay tilted her head curiously, scanning my face. "You are still coming, aren't you?" Her voice had gone a little tight and her smile, a little stiff. I knew it was a big night for the agency, with the launch of the perfume, but I couldn't see how it could matter all that much to Lindsay if I came or not. "You don't have a conflict, do you?" she pressed.

Her hand found my arm and squeezed harder than necessary. I rocked back half a step, jostled off balance less by her gesture than by the two thoughts in my head. *Why is it important to you?* and *You're following me.* Quickly, they folded into one thought: *What is so important to you that you're following me?*

We hadn't crossed paths because of synchronicity, coincidence, or planetary influences. We'd crossed paths because Lindsay was following me. She and her husband hadn't walked by the Carlyle on the way to Girasole coincidentally, she'd dragged him by because that's where Kyle and I were. She'd brought Wendy to the Lenox Lounge because she knew I was there with my friends. And now she was here, in front of Ronnie's office, because she knew where I was headed. Had she revealed herself to keep me from going in? Or to find out what I'd deduced since last night?

She shifted the pressure on my arm, trying to persuade me away from the entrance to Ronnie's building. "Want to see my shoes for tonight?" she asked. "I don't splurge on shoes very often, but I couldn't resist this pair. They make me wish

I was wearing a shorter dress, so they'd show more." Why didn't she want me to go in? Was she protecting Ronnie now, too? Was part of Lindsay and Wendy teaming up together last night to present a unified front in his defense?

I eased my arm from her grasp. "I really shouldn't play hooky," I said, inwardly grimacing at how phony it sounded. "But I can't wait to see your shoes tonight."

"Then you are coming," she said, relieved.

"As long as I get my work done and Eileen doesn't ground me," I assured her.

She gave an expansive, sympathetic sigh. "Bosses will make you crazy."

She ran her hand through her hair while I considered pulling mine out by the handful. "Hard to find one worth adoring," I said.

Her hand froze in midsweep. I braced myself for an angry retort or a heartfelt speech, but it was just that the charm on her bracelet was snagged in her hair. I stepped closer to give her a hand, but she turned away a little, gesturing with her other hand that she could handle it herself. As she did, my eye was caught by how the link connecting the charm to the bracelet caught the light. Or didn't, actually. The link was dull. Cheap. It didn't match the rest of the bracelet. As though the charm had been broken off and then replaced somewhere other than Tiffany. Quickly. Before anyone could notice it was missing.

I made myself breathe evenly and not leap to any conclusions. There are lots of ways for a charm to get pulled off a bracelet. There are a number of rationales for having a Tiffany bracelet repaired somewhere other than Tiffany. There are plenty of reasons for killing your boss.

Lindsay misinterpreted my freeze for awkwardness. "It's okay, I can get it," she said, tugging for a moment and then just pulling until a little knot of her hair came free with it. She unwound the hair from the bracelet with sharp little twists of her hand. Looking around for an appropriate place to discard it, she didn't find anything, so she tucked it in her jacket pocket. A place for everything and everything in its place, as my grandmother would say. Made me wonder what else Lindsay might have been capable of disposing of.

Picking a suspect on the rebound was certainly more dangerous than picking a man that way, but I suddenly couldn't take my eyes off Lindsay. Had I mistaken immense self-control for calm, since I'm not terribly familiar with either one, and overlooked her completely?

Everyone thought so highly of her, relied on her, yet they kept her at arm's length. The married one. The maternal one. The different one. As the Girls all cooed and clawed their way into Garth's good graces by way of his bedroom, she'd been shut out. How maddening would that be, to see your peers succeeding because there was a shortcut you couldn't take? People leap over a variety of moral boundaries in the course of a day, but this was a huge one. I could see why she hadn't crossed it, but I could also see how it would strike her as unfair. Especially if there was the rumor that someone was going to be elevated after the merger. She'd told me she and Daniel were frantic about money. Still, the slope from frustrated to homicidal was pretty steep. Had she really climbed it?

Suddenly self-conscious that I might be staring, I plastered on a smile. "Thanks for the invite, but I really gotta go. So cool running into you." Cool enough to give me goose bumps.

Her weight shifting uneasily, Lindsay smiled in return. "Absolutely."

I shuffled a bit myself, the two of us in an awkward *pas de deux,* choreographed by anxiety. She didn't want to head in any direction until she knew where I was headed and I was trying to figure out where to go so I could double back around and follow her. I wanted to be wrong about her because I'd enjoyed her company and I'd envied her relationship, but if I was wrong, I needed to find out as soon as possible.

Especially because she was picking up on it. "Are you okay, Molly?" she asked, stepping in a little and trying to take my arm again. I leaned away more than stepped away, not wanting to offend her or tip my hand any more than I might already have done.

"Yeah, I'm fine. Just thinking of all the things I need to do. How 'bout you?"

"Great."

"Good."

"Yeah."

We both paused in our fluttering at the same moment, locking eyes. What a fascinating place the world would be if we all said exactly what we were thinking all the time. If we didn't withhold and lie and dissemble and sugarcoat, just laid the truth out, plain and unadorned, and people responded in kind. Would the planet be a calmer, happier place because we were all living in harmony? Or would it be calmer and happier because we'd all killed each other off ages ago?

"I'm going to have to come back here later, might even have to wait until Monday," I said, breaking our face-off as gently as possible. "So glad I ran into you. I need to go get a dress. See you tonight." I grabbed her hand to squeeze it in farewell and was surprised by how clammy it was.

She pulled her hand away quickly and gestured back over her shoulder. "Shoes," was her farewell as she finally turned and hurried away. I moved to the edge of the sidewalk, as though preparing to hail a cab, but folded my arms and watched her. Watched her pass two shoe stores, then cross Madison. I was sure she hadn't been imprecise about the direction of the shoe store, but that she'd lied to me about where she was headed. So why lie and where was she going?

I went north to cross Madison there, watching Lindsay the whole time, to the point that I tripped over a stroller being pushed by a nanny who called me all sorts of names in a language I couldn't even identify and jostled more than my share of equally preoccupied walkers. Fortunately, no one took great offense or spilled their coffee on me. The only real damage I caused was snagging a guy's iPod earpiece wire on my purse and unplugging him from his morning's podcast, which displeased him greatly. But I couldn't stop to apologize because Lindsay was disappearing down a side street.

Women in Manhattan invest a great deal of time, money, and energy in standing out in a crowd, but at that moment, I would have forked over big bucks for gunmetal sweats like they made us wear in college P.E., anything to blend in and become invisible as I hurried after Lindsay. But then I realized, dressed like that I'd probably stand out even more than I did now because there were plenty of my peers dressed like me out and about, but I hadn't seen plain sweats in a long time. This was Big Apple camouflage: Dress like an individual to blend in.

Tailing someone on foot was new to me and I wasn't sure how close to get. Not that she was watching over her shoulder; she was walking quickly, head down. As I began to worry that she really was only shopping for shoes and other items for the gala, she stopped. Not in front of a store but in front of a church.

It squeezed the breath out of me for a moment, considering that Lindsay was being driven to the confessional by her concern that I was figuring out her culpability in Garth's death. Much as I wanted her to confess to me, I understood the impulse to settle accounts in her heart and soul first. But it didn't look like an easy decision. Even from a block away, I could read her indecisiveness as she paused at the bottom of the broad sweep of the front stairs. After a moment, she steeled herself, ran up the stairs, and disappeared inside.

I drifted closer to the church myself, then kicked myself for my lofty spiritual digression. She wasn't there to confess, she was there to see her husband. The church was St. Aidan's, where Daniel's group, Rising Angels, had its offices. I'd actually been to the church before, but had been so intent on following Lindsay this time I hadn't recognized the block. She could have a million different reasons to drop in on her husband in the middle of the day. Could her actual reason have any significance to me? How close did I dare go to find out?

Now I was the one who swayed indecisively outside the

church. There was no way I could pass it off as coincidence that I'd shown up at the church moments behind Lindsay and I couldn't think of any questions to manufacture as a reason for following her that didn't have big "I think you're guilty" balloons tied to them. Was there some angle I could present that entailed my needing to talk to Daniel, something about the impact of Garth's death on the families of his employees, the ripple effect of a homicide? No, if it felt like a reach to me, it was going to read like one to them.

Still, I couldn't walk away. The concept of Lindsay being the one who snapped and took out her frustration, resentment, or something I hadn't even considered yet was growing more compelling by the moment and I couldn't leave without trying to gather more evidence. Hoping I'd think of something clever and enticing to say when I saw Lindsay and Daniel, I crossed the street and tried to keep my heart from thumping out of my chest as I started up the stairs.

I was seven steps up when I heard Lindsay's voice at the top. A man's voice, presumably Daniel's, answered her. The center of my brain that improvises excuses and alibis went numb and the resolve flushed out of me like sweat. Glancing around madly, I backed down the stairs in search of some nook in which to conceal myself. Better yet, I spotted a street-level door to the left of the staircase. A weathered wood-burned sign over the doorway read: THRIFT SHOP.

I flung the door open and stepped in, just as Lindsay's and Daniel's voices dropped to my level. I stayed at the door, my hand wrapped around the knob, trying to catch my breath and praying they hadn't seen me. I wasn't proud of panicking, but I wanted to make sure I didn't play my hand too soon for a variety of reasons—setting a killer off again being pretty high on the list.

After a moment, I decided Lindsay and Daniel hadn't seen me, but just to be sure, I pried my hand off the doorknob and walked into the store. It was a claustrophobic warren of clothing, home furnishings, knickknacks, and books. Three older women with matching permed white hair and complementary cardigans sat stiff-backed behind the small cashier's counter, two crocheting and one knitting. They were watching me oddly, but who could blame them since I was acting oddly. I smiled apologetically, attempting to put them at ease. "May I look around?"

The smallest of the three, a pink dumpling of a woman, nodded emphatically. "Help yourself, sweetheart. That's why we're here." She gestured with a knitting needle that could easily impale me if I chose to misbehave. I couldn't be sure if that was her intended message, but I wasn't about to challenge her.

I thanked them and, surveying the various groupings and wondering which to poke through first, took a deep breath. Hovering above the musk of dust and wool and flannel, there was a strident layer of something so sharp and bright, it nearly made me dizzy. While I couldn't pinpoint its source, there was no doubt of its identity. It was, as they say, the sweet smell of Success.

I turned back to them slowly, not wanting to make too much a deal of this or to startle the little one with the big needle. "Do you have perfume here?"

The middle one, a slender, reedy creature, tapped on the counter with her crochet hook. "A few bottles of White Shoulders and there's half a carton of Britney Spears in the back."

"But I smell something else," I said, surprised that they didn't.

"Oh, that," the little one said. "Someone spilled something somewhere, but we couldn't find it." She pointed with the needle again, this time past me toward the outside wall of the shop. "Probably in those bags that haven't been unpacked yet."

Against the wall, a collection of plastic and paper bags were stacked in casual piles. Remembering the bags on Lindsay's office sofa, I drifted toward the heap. "Any reason they haven't been unpacked?" I asked lightly.

"Youth group's supposed to do that," the middle one said with a disapproving frown. "Haven't gotten around to it."

The third one, a solid block of a woman who hadn't

stopped crocheting since I'd entered, snorted. "Worthless bunch of snot-nosed brats."

"Mind if I look through them?" I asked, still drifting toward the pile. The scent grew stronger as I drew closer, unless I'd fallen prey to wishful sniffing. I couldn't decide which was headier: the scent or the possibility it was linked to Lindsay, the only point of intersection between the perfume and this church I could plot on my mental graph paper.

The Fates conferred wordlessly, then turned back and shrugged at me in unison. I took that as permission and knelt beside the heap. The smell evenly saturated the air here, so there was only one thing to do. Grab a bag and start digging.

I paused long enough to call Cassady and get voice mail, then call Tricia and get her. "Interested in a little shopping?" I asked. Out of the corner of my eye, I could see that the ladies had returned to their sewing and whispering to each other.

"Let me check if I'm still breathing. Yes."

I explained where I was and she said she was on her way. I pocketed the phone and unknotted the top of the first bag.

When Tricia arrived twenty minutes later, looking freshly laundered and coiffed, I was feeling stale and musty. The ladies perked up at her entrance; I don't know why, since there was absolutely nothing about her Missoni ensemble that proclaimed her as a thrift shop habitué. Then again, Tricia does have that effect on people. Including me.

She took a moment to survey me and the sprawl of bags around me before kicking off her Via Spiga pumps and joining me on the floor. "We could have met in my grandmother's attic to do this and there would have been a martini shaker involved as well," she said genially.

"If your grandmother's attic smells of Success perfume, I want to know who she's been playing bridge with because they might be tied to Garth Henderson's death," I told her.

Tricia looked at me in surprised delight. "Oh, this is work! Even better!" She pulled a faded Fordham sweatshirt out of the open bag and sniffed at it, which provoked several sneezes of impressive volume for such a delicate nose.

As we sat on the floor and went through the bags, trying to find the source of the smell, I couldn't help but remember the number of times we'd packed dorm rooms and apartments together, winding down one adventure and getting ready for the next, always strengthened by knowing we were moving forward together. I hoped that was going to remain a constant in my life. Of course, I'd always imagined us gathering in hospitals to celebrate births together, too, but so far we were only hanging out in E.R.s because of my misadventures. One step at a time, I suppose.

"What do you think of Aaron?" Tricia asked, recoiling from a bag of old shoes. She hastily tied it back up and put it in the "checked" pile.

Was she remembering the same things I was? "He seems interesting. Calming."

"It's been a while since she hibernated with someone like this. Wonder when it will wear off."

"Maybe it won't."

Tricia flashed a smile. "That day's coming, isn't it."

"And we'll adjust," I assured us both.

She nodded without looking at me. I was going to pursue that line of thought, but the next bag I opened released a blast of Success in my face like a booby-trap and I was the one who sneezed with sinus-rattling vigor. Tricia reacted to the smell, too, and leaned forward to peer into the bag with me.

It appeared to be predominantly towels and table linens, but nestled among them was a silk blouse. Brilliant red. Jewel tone. With intricate cutwork on the collar. And redolent of Success. I pulled the blouse out of the bag to examine it more closely and as it unfurled, a small gray object dropped from its folds and clattered to the floor between me and Tricia. A pistol looks so much smaller when it isn't being pointed at you.

Eighteen

DEAR MOLLY, IF I DO *the right thing for the wrong reason, do I still get credit—in the karmic sense? Does it diminish the act that it's done to please someone I care about and not because it's what the law or the culture or the company requires? Aren't I actually accomplishing twice as much this way, which is ultimately a good thing, even if it started out as a sneaky thing? Or if I have to work this hard to justify something, does that mean I shouldn't have done it in the first place? Signed, Means in Search of an End*

Detective Donovan looked at me and the gun with equal suspicion. Tricia was still behind the thrift store counter, trying to get the three little ladies to stop hyperventilating, so I was on my own with her new friend and his previously invisible partner, a raspy, reedy fellow named Novatny who came off as far too burnt for someone in his early thirties. Perhaps the constant joy of working with Detective Donovan took its toll.

Both the blouse and the gun were now in evidence envelopes and the detectives were debating the merits of having crime scene techs come in and examine the thrift shop more thoroughly. To their consternation, the thrift shop's methods for accepting donations were casual, bordering on the offhanded. Unless the items being dropped off were of remarkable value, donors were given a receipt with an umbrella statement such as "three bags of clothing" or "two boxes of housewares." Finer points were left to their tax accountants. The donors filled out names, addresses, and phone numbers, but no proof was required of any of the information. Normally, these receipts were only the concern of the IRS, not the NYPD.

Further complicating matters was the disposition of the donated material; as Tricia and I had already learned, the bags were often stacked against the wall until more flexible backs than the three older ladies' were available for unpacking, sorting, and shelving. There was no way to match receipts to bags, even if the donor had been truthful.

And it didn't help matters at all that while I could say I'd seen Lindsay in a blouse just like that one, it certainly wasn't a one-of-a-kind creation and her name wasn't exactly monogrammed on the collar. And the blouse had been drenched in a perfume Lindsay couldn't wear. Or had said she couldn't wear. But as tenuous as they were, there were too many connections here for me not to believe fervently that the gun was the murder weapon and belonged in official hands as soon as possible.

Still, Detective Donovan squinted at me as though he were in agony. "What exactly are you trying to do here?"

"The right thing," I said, doing my best to sound sincere and not indignant. It had actually crossed my mind to pay the little ladies whatever was required and leave with the blouse, the gun, and the bag they'd come in, and try to sort out the contents and my thoughts in the privacy of my apartment before I decided who to call. But then I considered the full import of the gun—if it did, in fact, turn out to be the gun that had killed Garth. I'd been a little high-handed with evidence in the past and been well-schooled in the complications that could cause once a case went to trial. I didn't want to make that mistake here.

But for some reason, Detective Donovan was having trouble accepting that. "So tell me again how you happened to find the murder weapon, here in this thrift shop, when we've been looking for it in all sorts of reasonable places for two months and haven't been able to put our hands on it."

"I didn't come here looking for it," I told him again, pleasantly and politely. "I ducked in here so Lindsay wouldn't see me, then I smelled the perfume and thought there might be a connection, so I started digging around." A very compact, orderly progression of events, it seemed to me, but Detective Donovan was still struggling with it and Detective Novatny had moved over to talk to Tricia and the little ladies again.

"You trying to play me, Molly?" Detective Donovan asked, anger starting to infuse his words and his expression.

Stung, I actually took a moment to formulate a response before I opened my mouth. I couldn't be sure if he was trying to provoke me or if he was genuinely suspicious and I needed to tread carefully. "Detective Donovan, I know we've seemed to be at cross-purposes previously," I said in my best let's-all-be-professionals voice, "but it's never been my intention to be anything other than helpful."

"Then what're you wasting my time for? You expect me to believe this is real, and not some sort of setup or decoy that you and Mulcahey have concocted?"

It was a toss-up which was more insulting: that I'd be interested in setting him up or that I'd do it with Peter. But the mud wrestling could wait. "Test the gun, Detective Donovan. If it's not the murder weapon, I'll apologize. If it is, you can."

"I don't owe you anything but a run to the precinct," he snapped, taking my arm.

"Excuse me?"

"We're going to get a formal statement from you to support your ridiculous story so I don't look like an idiot further down the road," he said.

"Wouldn't your time be better spent talking to Lindsay?" I asked, doing my best to stay polite.

"Based on what? Your theory? I need a little more to go on before I start dragging people in for questioning."

In a rare moment of restraint, I just nodded. "Okay."

As he released my arm, I couldn't tell if he was angry or

disappointed with my willingness to cooperate. "Okay then. Let's go."

He watched me carefully, as though he thought he was calling my bluff, but I just nodded in Tricia's direction. "Can I tell Tricia I'm leaving?"

He nodded, but Tricia was already hurrying over. "What's going on?" she asked. I sketched out the situation in the most diplomatic terms I could come up with and Tricia announced, "I'm going with you."

"That's not necessary," Detective Donovan assured her. "She's not being accused of anything, I'd just like to get a formal statement because of the unusual circumstances—"

"I'm going with you," Tricia repeated with added steeliness.

"Then let's get going because we all have somewhere to be later tonight, remember?" I smiled cheerily at Detective Donovan, but Tricia did not, leading me to wonder if his invitation to the gala was about to be rescinded.

Detective Novatny lingered behind to soothe the ladies and finish his examination of the shop while Detective Donovan escorted us to his precinct. Which was also Kyle's precinct, a fact I had blocked out as long as possible. But now it was inescapable, as Tricia and I passed a number of people I'd met at various social functions with Kyle. None of them reacted to my appearance in shock, which I hoped meant that Kyle had not put out a memo proclaiming me to be persona non grata, but more than one stopped to watch with interest as Tricia and I followed the frowning detective to an interrogation room, and it wasn't to admire our outfits.

The visit almost went smoothly. Tricia sat beside me in silent support, studying each and every one of Detective Donovan's statements and gestures, weighing them for true meaning and intent. I couldn't tell how the tote board was leaning because she was being remarkably impassive, but I could still sense a thorough evaluation taking place.

The detective and I went through the formalities of my making a statement, dotted the I's and crossed the T's, were civil to each other—it was just like it was supposed to be.

Crisp. Professional. I kept my mind focused on the task at hand and didn't get distracted—for more than a moment here and there—by wondering how all this would play out, whether Detective Donovan would still come to the gala, whether Lindsay would still come, whether she'd picked up her shoes. Even as I laid out how I'd come to find the gun and believe it was Lindsay's, I knew my theory sounded sketchy and presumptive, but I couldn't melt that icy lump in my gut that told me Lindsay was at the heart of all this. But I also respected that Detective Donovan had to approach this from a solid investigative angle that would hold up in court; hunches need not apply.

As we stood to leave, me trying to think of the proper way to express my appreciation that an awkward situation had turned out well, things shifted to redefine "awkward." Detective Donovan opened the door just in time for Kyle to stick his head in and say, "Heard you've got an interesting development," and then stop, surprised by the sight of me across the table. Whoever had mentioned the "interesting development" to Kyle had apparently not mentioned my involvement in it, leaving all of us with that slightly nauseous feeling you get from coming around a corner and seeing an animated discussion screech to a halt, which can only mean they were talking about you and not exactly in complimentary terms.

"Hi, Kyle," Tricia said with a touch of preemptive protectiveness.

"Tricia," he responded evenly.

I wanted to ask how he was, where he'd been, when we were going to talk again, but all I could manage was, "Hello."

With a similarly loaded nod, he returned the greeting, then glanced quickly at Detective Donovan before asking me, "What's going on?"

"I think I'm the interesting development."

Kyle started to pinch his bottom lip, then restrained himself and put his hand in his pocket. "Would make sense."

"I found a gun that I thought might be linked to the Henderson homicide, so I called Detective Donovan," I explained, wishing I didn't feel quite so much like a spelling bee contestant who was relieved that the semifinal word was one she at least recognized.

I had no idea what reaction to anticipate from Kyle, but I was unprepared for the look of surprise on his face, mainly because I could tell the surprise related to my having done the appropriate thing and not to the discovery of a potentially key piece of evidence. "That's great," he said quietly.

"Let's see what ballistics says first," Detective Donovan said.

I knew that wasn't what Kyle had meant and met his eye to acknowledge his approval of my following the rules for a change. I hadn't done it just to please him, I'd also done it because it was the right thing to do, but the fact that it pleased him was a delightful bonus. I so wanted to prove to him we could both do what we loved and make it work.

He allowed himself a small smile before turning back to Detective Donovan. "She's got a pretty great track record," Kyle said, then nodded to me. "See you later."

"Great," I said, feeling a weight I hadn't been aware of soar off the back of my head.

He looked at his watch reflexively. "Might have to meet you at the thing tonight."

He was coming to the gala. He was speaking to me and coming to the gala and coming home with me after the gala and we were back on track. Or he was at least coming to the gala and we could take it from there. "Okay," I said, suddenly nodding so enthusiastically it threatened to turn into my infamous bobblehead imitation. I cleared my throat as though that would stiffen my neck and get my head to stop bouncing. "See you there."

"Clearly, my day has gotten much more complicated, but I'll do my best to meet you there. As long as I'm still invited." Detective Donovan turned to direct the second half at Tricia and, in doing so, missed the perplexed look that ran across Kyle's face.

"That might depend on ballistics, too," Tricia said and

now both detectives looked perplexed. She smiled. "I'd prefer that you not use the event as an opportunity to arrest anyone I know," Tricia explained.

"Which brings me to a crucial point," Detective Donovan said sternly. Even Kyle reacted to his change in tone. "Stay away from the principals in this case."

"Could you give me a list?" I asked.

"Molly," Kyle said in quiet warning.

"I'm trying to cooperate. But our assessment of who the principals are at this point might be very different," I said, wanting to be helpful but also mindful of the article I had to write. I could stay away from Gwen and Ronnie for a while, I wanted to stay away from Lindsay, but I did have work to do.

"No employees of GHInc. or Willis Worldwide."

"What about tonight?" I asked, suddenly feeling like Cinderella facing down the ugly stepsisters at the front door.

"You can go. As long as you don't talk to any of these people."

"Who else am I going to talk to?"

"Me. I'll vouch for her," Kyle said with a quick look to Detective Donovan. Now at least Cinderella had a Prince Charming.

"You also need to stay away from St. Aidan's Church. And Peter Mulcahey."

I could feel the heat of Kyle's gaze on my cheek. Or maybe I was blushing. "I have no problem staying away from Peter."

"And the rest of them."

"Right. But—for how long? I need to tell my editor if this is going to interfere with meeting my deadline."

"He can't do that!" Eileen shrieked, an even more unnerving interaction than usual because she was standing on top of her desk and literally looking down on me, rather than squawking from her normal metaphorical perch of disdain. Suzanne dutifully stood by, perhaps to catch her should she fall, while an intensely focused and matronly woman in a black dress so plain it looked like a uniform did her best to hem Eileen's dress. Bull pen rumor was, the seamstress was from The Publisher's tailor shop and had been summoned to put finishing touches on what Eileen was wearing that night. Not in the gala, to the gala. But apparently the pressure of parading with the Beautiful People had destroyed Eileen's confidence in most of her wardrobe, several piles of which were slowly slipping off the sofa, making entering her office even more treacherous than usual.

"Actually, he can," Cassady explained, gracefully stepping into the role of *consigliore*. Tricia and I had encountered her outside the precinct, as she'd been rushing up the steps to come save me from myself. I hadn't even been aware that Tricia had been texting her, urging her to do just that, until Cassady arrived.

Thankful that we'd been allowed to leave as quickly as we had, Cassady had hustled us into a new cab and commanded that we be driven back to my office so she could rationally explain to my irrational boss why there could be a delay in finishing my article.

"There's the potential for charges for materially interfering with an investigation, obstruction of justice, aiding and abetting—"

"Aiding and abetting? I'm not going to help her," I protested.

"Her? Her who? Who do you think it is?" Eileen demanded, slithering to the edge of her desk. Tricia reached over and thoughtfully slid the phone and a full coffee cup out of her path before Eileen could kick them off.

"I'm advising my client not to discuss this matter with anyone until further notice," Cassady said as calmly as she might have inquired about the color of Eileen's nail polish.

The color of Eileen's face was more to the point. Pale with rage, she scowled down at Cassady, though with Cassady in four-inch Kenneth Coles and Eileen barefoot on the desk, the distance wasn't as great as Eileen might have liked. "Don't pull this Judith Miller shit on me. I will not be scooped."

"No, you won't be. Quinn Harriman's magazine is facing

the same restrictions," Cassady assured her. We'd made a few phone calls in the cab to be sure of that.

Not getting enough of a reaction out of Cassady, Eileen swung her fury in my direction. "I asked you for a simple profile—"

"You asked me to prove that Gwen Lincoln is innocent and that's what I'm trying to do. And I'm still going to do that before the deadline. All this means is you can't show up tonight and announce we've got proof Gwen didn't do it," I explained, trying to match Cassady's lightness of tone.

Eileen straightened up, petulantly yanking her skirt away from the seamstress. That's precisely what she'd hope to do—make her grand pronouncement, then sashay down the catwalk as the savior of the evening. This had nothing to do with journalistic ethics or competition or, heaven forbid, doing the right thing. This was all about Eileen being the star. If I'd been less focused on the story, I would've been more aware of that. "I'm very disappointed," Eileen said and I almost stepped out of the way to avoid the venom dripping from the words.

"So am I," I replied sincerely, "but I'll still deliver the article to you by its due date and I promise you, you'll be pleased then."

"I'd better be," she said in her threatening voice, which was growing nearly indistinguishable from her normal voice due to constant use.

"I, for one, can't wait to read the article that will not only clear Gwen Lincoln, but will explain to the entire city the role this magazine had in setting things right," Tricia said. "Your publisher will be able to dine out on this one for months because he gave you the freedom to pursue the story and you passed that along to Molly." A threatening tone never came within a mile of Tricia's voice, but Eileen pulled back like a toddler whose hand had just been slapped. Tricia had put the chain of command in her head and I could see that Eileen was already testing possible combinations of greed, ambition, and self-promotion to see what approach would benefit her best as she strove to take full credit for whatever I came up with.

Fine with me. As long as I was able to come up with it. And how I was going to do that when I'd been placed on double not-so-secret probation was beyond me. Having to hold back until Detective Donovan gave me the "all clear," at which point everything would be over except the Monday morning quarterbacking, was maddening. There had to be some way to talk to Lindsay before then without tipping my hand. The trick was to do it so there was no possibility of getting busted in any form by any party.

But doing anything necessitated getting away from Eileen, who was considering Tricia's view of the future and warming to it. Given what the Girls at GHInc. were willing to do to get what they wanted, Eileen's purely political conniving was almost refreshing.

Eileen let go of her skirt and gestured for the seamstress to return to her work. "Fine. But if I get scooped . . ."

"You won't," I promised.

"Then go work on something else and keep yourself out of trouble. And don't be late tonight. I don't want Emile to think my staff is rude."

Choosing discretion over zinger, I led Cassady and Tricia from the office, closing the door behind me to shield the tender hearts in the bull pen from the sight of our fearless leader dancing on the furniture. Save that for the gala.

Pausing by my desk, Tricia checked her watch. "Lunch would do us all much good."

"Is it that time already?" I asked, distracted by a half-formed thought buzzing around in the back of my brain.

"Time flies when you're being questioned," Cassady said. "Come on, let's find somewhere we can eat where we can protect you from the legions with whom you are not to have contact."

I hesitated, still trying to identify the thought. "Seriously, I'm not sure I'm hungry."

"What are you wearing tonight?" Tricia asked.

"I still don't know," I answered.

"First things first," Cassady said. "Unless you don't feel like shopping either."

"In which case we're taking you to the hospital," Tricia said. "But not the one Peter's in, because that would upset too many detectives."

"And we don't want to do that," Cassady emphasized, arching an eyebrow that Tricia chose to ignore.

"It's not that dire," I assured them. "Let's shop."

The palliative secret of shopping is the distraction. You get caught up in a vision of the future in which you'll be happy in this dress or at the place where you can wear these shoes and you stop thinking about your problems, disappointments, and deadlines for at least a few moments. But the magic wasn't working yet again. There I stood, back in Saks, surrounded by the stuff of daydreams, and I couldn't shake that gnawing feeling that I was missing something. Something important.

Tricia pulled a slinky satin sheath the color of lemon sherbet off a rack and draped it over her arm for my inspection. "This would look great on you. And bring out the highlights in your hair."

I looked at the dress, but all that was going through my head was, "*The Yellow Wallpaper.*"

"Whose yellow wallpaper?"

"Remember that English class we took sophomore year? Professor Alexander?"

"Charlotte Perkins Gilman, that *Yellow Wallpaper*?" Cassady asked from the other side of the dress rack.

"Where the woman's trapped behind the wallpaper and the narrator keeps seeing her trying to get out."

"Why are we discussing early feminist literature in the evening-wear section of Saks? It's not so much ironic as inappropriate," Cassady asked, exchanging a look with Tricia, who slowly hung the lemon sheath back up.

"This thought's stuck in my head, slinking around behind the wallpaper, and I can't get it to come out and identify itself."

"Molly, you're stressed. It's been a hectic couple of days.

Lots of shooting and not enough sleeping. You need to re-lax," Tricia said.

Cassady nodded firmly. "You have that great dark blue gown from Andrea Sebastian's wedding, wear that tonight and we'll go get lunch, maybe even an afternoon cocktail, and sort it out, whatever it is."

I agreed. My Visa balance didn't need to contend with another semiformal dress that I wouldn't wear often enough to justify and it might do my lurking thought good to contend with a glass of pinot grigio and a chicken Caesar. Then Tricia and Cassady each held a hand out to me, in friendship and support, and the lurking thought burst forth. This gnawing sensation hadn't been my frustration at being brought to heel by Detective Donovan. It had been my frustration at being taken in by Lindsay, who had presented herself as a friend. As I looked gratefully at my two best friends, I felt like an idiot not to have seen the machinations behind Lindsay wanting to help, to have dinner with Kyle and me, to cozy up to me. I tried to form a cogent statement about the nastiness of this particular brand of betrayal, but all I could think was: *Bitch*.

But as freeing as it was to let that thought out from behind the wallpaper, I was stunned by the next thought, which came so clearly that it might as well have been scrawled on the now-exposed wall: *Lindsay didn't do it*.

Nineteen

Tricia and Cassady spent the rest of the afternoon trying to convince me of three things: Kyle would make it to the gala on time, I needed to do something with my hair, and Lindsay Franklin had killed Garth Henderson. Even after the two of them left to get ready themselves, I tried to be won over by their trio of reasonable statements.

I knew I couldn't control Kyle's schedule, I could only have faith in his pledge to be there. And I couldn't do much to control my hair, but spending half an hour scorching myself with a curling iron also gave me time to stand still and listen to the inner voice that insisted Lindsay was innocent.

Yes, the blouse wrapped around the gun looked just like the ones I'd seen her in. Yes, she'd told me she took bags of donations to the thrift shop on a regular basis, which supported both the bags being there and no one at the shop being particularly concerned about the contents. Yes, she'd been prevented from advancing her career by a man who cared more about his libido than his livelihood and that could be enough to provoke a murderous rage. Yes, she'd essentially stalked me to keep track of where I was in my investigation.

But I couldn't get past the Success.

If Lindsay was highly allergic to the perfume—a fact her colleagues had attested to freely—how did she handle sufficient quantities to soak the blouse and make the hotel room reek without showing any adverse effects? As closely as this group watched each other, wouldn't someone have noticed if Lindsay had broken out in hives upon the death of their boss?

But if Lindsay didn't kill Garth, who did? And was she knowingly covering for the killer or had she been duped? I tried to imagine someone like Wendy or Tessa setting up someone like Lindsay, but once you've imagined someone pulling the trigger, it gets a whole lot easier to imagine them doing all sorts of antisocial things.

By the time Tricia buzzed me from downstairs, my hair had gained nothing but static electricity from my attempts with the curling iron, my chest and neck were blotchy from nerves, and even my kate spade sams, my favorite dress shoes, were pinching my toes—out of spite, it seemed. If I'd had the sense to recognize these as harbingers of the evening to come, I would've stayed home in my pajamas, turned on Turner Classic Movies, and built a bomb shelter in my bathroom.

Downstairs, Danny, our doorman, was making a marvelous fuss over Tricia. She did look magnificent in an ice blue vintage Armani, her hair swept up behind her ears with marcasite combs. She cooed over me, but I felt like I was heading to a costume ball, a bundle of nerves masquerading as a journalist.

"Try to put everything else out of your mind except the comic possibilities of your editor on the catwalk," Tricia said, knowing exactly what I was struggling with. "Don't think about your article until tomorrow."

"I'm not worried about the article," I said as she walked me out the door to the waiting cab. Cassady and Aaron were meeting us at the gala; Kyle and Detective Donovan were supposed to do the same.

"Liar," she said gently.

"Okay, the article isn't my primary concern."

"No, your primary concern is getting in the backseat of a cab in that slim skirt." Tricia clutched her evening bag in front of her, smiled expectantly, and waited for the show to begin.

Getting in and out of a cab elegantly is something of an art. In a gown, it's something of an impossibility. That's the real reason red-carpet walkers arrive at events in limos; limos come equipped with strong men who pull you to your feet, making you appear lithe and graceful. This cab came equipped with a large, sullen woman who wasn't about to move anything but the steering wheel and was quickly growing impatient with my reluctance to dive in.

Through an interesting combination of leaning, spinning, and stumbling, I was able to inject myself into the backseat and slither over far enough for Tricia to slide in beside me. I hadn't heard any stitches pop, my heels hadn't caught in my hem, and my straps were still riding in the proper position. I could only hope the rest of the evening would go as smoothly, especially because a special brand of anxiety was settling over me.

When I turned sixteen, my best friends conspired to throw me a surprise party. They even managed to persuade Jerry Shannon, the basketball player who sat behind me in English and on whom I had a grand crush, to come to the party. The exhilaration of walking into my friend Mary's basement and seeing Jerry there among my friends was matched only by the despair of realizing slightly later that he had brought along Bonnie Conneally, a cheerleader for our crosstown rivals, a girlfriend no one in my social group knew he had. The uneasy mixture of joy and disappointment stuck with me for days and, even now, I associate that uneasy brewing feeling in my stomach with that party.

Now I had another party I could associate it with. With each passing block, I grew more certain that Lindsay was covering for someone and might have done such a good job that she was going to take the fall for the whole thing. I didn't find it hard to believe that one of the other Girls would let her take the fall, but I struggled with her willingness to do it. Even as the maternal one, her instinct for self-preservation had to kick in at some point.

Unless she was partly culpable. Or considered herself so. Maybe she hadn't just disposed of the gun. Maybe she'd helped get it. Or helped plan the killing. Maybe this was as fully orchestrated as one of their campaigns, and just crafted to look like a spur-of-the-moment crime of passion to throw everyone off their trail.

So was it Wendy? They'd both pled allergy to the perfume, but Wendy's hadn't provoked much comment. Maybe hers was fake. It played out neatly in my head. Wendy, who thought she deserved to move ahead of the pack as the new company formed, confronted Garth about his decision to keep things the way they were. She'd forced him to drink for a charm, then lost control—striking him and then shooting him. She'd called Lindsay for help and Lindsay had literally cleaned up after her, which is how her blouse wound up covered in perfume and wrapped around the gun.

Or was it Tessa? Had she disposed of her bracelet because she was afraid it would tie her to the murder? Or was it one of the other Girls who had been so careful that she'd flown under my radar?

"You're detecting," Tricia chided softly.

"I can't help it."

"You did promise."

"Are you really interested in Wally Donovan?"

Tricia frowned. "Wally Donovan's intriguing, but you're evading."

"I just feel rotten. I think I pointed them in the wrong direction."

"Detective's remorse? It's not like you delivered her to the executioner. If the evidence doesn't support your theory, you know Detective Donovan will happily tell you so."

Tricia was right but that didn't give me the comfort it usually does. Anxiety was along for the ride.

I shook it free for a moment as we entered the ballroom at the Palace Hotel, which was like dropping down onto the surface of another planet. The air inside was dizzyingly thick with Success. The regal space had been draped in metallic fabric and lit like a techno-pop dance club, constantly spinning bold splashes of color across every surface, while a thudding bass line shot up from the floor, straight into your molars. A Plexiglas runway snaked among the tables in a circuitous route that was bound to delight the attendees and exhaust the models.

Above it all, twelve-foot-high banners on the walls proclaimed: SUCCESS. GET IT. TAKE IT. OWN IT. Each proclamation was paired with a picture of a devastatingly beautiful woman in an Emile-designed dress grabbing a bottle of the perfume with one hand and a devastatingly handsome man with the other, pulling the man by his tie or lapel or belt into a position of submission. Sex was moments from happening on each banner and the expressions on all the models let you know it was going to be steamy, spectacular, and sullen.

"I'm sold," Tricia said with a smile. "Where do I get mine?"

"The perfume, the man, or the clothes?"

"Yes."

"I'm just trying to imagine how big the swag bags have to be for you to get all three home."

"He can carry me, I'll carry the rest."

We made our way across the room, which was filling rapidly with a kaleidoscope of guests ranging from relatively conservative business types to outrageous fashion types and a little something for everyone in between. Cocktail hour was nearly over and the high pitch of forced laughter was a counterpoint to the thundering bass. Everyone moved grandly from point to point as though performing dance steps. It was like drifting through the opening number of a comic opera.

Our table was pretty central, at the corner where the runway turned back from its farthest projection into the room. It would certainly give us a unique perspective on Eileen and the other models as they swept by at shoulder level. Just as long as no one lost their shoe in my consommé, it would be entertaining.

Cassady and Aaron were at our table, still standing to better survey the crowd. Aaron was elegant in a Hugo Boss tuxedo and Cassady intensely classic in a black and white Chanel strapless. They made a stunning couple, both of them drawing approving glances from the people eddying by.

Cassady greeted us both with hugs and Aaron wryly kissed our hands. "Let me assault a waiter and get you both a glass of champagne," Cassady insisted. "Not that you can taste anything with that perfume drowning everything, but you can still feel the bubbles and the buzz."

I turned to help Cassady scan the room and found myself almost nose to nose with Lindsay. I gasped in spite of myself and she smiled. "Thank you," she said, thinking I was left breathless by her ruby red BCBG dress. "I love yours, too."

"Lindsay," was all I could say.

Tricia slid her arm through Lindsay's. "Such a great color on you."

I almost choked, but Tricia didn't bat an eye and didn't meet mine either. Instead, she skillfully turned Lindsay away from me, asking, "So point out all the most eligible bachelors in the room so I know on whom to focus my charms tonight."

Lindsay hesitated, glancing back toward me. "No offense, but I wanted to talk to Molly."

"It's okay," I said, grabbing my bag again. "Hang with them while I run to the ladies' room. We can talk when I get back."

Cassady stepped forward. "Which one of you came up with this wonderful campaign? I'm really impressed by its muscle."

Lindsay hesitated, debating whether to stray from the party line and give one person credit, and I walked away quickly, pretending I knew where the restrooms were, and thanking God for my friends.

But I wasn't more than a few steps away when a hand grabbed my arm with more than friendly force. Lindsay had shaken off Tricia and Cassady, no mean feat, and was determined to talk to me. "Let me go with you," she said, as though she were offering to accompany me behind enemy lines rather than to the restroom.

We all stopped, Lindsay caught between me and my friends. Tricia and Cassady looked as perplexed as I felt. I didn't want to break my promise to Kyle, but I felt awful leaving Lindsay hanging like this when I'd been questioning her guilt all afternoon. I remembered what Tricia had said about the value of dissembling, but this situation demanded the truth. "I can't talk to you," I said simply.

Lindsay released my arm slowly. "Why not?"

"Conflict of interest," Cassady explained.

"I don't understand."

"You will. Later," I said. When Detective Donovan comes to get you. But I couldn't say that or she'd run for the door. And that was an option I was reserving for myself.

"You should really go sit down, Lindsay," Tricia urged. "They're about to start the show."

The soundtrack had shifted to something more bluesy, full of synthesizer arpeggios. The Success theme song, I supposed. Up on the catwalk in black tie and tails and a fuschia shirt, Emile was yelling into a wireless mic, welcoming his friends and peers to his extravaganza. The crowd was applauding, whooping, or screaming, depending on their level of inebriation.

Lindsay wouldn't budge. "Why won't you talk to me?"

"Please go sit down," I said, glancing guiltily at the doors.

"What did I do?"

It was the question I'd been struggling with all afternoon and I was shocked at how disingenuous it sounded coming from her. "Nothing," I said flatly. "Right?"

The wounded expression on her face gave way to something more guarded. "What are you talking about?"

"She's not talking about anything," Tricia said, inserting herself between us. "We need to sit down and so do you." Tricia took me by the arm, blocking Lindsay's attempt to do the same, and walked me back toward our table.

If I'd just followed her and kept my mouth shut, it might have all been fine. But I couldn't do it. I had to say back over my shoulder, "Whoever you're covering for, I hope they're worth it."

"Molly!" Tricia hissed, yanking on my arm as though it were a cutoff valve.

"What are you talking about?" Lindsay repeated, sounding angry this time.

"Molly," Cassady warned.

"Tell me!" Lindsay insisted.

"Molly."

I have a short name, yet people are able to pack huge quantities of emotion into it. In this case, the fury Kyle compacted into two syllables was staggering and left me blinking in its wake.

"There's an explanation," I began.

"What a surprise," he said tautly. "We had a deal—"

Gwen Lincoln swooped down and cut him off. She looked terrific in her backless Trebask gown of emerald satin, as long as you ignored the fury on her face. "I can't imagine what's going on here, but you clearly haven't noticed that the program has begun. Now sit down, all of you, before I have you thrown out."

Kyle reflexively reached into his jacket pocket and pulled out his badge, showing it to Gwen and all the people seated nearby who were craning their necks and attempting to figure out what was happening in our unhappy little cluster.

The badge did not have the desired effect on Gwen. "Because you people haven't made my life miserable enough. Whatever it is you want, must you do it right here, right now?"

"I'm so very sorry, Gwen," Lindsay said, suddenly her steely self again, "this situation should never have gotten this far."

"Damn straight," Cassady muttered.

"I'll have security escort them out at once," Lindsay said.

The chorus of "What?"'s that answered her almost silenced Emile up on the catwalk, but Gwen hurriedly gestured for him to continue. He was bringing out the celebrity models, so most people were having no trouble ignoring us, but I worried that wasn't going to last much longer.

"If I leave, I'm taking you with me," Kyle told Lindsay.

"This isn't your case," she replied tartly.

"We all work in the same house," he explained, "and I'll help out a brother officer anytime I can."

Gwen looked at Lindsay with surprise. "What do they want with you?"

"It's a setup," Lindsay replied. "To make you look bad. To push you to say incriminating things about Garth's death." I had to hand it to her: these advertising babes are quick.

And she knew exactly what buttons to push with Gwen. Gwen sneered at Kyle. "How dare you come to my event and attempt to provoke me—"

"That's not what's happening," I protested.

"Stay out of this, Molly," Kyle said quietly.

"I'm getting security," Gwen announced and she hurried away.

"Who's her event planner? I would've been all over this," Tricia whispered.

"Why don't we talk outside?" Kyle suggested to Lindsay. I didn't know if Detective Donovan was outside, but it was reasonable to assume he would be soon.

"Where are you trying to take my wife?" Daniel strode up, his tuxedo jacket open, face flushed, looking for a fight. I hadn't even realized he was there.

Kyle showed Daniel his badge, then slid it back in his pocket. "This doesn't have to be unpleasant. Let's just take it outside." Kyle stepped forward to take Lindsay's arm and stepped straight into the wild right that Daniel threw, every ounce of his weight behind it. Kyle's head snapped back and he rocked off his feet. We all scrambled to help him—Tricia, Cassady, Aaron, and I—but we didn't react quickly enough. He fell with a loose, heavy thud, his head smacking the floor as he landed. He was out.

Above us, a radio DJ known for her sexually provocative talk was flashing some serious décolletage and streaming her own commentary about how hot she looked as she pranced by on the catwalk. She had the full attention of most of the room, but Kyle hitting the floor had garnered us increased interest from surrounding tables.

Two men and one woman stood and identified themselves as doctors. They, Aaron, Cassady, and Tricia immediately attended to Kyle, but I whirled on Daniel. "You son of a bitch."

Daniel wavered a moment, weighing the full impact of what he'd done by assaulting a police detective and then he took off. Sprinted away.

"Daniel!" Lindsay screamed after him, her voice so full of betrayal it ran through me like an electric current.

"Lindsay. Are you covering for Daniel?"

She caught herself on the back of a chair, but her knees still began to buckle as the color drained from her face. Her mouth worked, but no sound came out. So I took off after Daniel.

I waitressed one miserable summer in college and the slaloming between tables, dodging people and chairs and napkins on the ground, came back to me like riding a bike. Daniel headed toward the kitchen and I relished the thought of grabbing him and running him through the meat grinder, assuming they had one, but he made a sudden hard left toward the entrance to the backstage area where all the models, real and otherwise, were getting ready.

I would've expected the dozens of seminude women to scream or at least protest as Daniel raced through their midst, but most were pretty blasé about it. It wasn't until they realized I was chasing him and that Lindsay was now chasing me that they began to perk up. A few screamed, but mainly they covered themselves, cleared out of the way, and watched with interest. A stage manager ran over, headset flipped up, to hush them all while grabbing the next model and throwing her in line.

But no one made a move to stop Daniel. And the only person who tried to stop me was Eileen, swathed in impossible layers of teal tulle and hot pink silk, who attempted to stand in my path as I raced by her. "Molly Forrester, what the hell—"

I cut around her at the last possible second, my sights still on Daniel. "Stop him!" I yelled, trying to get someone to respond, but all they did was look in his direction. I raced on as he headed toward a set of double doors that led back into the service corridors of the hotel. Suddenly, I was skating, sliding on someone's silk chemise that had fallen on the floor. I pinwheeled madly, trying to keep my balance, and while I managed to stay upright, just barely, it slowed me sufficiently for Lindsay to catch up with me.

She grabbed me by the hair, but I twisted free. She clawed at me as I tried to go after Daniel and I turned around and smacked her across the face. She gasped as did several of the models. A few of them clapped.

"You don't understand," she wailed.

"Damn straight," I snapped, then turned back around to go after Daniel, who threw himself against the handles of the double door. Alarms whooped and emergency lights flashed. The stage manager let loose a piercing profanity and some of the models screeched and put their hands over their ears. The music paused out front for just a moment, then the stage manager jammed his headset back down, started barking into it, and grabbed Eileen and dragged her off for her entrance.

The music started up again. Daniel spun off the double doors, hugging the wall, trying to stay as far away from me as possible, while I clambered over chairs, clothes, and models to get to him. His path was blocked by a huge mound of equipment cases and he had no choice but to circle back around and come my way. I advanced on him, praying he didn't have a weapon and reassuring myself that he would have used it by now if he did.

He was cornered. I wasn't sure what I was going to do with him, but I had him trapped, his back against the catwalk. "Daniel, they've tested the gun. They've got you," I said, hoping he'd see the futility of attempting to flee.

"It's her gun." He pointed over my shoulder at Lindsay. I knew she was coming up behind me, but I didn't dare take my eyes off him to see exactly where she was.

"Daniel!" she screamed again.

"Shut up!" he screamed back and I threw myself at him, trying to be as aerodynamic as possible, but he moved too quickly and as I hit the floor, he climbed up onto the catwalk. Ignoring the pain in all the impact points and the possible damage to my dress, I scrambled up, kicked off my shoes, and climbed up after him, dodging the stage manager and following Daniel out into the blazing light of the ballroom.

"Molly!" Tricia screamed from somewhere out on the floor, but the lights were blinding and it was hard to see. I had to squint to see Daniel backing down the catwalk in front of me, gauging his possibilities for escape. People gasped and called out, rising from their seats. Emile asked everyone to remain calm, but that made everyone more nervous. I could sense the little flames of panic igniting all over the room.

Daniel suddenly stooped and grabbed a corkscrew out of a waiter's hand, then grabbed the model on the runway beside him and put the point to her neck. It was Eileen. She glared at me, her fury overriding her fear. "This is your fault, Molly Forrester!"

Daniel slid his hand up to cover Eileen's mouth and she had the good sense not to struggle with him. "Please let her go, Daniel," I asked. He shook his head.

"Please, Daniel," Lindsay said, drawing up even with me. I glanced at her briefly, but she was focused on her husband. She wasn't trying to take me out anymore, she wanted to help me bring him in.

He shook his head again, ferociously this time. "It was supposed to work."

"I know, honey, I know," she said, bitterness leaking into her voice.

"I didn't want to kill him."

A collective gasp rose from the crowd and there was a flurry of activity at every table. At least half the guests were taking out their cell phones to take pictures of what was going to happen next.

And what happened was that Eileen, impatient with her restraint and the interruption of her moment in the spotlight, bit Daniel's fingers as hard as she could. He screamed in pain and brought the corkscrew down like a knife, determined to return the favor. And I, acting out of instinct and not out of love for Eileen, tried my flying tackle again, with somewhat better success. I say "somewhat," because I managed to knock Daniel away from her and jar the corkscrew from his hand, but my trajectory was such that I took Eileen with us on our trip off the catwalk and onto the floor, breaking her arm and dislocating Daniel's knee. I rolled away with no injuries, other than those to my pride, my career, and my relationship.

I'd love to be remembered as a knockout, but this wasn't exactly what I'd had in mind.

Twenty

I USED TO THINK I was willing to do anything for love. Climb a mountain, write a sonnet, give up a throne. Then I discovered what some people actually will do in the name of love—get breast implants, wreck marriages, commit murder. So I decided that, while I like to think of myself as a true romantic, my willingness to make an eternal declaration of passion probably falls somewhere between getting a tattoo and getting a gym membership. I'll leave the messier stuff to other people. And do my best to learn while cleaning up after them.

Two days later, still nursing my bruised bones and ego, I tried to do some cleaning up, but Kyle wasn't interested. He'd come up with a plan of his own and he was going to see it through. I'd tried to dissuade him, but he's about the only human being on earth more stubborn than I am.

Even as Eileen, Daniel, and I flew off the catwalk, the police were bombarded with calls as people stopped taking pictures with their phones and started calling 911. Detective Donovan, in his tuxedo, arrived just ahead of the massive uniformed response. He thought he was coming late to the party with the bombshell news that the gun was registered to Daniel's secretary, who had reported it stolen a week before the murder. He found Kyle, groggy but conscious, handcuffing Daniel as the glitterati fled the ballroom.

Not that Daniel was about to go anywhere until the paramedics reset his knee. Kyle and Detective Donovan had a brief conversation with Daniel that included reading him his rights while waiting for the paramedics to arrive. Meanwhile, Tricia and Cassady picked me up off the floor and placed me at a table where Lindsay was crying quietly but continuously. Emile had already swept Eileen up into his arms and spirited her away to another table where everyone else from *Zeitgeist* was tending to her.

"This is all my fault," Lindsay sobbed as they eased me into the chair next to her.

Cassady sucked air between her teeth. "You have the right to counsel, honey, and I'd be embracing it pretty tightly if I were you."

"And you didn't kill Garth, so it's not your fault," I said, earning a dark look from Cassady.

"No, I didn't. Daniel did," Lindsay affirmed.

"Detective Donovan!" Tricia called, motioning for him to join us quickly. We all waited anxiously, wanting Lindsay to continue but not wanting to push her and perhaps make her shut up.

"Garth wouldn't sleep with me, so Daniel killed him," she said with jaw-dropping matter-of-factness.

"You have to run that one by me again," I said as both Tricia and Cassady grasped my shoulders so hard that I was going to have welts and permanently improved posture.

"They were all getting ahead by sleeping with the bastard. I wanted my chance. But he wouldn't sleep with me because I'm married."

Aaron appeared with a pitcher of water and a couple of goblets he'd procured from another table. He froze as he picked up Lindsay's conversation, until Cassady nudged him gently. She helped him pour water for all of us, but only Lindsay took her glass. We all waited while she took a drink; I know I was holding my breath and I'm pretty sure everyone else was, too.

"Daniel and I talked about it, examined the pros and cons. It seemed the only thing to do to maintain a competitive edge was . . . compete. So I let Garth know I was interested. And—he rejected me." She put her water goblet down with such force that the bowl snapped off the stem. Tricia took the pieces from her quickly, before she could hurt herself.

"Then why did Daniel shoot him?" I asked, worried that I knew the answer.

"Because he loves me," she said with forceful bitterness. "Because he wants to see me happy. Fulfilled. Successful. And it seemed like no matter what I was trying to do—get ahead at my job, get pregnant—Garth was blocking my path."

"How was Garth keeping you from getting pregnant?" Tricia asked with gentle bewilderment.

"We need help. IVF. And our salaries just aren't enough. But how could I get a raise when Garth wouldn't see me on the same level as the rest of them?"

"So you were going to sleep with your boss to get a raise," Cassady said, careful to clarify and not question.

"To have a baby. Save my marriage. Oh, God," she exclaimed. "You don't get it, do you? Garth wouldn't even give me the chance. That's all Daniel went to ask for. A chance. We'd turned ourselves inside out, looked at this a million different ways, and it seemed like the only option we hadn't tried. We convinced ourselves we could be okay with it as long as it got us where we wanted to be."

Lindsay took a deep, shuddering breath. "But Garth said no. To me. Damn him! I'm every bit as good as the rest of them. Maybe even better. At anything. At everything. But he said no." Her body shrank as tears squeezed through her tightly clenched eyelids, her breath catching raggedly. "It was okay to have me run a campaign or train one of those other—" She stopped as more tears spilled out. "But not to have me for . . ." Her face went slack and she let the last of the tears drop. "Because he didn't want me, we couldn't have anything we wanted."

I was thinking about reaching out to pat her hand, shake her, do something, when Lindsay suddenly jerked upright and looked at everyone with a smile that beamed with pride. "I think that hurt Daniel more than losing our chance for a baby. Garth turning me down."

This version of "Stand By Your Man" would have taken even Tammy Wynette's breath away. All we could do was stare at her in silence. I tried to imagine Daniel seeing himself in the role of defender as he marched into the hotel room and demanded that Garth sleep with his wife.

Detective Donovan joined us then. "Mrs. Franklin, your husband's being taken to the hospital; my partner's going to ride along with him. I thought you and I could have a chat."

Lindsay sniffed hard and I handed her a dinner napkin. "Pull up a seat, Detective Donovan, I was just telling everyone what happened," Lindsay said, gesturing imperiously to a chair.

"It would be more appropriate—" Detective Donovan began.

"I owe my friend an explanation," Lindsay said, moving the imperious gesture to me.

"No, you don't," I said, mindful of Cassady and Detective Donovan wanting to upholding the law, much as I wanted to hear the rest of the story.

"Daniel has his pride," Lindsay continued, oblivious to our concerns. "Maybe too much. You can't imagine what it took for him to go see Garth and explain our situation. He never intended to hurt Garth. He just wanted to make an impression on him, make sure Garth knew how serious we were about being willing to do anything . . ." She sniffed again, wiping her eyes and nose with the napkin.

"But Garth laughed at him," Lindsay resumed, her jaw tightening. "Daniel can't stand it when people laugh at him. So Daniel took out the gun and made Garth drink for his charm. But Garth kept laughing. That's when Daniel hit him—while he had my charm in his mouth. Which is why I didn't take it back to Tiffany to get it fixed. I was afraid they'd be able to tell there'd been blood on it. But after

Daniel broke Garth's tooth, Garth got really angry. They started fighting. And Daniel shot him."

"What about the blouse and the perfume?" Detective Donovan, the only one who wasn't speechless, asked.

"Daniel came home and started tearing apart my closet, telling me I couldn't go back there, couldn't work there anymore, because they didn't respect me. He took the sample bottle of Success and poured it all over my favorite blouse and told me how they were all pissing on me and I shouldn't have to take that, I was better than that." Her voice caught momentarily, but she took a deep breath and continued. "Then he told me what he'd done. And I told him I'd clean up the mess."

Lindsay looked at me expectantly and all I could say was, "Thank you for telling me."

"I enjoyed our dinner together. Daniel really liked your boyfriend," she said.

At first I thought it was a non sequitur, but then I understood she was expressing her regret for how things had turned out. I nodded and said, "Me, too."

Detective Donovan flipped his notebook closed. "Molly, the paramedics took Kyle, too. St. Luke's."

I looked over guiltily, not having seen him leave, as Cassady answered him. "Thank you, Detective. We'll get her there."

Detective Donovan held his hand out to Lindsay. "We should go now." She took his hand and stood up. We all stood, out of some instinctive etiquette, and watched Detective Donovan escort her out, past the billowing banners of women seducing Success. Or was it the other way around?

"You're barefoot," Cassady pointed out.

I looked down. I'd forgotten I'd kicked my shoes off in my final effort to catch up with Daniel. "Never leave a man behind," I said, summoning my resolve and leading them backstage. Fortunately, my shoes were pretty much where I'd left them. Tricia steadied me while I slid them back on. As I straightened up, I caught Aaron watching me with such a purely puzzled expression that I had to smile. "We know how to party, don't we, Aaron?"

"The partying is exceptional. The stopping needs a little work," he said, earning another smile for frankness.

"Okay, St. Luke's it is," I said. "And let's hope different nurses are on duty."

This time, Tricia, Cassady, and Aaron waited outside while I went into the E.R. examining room. Kyle was sitting on the side of the gurney, looking tired and miserable, while a freshly starched doctor tried to get him to lie back down. "You're not going anywhere," the doctor said.

"I can't take him home?" I asked.

The doctor looked at me in surprise. "You the girlfriend?"

"Yes."

The doctor looked back at Kyle. "You said she wasn't coming for you."

I tried not to wince while Kyle said, "I said I didn't know when she was coming for me."

The doctor's expression made it clear he didn't think he'd heard Kyle wrong the first time, but he wasn't going to argue the point. Instead, he recited discharge orders to me: to wake him periodically, and bring him back immediately if he showed signs of lethargy, disorientation, or nausea. "Sounds like a fun night," I said as cheerily as possible.

Kyle was gracious to Cassady, Tricia, and Aaron, but everyone knew he needed to get home. I urged them not to let their fancy duds go to waste as we got into a cab and headed back to my apartment.

"So it was the dweeb we had dinner with," Kyle said after several blocks, just at the point where I thought he wasn't going to say anything at all. "Because he tried to pimp his wife and it didn't work. What the hell's wrong with people?"

"You didn't like him. You've got good instincts," I said.

"If I had good instincts, I wouldn't have wound up on the floor," he said. "Damn sucker punch."

I stroked his hair and he caught my hand, not pushing it away, but holding it tight against his head, as though he were leaning into it. Worried I was hurting him, I tried to pull my hand away, but he wouldn't let me. He held it there until the cab pulled up in front of my building.

I set the alarm clock so we'd wake up every two hours, but I wound up not needing it. I couldn't sleep. I lay beside him for a long time, watching him breathe, studying his profile in the twilight of the bedroom. He woke up quickly at each alarm, but went back to sleep just as quickly. After a while, I sat up and pretended to read, but I didn't absorb anything.

I couldn't stop thinking about the empire Garth had created, one where people had stopped valuing themselves for their talents, their individuality, and started measuring themselves by their appeal to one megalomaniacal tyrant. In the scramble for success, they'd lost their bearings. No wonder some of them had crashed. It wasn't just Lindsay and Daniel. Look at the knots Wendy had tied herself in, or Gwen and Ronnie trying to revive an old affair to convince themselves they could create something special in the rest of their lives. And these were the people who told the rest of us what we were supposed to want out of life.

Come morning, the gala was inescapable. Between the press that had been covering the event, Emile's videographers, and all the camera phones, every outlet had pictures of some part of the melee. As a generally out-of-focus blur, I made out slightly better in the pictures than Eileen, who was generally caught in mid-fall with the expression of a small child whose large ice cream cone has just been snatched away by the neighbor's German shepherd.

She called bright and early, as she adores to do, to inform me that Emile was fashioning sleeves to slide over the cast she'd be wearing on her forearm for the next month and to ask me when my article would be ready.

"I'm still sorting things out, Eileen," I said. "Can't we talk about this later?"

"Don't you get temperamental on me. Any other editor would fire a writer for doing what you did."

"Are you talking about solving the case or saving your life?"

"I'm talking about assaulting me in front of hundreds of my dearest friends."

There were so many things wrong with that sentence, I barely knew where to begin, so I opted for the easy out. "I'm sorry about that part."

"And the other part is why you still have a job. Get to work," she snarled and hung up. Expecting a thank you was too much, I knew, but a girl can hope.

As I put down the phone, I saw that Kyle was awake and looking at me intensely. "Hey, did the phone wake you?"

"Maybe. That Eileen?"

"Yeah," I said, suddenly self-conscious of my talk of breaking cases and saving lives. "Just the usual flinging of hyperbole. How do you feel?"

He didn't answer for a moment, then said, "I'll be fine."

He was quiet while we made breakfast, while we ate, and when the first bouquet of flowers arrived. It was a huge spray of orchids and other exotics and the card read: *Thank you, Gwen Lincoln.* The second bouquet, ridiculously large and rich with roses, was from The Publisher. The card read: *Looking forward to the article.* The third bouquet was from Peter: *Can't think of anyone I'd rather have scoop me.*

Kyle looked at the bouquets for a long time—couldn't avoid it, actually, since they consumed half the living room—and then said, "Congratulations. You were right."

"I wasn't. I didn't figure out it was Daniel until the last second."

"You knew it wasn't Gwen and you stuck to your guns. Even when I told you to stop."

"I'm sorry about that."

"You shouldn't be. And I shouldn't put you in a position where you feel you should be."

"You don't."

"Yes, I do. I'm gonna take a shower." He walked out of the room before I could stop him.

I paced outside the bathroom for two full minutes, then took the plunge, stripping off my nightshirt and getting in the shower with him. It was a small shower and the physics of our both being in there would have amused Aaron, but I couldn't wait another moment to wrap my arms around Kyle, to kiss him, to meld myself with him, and wash away his agitation.

The rest of the day went well. We stopped answering the phone, watched old movies, listened to music, and lost ourselves in each other. It was wonderful to let everything else fall away. Until he said, late that night, "This works so well. Too bad there's a world out there."

I felt like someone was choking the air out of me. "But it's you and me against that world, right?" I managed.

"I love you, Molly," he answered.

"I love you, too."

"Then we better figure out how to fix this."

I could taste the tears in my throat before I felt them in my eyes. "Fix what?"

"You know what," he said, gently and sincerely. "We both love what we do and we're both good at it. But if it's gonna have us crashing into each other all the time . . ."

"We'll figure something out."

He nodded. "Yeah, I know we will. Sooner or later."

I didn't sleep much more that night, worried that I'd wake up and he'd be gone. But he was there in the morning. He didn't start pulling his stuff together until after breakfast.

"You don't have to leave," I told him.

"A little perspective would be good for both of us."

"No, I need you," I protested.

He slid his hand up under my hair and pulled me to him. "It's gonna be all right," he whispered. "I'll call you." He kissed me with such tenderness that it hurt, picked up his duffel bag, and left.

I stared at the closed front door for a long time. And thought about Lindsay and Daniel. They'd destroyed their relationship, their lives in their desperation to build what they saw as the perfect future. Willing to do anything, they'd lost everything instead. How much sacrifice should love demand? Wasn't there a way to have passion and balance? Does there have to be a choice between who we love and what we love to do?

I'd gone through two boxes of Kleenex by the time Tricia and Cassady arrived. Cassady quickly pointed out that Kyle had not returned my key and Tricia reasoned that a lesser man would have told me I needed to find a different job if we were going to stay together. Some solace, but not enough to get rid of the debilitating ache in my chest.

Cassady insisted that brunch, with many mimosas, was the only sane course of action and they dragged me to the bedroom to persuade me into appropriate attire. "Where's Aaron?" I asked as Cassady presented me with my favorite JCrew white blouse.

"He had atoms to split or some such thing, so I told him I'd talk to him later."

"And you never got to spend any time with Detective Donovan," I said to Tricia as she handed me my black slacks.

"I think that was adrenaline, not attraction. Moving on," she said brightly.

"I'm not, am I? Moving on, I mean?"

"Not if the man's as smart as we've always given him credit for being," Cassady said.

Tricia swept my black Belle sandals out of the closet. "It's the bumps in the road that make the trip interesting."

Cassady laughed. "Which maiden aunt taught you that?"

Tricia frowned. "Aunt Jessica. And I've always thought it was quite astute."

"It belongs on an embroidered pillow, underneath a Persian cat that eats shrimp twice a day." Cassady threw her arm around Tricia's shoulders and glanced over at me. "I don't know about taking any advice from this one, but not to worry, I'll get you through this."

"We both will," Tricia said, her arm around Cassady's waist.

"Whether I like it or not, right?" I said. They laughed appreciatively and I smiled a bit, reassured by knowing that, with faith in the people you love, you can get through anything. At least, that's the hope.

KEEP READING FOR AN EXCERPT FROM
SHERYL J. ANDERSON'S NEXT MYSTERY

Killer Riff

COMING SOON IN HARDCOVER FROM
ST. MARTIN'S MINOTAUR

1

"I CAN'T BALANCE MY DIET, so how am I supposed to balance my life?"

Tricia nodded sympathetically. "Everything you've been hoping for. For it to all happen at the same time—it's just criminal!"

Coming from anyone else—in fact, coming from my other best friend, who was also at the table—it would have sounded at the very least snarky. More probably, it would have sounded like a righteous putdown. But coming from Tricia Vincent, it was a sincere and heartfelt expression of how Fate can take something that should be glorious and turn it into a major kick in the teeth.

Cassady Lynch pushed a glass of champagne across the table to me. "I thought we were here to celebrate."

"That was before I had two things to be happy about." Two things that clashed with each other with all the vigor of freight trains colliding at top speed. On the one hand, I had the professional promotion I'd been dreaming of. On the other, the romantic redemption I'd been yearning for. But since professional issues were responsible for derailing the romance to begin with, I felt smacked by an Olympian dose of irony, with no clear vision of how—or if—I could make this work.

Things had been much more promising earlier in the afternoon as I'd stood nervously in my editor's office, listening to her proclaim, "Molly, I'm going to make you happy and it just kills me."

Gotta give the boss lady this: You always know where you stand with her. Usually, that place is akin to the crumbling lip of a rumbling volcano, but there's never any question it's exactly where Eileen wants you to be. So she gets points for honesty, if nothing else. The problem is, from that point, it can be pretty tricky to see where she's headed and, even though I should know better by now, I always try to figure that out. For the most part, it's an exercise in futility, but it's the only regular exercise I get.

On this particular occasion, looking ahead was especially tempting because Henry Kwon was somehow part of the equation. He was slouched on the couch in Eileen's office. I couldn't tell if that was an expression of how relaxed he was about what was happening or about how impossible it is to sit properly on that ridiculously unyielding piece of furniture. Even so, he looked great—he always looks great—and he was smiling. What could that mean? I looked him in the eye and his smile grew.

Having a handsome man smile at you is rarely a bad thing. But this particular handsome man was also the associate publisher of our magazine, so the potential reasons for his smile were all the more intriguing. And the fact that he was flat-out gorgeous didn't hurt. Especially since I had been painfully single for seven and a half weeks and deeply missed having someone gorgeous smile at me.

Pushing that distraction from my mind, I did my best to concentrate on decoding what Eileen and Henry were up to. Even though I've been out of school more years than I care to admit, I still feel like I've been summoned to the principal's office when I have to go into Eileen's lair. So, even though Eileen was suspiciously proclaiming that she was going to make me happy, my perpetually fluctuating self-worth and guilty conscience were conspiring to make me nervous. That annoyed me because I don't like letting Eileen get to me. I particularly didn't want Henry to think of me as anything but cool and controlled.

I tried to dismiss that feeling that I'd done something wrong and focus on the positive sheen to Henry's smile. Eileen was too savvy to have pulled him into something political between the two of us, so this had to be substantial. It had to be about something pretty darn good, too, if even Eileen was forced to admit it would make me happy. Were they moving my advice column to a different position in the magazine? Expanding it? Or was I being traded to another magazine for a copy editor and an assistant to be named later?

"The Publisher was very impressed with the article you wrote about Garth Henderson's murder," Henry said smoothly.

I nodded, remembering the huge bouquet of flowers The Publisher had sent me after I'd helped nab Garth's killer. Although I had wondered if part of the grandness of the arrangement was because I'd sent Eileen flying across a densely populated hotel ballroom in the process. The Publisher, after all, is known for his sense of humor. "I appreciated the flowers very much," I said.

Eileen grimaced as though bracing herself to taste something foul. "So he wants you to do it again."

It took me a moment. "A follow-up? An article on the trial?"

"No," Henry said, "not that specific. But we do want you to focus on feature articles from now on."

I actually considered fainting. Millions of microscopic helium balloons launched themselves in my head, trying to push off the top of my skull, and my hands tingled and sweated simultaneously.

"Features?" I repeated, knowing it didn't sound bright, but that it beat standing there gaping in silence.

"We've been discussing new ways to increase the profile of the magazine and including more substantial editorial content is absolutely key. The investigative articles you've done are exactly the kind of thing we're looking for. So we want that to be your new focus and we'll use it as a springboard for further growth of the entire publication." Henry's smile grew. "No pressure."

And no pressure just because this was what I'd always wanted, because this was a dream coming true, because I knew I could really make something of this break.

"Thank you," I said, wishing I could be eloquent and charming, but so completely caught by surprise that two words were all I felt able to string together. I'd been working toward this for such a long time, trying to move into feature writing, grabbing chances when they came my way and proving myself, but never getting the bump. In the last few weeks, I'd actually been quietly checking out opportunities at other magazines because I figured I was never going to be released from my existence as an advice columnist while I was working for Eileen. She's not the sort to recognize and nurture potential; she's more the crush-or-curry school of management, specializing in picking favorites, usually attractive young men, and whipping everyone else with delight and regularity.

Small wonder it was killing her to give me this break. Or, more correctly, to sit there and watch Henry give it to me and not be able to do anything about it but scowl. I knew part of her unhappiness was because of her aforementioned aversion to making me happy, but there was more at stake here, too. She'd been brought in to "put teeth" in the magazine. If The Publisher and Henry felt that wasn't happening fast enough and that they had to get involved in the process, perhaps Eileen was spending some time standing on that volcano lip herself.

"There is a catch," she said with a crinkle of her little nose that was sharp enough to burst my bubble. I kept smiling. How bad could the catch be if it was part of becoming a feature writer?

Henry frowned, one of those polite frowns bosses use to soften a blow. My stomach lurched, like the feeling you get on the first dip on the roller coaster, the one that's the tease for that huge first drop. "This isn't my usual style," Henry explained, "but we have your first subject, already approved by The Publisher and Eileen."

My breath came back with a happy puff. "That's fine," I said, immediately feeling better because I couldn't imagine an article they'd come up with that I wouldn't be willing to write.

"And he's dead, just the way you like them. Sadly for you, though, he got there all on his own. No conspiracy, no mystery. Nothing to solve, just an article to write," Eileen said with enough precision that I knew I was being warned as much as I was being informed.

I understood why she was concerned, given my track record of digging into a story where everyone thought there were no unanswered questions and winding up in the middle of a homicide investigation. She didn't approve, even though I always met my other deadlines; had I fallen on my face with one story, I have no doubt she would have taken great delight in sending me packing. But I'd worked hard and been fortunate, other than losing my boyfriend. Now, here at last, was the step up I had been striving for the whole time. Whoever this person had been, I would dive in and do a great article to prove The Publisher's faith in me—and Eileen's inability to erode it—were all for the best.

"It's not all about him," Henry said, cutting a look at Eileen. They'd already discussed this and not altogether happily. I wondered which was upsetting her more, the choice of subject or my promotion. Henry continued, "It's about his daughter keeping his legacy, that sort of angle. Right?"

Eileen gave him the kind of smile you give the dentist after he's shoved the x-ray film as far back in your mouth as it will go. "Right."

Henry's marvelously dark eyes swung back to me. "My sister went to college with Olivia Elliott. Russell Elliott's daughter."

I nodded in recognition. Russell Elliott, a renowned rock-and-roll producer who had started out as the manager of one of my favorite bands, had died three weeks before, alone in his Riverside Drive apartment with music on the stereo and a highball glass in his hand. While the print media politely conveyed the medical examiner's finding that it was an accidental overdose of prescription medication mixed with alcohol, the Internet and tabloids feasted on the similarities between Russell's death and that of the lead singer of the aforementioned band. Message boards blazed with theories about suicide, old affairs, demons from the past, and other uncomfortable things it has to be tough to hear when you're mourning the loss of your father.

Olivia had attempted to drown out the rumors by throwing a monumental post-funeral bash that had been attended by a blinding array of rock royalty. It hadn't quelled the loose talk, but it had put a pretty gloss on it; people were whispering now instead of proclaiming.

"As you can imagine, she's pretty shattered. She's also unhappy with what's been written about her dad since he died. And I get her point. I don't know how familiar you are with Russell's work—"

"I had a poster of Subject to Change on my bedroom wall in high school," I admitted.

Henry laughed in understanding. "I spent my entire junior year trying to get my hair to look like Micah's."

Micah Crowley had been the dark, brooding, and intensely sexy lead singer of Subject to Change Without Notice, a blues-based rock band that ripped through the chatter of the hair bands in the late '80s, helping pave the way for grunge and roots rock. Russell Elliott had been Micah's best friend in college and became the band's manager. Depending on which stories you believe, Russell was largely to thank for guiding the band's artistic development, or Russell was mainly responsible for the infamous fights with producers, session musicians, and record executives, which were part of the band's history. Toward the end, Russell had begun producing the albums; again, either because he was shaping and protecting their vision or because no one else wanted to put up with the drama. But no matter how it was told, the story ended the same way: Micah Crowley overdosed in 1997 and the band fell apart.

After Micah's death, Russell had become guardian of both the band's music and Micah's family. He'd also developed a solid reputation as an innovative producer who didn't throw temper tantrums any more—either because he'd cleaned up his act or because it had actually been Micah throwing them—who'd launched several successful acts in the last couple of years on his own label. His most recent star was Jordan Crowley, one of Micah's sons.

"Are you sure the poster wasn't on your ceiling?" Eileen said with a sniff in my direction.

"Did you like them or were you too old for such foolishness by then?" Henry asked her. My admiration for him doubled on the spot as she blinked slowly, searching for a response.

"I'm more classically oriented," she replied. I wanted to ask if she meant Beethoven or disco, but decided not to push my luck in the middle of such a crucial conversation.

"I'm glad you bring a familiarity with the band to the piece," Henry continued to me. "Thing is, Olivia feels all the press surrounding her dad's death has been about how he took care of Claire and Adam, and now Jordan, after Micah's death. That he's viewed as part of Micah's legend, so his own larger contributions to the music industry have gotten short shrift. My sister mentioned it to me in passing, but I see an intriguing story there. And coming from the daughter's point of view, it's perfect for *Zeitgeist*. And for your first assignment as a full-time feature writer."

Squealing with glee on the inside, I strove to be polished and professional on the outside. "Thank you, Henry. Eileen. I can't tell you how much I appreciate this opportunity," I said.

"Personally, I think it's overdue," Henry said, standing. Eileen glared at him so hard it made her roots show, but he ignored her. "Morgan in legal will talk to you about the new contract, pay structure, all that." I'd been so thrilled about getting my dream job that I hadn't even thought about it meaning a raise, too. *Suh-weet*. He held out a business card. "Here are Olivia's numbers. She's expecting your call, keep me apprised."

We had a brief diploma-exchange tangle as I tried to both take the card and shake his hand, but he smiled at the right moment and made me feel much calmer. "Thank you," I said, looking him right in the eye and trying to convey my gratitude and excitement. "Sadly, words escape me."

Henry laughed warmly. "Just make sure they're back by deadline. Congratulations, Molly." He nodded at Eileen. "Have fun replacement shopping."

I'd intended to follow him out of the office, but that pulled me up short. "Replacement shopping?"

Henry paused in the doorway. "Your column. We're going to keep you too busy for you to stay with it."

I was surprised by the sharpness of the sting as the news pierced my spinning brain. Of course I had to give up my column. That was a good thing. I'd been eager to move beyond dispensing advice to the distraught, obsessive, and lovelorn for a long time. Still, I found myself feeling possessive and even a little sad. I'd created "You Can Tell Me," and it was odd to think of handing it over to some unknown party. Unless they'd already figured that part out. "Do you have someone in mind?"

Henry shook his head, gesturing to Eileen. She pursed her lips and turned to me. "I'm still absorbing this happy news, so I haven't considered its repercussions."

"I'd like to open it up to magazine staffers, if you think that's feasible," Henry suggested. "We should be doing more promoting from within."

Eileen's lips unpursed and curled into a smile. "Oh, yes. Let's make it a contest. Our own little *American Idol*. Post some letters and have people answer them. Best answer gets the job."

Henry wasn't going to let her get away with being sarcastic. He opened his arms in a grand gesture. "I love it. Great idea."

Eileen's nostrils flared. "You're not serious. Can you

imagine the dreck they'll produce?" She wiggled her French-tipped fingers in the direction of the bull pen outside her office door, where most of the junior editorial staff sat. "Who could we even trust to screen the responses?"

"No one but you," Henry replied. I wasn't sure which was more entertaining: Eileen's discomfort or Henry's pleasure in it. This was a whole new take on Eileen's position in the organization and I found it fascinating.

"It's Molly's column," she protested with the annoyance of a big sister who's been asked to baby-sit on a Friday night.

"So you and Molly can screen them together, then the three of us will sit down and make the final selection. How's that sound?"

"Great," I said quickly.

Eileen smiled jaggedly. "I look forward to it."

"It'll be a party," Henry said with a smile and a wink as he walked out of the office.

I started to follow him, but Eileen had another idea. "Molly," she said with a thick coating of ice.

I turned around and launched a preemptive attack. "Eileen, I really can't begin to tell you how much I appreciate this. I know we've had our differences, but I also know that you're going to be very pleased by what I bring to the magazine from this new vantage point."

Startled, Eileen took a moment before responding. "Isn't that sweet. I just want to make sure we understand each other."

"About?"

"About how this really changes nothing."

"Except what I'm doing."

"Yes, but you're still doing it for me."

She rose to walk around her desk and get closer to me. It wasn't going to lead to a congratulatory hug, I knew that much. For a flickering moment, I had thought this promotion might lead to a better relationship with my boss because I'd be doing what I was supposed to be doing, not pushing to do something more. But I could tell by the way her petite shoulders squared as she advanced on me that this was only going to fan the flames. She'd been working hard to keep me in my place, wherever she perceived it to be, but now Henry had lifted me out of it. Was her new hobby going to become trying to trip me up so Henry would withdraw the promotion? It sounded paranoid, but working for Eileen for any extended period brings that out in people.

"I'm sure you're going to do good work. And I simply won't publish it if it isn't," she said as she stopped in front of me. "Just remember, The Publisher giveth but the editor taketh away."

"That won't be necessary," I assured her. I thought about hugging her just to see what she'd do, but decided not to start off my new gig by pushing my luck. Besides, I was pretty sure her head would explode and that wouldn't be pleasant for anyone.

Eileen tilted her head to the side, like a cat deciding whether to play with a mouse or eat it. With an exasperated sigh, she said, "Write a sample question for your column and give it to me. I'll write a memo to the staff about the process of being named your heir."

"Thank you," I said, backing toward the door.

Her lips twitched in the vicinity of a smile. "I had no idea you and Henry were so close."

"We're not," I said, hoping that she wasn't suggesting what I was sure she was suggesting.

"So this brilliant idea leapt into his head all by itself."

"You'd have to ask him," I said, certain she already had and hoping she'd been more graceful with him than she was being with me.

"Fine. Be coy, even though it doesn't suit you."

"Eileen," I ventured, emboldened by the glorious news, "maybe he just thinks I'm a good writer."

"Of course, how silly of me," she oozed. "Merit."

"Isn't that how you got your job?" I asked.

I meant it as a point of perspective, but I could tell it struck a deep and dissonant chord. Eileen's carefully plucked eyebrows knotted together and she pointed to her office door. "Weren't you leaving?"

I hustled out the door and into the office bull pen, puzzling over what key point of Eileen's past I had tripped over as her door slammed behind me.

"That went well."

Skyler Christopher was Eileen's current assistant, a job that turns over so often there should be a turnstile by the desk. A sloe-eyed brunette given to tight sweaters and tighter skirts, she'd been a startling choice, given Eileen's track record of selecting gay men and dowdy women to guard her office door. Then the grapevine reported her grandparents were pals of The Publisher. Eileen doesn't like anyone sharing her spotlight, but she also doesn't miss a chance to be political. Skyler struck me as too smart to last long in her current position, but she was fun to have around in the meantime.

"She's very happy for me," I said.

"I can tell. Congratulations, by the way."

"Thanks."

"So who's going to get your column?" She said it casually, her eyes never leaving her monitor, but I could hear the steely purpose under the question. Three weeks on the job and already looking for her next move. Who could blame her?

"Whoever writes the best response to a sample question. Unlock that inner Ann Landers and go for it," I said and her eyes swung up to meet mine for just a moment. We exchanged smiles and I headed back to my desk to start spreading the news.

I was tempted to email everyone so there wouldn't be a question about who got called first. But that was quickly supplanted by the desire to call my boyfriend. And it wasn't until my hand was actually on the phone that I remembered I couldn't call my boyfriend. And it wasn't until my hand was actually on the phone that I remembered I couldn't call my boyfriend because he wasn't exactly my boyfriend anymore. Mainly because of stories like the one Henry had liked so much.

Kyle Edwards, the man about whom I continued to be ab-

solutely nuts, was an NYPD homicide detective. As supportive and understanding as he tired to be, my attraction to dangerous stories had led to an impasse in our relationship.
He'd decided we needed to take a break and I certainly felt
broken. Since the split began, we'd only talked a couple of
times; in the last three weeks, we hadn't talked at all, which
I tried to ascribe to our individual schedules even though I
knew it was really our individual stubbornness that was to
blame.

So I went back to pre-Kyle mode and called my best
friends to tell them. Tricia was with a client but when I explained to her assistant that I had big news and Tricia should
call me when she got a chance, her assistant put me on hold
and Tricia picked up immediately.

"What big news?" she asked cheerily.

"It can wait. Take care of your client."

"It can wait, but I can't. Besides, they're trying to decide
on linen colors and I may not be able to get back to you until sometime next week." Tricia Vincent is an event planner,
the key to her success being that you feel like you're sitting
down with that one friend whose own style and look you se-
cretly covet and getting great personal advice from her. "I'm
trying to convince them that gray napkins will look dirty, not
elegant, and it may take a while. Tell me."

So I told her about my promotion and delighted in her
gasp of pleasure. "Yes! Are you jumping up and down right
this very minute?"

"Actually, no. Wrong shoes."

"Fine, I'll jump for you. And I'll meet you for champagne
at the place of your choosing at 6 p.m. Unless you and Cassady have another plan in mind."

"I haven't talked to her yet."

"How flattering. I'm sure it was just my turn to get called
first, but I'll pretend it was a deliberate choice. Let me know
what she says about six o'clock." Tricia blew kisses into the
phone and went back to her napkin dilemma.

It's become something of a game over the years: This issue of who gets called first when something important hap-

pens or even when something inconsequential but emotionally resonant occurs. But underneath is the exquisitely comforting knowledge that the three of us have a bond that can withstand anything. So far.

As I reached for my phone to call Cassady, it rang. Expecting it to be her being psychic, I snatched it up and breezily said, "Hello there."

"Molly, it's Ben Lipscomb and everything's okay." Despite Ben's quick reassurance, there was still time for my heart to stop for a moment as my mind raced through all the terrible reasons Kyle's partner might call me out of the blue. Emergency rooms or worse headed the list, but I didn't get much past them before his disclaimer sunk in.

"Nice to hear your voice, Ben," I said genuinely. Ben is a big man who's intimidating and imposing in the field, but gentle and charming at the core. I suddenly realized I missed him, not just because he was Kyle's partner but because he was a good guy and you can never have enough of them in your life. "What's up?" I continued, trying not to sound breathless.

"I just wanted to call and check on you."

"Really?"

"'Cause that's what people do when they care about other people. They call and they check on them."

It was less a rebuke than an instruction, but I still winced. "I have called."

"Not lately."

"Who's keeping track?"

"Who's admitting to it or who's pretending not to? Just because I'm the one calling to check in doesn't mean I'm the only one thinking about you."

I found myself grinning at the unmasking of Ben Lipscomb, decorated homicide detective, as Ben Lipscomb, old-fashioned matchmaker. "Ben, what are you up to?"

"Molly, when you do what I do for a living, you see way too many people whose lives go wrong because of bad decisions. So, I try to make a point of getting the people around me to make good decisions while they can."

I had a sudden vision of willowy blondes—Naomi Watts and Uma Thurman, to be exact—dressed in Badgley Mischka cocktail dresses with navel-baring necklines, advancing on Kyle like panthers stalking prey. Was Ben trying to tell me someone else had entered the picture? "While they can?" I repeated as a request for clarification.

"Wasting time on pride is stupid, if I may be frank."

I started to protest that pride wasn't the issue here, but the words wouldn't come out, probably because they weren't true. Kyle and I hadn't broken up solely because of pride, but it was a large part of the equation. In our painfully few recent conversations, all we'd done was acknowledge the impasse, not even beginning to see a way around or through it. The crux was, he worried about my getting hurt while writing about a crime, and I couldn't see that as anything but a demand to choose between him and my job.

My job. What elegant timing. It wasn't going to make it any easier to get back together with Kyle when one of the first things I'd have to tell him would be that I was a full-fledged feature writer now, which would fan the flames under all his worries. However, thinking optimistically, it might be fine. Russell Elliott hadn't been murdered, so there wasn't going to be any danger involved in this assignment. Which would give me the opportunity to show Kyle I could juggle my job and his concerns. Let him get used to the idea that he didn't have to fear for my safety and buying us time to get everything back on track.

It was going to be a touchy conversation, but suddenly I couldn't wait to have it. "Does he want me to call him?"

"Clearly, he doesn't know what he wants or I wouldn't have to be looking after him like this."

If he'd been in the room with me, I would've hugged Ben Lipscomb. "If I call him, will he call me back?"

"That's my plan."

"You're a wonderful person, Ben."

"Yeah, and there aren't many of us, so we have to stick up for each other."

"I appreciate it."

"You do know that this conversation never happened."

"Even though I'm very glad it did."

"Hope I see you soon, Molly."

"Me, too."

I hung up and grinned at the phone. A promotion and an indication that Kyle would be open to getting back together. It was turning out to be a pretty darn spectacular day. But as I started to dial Kyle's number, my excitement did a nice little tuck and roll and transformed into anxiety. What was I going to say? How was I going to start? Was it going to look like I was calling today because of the new job? How many wrong ways could he take that? Confronting those questions made my stomach flip again, so I dialed Cassady instead.

"It's about damn time," was her response to my news. Cassady's a lawyer and I always appreciate her incisive take on things.

"The job or the call from Ben?"

"Both. Your stars are aligning, sweetheart, and you better take advantage."

"I know, but I can't exactly call Kyle and say, 'Just wanted to let you know I got the job you were dreading when we were together. Wanna come back?' "

"Then don't say that."

"Thank you, counselor."

"What's wrong with calling him to let him know you've been thinking of him, then just allowing the job news to work its way into conversation in due course? Besides, this is a murderless story. Doesn't that solve a lot of problems right there?"

"I hope so."

"Call him."

"It's not that simple."

"Of course it is."

"How many times have you called an ex just to say you were thinking of them?"

"I never think of my exes."

"Comforting."

"Yes, but I come from the scorched-earth school of dating, while you are one of those irritating girls who can be taken home to Mother when things are going well and remembered fondly after they tank."

"Do I apologize at this point?"

"Not to me. But you could always run a mea culpa past Detective Edwards."

"Wait. It's not all my fault."

"No, but there's this fascinating concept we call 'contributory negligence' which might apply."

I had no worthy response. It was easy to say that my relationship with Kyle winding up on the rocks wasn't all my fault, but it was impossible to say I wasn't partly to blame.

"I'll take your silence as an admission that you're at least going to think about it. Nothing wrong with a little show of vulnerability, Molly. I happen to think Kyle struggles with your lack of it, so he might respond to a quick flash here."

"Maybe." I did need to think it through, though, rehearse it in my head a bit. This conversation was too important to improvise.

"Don't start thinking," Cassady said presciently. "You'll talk yourself out of it and that would be a huge mistake."

"Did Ben call you?"

"No, but he should have. Great minds and all that."

"Could we move on for the moment? Will you join Tricia and me for a little celebration this evening?"

"Only if you've called Kyle by the time I see you."

I hesitated, trying to manufacture a plausible excuse, but Cassady cleared her throat impatiently. "I promise."

"That wasn't so hard."

"That wasn't calling him."

"That won't be hard either."

"Says the woman who's never done it."

"Show me the way. The Bubble Lounge at six."

"Bring Aaron, too," I added. Aaron was a droll physicist who was demonstrating impressive longevity in the role of Cassady's boyfriend. It can be difficult to integrate new men into our circle, but Aaron had slid into the dynamics with ease and bemusement.

"I believe he has a seminar, but I'll ask, just to show you care. Will you be bringing Kyle?"

"Pace yourself. And me," I requested before exchanging good-byes and hanging up.

I left my hand on the phone, as though breaking the connection would let what resolve I'd summoned while talking to Cassady drain away. Was I making this all too hard? Was it really as simple as calling Kyle and saying, "I miss you and I'd like to see you"? But that wasn't simple at all—if, in fact, that was even the question to ask. Had years of writing an advice column in a woman's magazine taught me nothing?

Dear Molly,

Why are the most important questions in life the hardest ones to ask? Like, "Am I happy?" and "Is this really what I want out of life?" and "Do you still love me?" If I hesitate to ask these questions, is it because I'm afraid of the answer or because I already know the answer? Is it better to have called and asked than never to have called at all? Signed, Reach Out and Touch No One

Framing my problem as someone else's letter always gave me clarity and perspective and this time was no different. I wasn't being proud, I was being a coward. If I was really that afraid of Kyle rejecting me, then it was better to get it out in the open and get it over with. Yank the Band-aid off instead of peeling it back, bit by painful bit. I took a deep breath, lifted the receiver, and began to dial his number.

"Sorry, am I interrupting?"

My finger hovered over the last digit and I plunked the receiver back down, embarrassed by the accompanying sense of relief. I smiled at Dorrie Pendleton, the editorial assistant who fidgeted before me, frowning nervously. Dorrie did everything nervously, but she also did it dependably and well. She even dressed dependably and well, just this side of tweeds and sensible shoes, which made her stand out in our pool of burgeoning fashionistas, but she seemed oblivious to the contrast. "What can I do for you, Dorrie?"

"Is it true that staffers are going to be given an opportunity to submit work for consideration for replacing you on 'You Can Tell Me'? Not that anyone would really replace you, but—"

Impressed by how efficiently the rumor mill was operating, I held up my hand. "I appreciate that, but I'm sure one of you will prove quite capable of filling my Kate Spades. Eileen's going to circulate a memo about the process."

Dorrie perched in the chair beside me, leaning forward to create the illusion of intimacy. She had to be just as aware as I was of the number of our colleagues who were suddenly easing back in their chairs to catch a snippet of our conversation. "Your column sets this magazine apart. It's crucial to maintain its integrity and insight."

"Thank you." I smiled, bracing myself for the pitch for herself as leading candidate that had to be coming.

"And I'm so relieved that the rumors about Eileen forcing you out turned out to be wrong."

My smile locked into something that felt more like a grimace. "Yeah, me, too," I managed out of one side of my mouth. Hearing my private paranoia voiced as office gossip was unsettling, even in light of this afternoon's events. Had talk about my leaving the column because of my new position been misunderstood or had Eileen really been trying to get rid of me? Either way, why was I the last to know?

"You're an inspiration," Dorrie continued, but her adulation was making me uncomfortable now and I started edging out of my seat.

"Thanks again and good luck in the competition," I said as I stood up, even though I wasn't sure I knew where I was headed.

"No. Thank you," Dorrie said and she quickly slipped back to her desk, leaving me to stand awkwardly beside mine and realize that at least four people had dropped the subterfuge of working while eavesdropping and were staring directly at me. I considered blowing them a big kiss, but discretion being something I'm not known for, I gave it a try; I grabbed my cell phone and headed for the elevator.

There's nothing like not wanting to confront one problem

in your life to make you willing to confront another. I'd barely stepped out into the constant rumble of Lexington Avenue before I'd flipped open my phone and speed-dialed Kyle. I had no idea what I was going to say, but I was determined to say it.

He answered on the second ring, before I had a chance to change my mind. "Hey," he said and my knees wobbled and my eyes dampened with the sudden sharpness of missing him.

"Hey," I replied with all the eloquence I could muster. "Am I interrupting?"

"No. How are you?"

"Miserable," I said without thinking.

"Good."

"What?"

" 'Cause I am, too."

"Sounds like something we should talk about," I said, resisting the impulse to shout over the blood rushing in my ears.

"Good idea. What are you doing tonight?"

Anything you suggest, I thought, but I swallowed hard and said, "I'm meeting Tricia and Cassady for drinks at six. Care to join us?"

"No. No offense to them, but I just want to see you." I was about to break a cardinal rule and offer to cancel on them, but he continued, "Where are you meeting them? I can meet you somewhere near there afterwards."

"The Bubble Lounge."

"Champagne before dinner? Why? What happened?"

The downside of being involved with a detective, but hesitating now would only make it worse. "I got promoted. They're making me a feature writer. My first article is about this woman, Olivia Elliott, who's trying to protect her late father's legacy. It's not about his death, he just happened to die and now she's trying to make sure he gets remembered properly," I over-explained, wanting it perfectly clear that this was a homicide-free assignment and nothing to worry about.

There was enough of a pause for sweat to bead along my spine before he said, "Russell Elliott, the music guy?"

"Yes."

"I loved Subject to Change Without Notice."

"Yeah, me too."

"That's great."

"Our similar taste in music?"

"Your new job."

"Is it?"

"Isn't it?"

"I hope so."

"Then it will be."

"Thank you."

"Okay, count me in for the champagne. But I'd like dinner to be just the two of us."

"Absolutely," I said, wondering if my hands would have stopped trembling by then.

"See you there."

"Yes."

"I'm glad you called."

"Me too."

I stood there on the sidewalk, catching my breath and blessing Ben Lipscomb at the same time. The tiny helium balloons returned and I felt like I could float all the way to Central Park with one decent gust of wind. I had to do something with all the adrenaline that was coursing through me or I was apt to start grabbing strangers as they walked by and hugging them, inviting them to dance, and otherwise making a fool of myself. Determined to channel my energy a bit more productively, I fished Olivia Elliott's business card out of my pocket. I considered calling her office number, but decided it would be simpler to leave a message on her cell phone than to explain myself to a receptionist.

"Olivia Elliott."

Her voice had the dusky richness of a jazz DJ and caught me by surprise. I hadn't expected her to answer, so it took me a moment to frame my response. "Ms. Elliott, my name is Molly Forrester and I'm a writer for *Zeitgeist* magazine. Henry Kwon talked to you—"

"Yes, yes, and Henry spoke highly of you. I'm so pleased you'll be doing the article about my dad."

"Thank you. I was—am—a fan of his, especially his work with Subject to Change."

"Very kind. Though I need you to understand from the outset that I'm not interested in participating in an article that will be yet another rehash of Dad's so-called glory days."

By the end of the sentence, all silkiness was gone from her voice, replaced by a sharp, bitter edge. I waited a respectful moment before replying. "Henry and I discussed your concern that his contributions to contemporary music are being overlooked, so I thought we could focus on your role in assuring your father is remembered properly."

"And I can't really do that until he's buried properly, can I?"

"I'm not sure I follow."

"Ms. Forrester, I assumed Henry had chosen you for this article because of your body of work. I thought you'd be more attuned to the central issue here."

"And that issue is?"

"No one seems to care that my dad was murdered."